THE CAREER OF NICODEMUS DYZMA

TADEUSZ DOŁĘGA-MOSTOWICZ

THE CAREER OF
NICODEMUS DYZMA

A NOVEL

Translated from the Polish by
Ewa Małachowska-Pasek and Megan Thomas

With an introduction by
Benjamin Paloff

NORTHWESTERN UNIVERSITY PRESS
EVANSTON, ILLINOIS

Northwestern University Press
www.nupress.northwestern.edu

10 9 8 7 6 5 4 3 2 1

Library of Congress Cataloging-in-Publication Data

Names: Dołęga-Mostowicz, Tadeusz, author. | Małachowska-Pasek, Ewa, translator. |
    Thomas, Megan, 1977– translator. | Paloff, Benjamin, writer of introduction.
Title: The career of Nicodemus Dyzma : a novel / Tadeusz Dołęga-Mostowicz ;
    translated from the Polish by Ewa Małachowska-Pasek and Megan Thomas ; with an
    introduction by Benjamin Paloff.
Other titles: Kariera Nikodema Dyzmy. English
Description: Evanston, Illinois : Northwestern University Press, 2020.
Identifiers: LCCN 2020022217 | ISBN 9780810142879 (paperback) | ISBN
    9780810142886 (ebook)
Subjects: LCSH: Poland—Politics and government—20th century—Fiction. | LCGFT:
    Political fiction. | Satirical fiction.
Classification: LCC PG7158.M6 K313 2020 | DDC 891.8537—dc23
LC record available at https://lccn.loc.gov/2020022217

CONTENTS

Benjamin Paloff

The Actual Impostor (A Backstory)

As sometimes happens with literature in translation, looking immediately to where the text comes from can obscure how it has perhaps been with us all along, poorly disguised, hidden in plain view. Such is the case with *The Career of Nicodemus Dyzma* (1932), one of the most popular and influential novels published in Poland between the world wars. For American readers at the beginning of the twenty-first century, this novel's backdrop ought not to be Warsaw's endemically corrupt political establishment of the thirties, but the vibrant New York literary scene of the seventies and eighties, where the almost mythically eccentric figure of Jerzy Kosinski—much-feted émigré intellectual, award-winning novelist, inveterate obfuscator, and by turns ardent free speech advocate and *célèbre* without a *cause*—found himself dogged by a persistent rumor. In such highly visible pages as the *New York Times* and the *Village Voice*, Kosinski's supporters and detractors, who had long debated the author's slipperiness with biographical fact, could not get past one persistent question, that of whether his most successful work, the short novel *Being There* (1970), which Hal Ashby made into an acclaimed 1979 film starring Peter Sellers and Shirley MacLaine, had been plagiarized from a Polish novel that had never been translated into English.[1]

It was not mere rumor. The book now before you is *that* book—the novel Jerzy Kosinski ripped off when he wrote *Being There*.

"Ripped off" more accurately reflects the relationship between Kosinski's text and its predecessor than "plagiarism" would. *Being There* is not a word-for-word copy of Tadeusz Dołęga-Mostowicz's *The Career of Nicodemus Dyzma*. Kosinski's book is, for one thing, much shorter and is written in a style poised between its author's wry knowingness and a manufactured, fabular naiveté, conveyed in Ashby's film by Sellers's otherworldly affect and, just before the closing credits, his literally walking on water.

And whereas Dyzma is a street-smart, small-time hustler, Kosinski's hero is a man permanently arrested in his intellectual and social development, thrust by chance into the company of the rich and powerful and named, with a fabulist's subtlety, "Chance." Both figures survive by saying nothing when possible or, when they must speak, simply repeating what they have overheard. The novels share plot points both major and minor and even some significant episodes. Not coincidentally, *The Career of Nicodemus Dyzma* had been Jerzy Kosinski's favorite book in his youth.[2]

This, then, is the first of several misfortunes to befall Dołęga-Mostowicz's most infamous creation along its journey into English: its imposter beat it by half a century.

Not Being There

Tadeusz Dołęga-Mostowicz was one of the most popular writers in Poland in the 1930s, and *The Career of Nicodemus Dyzma* is widely acknowledged as having been his most successful work, reprinted in multiple editions and frequently adapted for stage, television, and film. Yet Dołęga-Mostowicz had already achieved public notoriety before publishing his first serialized novel, *Ostatnia brygada* (The last brigade), in 1930. Following his service in the Polish-Soviet War, he had spent most of the 1920s working in journalism, quickly rising to become an editor at *Rzeczpospolita*, a major daily newspaper that to this day remains a vital part of public discourse in Poland. There, he regularly published columns critical of the cozy relationship between the old aristocracy and the government, and especially against the authoritarian inclinations of Józef Piłsudski's ruling Sanacja movement. Not all of the attention this work brought its young author was welcome. In early September 1927, a little more than a year after the May 1926 coup d'état that had brought Piłsudski to power, Dołęga-Mostowicz was forced into a car, driven to the woods outside of Warsaw, beaten senseless, and left for dead, an event that is tragically reimagined in *The Career of Nicodemus Dyzma*. Though no one was ever tried for the crime, the evidence clearly pointed to Piłsudski's circle. Or rather, because the evidence clearly pointed to Piłsudski's circle, no one was ever tried for the crime.

Dołęga-Mostowicz achieved a kind of revenge in his turn to fiction, memorializing the hypocrisy and rapacity of self-styled "patriots" in characters who have left a lasting impression on the Polish language and the national consciousness. Dialogue-heavy and action-driven, with only brief bursts of cynical commentary from the author, his books read cinematically, a deliberate feature of their design: Dołęga-Mostowicz himself was in high demand as a screenwriter, producing both adaptations of his work and original screenplays depicting his beloved characters' later adventures. Michał Waszyński (born Mosze Waks), the Jewish director and producer whose work helped shape the early history of Central European film, brought no fewer than five of Dołęga-Mostowicz's novels to the silver screen between 1933 and 1938.[3] The first film adaptation of *Dyzma*, directed by Jan Rybkowski with the great comic actor Adolf Dymsza in the leading role, appeared in 1956. The same director teamed up with the cinematographer Marek Nowicki in 1979 to make a televised miniseries (now with Roman Wilhelmi, another legendary actor, as the title character) that enjoys a cult status to this day. A much looser film version followed in 2002. This is to say nothing of the many times *Dyzma* has appeared on stage or in popular song.

But the greatest honor bestowed on Nicodemus Dyzma, a farce of a human being who becomes a tragedy for the nation, comes from the Polish language itself, where his name has come to signify all manner of public fakery. A "Dyzma" is a phony, a fraud, especially one whose trickery depends on others' assumptions, self-deceptions, and moral shortcomings. A Dyzma feels no compunction about inveigling his way into privileges he has not earned or swindling the greedy and gullible, but he prefers fostering false assumptions to outright lying. Lacking the burden of any competency beyond the ability to inspire others' confidence in his nonexistent talents, a Dyzma is constantly failing upward. He answers questions with questions and deflects accusations simply by repeating them against the accuser. Rather than tell you what you want to hear, he smiles enigmatically and lets you say what you want to hear yourself.

This passage from character name to allusive noun is no mean feat. We know the world, and the people in it, through *scrooges* and *romeos*, through *mad hatters* and all their *quixotic* folly. In English, we might say that Dyzma has passed from *the* to *a*. Anyone can be a Dyzma; they are everywhere. And while the Polish language's lack of grammatical articles may dampen this formulation, a Dyzma never quibbles with details when fame and fortune are on the line.

The author, unfortunately, was not privileged to enjoy the afterlife of his greatest creation. When the Soviet Army invaded Poland on September 17, 1939, Dołęga-Mostowicz, now a corporal in the Polish reserves, was mobilized to the east. He didn't survive the week. His works were later banned in Stalinist Poland—hardly surprising, given that in the span of twenty years he had twice taken up arms against Russian occupation—and reappeared only with the Khrushchev Thaw in 1956. By that point, the attentions of the Polish literary establishment were directed elsewhere: to literature's responsibilities to history, its tensions with ideology, its role in rebuilding a society that had been demographically, materially, and psychologically devastated. The best Polish criticism in the postwar period tended to ignore the popular literature of the 1930s and the chaos it reflected, preferring instead the reevaluation of the avant-garde that brought such writers as Bruno Schulz, Witold Gombrowicz, and Stanisław Ignacy Witkiewicz into the canon. An important novelist like Zofia Nałkowska, whose works had enjoyed widespread critical and popular acclaim before the war, would have to wait until a new millennium for most of her major works to become available in English. Tadeusz Dołęga-Mostowicz had to wait a little longer.

This sets up one of the oddest contradictions in the history of modern Polish literature. On the one hand, *The Career of Nicodemus Dyzma* has been continuously recognized as relevant, as evidenced by its reeditions, by its regular reinterpretations for stage and screen, and in the Polish language itself. On the other, our most substantial histories of this period in Polish literature treat it as though it does not exist. Jerzy Kwiatkowski's substantial survey of interwar literature mentions the book in passing as "perhaps the best and most scathing" of novelists' fictional assessments of national politics between the wars.[4] Czesław Miłosz's *The History of Polish Literature*, clearly reflecting its author's disdain for popular fiction, mentions neither the novel nor its author.[5]

It is, rather, in political journalism that Nicodemus Dyzma might be invoked. His name signals the credulity of self-interested elites and undereducated masses as they coalesce around any would-be strongman. Jerzy Urban concluded his satirical essay "Dyzma" (1974), about a fraud posing as an economist, with testimony from the malefactor's erstwhile employer, who declares that he would hire him again in a minute because good economists are hard to come by.[6] Witold Bereś and Jerzy Skoczylas entitled the book collecting their satirical profiles of populists and political manipulators, which first appeared in the pages of the daily newspaper *Gazeta Wyborcza*, simply *Nikodem Dyzma 2000*, and notably offered no explanation for their choice, since any reader would know exactly what they meant.[7] Today, one finds casual references to Dyzmas not infrequently in Polish editorials, not least because the rise of populist politics has made the beginning of the twenty-first century an especially fruitful time for Dyzmas all around the world.

A Hero of Our Time

An older novel's prominence within a particular time and place often suffices to recommend it to the contemporary reader, particularly when that reader already has an interest in the circumstances that gave rise to that novel in the first place. And *The Career of Nicodemus Dyzma* does indeed provide an illuminating portrait, albeit an irremediably pessimistic one, of Polish society in an especially turbulent political era. And yet, more than its biting wit and sinister charm, more than the special place it holds in the Polish language and political imagination, more even than the remarkable artistry of this first English translation, *The Career of Nicodemus Dyzma* demands our attention because it so accurately represents the geopolitics and globalized culture in which we are now living. One need not interpret Dołęga-Mostowicz's book at all broadly to remark dramatizations—not merely general parallels, but quite specific tableaux!—of episodes from recent politics in Brazil, Hungary, Turkey, the United States, the United Kingdom, and Poland itself. The uncanny is baked into the reading experience as we hear the rhetoric of our own politicians and their surrogates spoken almost verbatim by Dołęga-Mostowicz's characters nearly a century ago.

This is not a demonstration of the novelist's prescience. Rather, Dołęga-Mostowicz had a deep appreciation of human weakness and of how it perpetuates and amplifies itself across a society. For while *The Career of Nicodemus Dyzma* is unquestionably a character portrait, it would be a mistake to assume that the eponymous hero is the character being portrayed. Rather, Dołęga-Mostowicz has provided us with a sharp portrait of the *national* character, the general set of conditions that allow Dyzmas to thrive. A Dyzma, after all, does not corrupt so much as he allows our own corruption to achieve its full flower. A Dyzma does not rally an angry crowd; he slips into the crowd just as they're gaining strength and, within minutes, is leading them in whatever chant they have already begun.

Who among us, then, can be a Dyzma? Certainly, those of us who, through the fortuitous alignment of our own opportunism and someone else's desperation or wishful thinking, have found ourselves enjoying rewards we haven't earned for services we cannot perform. An athlete who wild cards into an elite competition could well be a Dyzma. Advanced university courses, particularly those regarded as prerequisite to a desirable fellowship or employment, might have several Dyzmas. Anyone who uses a misdirected invitation to crash an exclusive party, as the character Nicodemus Dyzma does in the novel's opening pages, is almost certainly a Dyzma. But it is in the sphere of politics that a Dyzma thrives. Political commentators the world over have colorful terms to describe those who readily spout populist beatitudes while cutting backroom deals to defraud the populace, who preach temperance and rectitude only to create the conditions that allow them to reject both. In Polish, these people are very likely to be called Dyzmas.

Whatever we call them, Dołęga-Mostowicz understood who they are. They're us.

Notes

1. One of the most interesting and substantial of these volleys came from John Corry, who in 1982 published an extensive defense of Kosinski in the *New York Times*, where he derided insinuations that Kosinski was a plagiarist as disinformation spread by Polish communists. "Few people in New York literary circles," Corry wrote at the time, "seem to know the name of the novel Mr. Kosinski supposedly plagiarized; many people, however, have heard the rumor. It hangs around, billowy and undefined." John Corry, "17 Years of Ideological Attack on a Cultural Target," *New York Times*, November 7, 1982, sec. 2, 1. Corry does go on to name Dołęga-Mostowicz's novel and to summarize the basic plot similarities with *Being There* before concluding, "Polish scholars in the United States dismiss the charge of plagiarism." The contemporary scholarly and critical consensus is that Kosinski's *Being There* is indeed based largely on Dołęga-Mostowicz's novel.

2. James Park Sloan, *Jerzy Kosinski: A Biography* (New York: Dutton, 1996), 65. Sloan offers the most intriguing defense of Kosinski's appropriation of Dołęga-Mostowicz's novel, namely, that it was his own life and career that Kosinski had modeled on the character of Nicodemus Dyzma, and that he then based *Being There*'s Chance Gardiner on himself: "To Kosinski . . . the book was far more than a work of literature. It was more on the order of a blueprint, a plan of action for life." Sloan, *Jerzy Kosinski*, 66.

3. Waszyński is best known today as the director of *Der Dibuk*, the most important Yiddish-language film produced in Poland before the Second World War.

4. Jerzy Kwiatkowski, *Dwudziestolecie międzywojenne* (Warsaw: Wydawnictwo Naukowe PWN, 2000), 284.

5. Czesław Miłosz, *The History of Polish Literature*, 2nd ed. (Berkeley: University of California Press, 1983).

6. Jerzy Urban, "Dyzma," in his *Wszystkie nasze ciemne sprawy* (Kraków: Wydawnictwo Literackie, 1974), 114–18. English translation: Jerzy Urban, "Dyzma," trans. Abraham Brumberg, in *Poland: Genesis of a Revolution*, ed. Abraham Brumberg (New York: Vintage, 1983), 147–50.

7. Witold Bereś and Jerzy Skoczylas, *Nikodem Dyzma 2000* (Warsaw: Prószyński i S-ka, 2000).

THE CAREER OF NICODEMUS DYZMA

Chapter 1

The restaurant owner signaled to the piano player, and the tango broke off midmeasure. The dancing pair lurched to a halt in the middle of the floor.

"Well, Mr. Director?" asked the slender blonde, freeing herself from her partner's embrace and heading to the little table where a beefy, sweaty-faced man was rising to his feet.

The owner shrugged his shoulders.

"Will he do?" she asked coolly.

"No way. He's got nothing, no moves, no pizzazz. If he was at least a little handsome, that would be something, but . . ."

The dancer came closer.

The blonde ran an appraising eye over his threadbare clothing, his thinning, walnut-colored hair, slightly frizzy and parted in the middle, his thin lips, and his jutting lower jaw.

"And you've danced somewhere before?"

"No. I mean, I've danced before, but privately. It was even said that I was a good . . ."

"Where, then?" the restaurant owner asked indifferently.

The aspiring taxi dancer cast a sad glance around the empty room.

"Here and there back home, in Łysków."

Fatso burst out laughing.

"Warsaw, my dear man, is not Łysków. Here you need elegance, my dear man, some flair, a little panache. I'll be straight with you: you're not cut out for this; it's better you start looking for a different line of work."

He turned on his heel and made for the buffet. The blonde hurried off to the dressing room. The piano player closed the lid over the keys.

The would-be taxi dancer slung his coat listlessly over his shoulder, squeezed his hat onto his head, and headed for the door. A young waiter passed by with a tray of canapés, and their intense, delectable aroma made his nostrils twitch.

The street was flooded with hot sunshine. It was close to noon, and there weren't many people out. He plodded in the direction of Łazienki Park.

Pausing at the corner of Piękna Street, he reached into his waistcoat pocket and fished out a coin.

My last one, he thought.

He approached a cigarette kiosk.

"Two GPCs."

He counted his change and stood vacantly at the tram stop. Some old man leaning on a stick cast a filmy glance his way. An elegant woman with a dozen packages in her arms kept craning her neck in search of the next tram.

Beside him, squirming impatiently, a boy was waiting with a book under his arm. Actually, it wasn't a book so much as some sort of portfolio bound in gray linen; when he stood in profile one could see what was inside, a wad of letters and the edges of a couple dozen delivery confirmation receipts.

He observed the boy and recalled that he himself had carried a similar portfolio as Notary Winder's office boy back before the war, before he'd become a clerk at the Łysków post office. Except the notary had used blue envelopes, and these were white.

The number 9 was approaching, and the boy took a running leap onto the rear platform, but his portfolio knocked against the railing and letters scattered everywhere.

Small Fry's lucky it's not raining today, the failed taxi dancer thought as he watched the boy scoop up the letters. The tram pulled forward, and a letter slid down the stairs and fell to the pavement. The failed taxi dancer picked up the white envelope and began to wave it at the departing tram. But the boy was so busy gathering the rest of the letters that he didn't notice.

It was an exquisite envelope of handmade paper, with a handwritten address:

> *The Honorable Chairman Artur Rakowiecki, 7 Ujazdowskie Avenue*
> *no. 3.*

Inside (the envelope wasn't sealed) there was an equally exquisite card folded in half. On the front, there was something printed in French, and on the back, probably the same thing, but in Polish:

> *The Chairman of the Council of Ministers has the privilege of requesting your Honor's presence at a banquet that will be held on the evening of July 15 at 8:00 p.m. in the lower salon of the Hotel Europejski in honor of the arrival of His Excellency the Chancellor of the Austrian Republic.*

Some small print at the bottom added: *Formal attire only.*

He read the address again: 7 Ujazdowskie Avenue.

Should he deliver it? And maybe pick up a zloty or two? It wouldn't hurt to try. After all, number 7 was barely a few dozen steps away.

The resident directory showed apartment number 3 on the first floor next to the name A. Rakowiecki. He went upstairs and rang once, twice. Finally, a housekeeper arrived and announced that Mr. Chairman had gone abroad.

"Too bad."

He shrugged and, still holding the letter, started toward home. A good half hour passed before he reached Łucka Street. He made his way up the creaky stairs to the fourth floor and pushed open the door. The cramped room's stale fug billowed into his face, and with it the acrid smell of scorched onions and hot grease and the aroma of drying diapers.

From the corner, a woman's voice brayed, "Shut that door! There's a draft, you're going to give my kid a cold!"

He muttered something under his breath, took off his hat, hung his coat on a nail, and slumped down by the window.

"Well?" said the woman. "So again you found nothing?"

"Again . . ."

"Look, Dyzma, I'm telling you, you're out there pounding the pavement for nothing. It's easier to earn your daily bread out in the country. You know—peasants."

He didn't answer. He'd been out of work for three months already, ever since the closing of Bar Under the Sun, where he'd earned five zlotys a day, plus dinner, for playing the mandolin. True, the employment agency had then found him work at the railway hub, but Dyzma failed to hit it off with the engineer or the foreman or, for that matter, any of the laborers, and after two weeks they'd given him notice. Whereas in Łysków . . .

The woman's thoughts were along the same lines, because she asked, "Dyzma, wouldn't it be better to go back where you came from, back to your family? Maybe out there they can find something for you to do."

"But I already told you, I don't have any family."

"They're dead?"

"They're dead."

Mrs. Barcik finished peeling the potatoes and, setting the pot on the fire, began: "Because here in Warsaw, people are different and there's no work. My man gets only three days a week, you know, and that's barely enough for us to eat, and the boss, whatshisname, that Purmanter or whatever, says they might just close down the factory because of something to do with the price of commode-ities. And if it wasn't for Mańka, we wouldn't have the money for rent. That girl works herself to the bone, but it doesn't even matter. If she doesn't catch herself a customer at least twice a week—"

"She should watch out," Dyzma interrupted, "that they don't catch *her*, working without papers like that . . . yeah?"

Mrs. Barcik changed the baby and hung the wet diaper over the stove.

"Don't jinx it!" she answered curtly. "And keep your nose out of other people's business. You, who hasn't done a lick of work in three weeks, who only takes up space. You're not even a real tentant."

"I'm going to pay," Dyzma muttered.

"Maybe you'll pay, maybe you won't. And fifteen zlotys might be half-free but still, I'm not made of money. And you, even when you do manage to land a job, you just get fired right away . . ."

"Mrs. Barcik, whoever told you that?"

"Oh yeah, some big secret. You said it to Mańka yourself."

Silence fell.

Dyzma turned back to the window and stared out at the shabby court-yard wall. Indeed, misfortune seemed to haunt him. He could never stay in one place for very long. He was expelled from his fourth year of secondary school due to a stubborn lack of diligence. His job with Notary Winder had lasted the longest, probably because little Nicodemus Dyzma's German was just passable enough to understand where it was he was being sent. Then came the post and telegraph office, the meager pay and the constant nagging and nitpicking of the postmaster. Then the war, the telegraph battalion supply unit where after three years of service he'd advanced only to private first class. And then back to the post office in Łysków, at least until the staff cuts came. The parish priest found him a job in the reading room, but he barely made it through the winter, since by April it was clear that he couldn't keep the bookshelves in any kind of order.

As a matter of fact, the most interesting thing about it was—

Dyzma's reverie was interrupted by a whistle blast from a nearby factory. Seeing that Mrs. Barcik was starting to set the dinner table, Dyzma pulled himself to his feet and made his exit.

Although his legs ached, he aimlessly wandered the sun-roasted streets. Staying in that apartment, enduring Walenty Barcik's cutting remarks and Mańka's disdainful jibes, and especially having to watch them eat: it was beyond his strength. He was already on day two of putting nothing in his mouth besides the cigarettes into which he had sunk his last pennies.

Passing a meat market from which wafted the tantalizing aroma of kiel-basa, he held his breath. He tried to wrench his head away from the store's windows, but his hunger would not allow itself to be forgotten.

Nicodemus Dyzma realized with perfect clarity that there were no greener pastures awaiting him.

Did this scare him? Not in the least. The Nicodemus Dyzma psyche—lucky for him—was bereft of imagination. The scope of his plans and expectations didn't extend beyond the boundaries of the very next day, and just as he'd made it through last week by selling his watch, he would survive the next by cashing in his coat and tails and patent leather shoes.

True, buying this outfit had entailed no small amount of scrimping and sacrifice; true, it was to this suit that he'd bound his dreams of the easy money of a taxi dancer and the radical improvement of his lamentable material circumstances—but now, when after multiple attempts he concluded that no one wanted any part of his taxi dancing, he resolved, without pain, to part with his splendid attire.

It was already close to six when he settled on this final decision and turned back toward home.

In the apartment there was only Mańka, a frail brunette with a nervous demeanor. Evidently this was one of the evenings she had to go out and make some money, because she was sitting by the window putting on makeup. Seeing as she was sitting on his suitcase, Dyzma, not wanting to interrupt, positioned himself in the corner and waited.

The girl was the first to speak:

"Hey, you. Turn around, I'm getting dressed."

"I'm not looking," he said.

"Good, because you'll never get a taste of this."

He swore. The girl gave a short bark of laughter and pulled off her dress. Indeed, he didn't pay her any attention, unless you counted the extreme extent of his irritation with her. How satisfying it would be to smack her in the mouth and throw her out the door. She teased him systematically, doggedly, with a kind of inexplicable passion. It's not that he found it an insult to his masculine ambition; his life had yet to offer the conditions under which such a thing could possibly develop. It didn't even wound his dignity—he'd never had a whole lot of that—and in this instance he wasn't even bothered by the class difference between them: he, an unemployed "intellectual laborer," and she, this girl. He was just sick of the constant ridicule.

Meanwhile she got dressed, threw a scarf over her shoulders, and stood before Dyzma, flashing her large white teeth.

"What do you think? A nice dish?"

"Go to hell!" he spat furiously.

She chucked him under the chin but snatched back her hand when, with a sudden swing of his fist, Dyzma struck her outstretched arm.

"Ugh, you louse!" she hissed. "Good-for-nothing woman beater! And he has the nerve to touch me. Just look at him, what a bum . . ."

She went on talking, but Dyzma had stopped listening. He began to open his suitcase, calculating to himself that he could maybe get fifty zlotys for the tailcoat. He'd paid seventy at Kiercelak Market. The patent leather shoes could go, too, at a loss of eight, maybe ten zlotys.

The baby had begun to wail mercilessly, and after a minute Mrs. Barcik came running from the neighbor's. It was only then that Mańka wrapped up her tirade and, slamming the door, finally left.

Nicodemus Dyzma opened his suitcase and took out his suit.

"Oh ho," laughed Mrs. Barcik. "I guess you're headed to a wedding or a ball or something."

He didn't answer. He carefully folded the pants, waistcoat, and tails, wrapped them in newspaper, and asked for a piece of string. Walenty was back; Mrs. Barcik was heating up potatoes for supper, and again the room filled with the smell of melted fat.

"What, are you going to Kiercelak?" Walenty asked.

"Yes, to Kiercelak."

"But today's Saturday. There aren't going to be any Jews there, and our own people hardly ever buy secondhand. And even if they do it's for next to nothing."

Fat was sizzling in the pan. Dyzma swallowed hard.

"So let it be for next to nothing."

Suddenly he remembered that he hadn't checked the suit's pockets. He quickly unwrapped the package. Indeed, there was a glazed cigarette holder in the pants pocket and a handkerchief in the tailcoat. As he slipped both objects into his pocket, his fingers brushed against something unfamiliar. Some kind of card stock . . . Aha, it was that letter he'd found. The invitation.

He took out the envelope and read it again. When he reached the fine print at the very bottom, something unexpectedly lodged itself in his brain: formal attire only.

His eyes turned to the tailcoat. A banquet . . . Food, lots of food, and for free!

I'm a madman, he thought, but he read the invitation again: "July 15 at 8:00 p.m."

The idea refused to go away.

"Walenty, is today the fifteenth?"

"It's the fifteenth."

"And what time will it be?"

"Well, it *will* be ten, but right now it's seven."

Dyzma stood motionless for a moment.

And what's the worst they could do to me? he thought. At worst, they'll just throw me out. Besides, there's sure to be a ton of people there . . .

He took out his shaving kit and began to change his clothes.

Back when he worked at the reading room, during the long preprandial hours when there was almost nothing at all to do, he'd sometimes, out of sheer boredom, read books. He'd often happen upon descriptions of balls and banquets thrown by various counts and ministers. He knew—if the descriptions were to be believed—that at such large parties there were usually a lot of people who didn't know each other and that therefore he might be able to pull off this seemingly risky venture. Especially if he didn't stand out among the guests.

The Barciks were sitting at the table, gobbling potatoes and washing them down with tea.

Food, a whole lot of food, thought Dyzma. Meat, bread, fish . . .

He washed himself over the sink, ran a comb through his coarse hair, and pulled a starched shirt over his head.

"Didn't I tell you he's going to a wedding?" Mrs. Barcik said. Her husband glanced up at their lodger and muttered, "What's it to us?"

With some difficulty, Dyzma buttoned his stiff collar, knotted his tie, and put on his tails.

"Food, lots and lots of food," he whispered.

"What did you say?"

"Nothing. Bye."

Fastening his gabardine coat, he slowly descended the stairs.

Dyzma examined the invitation by the light of the nearest lamppost and found that it didn't specify the addressee's name. He tucked it back in his pocket, then tore up the envelope and tossed it down a drain.

His ability to navigate the city was still rather weak, and he hesitated a moment, finally deciding to follow a familiar route. He went down Żelazna Street, and at the corner of Chłodna he turned back toward the church. From here he could see Elektoralna and Bank Square.

The street in this working-class district seethed with nightlife. The wheezing of concertinas poured from the open doors of various taprooms, and all along the litter-strewn sidewalks groups of teenagers and young workmen in unbuttoned jackets and collarless shirts sauntered to and fro. Young girls, their arms linked in clusters of threes and fours, giggled and whispered among themselves. Older women with children in their arms stood in doorways or perched on stools outside their apartments.

Quitting time, Dyzma thought.

There was a crowd on Elektoralna as well. Observant Jews filled not only the sidewalk but also the street. When he reached Theater Square, the clock tower on the town hall showed it was already five past eight. He picked up his pace and was soon standing before the hotel.

He watched how one gleaming automobile after another pulled up, how from each there emerged elegant ladies and gentlemen decked out in furs despite the heat.

He was more than a little daunted.

How would he manage to act like one of them?

But hunger prevailed. Food, food at any cost! So what if they eventually threw him out? That would hardly be the end of the world, after all.

He gritted his teeth and went in.

Before he knew it, a servant had relieved him of his coat and hat and some excessively polite gentleman had led him to the door of a hall and, with an obsequious gesture, was even opening it for him.

The white of the cavernous hall, the black blotches of tailcoats, all the colors of the ladies' dresses—Nicodemus Dyzma's head was spinning. The mingled perfumes and the hubbub of voices were practically intoxicating.

He was standing stock-still by the door when he suddenly realized that, right in front of him, there was someone with his head politely bent and his hand extended. Dyzma automatically took hold of it.

"Sir, allow me to introduce myself," the man said. "Antoniewski, personal secretary to the prime minister. On behalf of the prime minister, please allow me to thank you for gracing us with your presence. Hors d'oeurves, if you please, are this way."

The words had hardly left his mouth when he bounded over to two slim gentlemen who had just arrived.

Nicodemus Dyzma wiped the sweat from his forehead.

Thank God! Now, let's do this . . .

He quickly got ahold of himself and began to take stock of the situation. He saw that men and women were either standing around several large tables and eating with plates in their hands, or they had found seats at smaller tables. He resolved to overrule his hunger as long as he could so that he might observe further how these people behaved. He scanned a table crammed with platters of all sorts of strange food, the likes of which he'd never seen. He'd have been more than happy to seize any one of these platters and scurry off to devour its contents in the corner. But he kept himself in check and simply watched.

At last he determined it was time to figure out where to find a plate. When he located one, along with a fork, he heaped it with some kind of salad and a big hunk of pate. His mouth was watering. He couldn't tear his eyes away from his plate. Suddenly, as he was turning to look for a more secluded area, he felt a rather strong blow to the elbow. His plate, knocked from his hands, slammed onto the floor.

Rage swept through him. Right there for everyone to see, some over-weight gentleman had unceremoniously elbowed his way past him without even deigning to turn around and apologize for his clumsiness. Had Dyzma been able to contain his fury, he surely might have tempered his reaction. Now, however, he was certain of one thing only: he'd had a plate of food, and this fatso had knocked it right out of his hands.

He caught up with the culprit in two quick steps and grabbed hold of his elbow.

"Watch yourself, goddammit, you knocked the plate out of my hand!" he roared in the man's face.

The assailed man's expression was one of full-blown astonishment, even terror. He stared at the floor and, obviously discomfited, began to beg Dyzma's pardon.

Silence had fallen around them. A waiter came running to clear away the mess, and a second waiter handed Dyzma a new plate.

Even as he loaded his plate with another helping of salad, he didn't register the folly he'd just committed; that happened only when he'd simmered down and found himself an out-of-the-way spot to eat. He suddenly understood that he would undoubtedly be thrown out the door any minute now. He wolfed down his food in order to maximize his intake.

Meanwhile, the room was becoming more and more crowded, and Dyzma, to his relief, saw that no one was paying him any attention. He was emboldened to fill his plate again. As he chewed, he spotted a tray with glasses of cognac. He drank two, one after the other. Now he felt himself on firmer ground. As he reached for a third, he was amazed to see that the adjacent glass, lifted by somebody else's hand, clinked lightly against his own.

At the same time, a voice reached his ears.

"Will you allow me to join you, sir?"

Next to him stood a tall, brown-haired man in a colonel's uniform and with a somewhat ambiguous smile on his face.

They raised their glasses and drank. The colonel extended his hand.

"I'm Wareda."

"I'm Dyzma," he replied in an identical tone, pressing his hand.

"I congratulate you," the colonel said, leaning toward Dyzma, "for putting that Terkowski in his place. I saw the whole thing."

Dyzma's cheeks flushed.

Ah, okay, he thought. Now I'll be shown out. But they start so politely . . .

"Hee hee," Colonel Wareda quietly chuckled. "Even now, the very mention of that numbskull still gets your blood up. I congratulate you, Mr. . . . Dyzma. Terkowski hasn't been taught a lesson like that for a long time. To your health!"

They drank, and Dyzma began to catch the drift of the situation, inasmuch as he understood that this colonel had a bone to pick with this fatso Terkowski.

"It was nothing," he replied. "It's really just a shame . . . about . . . the plate and the salad."

Wareda burst out laughing.

"Good one! My, but you're a wicked fellow, Mr. Dyzma. To your health!"

"You know," he added a moment later, setting his glass down, "that's a first-rate gibe: Terkowski's nothing, but it's a real shame about the salad!"

He was immensely pleased, and while Dyzma couldn't quite work out why that was, he laughed, too, through a mouthful of canapé.

They strolled over to a window, and the colonel offered him a cigarette. He'd barely managed to light it when they were approached by a stocky man with grayish-blond hair and glassy eyes. He was gesticulating energetically.

"Wacek!" he cried. "Give me a cigarette! I forgot mine."

Once again, the colonel held out his silver cigarette case.

"At your service. Allow me to introduce you. Mr. Dyzma, Minister Jaszuński."

Within himself, Dyzma cowered and quailed. Never in his life had he seen a minister. Working at the Łysków post office, he'd heard tell of ministers, but even in the word itself there was something unreal and abstract, something remote and unreachable . . . He shook the hand extended to him reverently.

"Picture this," the colonel began. "Just moments ago, Dyzma had a little incident with that nitwit Terkowski."

"Ah! So you're the one? Do tell!" the minister said with relish. "I heard, I heard. Well, well, well!"

"And that's not all, just listen," the colonel continued. "When I congratulated him, Dyzma said, 'Terkowski's nothing, but it's a shame about the salad!' Just imagine, the salad!"

They both exploded with laughter. Dyzma joined in without conviction.

All of a sudden, the minister broke off, and he said meaningfully, "Well, such is the fate of an egomaniac like that. He pushes his way around, that boor, with no shame whatsoever, until finally someone gives him a taste of his own goddamn medicine, and afterward it's worth less than—"

"—a salad!" Colonel Wareda finished.

Again they dissolved into merriment, and the minister, taking Dyzma by the arm, said gaily, "In any case, Mr. Dyzma, I sincerely congratulate you. Sincerely. If our country had more men like you, dear friend, men who don't let themselves get pushed around, our standing in the world would be very different indeed. We need strong men."

Several others drew near. Dyzma's full stomach, along with all the cognac he'd drunk, had soothed his frayed nerves. At first, he'd thought they must have him confused with someone else who bore the same name (perhaps some relative of his here in Warsaw?); only later did he piece together that they considered him one of their own, almost certainly because of how he had set that Terkowski straight. And who exactly was Terkowski? Probably also a noted figure of some sort.

Weighing the situation, he concluded that the most prudent move would be to leave immediately. An elderly gentleman standing nearby, whose gaze was clearly tracking him, had begun to be a source of unease. The old man was even executing subtle maneuvers to allow him to try to catch Dyzma's eye.

Who the hell is this? he thought. What does this old guy want from me?

The answer came quickly. The elderly gentleman stopped a passing waiter and spoke a few words to him, motioning in Dyzma's direction. The waiter bowed and, approaching Dyzma, reported, "That gentleman would like to speak to Your Honor for a second."

It was no use. Escape was out of the question. Nicodemus took three steps and cast a glum look at the gray old gentleman. That gentleman, however, grinned and began speaking in an obsequious, twittering voice:

"My deepest, deepest apologies to Your Excellency, but if I am not mistaken, I had the honor of meeting Your Honor at last year's Congress of Industrialists in Kraków. Do you not remember? In April? Leon Kunicki?"

He spoke quickly and with a slight lisp. He urgently thrust a small, nervous hand at Dyzma.

"Leon Kunicki."

"Nicodemus Dyzma. But you're mistaken. I've never been to Kraków. It must have been someone who looked like me."

The old man began to apologize and excuse himself, the words and expressions tumbling from his lips so rapidly that Dyzma could barely grasp their meaning.

Yes, yes, of course, the old eyes weren't what they used to be, distractions, please forgive him, ah but how pleased he was, he knew almost no one here, it was unfortunate, no one with whom to share a few words, he'd even had specific business to settle here, which is why he'd asked a friend to wrangle him an invitation, but it's difficult to manage when one is old . . .

"I was actually," he continued in the same tone, "I was actually so glad to meet you again, and to see what a close relationship you have with our venerable minister of agriculture, because I'm thinking to myself, this friend, he can do me the favor of presenting me in a good light to Minister Jaszuński. But no, I truly, truly beg your pardon."

"It's nothing."

"Oh, no, no, I tore you away from a nice conversation with that very minister, but, you see, I'm just a provincial, and in the countryside where I'm from, everything, Most Esteemed Excellency, everything gets settled cordially, in a simple way . . ."

How he jabbers on, thought Dyzma.

"So, my deepest apologies," the old man lisped. "But while we're on the subject, if you could be so kindhearted as to do a favor for an old man, what could it possibly cost you?"

"What kind of favor?" Dyzma was surprised.

"Ah, I don't impose, but if Your Excellency were only willing, for example, to introduce me to the minister, he would, at once, treat me, you know, as someone who comes with the recommendation of a friend."

"A friend?" Dyzma was frankly astounded.

"Hee hee, deny it if you must. I heard how Your Excellencies were talking; I'm old and half blind, but my ears work just fine. I have no doubt that if you introduce me, if you, for example, say to the minister, 'My dear Minster, allow me to present my dear old friend Leon Kunicki! . . .' Oh! What a difference it would make . . ."

"But sir!" Dyzma protested.

"I don't impose, I don't impose, hee hee, but I would be grateful a hundred times over, yes, a hundred times over, and what could it possibly cost you?"

Suddenly, the door to the next room opened. There was a commotion, a small crowd at the entrance. Minister Jaszuński, ambling past Dyzma and Kunicki with two other gentlemen, smiled at Dyzma and said to his companions, "There's our man of the hour."

Kunicki practically shoved Dyzma forward and took a deep bow before the minister. Seeing no other way, Dyzma blurted out, "Minister, sir, allow me to acquaint you with Mr. Kunicki. He's my dear old friend."

A surprised look appeared on the minister's face. But he didn't have even a moment to answer because Kunicki, pumping his hand, had immediately launched into his spiel, how happy he was to make the acquaintance of such an outstanding statesman, whose fatherland, and agriculture in particular, and forestry to an even greater extent, owed him a debt of gratitude, and he would remember this moment until his dying breath, because he, as an agriculturalist and lumber industrialist, knew the great value of his services in this field, and that by no means all, unfortunately, of the minister's aides were capable of understanding the greatness of his forward-thinking concepts, but there was always a fix for that, and that he, Kunicki, owed an unpayable debt of gratitude to this kind, beloved Mr. Dyzma, who had deigned to introduce them.

The lisping torrent of speech flowed so rapidly that the minister, increasingly dumbfounded, was only able to utter, "Very nice to meet you."

But when the relentless old man began to speak of the state forests in the Grodno region and lumber mills of some kind, which . . . , the minister broke in drily:

"I mustn't permit myself to take up such matters at a party. Otherwise, I'd have no work to do at the ministry."

Extending his hand to Dyzma, he nodded at Kunicki and walked away.

"He's a tough nut to crack, that minister," said Kunicki. "That's not what I imagined. Is he always like that?"

"Always," Dyzma replied, just in case.

The reception was over. Most of the partygoers, however, adjourned to the neighboring dining room for dinner.

The old man had clamped on to Dyzma for good. He positioned himself next to him at the table and nattered away without pause. Dyzma's head was beginning to spin.

Admittedly, the chief culprit in this state of affairs was the cognac, to say nothing of the several glasses of wine, but Dyzma was starting to feel drained and sleepy. And to make matters worse, he felt compelled to continue his eating and drinking, which—considering the incredible amount of food he was putting away—was downright exhausting. Dyzma longingly pictured his own narrow cot, which he'd unfold under the window as soon as he returned to Łucka. Tomorrow was Sunday; maybe they would even let him sleep until ten.

Meanwhile, Kunicki was clutching his arm.

"My dear sir, don't even think of refusing me, it's only just eleven, drink with me, sir, a glass of good Hungarian! I'm staying here, at the Hotel Europejski, right on the first floor! I have for you, sir, a very important business matter. Ah, so you won't refuse me after all, sir! Let us sit, sir, in peace and quiet, in comfort, over a good wine . . . Well? For half an hour, for fifteen minutes."

He more or less dragged Dyzma along as he spoke. They left the vestibule and soon found themselves in a spacious room. Kunicki ordered more Hungarian wine.

Down below, a revolving glass door was in constant motion, its cylinder expelling men and women dressed to the nines. A doorman standing at the edge of the pavement announced the arriving automobiles.

"A car for Minister Jaszuński!"

A gleaming limousine pulled up, and the minister, saying goodbye to Colonel Wareda, asked, "Listen, Wacek, what was that fellow's name, the one who laid into Terkowski?"

"A capital fellow!" the colonel declared resolutely, wobbling a little on his feet. "His name's Dyzma, that was a first-rate tongue-lashing . . ."

"He seems to be a landowner or some kind of industrialist because, you know, he's friends with the famous Kunicki, the one that was mixed up in that affair with the railway ties."

"I'm telling you, he's a terrific fellow, a real straight shooter, this guy."

"Yes, he sure has a powerful personality. I'm a believer in phrenology. His skull juts forward and his jaw is well developed. I'm a believer in phrenology. Well, buh-bye!"

The motor whirred and the doors banged shut. The colonel remained on the sidewalk.

"Boy, is he plastered," Wareda said to himself. "What the hell does personality have to do with chronology?"

Chapter 2

On the table stood a low lamp with a green shade, its light illuminating only a small circle of plush tablecloth, a box of cigars, a mossy old bottle, and two glasses of amber liquid. The room around them was so dark that the contours of the furniture seemed to dissolve into the murk.

Dyzma was sunk deep in an overstuffed chair. He felt exceptionally sluggish and so drowsy he surely would have fallen right to sleep listening to this monotonous voice, these muffled, lisping words like tiny beads rapidly threaded one after another on a thin string, if not for, at the opposite side of the table, the diminutive figure of Kunicki, his white dickey and silvery-gray hair aglow, intermittently emerging from the gloom into the circle of lamplight.

Then those small, sharp, insistent eyes would bore through the darkness in their attempt to meet Dyzma's gaze.

"So you see, sir, you see how hard it is with these two-bit provincial officials and their red tape. Hamstringing and harassment. They hide behind regulations, they use rules as an excuse, but it's all just to ruin me, to take bread from the mouths of my workers. Mr. Dyzma, you, God's honest truth, you are my only hope, my only hope."

"Me?" Dyzma was incredulous.

"You," Kunicki repeated with conviction. "You see, sir, I've already been to Warsaw four times in regard to this matter, and I said to myself, if I don't blow this tyrant out of the water now, this dimwit Olszewski, if I can't get a decent contract on state forest lumber from the Ministry of Agriculture—that's it! I'm liquidating everything! I'll sell it to the Jews—the sawmills, the furniture factory, the paper mill, the cellulose factory—they'll get it all for next to nothing, and as for me, I don't know, I'll shoot myself in the head or something."

"To your health, Mr. Dyzma," he added after a pause, and he drained his glass in one gulp.

"But how can I help you?"

"Hee hee," Kunicki chuckled. "That's a good one, sir. Just a tiny little favor, just a little . . . Oh, yes, sir, I am well aware that it would take up some of your valuable time, and the . . . and yes, there are costs, but with your connections, ho . . . ho!"

He slid his chair closer. His tone suddenly changed.

"My dear sir. I'll be straight with you: if some miracle worker stood in front of me and said, 'Kunicki, I'll try to take care of this matter for you, I'll fire this idiot Olszewski from the State Forestry Board of Directors, I'll replace him with somebody who listens to reason, and I'll try to get you a good quota of lumber, what would you give me for it?' Well, in that case I would answer without hesitation: 'Mr. Miracle Worker, thirty, no, let's make it thirty-five grand in cash, I swear to God! Ten thousand down to cover the expenses, and the rest when the deal is done.'"

Kunicki stopped and waited for an answer. But Dyzma was silent. He'd understood immediately that this old man was offering him a bribe for something that he, Dyzma, he, Nicodemus Dyzma, even if he racked the entirety of his brains, was unable to do. The enormous sum, a sum so beyond his reality it even outstripped his wildest dreams, further underscored the incongruity of the whole exchange. If Kunicki had offered him three hundred or even five hundred zlotys, the deal would have lost its abstract unattainability and appeared instead as a lucrative opportunity for Dyzma to fleece the old man. It occurred to him that maybe he could blackmail this Kunicki with the threat of denouncing him to the police. Maybe he could get himself a payoff of fifty zlotys or so. Jurczak, the court clerk in Łysków, once made a quick hundred this way. Nah, but the clerk had been at his own office, he was an official . . .

Dyzma's silence unnerved Kunicki. He didn't know what to make of it. Was his speech too blunt? . . . Had he offended Dyzma? . . . It would be catastrophic. He had already exhausted all his connections and influence, he had wasted a whole lot of money and time, and if this opportunity slipped through his fingers . . . He resolved to repair the damage and soften the bluntness of his proposition.

"Of course, these days miracle workers are few and far between. Hee hee . . . And one would be hard-pressed to ask even the kindest, most generous friend to take care of issues he's only heard about secondhand. Am I right?"

"True."

"You know what, I have an idea! Mr. Dyzma, my dear friend, do me the favor of visiting me in Koborowo for a couple of weeks. You can relax, make the most of the countryside, the air is terrific, you can ride a horse, I have a motorboat on the lake . . . And while you're there you can have a look at my holdings, my sawmill. So, my dear man?! Is it a deal?"

At this new offer, Dyzma's mouth dropped open in surprise. But Kunicki was indefatigable in his pursuit of the matter: he praised the countryside, the pine forest, the benefits of relaxation; he assured Dyzma that his ladies would appreciate the wonderful diversion of a visitor from Warsaw.

"But, sir," Dyzma interrupted. "There's no way I can think about resting right now. Unfortunately, I've had altogether too much rest lately."

"Oh, there's no such thing as too much."

"I'm unemployed," replied Dyzma, smiling wanly.

He expected to see a look of surprise and disappointment on Kunicki's face, but instead the old man burst out laughing.

"Hee hee, what a comedian you are! Unemployed! Of course, these are tough times for trade and industry. It is hard to get a lucrative post; then again, in civil service there's plenty of recognition, but not much income. Even at the executive level, the pay for working in an office is nothing to write home about."

"I know a little something about that," Dyzma agreed. "I myself spent three years in the state sector."

Kunicki suddenly got the picture. So that's your angle, you sly dog, he thought. Well, so much the better, you just want everything to appear above board.

"My good man," he began, "from the moment I met you, I felt it in my bones that you were sent to me by God. Let's hope that turns out to be the case. Dyzma, sir, my dearest Nicodemus, it just so happens that everything is falling into place. You are looking for a good position, and I've reached that age when a man doesn't have the power he once did. My dear friend, don't be put off by my boldness, but what would you say, sir, if I were to propose that you take up, so to speak, the general administration of my estate and industrial facilities? And don't go thinking it's a two-bit operation. As you'll see, it's quite substantial, a good deal of machinery."

"I don't know if I could. I know absolutely nothing about any of that stuff," Dyzma said truthfully.

"Oh please, my dear sir," Kunicki protested, "you can familiarize yourself easily enough. Besides, I can manage quite well when I'm there, but you know, these trips, these talks with various offices, getting in good with guys like this Olszewski, trying to settle matters at the ministries, I'm already too old for all that. These days you need an energetic, well-connected man who can take these Olszewskis down a peg or two, and, well, someone young. You're not even forty, my dear man, am I right?"

"I just turned thirty-six."

"Ah, such youth! My dearest sir, please don't refuse me. You'll have comfortable quarters, either with us in the manor or in a separate annex, whichever you'd like. Horses if you want them, an automobile at your disposal. You'll eat well, it's not far from the city, and if you want to visit your friends in Warsaw, you're more than welcome. In other words, zero inter-ference. And as for the terms, I'll leave that to your discretion."

"Hmm," Dyzma murmured, "I really don't know."

"So, let's say a thirty percent cut of any increased revenue, agreed?"

"Agreed." Dyzma nodded, unclear what he was agreeing to.

"And a salary of, let's say . . . two thousand a month."

"How much?" Dyzma asked in astonishment.

"So, two thousand five hundred then. Plus all travel expenses. Deal? Let's shake on it!"

Dyzma dazedly shook Kunicki's dainty hand.

The old man, flushed and grinning, lisping on and on without a second's pause, pulled out an enormous pen, covered a scrap of paper with a dozen lines of small, rounded letters, then handed it to Dyzma. And when "my dear Mr. Nicodemus" signed his name with great precision and a highly sophisticated ornamental flourish, Kunicki drew a number of rustling banknotes from his fat wallet.

"Here's five thousand up front, and now . . ." And he began to elaborate on Dyzma's departure and its attendant issues.

Well, old Kunicki, he was thinking to himself, let no one say that you can't take care of business.

Sure enough, Leon Kunicki was renowned for his exceptional cunning; it was a rare thing for him to lose out on one of his deals, which were shrewdly selected and closed with lightning speed.

A few minutes later, Dyzma's footsteps had faded away down the corri-dor, and Kunicki was standing alone in the middle of the room, rubbing his hands together.

Dawn was breaking. The last few specks of stars, already barely visible, were melting away into the celadon firmament. Orderly rows of streetlamps glowed with a sickly white light.

Nicodemus Dyzma walked the streets, the sharp, slapping echo of his footsteps resounding loudly in the emptiness.

His mind was swarming with recollections of the events of the evening he had just passed, a motley tangle of flickering impressions that chased each other around and around but were impossible to pin down. He under-stood that these events were of enormous importance to him, but he was unable to grasp their essence. He could sense he'd fallen into good fortune of some kind, but as for its basic substance, what it all meant, where it came from and why—he couldn't make heads or tails of it.

The longer he thought about it, the less likely everything seemed to him, the more fantastical and preposterous.

Then he stopped, terrified. He carefully reached into his pocket, and, when his fingers located the thick wad of crisp banknotes, he smiled to himself. Suddenly he registered one important thing: he was very, very rich. He ducked into an archway set back from the street and began to count. Jesus, Mary, and Joseph! Five thousand!

"So much cash!" he cried aloud.

Conditioned by years of living hand to mouth, Dyzma had one natural reflex: he must drink to it! And even though he was neither hungry nor thirsty, he turned onto Grzybowska Street, where—as he knew—Icek's pub was still open. He prudently pulled out a hundred and put it in a separate pocket. Flashing around a pile of money like this at Icek's wasn't the best idea.

Despite the hour, Icek's was packed. Droshky drivers, cabbies, waiters from just-closed restaurants, pimps drinking away the nightly earnings of their "fiancées," riffraff from the suburbs returned from pursuing that evening's prey—they filled the two small rooms with a low hum of conversation and clinking glasses.

Nicodemus drank two glasses of vodka and nibbled on a cold pork cutlet with pickle. It occurred to him that it was Sunday morning and Walenty would not be going in to work.

Let those rubes get a taste of real class, he thought.

He ordered a bottle of vodka and a kilo of sausages, scrupulously counted the change, and left. He was already nearing Łucka Street when he suddenly spotted Mańka. She was leaning against a wall and staring into space. He didn't quite know why, but he was tickled to encounter her here.

"Good evening, Miss Mańka," he called cheerfully.

"Good evening," she replied, looking at him with surprise. "What are you doing wandering around all night?"

"And why hasn't little Miss Marianna gone to bed?"

"Maybe I will right now," she answered with resignation.

Dyzma looked her up and down. She seemed prettier than usual. She was thin, that was true, but had a nice shape all the same.

How old is she? he wondered. She can't be more than seventeen.

"Why is it that Miss Marianna's so sad?" he asked.

She shrugged.

"If you'd been slinking around the street like a dog for three nights in a row without a single thing to show for it, you'd hardly be jumping for joy either."

Dyzma felt sorry for her. He reached into his pocket and pulled out a roll of tens.

"I can lend you something. Is twenty enough?"

The girl looked at the money with astonishment. She was quite aware that as of yesterday afternoon the lodger hadn't had a penny to his name. Where could he have gotten all these banknotes? Maybe . . . maybe he stole them from somewhere. That might be precisely the reason he'd put on that tailcoat in the first place. Anyway, she thought, what's it to me?

Nicodemus handed her two bills.

"Take it."

Mańka shook her head in refusal.

"I don't want it. I won't take it. I won't have anything to pay you back."

"So then you don't need to pay me back."

"I don't want it." She knit her brow. "Look at him, the big spender."

She turned away and added softly, "Unless . . . I just don't want it for nothing. Unless you go with me."

"Uhh," Dyzma mumbled, flushing.

Mańka looked him in the eye.

"You don't want me?"

"What? It's not that . . ."

"Some man *you* are!" she suddenly exploded in exasperation. "Oooh, I bet you can't even get it up!"

She spun around and started the long trudge toward home.

"Miss Marianna!" he called after her. "Wait, we'll go."

She stopped, and when he had caught up with her, said, "And the hotel is five zlotys extra."

"Fine," he replied.

They went through the narrow streets in silence.

A sleepy hoodlum in a plush waistcoat opened the door, led them to a small, dirty room, and held out his hand. Dyzma paid.

A shaft of bright sunlight shone through the gray and moldering lace curtains. The room was dank, airless, and smelled of mildew.

"Maybe we should open the window?" Mańka asked.

"Time to go home. It's already late, probably ten o'clock," Dyzma said.

Mańka was in front of a small mirror, brushing her thick black hair with a chipped comb.

"Did you find a job?" she asked indifferently.

Dyzma was suddenly overcome by an irresistible desire to impress Mańka. He pulled all the money from his pocket and laid it out on the table.

"Take a look," he said with a smile.

Mańka turned her head, and her eyes widened. For a long time she just gaped at the banknotes spread before her.

"So much cash . . . so much cash . . . and in five hundreds! Goddamn!"

Nicodemus was relishing the effect.

The girl grabbed hold of his hand.

"Listen! You got *work*?" she asked with awe.

Dyzma laughed and, just for fun, answered, "Mm-hmm."

Mańka carefully stroked the money with the tips of her fingers.

"Tell me . . . tell me . . ." she whispered. "Was it *wet* work?"

He nodded.

She was silent, her eyes full of fear and admiration. She never would have imagined that this quiet lodger, this loser . . .

"With a knife?" she asked.

"With a knife."

"Was it hard?"

"Ehh," he answered. "He didn't make a peep."

She shook her head.

"But he had a lot of dough. . . . A Jew, maybe?"

"A Jew."

"I didn't know . . ."

"What didn't you know?" Dyzma asked as he began to put away the money.

"I didn't know that you were such a . . ."

"Such a what?"

"Well, such a . . ."

She suddenly cuddled up to him.

"And if they nail you?"

"Don't worry. I can manage."

"Did anybody see you? . . . Maybe you left some trace behind? You really need to watch out. Cops, you know, they can even find fingerprints."

"They won't catch me."

"So tell me, did doing it give you the creeps?"

He laughed.

"There was nothing to it. Let's head home. And here's a little something for a new dress."

He laid a hundred zlotys in front of Mańka. The girl threw her arms around his neck and began to kiss his mouth over and over again.

They didn't talk on their way home. Nicodemus was gratified to note that the young girl's attitude toward him had changed almost instantly. He quickly realized, however, that it was not the money that had so aroused Mańka's awed respect, but his fabricated yarn of criminal derring-do. Although he was flattered by this change, he was ashamed that he didn't actually deserve it. Which is why he could never admit to her, not for anything, that it was all a fairy tale.

"Now, watch it, Mańka," he said as they climbed the stairs. "Not a word of this to anyone at home. Understand?"

"Yeah, sure."

"And now I'm going to have to go away for a while, you get it, right? . . . It'll be safer . . ."

"I get it. But you'll come back?"

"I'll be back."

Their lodger showing up together with Mańka made no particular impression on the Barciks. The vodka and sausage, however, were received with respect. Walenty's wife promptly covered the table with a green oil-cloth, and everybody sat down to breakfast. A glass that had once upon a time been a mustard jar made the rounds from hand to hand, and since it was rather capacious, Dyzma was soon pulling out five zlotys and Mańka was running down to buy another bottle. Meanwhile, Nicodemus paid the overdue rent.

When the girl came back, he said, "Well, you should congratulate me. I found a good job."

"Where?" Walenty asked.

"Not in Warsaw. In the provinces."

"Didn't I tell you?" Walenty's wife nodded. "It's easier to earn your daily bread out in the country. You know, peasants."

They drank to his health, and when the bottle was empty, Nicodemus unfolded his bed, undressed, tucked the vest containing the money under his pillow, and almost instantaneously fell asleep.

Walenty sat quietly for a moment and then, having become more than a little drunk, burst unexpectedly into song. This was met with fierce disapproval from Mańka.

"Be quiet, goddamn it, can't you see the man is sleeping? Let him get some rest."

Silence fell. Walenty put on his cap and left, and his wife went over to the neighbors to crow about the vodka their lodger had bought for everyone to toast his new position.

Mańka pulled a batiste handkerchief from the closet to cover the sleeping man's head. After all, the room was full of flies.

Chapter 3

It took Dyzma the entire morning to prepare for his departure. Fully aware that he would have to look the part, he had done no small amount of shopping. He'd bought several changes of underwear, a few neckties, a new shaving kit, some extremely yellow shoes, and two off-the-rack suits that very nearly fit. He'd also acquired some beautiful leather suitcases and a whole host of little odds and ends.

Back in Łysków, Notary Winder's son, a student from Lviv, was considered the embodiment of elegance by the entire town; many a time Nicodemus had admired the fanciness of the various toiletries he kept in his room. So now, while shopping, he had tried to let the taste of the notary's young son be his guide.

His capital was sorely depleted, but Dyzma was pleased with himself.

Everything was taken care of by six; the train didn't leave until half past seven. Mańka, who had initially promised herself that she'd see Dyzma to the station, was so intimidated by his new paraphernalia that she didn't even dare offer her company.

Only when he was leaving did she run out after him, following him into the street and giving him a passionate kiss. Then she helped him with his suitcase and, as the cab pulled away, called out, "You'll come back?"

"I'll come back!" he shouted in return.

Traveling second class was markedly more comfortable than third class. For one, instead of hard benches, there were springy couches. For another, the passengers here were considerably nicer, and, unlike in third class, the railway service treated him with actual politeness.

Dyzma delighted in his first trip under these conditions, which gave him the sensation that he was a real somebody and that not only Łysków's postmaster, but even both Winders, father and son, could not fail to be impressed if they could only see him now.

The few people who had taken seats in his compartment soon disembarked, and then only Dyzma remained. He didn't want to sleep. Besides, it was necessary to think this whole matter through.

By now he understood very well that Kunicki's astonishing proposition was because that sly old fox took him for a man of influence, with a close relationship to Minister Jaszuński. Dispelling the illusion would obviously be tantamount to setting this unbelievably high salary on fire. Ergo, for the sake of keeping it going as long as possible, he'd need to marshal all his cunning to bolster Kunicki's erroneous conviction. Room and board would be free. Which meant that expenses would be limited to just a few dozen, maybe a hundred zlotys per month. Which meant two thousand four hundred in savings!

Well! If he could manage to hang on at least for three months . . . Or maybe even half a year? . . .

He smiled to himself. Afterward, he could maybe set himself up lending money at interest and live like a lord, doing nothing at all.

He just needed to string the old man along for as long as he could and stay on his toes so he wouldn't give himself away. Speak as little as possible in general, and about himself, not a single word. Old or not, Kunicki appeared to be nobody's fool, and if even the slightest suspicion was raised, the whole thing would come crashing down.

It was already dawn when the conductor came in and announced their arrival at the Koborowo station.

Dyzma's anxiety spiked. Had Kunicki remembered he was coming on this train?

Evidently he'd remembered after all. Immediately upon disembarking, Dyzma was approached by a liveried footman.

"You are the honorable gentleman for Master and Madam Kunicki?"

"Yes."

"A car is waiting in front of the station, Mr. Administrator, sir," Kunicki's man said as he picked up the suitcases.

Settling back in the luxurious car, Nicodemus thought: the Honorable General Administrator of the Koborowo estate. I'm going to have to treat myself to some business cards.

The road was flat as a tabletop. They drove along the railway track for a while and then through more picturesque scenery, past a ramshackle water mill teetering over a rounded bridge, and then, turning right, past a number of factory buildings clustered around railway sidings.

From here, there began a long avenue flanked with maples, at the end of which loomed a grand manor house, stylistically a little all over the place and trying more than a little too hard, but harmonious in its own odd way. The car made a half-circle around the perimeter of the lawn and stopped at the forecourt. The front door opened and a chambermaid appeared to help the footman attend to the suitcases. The second Dyzma removed his coat, a somewhat disheveled Kunicki, clad in a long foulard dressing gown of such lurid floweriness that Dyzma at first took him for a woman, burst into the foyer.

Kunicki, beaming and lively as quicksilver, threw his arms around his visitor and proceeded to unleash a mighty volley of verbiage, his torrent of speech even faster and lispier than it had been in Warsaw, although its tediousness was unchanged. The first question for which he paused for an answer was, "Would my dear sir prefer to live here in the manor? Or else in the annex in the park?"

The dear guest replied that it was all the same to him, and so he was led to a set of beautifully appointed rooms on the ground floor. It was explained to him that this would be quite convenient indeed, since he could bypass the other rooms and the foyer by simply exiting right onto the terrace; meanwhile, the entrance to the bath was in the corridor just next door. Perhaps he wished to bathe after his journey? A bath had been prepared for him, and later, if he was not too tired and was willing to come to breakfast in the dining room, Kunicki and his ladies would be most pleased.

When Dyzma was finally alone, he quickly unpacked his suitcase, arranged his things in the wardrobe, and then made his way to the bathroom. Never before had he washed himself in a bathtub. Right away he deemed it considerably more comfortable than the crowded bathhouses. In fact, lately he hadn't even been able to afford those; his bathwater, which afterward had taken on a distinct new hue, could eloquently attest to that. Dyzma made several attempts to manipulate the tub before he located the chain to the drain and, pulling it, allowed the compromising liquid to find its way out. He rinsed the tub, dressed and combed his hair, and when he returned to his room, he was amazed to find that, during his absence, servants had tidied his clothing and shoes.

Damn! They don't let you lift a finger around here! he thought with admiration.

He'd hardly managed to knot his tie when he heard a knock at the door. There was Kunicki, all freshened up and voluble almost beyond human measure.

The room to which he led Dyzma, which really deserved the appellation "hall," was completely lined with a type of dark wood whose primary effect was to produce a sense of intimidation. Along the walls stood magnificent credenzas and glazed cabinetry, their interiors shimmering with the silver and crystal riches stuffed within, and on the smallish white table, there appeared four settings of luxury tableware that would suffice to serve the entire staff of the Łysków post office.

"My ladies will be along in a moment, just as soon as they finish their toilette. In the meantime, perhaps you might care, my dear Nicodemus, sir, to see the other rooms on the ground floor, since the rooms upstairs, hee, must remain unseen for now, you understand, sir: the ladies. What do you think of my abode? I did it all myself. I designed everything, from the architectural instructions to the smallest piece of furniture."

He took Dyzma's arm and trotted alongside him, trying to catch his eye whenever he could.

The manor and, indeed, the whole of Koborowo, he explained, was his pride and joy: "Yet back in the day, there was nothing here but wilderness, just a house in the middle of nowhere, fit for demolition, nothing but ruined farm buildings and fallow fields. But today—a gold mine, a gem, impeccably and systematically run. The sweat of my brow, dear sir, is what got this place back on its feet."

Soft carpets muffling their footsteps, they passed through room after room outfitted with a lavishness Dyzma had never come close to imagining.

Gilded bronze, paintings in ornate frames, gleaming furniture, enormous mirrors, fireplaces of marble and malachite, gold-embossed leather and fabrics Dyzma couldn't begin to identify—everything simply screamed money. The thought occurred to Dyzma that, if the mansion and all its trimmings were convulsed by a sudden earthquake, gold would spray out in every direction.

"Well, what do you think?" asked Kunicki when they found themselves back in the dining room, but Dyzma had no time to answer; the doors opened and in came the ladies they had been awaiting.

"Allow me," Kunicki said, bringing Dyzma forward, "to introduce you: Mr. Dyzma."

The older one, a fair blonde, took his hand with a smile.

"It's very nice to meet you. I've heard so much about you."

The younger woman, a brunette with a boyish appearance and an air of alert energy, shook Dyzma's hand firmly, looking him up and down with a brazenness that left him flustered.

Luckily, there was no need to respond, since Kunicki was rattling on without pause. Which meant that Dyzma had time to consider the two women. The blonde couldn't be older than twenty-six, and the brunette was maybe twenty or twenty-one. This surprised him, because he distinctly remembered Kunicki referring to his wife and daughter. Whereas these two could be sisters, although they didn't look much like sisters. You couldn't call the blonde slim, but she was shapely and supple. Her mouth was small but her lips had a sensual fullness, her face a gentle oval with immense, almost disproportionately large blue eyes that suggested a dreamy nature. Her elegant summer dress, raw silk, revealed a neck and shoulders of dazzling paleness.

Next to this pastel beauty, the younger of the two—with her narrow knit eyebrows, her short, mannishly cropped chestnut hair and its coppery sheen, her English blouse buttoned to the neck, her dark-green necktie and sun-bronzed face—stood in stark contrast. There was something defiant in her hazel gaze. More than anything, though, Dyzma was struck by the shape of her ears. The brunette sat with her profile to him, and he had to stop himself consciously from staring at them. He had never been one to pay any attention to the ears of the people he met. Only now did he realize that ears could have their own individual expression, that they might be beautiful, they might call to mind some exotic flower of a springy, succulent consistency, and he was riveted by their shape. Kunicki had little red ears that came to a sharp point on top, and the blonde's were obscured by her fluffy hairdo.

These observations of Dyzma's didn't interfere with his vigilance in adjusting his movements and methods of eating to most closely resemble those of his company so as not, through improper behavior, to expose the lack of what Notary Winder had called "good breeding," which he presumed meant "looking like a lord."

Kunicki talked without stopping, describing at great length Koborowo's various virtues and deficiencies, itemizing his property, characterizing the temperaments of individual horses, and drawing up a schedule by which he'd be able to show it all to his beloved Mr. Dyzma.

"So far, I've only managed to show you around the ground floor."

It was only when Kunicki took a sip of coffee that there was sufficient pause for the blonde to ask, "And how did you like it, sir?"

"Very expensive looking," Dyzma replied artlessly.

The blonde's cheeks flushed red. Her eyes shone with inexpressible regret.

"It is, if you please, my husband's taste, not mine."

"Hee hee," laughed Kunicki. "That's exactly what I told Mr. Dyzma. Just imagine, sir, that was the very first scene Nina made as my wife, hee hee, that's just what she did to me when we came to Koborowo after the wedding. I suppose that's feminine gratitude for you. Here I was, bending over backwards to feather my lady's nest, and still she made a scene. Just imagine—"

"Please stop," Nina broke in.

"I don't understand you, Papa," the brunette added. "Why are you saying things to Mr. Dyzma that bore him and upset Nina besides?"

"But I'm saying nothing, nothing at all, my dear. And anyway, it's about time we relieved you of our company, because I need to show Nicodemus all around Koborowo. I tell you, sir—"

"Perhaps Mr. Dyzma is tired," Nina interjected.

"God forbid," Dyzma countered.

"Well, well. You see, you see," Kunicki lisped with satisfaction. "We men of business, we're champing at the bit to get down to serious matters, matters of only the most vital importance."

"Papa, don't put words in Mr. Dyzma's mouth," his daughter interrupted. "I doubt that everyone considers railroad ties and scraps of timber to be matters of the most vital importance. Am I right, sir?" She turned to Dyzma.

"Well, of course you're right," Dyzma replied cautiously. "There are matters considerably more important than that."

Kunicki chuckled and rubbed his hands.

"Yes, yes, there are more important matters than railway ties. For example, the business of securing a higher lumber quota and the question of obtaining supplies!"

He laughed, very pleased with himself.

The blonde stood and nodded her head.

"We won't intrude on you gentlemen," she said coldly.

The brunette also rose and, before Dyzma could figure out exactly what this family conflict entailed, both had left the dining room. Dyzma hadn't expected breakfast to be over so quickly. In an effort to avoid looking like a glutton, he had eaten very little, and now he was hungry.

The footman announced that the horses were ready.

"Well," said Kunicki, putting on his hat. "There you go. Don't be put off, sir, but there's always some kind of big misunderstanding between me and my wife. She's an idealist, sir, a romantic, all kinds of dreams in her head—she's still young. And my daughter? . . . Hmm . . . Kasia takes her side, she's still a chit of a girl. And you know how it is with gals, they always stick together."

In the forecourt stood an impressive carriage, a kind of elegant two-wheeled cabriolet pulled by a pair of bays. They settled comfortably into the soft cushions and Kunicki cracked the whip. The horses broke into a trot.

"Pretty little nags, right?" Kunicki winked. "I bought this pair at an agricultural exhibition in Lublin. Top-notch, don't you think?"

Indeed, they ran like a house on fire, and Dyzma thought they were splendid.

"First I'll show you my railway department," Kunicki said. "Twenty-two kilometers of track with two branches. We're going to the first one, in my forest."

They turned at an avenue of maples and rode for a good half hour past fields dense with ripe rye. The air was still, but out here the heat was more bearable.

"Nice harvest," Dyzma remarked.

"Yes, yes," Kunicki answered sadly. "Too nice, too nice, unfortunately."
Nicodemus burst out laughing.

"You say that like it's a bad thing!"

"And you don't think it is?" Kunicki asked, surprised. "After all, it's a disaster for agriculture."

Dyzma was tempted to tell him he didn't understand, but he held his tongue. Better to be circumspect.

"A disaster," Kunicki repeated. "Prices are dropping like a stone. In two months, we'll be selling it for chicken feed. It's a high-yield disaster, dear sir."

Aha, Dyzma thought. You see, who would've thought! But best to say as little as possible, and for Christ's sake, don't ask questions.

"Well, sure, that's understandable," he said in a loud voice. "It's just that I don't agree that it's as bad as you make it out to be."

He fell silent, and it occurred to him that he needed to add something in order not to appear naive. Which is why he said, casually and somewhat randomly, "Grain's going up."

"Bah! But that's only if the government starts stockpiling grain."

"And who said they weren't?"

"What are you telling me?!" Kunicki leapt up.

Dyzma was afraid he had made some ridiculous fundamental error but was immediately reassured when he saw the gleam in his companion's eye.

"Hot damn! What are you saying? Has it already been decided?"

"For now, it's the plan . . ."

"My dear Nicodemus! What an absolutely brilliant idea! Brilliant! After all, it's the government's duty to protect agriculture; the country's welfare is entirely dependent on agriculture, for God's sake. Hell, in this country there's nothing less than an obsession for tinkering around with the economy. But Poland is seventy percent farmers! Seventy percent. Not industry, not mining, not commerce, but agriculture and agricultural products, livestock and lumber—it's the basis for everything! What's good for agriculture is good for everyone—for manufacturers, for wholesalers, for workers! Mr. Dyzma, you really should, sir, you have a sacred duty to your fatherland, to use every bit of your influence to push this brilliant project forward! So the government is going to buy up all the surplus! My God! Koborowo and the house alone . . ."

As he began to mentally calculate the potential profit, Dyzma spoke up again.

"It's just a matter of money. There isn't any money."

"Money, money? That's nothing." Kunicki was on fire. "A trifling detail. After all, the state can issue bonds. Grain bonds for, say, a hundred million zlotys. Pay the bonds and that's that. Charging interest, obviously, at, let's suppose, five percent, or even six. What do you think, sir? For six years, let's say. And I'll be damned if during that stretch there aren't at least two boom years, right? So then we sell the entire grain supply abroad and make a bundle. What do you think? And tremendous benefits: *primo*, sustained high prices that'll really save our hides, and *secondo*, increased circulation, because, of course, the bonds must be unregistered bearer bonds. And that way the state can give the domestic market a real shot in the arm, to the tune of a hundred million—now there's a sum that will surely have a salutary effect on our catastrophe of a cash situation. Hot damn! You simply must talk to Minister Jaszuński about this . . ."

"We've already talked about it at length, and who knows . . ."

He broke off, and at the same time thought, This old guy's got a hell of a good head on his shoulders. With a brain like that, he could even be a minister!

Kunicki pursued the matter unflaggingly. He rolled out various arguments, put forth reservations and doubts—which he immediately smashed with the power of his logical reasoning—on and on he lisped, his words tumbling out one after the other while he flourished his whip with emotion.

Meanwhile, the road had curved back into the woods, and they were making their way through tall pines.

In a vast clearing, cords of lumber were stacked along a narrow-gauge railway. A miniature steam engine had just begun to puff and hiss in the effort to move a dozen or so wagon cars loaded with great logs. Two rows of workers were helping it along, pushing the wagons from either side.

The workers doffed their caps with a reluctance that bordered on hostility. A weather-beaten figure in a gray jacket approached their carriage and was starting to say something when Kunicki cut him off.

"Mr. Starkiewicz, say hello to Mr. Dyzma, general administrator."

The figure took off his cap and gave Dyzma an appraising look. Dyzma bowed slightly.

For a few minutes, while Kunicki grilled Starkiewicz on various particulars, Nicodemus looked curiously around at the masses of accumulated lumber, the barracks slapped together with old planks, the clearing with its whistling saws and moaning axes. When they moved on, Kunicki launched into an expert lecture on the many different grades of wood, the state of their utilization, and the tribulations of obtaining a permit to fell one's own timber, a stand of trees in this very vicinity. He quoted articles of law, figures, prices, and from time to time he glanced at his companion's face, which wore an expression of scrupulous attention.

In truth, Dyzma was flailing in a sea of panic. His consciousness was being buried alive under an increasingly berserk avalanche of concepts and ideas about which he had not the slightest understanding. He felt like a man beneath a toppled haystack. He'd lost all orientation and realized he was singularly ill equipped to deal with this state of affairs, and not by a long shot would he be able to control the situation enough to avoid disgrace and humiliation—to avoid, to put it plainly, ratting himself out.

They'd already toured the lumber station in the state-owned woods, the sawmill by the railroad terminal, and the furniture factory, and by the time they had finished their visit to the paper mill as well as some warehouse or another, the muddle in Dyzma's head had grown to such a degree that he would've been glad to flee the scene right then and there. Looming before him was a towering mountain of incomprehensible business matters, bizarre and mysterious interconnections; he'd just met so many new people, these managers and directors, who spoke with such authority and with so many acronyms and abbreviations that Dyzma had managed to grasp nary a thing.

Dyzma's only consolation was that Kunicki was oblivious to his misery, instead interpreting it as diligent observation and considered deliberation. Clearly, he was so absorbed in the role of providing information to his new administrator that he didn't have time to notice said administrator's gloom.

It was already close to three when they stopped once again in front of the manor.

"So you see, sir," Kunicki said, handing the reins to a stableman, "my Koborowo is a substantial complex. Substantial and, God knows, logically and methodically designed to turn a good and steady profit. If in practice that's not always the way it works out, it's only because of our bureaucracy and flip-flopping agricultural policies. But even under these conditions, it's possible to do so much, so very much indeed, well, but now that's *your* purview and responsibility, my dear Nicodemus, sir."

It was just the two of them at lunch, since the ladies had taken the car to Grodno for some shopping. At Koborowo, one ate both superbly and copiously, which helped explain why, when they'd taken their black coffee in Kunicki's office, Dyzma felt so extraordinarily sluggish.

Meanwhile, the quicksilver Kunicki was back to elucidating the Koborowo economy. He opened cabinets and drawers, reached for files, pulled out bills and correspondence, all while ceaselessly chattering away. Nicodemus was approaching abject despair when the old man, his small, busy hands compiling a fat pile of books and papers, finally wrapped it up:

"I see that you're a little tired, and besides, one should, after all, get some rest after traveling. So then, if you'll allow me to have these materials sent to your room, you can go over them this evening. All right?"

"Yes, with pleasure."

"What would you say to a little catnap right now, my dear Nicodemus, how does that sound?"

"Well, you know, surely . . ."

"So, a nice little snooze, a nice little snooze, I'll see you to your room. And kindly do have a look at the date in question in the correspondence with the director of national forests. It's scandalous, after all, to be left hanging for three months without an answer, because . . . well, more of this later. Get some rest, sir. We'll have dinner at eight."

Nicodemus took off his shoes and stretched out on the bed, but he couldn't fall asleep. Thoughts swarmed mercilessly, almost painfully, inside his skull. What was he going to do? What was he going to do? . . . Resign on the spot and admit everything to the old man? Try to make sense of such hopelessly difficult and complicated materials? If he could somehow get a handle on it, he could hang on to Koborowo for two, maybe three months . . . Because fat chance of holding out longer than that. After all, the old guy had only hired him in order to get various concessions from the minister . . .

Such a slippery old codger, yet he still fell for it . . . But how am I going to manage? Aw, to hell with this . . .

Those two hours of rest were more exhausting than the entire busy morning and afternoon put together. He'd smoked a dozen cigarettes down to stubs, and the cloud that had filled the room was starting to get to him. He stood and went to the adjacent office. The desk was covered in the files, books, and documents with which it was his job to acquaint himself.

He uttered a few heartfelt curses and turned back. Then he remembered he could open the door to the terrace and go out into the park.

The beautifully maintained park certainly took up quite a lot of space. Dyzma, as he walked along, couldn't make out where it ended. Paths and avenues ran like smooth little rivulets of water in every direction among old oaks, chestnuts, lindens, and maples.

You could get lost out here, thought Dyzma, looking around him. As a precaution, he noted that the manor was on the north side.

Here and there, under the giant trees, a stone or wooden bench popped up. After strolling for ten or twenty minutes, Nicodemus chose a shady bench set back from the path and sat down. At once, the torturous thoughts returned: What will I do? How can I manage to work this out?

All of a sudden, he heard whistling and then hurried footsteps right in front of him. He looked around. Striding down a narrow avenue was a young man in exceedingly elegant clothes, a monocle glittering in his eye. Trotting behind him on bandy little legs was a miniature pinscher with a head like a bat. The little dog noticed Dyzma and immediately started to yap. The young man stopped and turned, fixing his eyes on Dyzma and taking his measure. He was around thirty years old, tall and lean. His height was augmented by his disproportionately long neck, which culminated in a round face so tiny and pale that it called to mind that of a sickly little kid. The haughty, contemptuous expression on its features made a stark contrast, as did his huge red-rimmed blue eyes and their look of venomous irony. Caught in their gaze, Dyzma was rattled, all the more so because the young man just stood there and stared at him insolently.

Who the hell? Dyzma thought.

The man pointed a very long index finger in Dyzma's direction and asked—squawked, really, "Who are you?"

Not knowing what to do, Dyzma rose to his feet.

"I'm the administrator, the new administrator . . ."

"Your name?"

"Dyzma, Nicodemus Dyzma."

The dog yapped, jumping gracelessly around the legs of its master.

"Oh? Dyzma, is it? . . . I've heard about you. I am Count Ponimirski. Sit down. Quiet, Brutus! You'll notice I named him that because it makes no sense, because why should a dog have a name that makes any sense? Sit down!"

Dyzma sat. This count was making a remarkable impression on him, inspiring dread, disgust, curiosity, and sympathy all at the same time.

"I heard," the count continued, quickly flicking the tip of his tongue over his bloodless lips. "I heard. Apparently, that scoundrel brought you here because you're some kind of somebody. I consider it my duty, as a gentleman, to alert you to the larcenous character of my lovely little brother-in-law."

"But who are you talking about?" Dyzma was puzzled.

"Who? Why, that swine Leon Kunik."

"Mr. Kunicki?"

"Damn him to hell!" the count cried. "Again with Kunicki? How is it Kunicki? Where does Kunicki come from?! Kunicki is a fine noble name that that parasite appropriated for himself! He stole it, do you understand? He stole it! His name is just Kunik! I took it upon myself to investigate. Son of Genowefa Kunik, mangle woman, and father unknown. Yes, the beneficent Countess Ponimirska, granddaughter of the Duchess de Rehon, is nowadays merely Mrs. Kunik."

"I don't understand," Dyzma began warily. "Does that mean you're Mr. Kunicki's brother-in-law?"

Ponimirski leapt up like he'd been shot through with an arrow. His heretofore bloodless face went suddenly and violently red.

"Silence! Silence, you, you . . . !"

"Why, I certainly beg your pardon!" Dyzma was alarmed.

"Don't you dare, not in my presence, refer to that scumbag as anything other than Kunik, or that swine Kunik, or even that charlatan Kunik! Least of all Kunicki! . . . My brother-in-law is the mangy usurer and swindler Kunik, the peasant bastard Kunik! Ku-nik! Ku-nik! Repeat after me: Ku-nik! Do it! . . ."

"Kunik," Dyzma mumbled.

Ponimirski, mollified, sat down again, and he even smiled.

"You didn't know this about him? My Brutus didn't know, either, and even groveled under my brother-in-law's feet, at least until he gave Brutus a kick. That beast!"

He lapsed into pensive silence, then added, "Both of them: Kunik's a beast and the dog's a beast, too . . . As a matter of fact, I'm a beast as well . . ."

He burst into startling laughter.

"If you'll excuse my frankness, you're a beast, too."

He laughed some more, and Dyzma made a mental note: he's a madman.

"Do you think that I'm a madman?" Ponimirski suddenly grabbed Dyzma's arm and pulled him close so they were face-to-face.

Dyzma flinched.

"No," he replied unconvincingly. "Of course not, God forbid . . ."

"Don't deny it!" shouted the count. "I know you're thinking it! Anyway, I'm sure that Kunik has already prejudiced you against me. And perhaps my sister has, too? Tell me, for after all, she will also have been corrupted by that pig, that vulture. What has Nina told you?"

"Nothing at all, nobody's told me anything."

"No one?"

"I give you my word," Nicodemus assured him.

"They've apparently decided you shouldn't have the honor of meeting me. Do you know they've forbidden me from setting foot inside the manor house? That I've been ordered to eat in solitude? That I'm not free to leave the park, because Kunik has ordered the servants to give me a lashing if I do?"

"But why?"

"Why? Because I'm inconvenient, because my aristocratic manners offend that parvenu, that mangle woman's bastard, because *I* should be the master here, not that villainous stray, because he can't stand it that I, the true heir to Koborowo, I, a scion of the family, should be lord of our immemorial family seat!"

"So Mr. Kunic—, Mr. Kunik got Koborowo in your sister the countess's dowry?"

Ponimirski hid his face in his hands and was silent. After a while, Dyzma noticed that his long fingers—his almost unbelievably long fingers—were dripping with tears.

What in goddamned hell?! he swore to himself.

The dog had begun to whine insistently and paw his master's legs. His master took out a highly perfumed handkerchief, wiped his eyes, and said, "Forgive me. I have a slight nervous condition."

"It's quite all right . . ."

The count twisted his mouth in a venomous smile.

"What is this 'It's quite all right'? Look, Mr. whatever you're called, I'm crying merely because I wish to cry. You sound like an Englishman when you say that . . . But anyway, surely *you* don't understand English? . . ."

"No, I don't."

"But that's marvelous," said the count happily. "I wouldn't want to cause you any distress; I've grown fond of you!" He drummed his fingertips on his knees. "Therefore, whenever I feel the need to give you a dressing down, I'll do it in English. All right? . . ."

"All right," replied Nicodemus with resignation.

"But that's not the point. I must inform you that, although Kunik is a swindler who cheated my family out of Koborowo, you should not undertake to defraud him, because someday I will bring him to trial and take Nina under my guardianship. What time is it?"

Dyzma pulled out his watch.

"Half past seven."

"What? Already? Ugh, I must get to the annex, they won't give me my dinner any later. I bid you farewell. It's a shame, there are still many more things I wanted to tell you. Come here tomorrow at the same time. You'll come?"

"Fine, I'll come."

"One more thing. For the love of God, don't let anyone know that you saw me, that you spoke with me. Give me your word of honor!"

"You have my word."

"Well, I suppose I believe you, although both your name and your appearance suggest that you come from common rabble and, after all, peasants have no honor. I bid you farewell."

He turned on his heel and, with great springy steps, bounded away down an avenue of maples. The little pinscher, running and leaping maladroitly, followed him.

"A madman," Dyzma said loudly, when they'd disappeared around a bend. A madman for sure, but the things he told me . . . There's always some kind of dirty business with any of these gentlemen types . . . Maybe what he said was true . . . Dammit . . . So it's Kunik, and he says he's a scoundrel . . . Maybe better to let sleeping dogs lie . . .

He threw up his hands and lit a cigarette. In the distance, he heard a low, deep gong. Dinner.

Chapter 4

Dinner consisted of several dishes served by a stiff and noiseless servant. The mood was slightly better than at breakfast. Kunicki, or rather Kunik, was less single-minded about business and Dyzma. Instead, he turned his verbal hose on his wife and daughter, asking all about what kind of shopping they had done.

Lady Nina responded politely, albeit coldly, while Kasia rarely deigned to mumble even a short "yes" or "no"; most questions addressed directly to her were met with disdainful silence. Even after his bizarre conversation with Ponimirski, Nicodemus was still completely at sea as to the origin of the daughter's contempt, a contempt that was entering the territory of offensive impertinence. He wanted to figure this obscure situation out somehow, and although he puzzled over how to do it in the most tactful way, he failed to come up with anything.

After dinner, Kunicki invited the company for a walk, and although Kasia just shrugged, Nina agreed.

"Yes, it would be a pleasure."

She and her husband, who tapped along with his thick walking stick and left a trail of cigar smoke in his wake, led the way. They headed into the park, but not to the part with which Dyzma was already familiar. That part was dense with ancient trees, whereas here there were mainly lawns and flowerbeds, and only occasionally were there clumps of picturesquely slender trees silhouetted against the dark sapphire of the sky.

Nicodemus was obliged to accompany Kasia. They proceeded in silence, and since utter stillness prevailed in the park, they could hear the low murmur of the Kunickis' conversation. How ridiculous they looked together! He, a little old man, with all that irritating fidgeting and constant gesticulating, and this young, slim, almost statuesque wife walking sedately alongside him, her steps even and smooth.

"Do you play tennis?" Kasia asked.

"Me? No, miss, I don't know how."

"That's strange."

"Why strange?"

"Well, nowadays every gentleman plays tennis."

"I never had time to learn the game, miss. I only know billiards."

"Really? That's interesting, you can tell me . . . Excuse me," she said suddenly, and ran off toward a flowerbed.

Dyzma had stopped, not knowing what to do, when Kasia returned holding several stems of a tobacco plant in her hand. The flowers' fragrance was intoxicating even from a distance. She brought them close to his face. Assuming they were a gift, he blushed and reached out his hand.

"No, no! They're not for you. Just smell them. Aren't they fabulous?"

"Yes, they smell nice," he said, abashed.

"You must be very conceited, by the way."

"Me? Why?" His surprise was sincere.

"Well, because you immediately thought that the flowers were meant for you. You probably get flowers from women all the time, don't you?"

Dyzma, who had never once received any flowers from any woman, said, just in case, "Sometimes."

"You're apparently quite famous in *le monde* of Warsaw, quite a powerful man."

"Me?"

"My father told me. But in any case, you actually look like . . . Aha, and you play billiards?"

"Since I was a kid," he responded, recalling a small, smoky snooker room in the back of Aronson's cake shop in Łysków.

"We have a billiard table at home too, but none of us knows how to play. If you could find a little time for me, I'd love to learn . . ."

"You, miss?" he asked in surprise. It had never occurred to him that a woman might play billiards. "But it's a man's game."

"Men's games are exactly what I like. Will you teach me?"

"It would be my pleasure."

"We can even start right now."

"No," Dyzma replied. "I have a lot of work to do today. I need to get the hang of the bookkeeping, the accounts."

"Hmm, you aren't a man of excessive courtesy. But that fits your type."

"And is that good or bad?" he ventured.

"Is what good or bad?" she asked coolly.

"Well, that I'm that type."

"You know, sir . . . I'll be honest. I like dealing with people who constitute a certain positive value, as long as they don't remind me of my dad. But right up front, I'd like to emphasize and, hmm . . . clarify, that . . . Will you be angry if I'm frank with you?"

"God forbid!"

"I don't care to get close."

"I don't understand."

"Do you like to dot your *i*'s and cross your *t*'s?"

"Huh?"

"I can see that you also like situations to be crystal clear. Very well, then. Even if I'm friendly with you, I don't want you to jump to the wrong conclusion. In other words, you'll get no flowers from me."

He finally understood what she was getting at and laughed.

"I wasn't counting on that at all."

"Great. It's best when matters are made clear."

He didn't exactly know why, but he felt insulted and said, almost without thinking, "You're right. And I'll be frank with you in return. You're not my type, either."

"Is that so? Even better," she said, somewhat surprised. "This mutual understanding will allow us to study billiards."

The Kunickis had turned back to join them. Kasia took Nina's arm and handed her the flowers, saying, "These are for you, Ninette, you like tobacco . . ."

Kunicki threw her a look in which Dyzma, despite the dusk, could detect distinct anger.

"What's with this display?" he hissed, lisping heavily.

Nina, embarrassment flashing across her face, quietly said, "It's a pity you plucked them. A flower's life is short enough as it is."

They parted in the hall, wishing each other a curt goodnight. But Dyzma didn't think about going to sleep. He resolved to try, at any cost, to familiarize himself with the documents related to Kunicki's financial affairs. These were highly complicated matters, bristling with numbers and crammed with hostile and incomprehensible words he either didn't know at all, or ones he knew but that were used in mysterious ways he couldn't understand. Inventory, discount, traction, semimanufactured items, protective custom duty, reinsurance, compensation, tendency, boom, an equivalent; beads of sweat covered Dyzma's forehead.

He began to read aloud in a low voice, but that didn't help either. He simply stopped understanding what the sentences he was saying meant; elusive, emptied of their sense, they fled from his consciousness.

Nicodemus kept leaping up from the desk. He ran around the room, exploding with curses and beating at his temples with clenched fists.

"But I have to, I have to," he repeated doggedly. "I have to figure this out or I'll lose it all."

Again he began to read, and again he leapt up.

"No, it's useless, my head will explode and I won't understand a thing."

He went to the bathroom, turned on the cold water tap, and held his head under the stream for a couple of minutes, thinking, Maybe it'll help, maybe it won't.

It didn't. He spent the entire night riffling through papers and documents, and his only reward for that torture was a massive headache. His murky, fragmentary conceptions of Koborowo's complex economy would not suffice, not by a long shot, to discuss the business with Kunicki, let alone allow him to administer the estate.

"What do I do? . . ."

He thought long and hard about it and decided, no matter what, that he wasn't giving up without a fight.

"Just hold on for as long as you can, and maybe, in the meantime, rescue will come from somewhere."

It was already after eight in the morning when Kunicki found Dyzma sprawled among the books and papers on his desk.

"My dear Mr. Nicodemus!" he cried with mock indignation. "Whatever are you doing? You haven't slept at all! Diligence, yes, but health is also important."

"I'll be fine," Dyzma responded. "When I start something, I don't like to interrupt myself."

"You're a determined man. So, how did you find everything?"

"Well, not bad."

"But you must admit, dear Mr. Nicodemus, that all the documents are exceptionally maintained. Clear, systematic, accurate . . ."

"Indeed," he said. "Very well maintained."

"Aren't they? You're right. I do it myself. And knowing this machinery inside and out, knowing every stick and every cog, is the best guarantee that my staff won't cheat me. But now, put aside this work, please. Breakfast will soon be served. You'll have time enough to work because I won't be bothering you today. I have a building audit in the paper mill, and then I'm off to see a forest in Kociłówka."

When they entered the dining room, the ladies were already at the table.

"You look pale," Lady Nina observed.

"My head hurts a little."

"Because, my dear ladies, Mr. Nicodemus didn't sleep a wink, do you believe it? He spent the entire night over the books."

"Maybe you should take a headache pill?" Lady Nina asked.

"It's probably not worth it . . ."

"Take it please, it will help you."

She asked the servant to fetch a box with some pills, and Dyzma had to take his medicine.

"You know, Nina," Kasia said, "Mr. Dyzma is going to teach me to play billiards."

"Do you play well?"

"I'm so-so," Dyzma said. "I used to be pretty good."

"Perhaps we can start right after breakfast?" Kasia proposed.

"I will watch your lesson," Lady Nina added.

"Oh ho," Kunicki laughed. "I'm afraid that you want to snatch Mr. Nicodemus away from me entirely."

"My husband is jealous of you," Lady Nina said, smiling, and Dyzma noticed how kindly she looked at him.

"She must be a very good person," he thought.

Right after breakfast, Kunicki said goodbye to them and trotted out to the car that was waiting for him.

Kasia ordered the billiards to be prepared, and all three went to the billiard room.

The lesson began with a demonstration of the hand position and the proper stick grip. Then Dyzma explained how to strike a cue ball. Kasia quickly grasped the basics, and since she had a steady hand and a good eye, Dyzma issued a verdict:

"You'll be a good player, you just need a lot of practice."

"So, is Kasia a clever student?" Lady Nina asked.

"She's doing very well for her first time."

"And what is the hardest part of billiards?" Kasia asked.

"The hardest is the carambole."

"Show me how to do it."

Dyzma arranged the balls and said, "Now pay attention. I'm going to strike the cue ball so it hits the remaining two."

"But that's impossible, they're not lined up."

"Exactly," he smiled, pleased with the impression he was making. "The whole art of carambole is when my ball hits the side rails in certain places, it goes in certain directions. And this is what it looks like." He lightly struck his cue ball and, to the ladies' admiration, made a perfect carom.

"Such geometry!" Lady Nina said in surprise.

"Ha," Kasia added. "I'll never achieve such perfection."

"Perhaps you'd like to try it?" Dyzma said to Nina.

"Oh, no, it's no use with me," she said, picking up a cue stick nonetheless. She didn't know how to position her left hand to make a good support, and Dyzma had to configure her fingers. He noticed then that Nina's skin was very smooth. It occurred to him that these hands had undoubtedly never done a day of work. What luck, he thought, to be so rich you don't need to lift a finger, everything is done for you.

"Well, sir," Nina said, "you obviously don't want to teach me."

"I apologize. I got lost in thought."

"I'm curious. What were you thinking about?"

"Eh, it's nothing. I just touched your hand, Madam, and was thinking that such delicate hands probably hadn't seen any work."

Lady Nina blushed.

"You're right. I've been ashamed of it for a long time, but I lack the will-power to take on some sort of work, to actually go through with it. Perhaps I'm idle due to the circumstances being what they are."

"Of course, why work when you have so much money?" Dyzma said baldly.

Lady Nina bit her lip and looked down.

"You are a very harsh judge, but I admit I entirely deserve this biting irony."

Dyzma didn't understand and started to puzzle over what exactly she was talking about.

"Mr. Dyzma's a blunt man. He tells it like he sees it," Kasia opined.

"That, however, is a rare virtue," Lady Nina added.

"Although not always pleasant for the people around him," Kasia clarified.

"But useful. I prefer the unvarnished truth to insincere flattery."

"Oh, that doesn't seem to be in Mr. Dyzma's repertoire. Please tell us, sir," Kasia said, wanting to provoke him, "do you pay compliments to ladies?"

"Yes, I do. If some lady is pretty, I can tell her that."

"That's all? Well, what would you tell me, for example?"

"You, miss? . . . Hmm . . . ," he said thoughtfully, stroking his protuberant jaw.

Kasia burst out laughing.

"You see, Nina, look how hard it is for him! So, sir, just say one thing. If you're unable to speak well of me in general, maybe you can find some detail about my features that's worthy of flattery."

A slight blush glowed beneath the silky down of her peach-colored cheeks. He thought that she was lovely but somehow alien, and there was something oddly predatory in the intense gaze of her hazel eyes when she fixed them on Nina.

"Indeed," he answered. "You have pretty ears."

"Oh! . . ." She was surprised. "That's not what I expected to hear from you. You know, Master Bergano himself honored me with the same compliment last winter on the Riviera."

"And who is Bergano?"

I slipped up, he thought to himself, and added out loud: "I don't know much about art. It was never an interest of mine."

"But that doesn't prevent you from sharing the taste of a great artist," Lady Nina said kindly.

Kasia set her cue stick down and declared that she was done with billiards for today.

"Well, now I'm off to change. Would you care to go riding with me, sir?"

"Thank you very much, but I still have plenty of work to do," Nicodemus answered.

"Well, I'll go on my own, then. Bye, Ninette." She put her arms around Lady Nina's neck and gave her a kiss on the lips.

When she'd disappeared behind the door, Dyzma said, "Your stepdaughter doesn't love you like a stepmother..."

Lady Nina suddenly turned away and walked toward the window.

"We love each other like sisters."

"Because," observed Nicodemus, "there must not be much of an age difference between you ladies. At first, I took you for sisters. Only you're completely different types."

"Oh, yes," Nina confirmed. "Our personalities, our dispositions, our views—they're all diametrically opposed."

"But you love each other."

Lady Nina did not answer, and Dyzma, not knowing what else he could say to sustain the conversation, decided to retreat to his room.

"I have to go. My respects to you."

She nodded and asked, "Do you need anything, perhaps?"

"Oh, thank you, Madam."

"Please don't hesitate, sir, to give the servants any instructions..."

"Thank you."

He bowed and left. For a few moments, Nina watched the ungainly motion of his blocky figure and his thick, red neck as he tromped away through the long enfilade of rooms.

"So, this is what a powerful man looks like," she thought. "Strange. And yet... Oh, you eternal dreamer!" She laughed and, clasping her hands to her chest, gave her body a delicious little stretch from head to toe.

Dyzma was making another attempt at Kunicki's documents, but it was going even worse than it had the night before. He was nowhere close to getting his bearings amid this dense forest of digits.

"The hell with this!" he swore. "Clearly I'm dumb as a bag of hammers."

He cast his mind back to secondary school. There, when he didn't understand something, he could at least learn it by rote. It was drudgery, sure, but it was always a good way out. And, when he couldn't manage to memorize all of it in time, he could always pretend to fall ill and not go to school . . . But here, there was no escape, none . . . After all, this stuff was impossible to memorize, and falling ill was . . . It suddenly occurred to him:

And if I should fall ill?

But so what?

It could always delay his firing for a few days, maybe even for a couple of weeks . . .

Now this was a thought! A great thought! In the meantime, something might happen, something might change . . .

Yes. He made up his mind: It's decided. I will fall ill, starting tomorrow, and that's that.

He spent a long time picking a suitable disease. A contagious one wouldn't work because they might send him to the hospital. His stomach also needed to remain healthy, otherwise they wouldn't give him food . . .

And what about rheumatism? . . .

He was pleased. That would work best, because even if they called the doctor, he wouldn't know the difference.

When the servant came to summon him for dinner, Dyzma's plan was ready. He was to have an acute attack of rheumatism in his right arm and right leg. This evening at dinner, he would start complaining of pain, and tomorrow morning he would not get out of bed at all. His satisfaction with this plan had put him in an excellent humor.

Everyone at the table was in a cheerful mood. The absence of the gentleman of the house clearly had a positive effect on the ladies' disposition. There was talk of Kasia's planned departure to Switzerland, where she would study medicine.

"Are you going to practice after graduation?" Dyzma asked.

"Of course."

"We can be your patients," Lady Nina laughed.

"You can, yes," Kasia said, "but Mr. Dyzma can't."

"You're hardhearted. And if I got sick, and there's no doctor nearby?"

"But you misunderstand me. I'm going to be a doctor of female maladies."

"Oh, really? That's a pity. I suffer from rheumatism myself, and that's more of a man's complaint."

"That depends," Lady Nina noted, "on whether it was acquired in a manly way."

"During the war," Nicodemus replied.

"Were you an officer, sir?"

"No, an ordinary private."

"How beautiful," said Nina. "Many remarkable soldiers served in those gray uniforms back then."

"The uniforms were green," Dyzma corrected her.

"Of course, the color of hope, as you so subtly point out. Were you injured, by any chance?"

"No. Rheumatism is my only war memento."

"Well, and medals, certainly?" she asked.

Nicodemus had no such decorations, but he lied:

"Virtuti Militari. And I was promoted besides, and almost became a general."

"How so?"

"I was appointed senior private, and I would surely have been promoted to the rank of general if the war hadn't ended."

"I can see you have good memories of the war, though."

"It was the most beautiful time in my life," he said honestly.

"I understand you. Although I myself, as a woman, would not be able to feel any joy among the dying and wounded, I realize that a true man can find, in war, an environment that stimulates his most masculine instincts. Brotherhood, combat . . ."

Dyzma smiled. He recalled the barracks of the telegraph battalion, chickens raised by a sergeant, hot coffee and monotonous, idle days . . .

"Yes, the wild beast within," he confirmed.

"My dear," Lady Nina said, as if referring to a conversation already in progress, "you must admit, though, that there's a kind of charm there, one that strongly affects women in particular."

Kasia shrugged.

"Not all of them."

"Women," Dyzma said, "generally prefer brute strength over flabbiness."

"Let us not boast *too* much, sir," Nina laughed.

They talked for a few more minutes, and then Dyzma went to his room. He remembered he had arranged a meeting in the park with that crazy count, from whom he could learn plenty of interesting things about the whole of Koborowo society.

Checking that no one was around to see him, he opened the terrace door and chose a pathway that seemed to be the shortest route to the stone bench under the old linden tree. He couldn't find it, however, and was losing hope that he'd be able to meet up with Ponimirski when he heard the yapping of a nearby pinscher.

He's here! he thought with relief.

Indeed, he saw the clumsy little dog leaping around the trunk of a forked chestnut and barking furiously. He looked up and beheld, to his amazement, the young count sitting right there in the fork of the tree.

"Ah, you came," he called from above. "Perfect."

He jumped nimbly to the ground and nodded to Dyzma.

"You didn't denounce me to Kunik, did you?" he asked warily.

"God forbid. Besides, he isn't home."

"Good. Were you surprised that I was sitting in a tree?"

"No, why would I . . ."

"You see, it's atavism. Sometimes, an irresistible call sounds from within a man to return to the primordial forms of existence. Haven't you noticed that, Mr., Mr. . . . Well, what are you called?"

"Dyzma."

"Aha, Dyzma. A stupid surname. And your first name?"

"Nicodemus."

"Strange. You don't look like a Nicodemus. But that's beside the point. My Brutus doesn't look like a Brutus either, and I don't look like a George. So you're telling me that scoundrel has left?"

"Just for a day."

"He's probably working on a new scam. Do you know that he snatched Koborowo out from under us?"

"I haven't heard anything about that."

"Then listen. Kunik dealt in usury. And because my father was no stranger to spending money, and then the war came along and seriously undermined the state of our finances, Kunik easily entwined himself in our interests and ended up talking Papa into a fictitious sale of Koborowo."

"What do you mean, 'fictitious'? Like, fake?"

"I don't know, I'm not familiar with all the little details. Suffice it to say he committed a disgusting flimflam of some sort and appropriated the estate. At any rate, he'll end up in prison someday."

"Right . . . ," Dyzma proceeded with caution. "In that case, why did Your Excellency's sister get married to Kunic . . . Kunik?"

"Out of love for our father. Father wouldn't have survived leaving Koborowo, and that villain sniffed it out and presented him with a deal: if Nina became his wife, he would transfer the Koborowo title to her, and therefore our ancestral estate would remain in Ponimirski hands. My sister sacrificed herself and was punished mightily for it, since a year later our father died anyway and that villain gypped Nina out of some bills of exchange, bills amounting to a huge sum of money, and plenipotentiary powers, too. Thanks to that, my sister can't lift so much as a finger in regard to her own estate because this lowlife Kunik has full authority."

"And what does his daughter have to say about it?"

"That Kasia? She's a piece of work, too. But she hates Kunik because he supposedly heaped terrible abuse on her mother."

"Is she dead?"

"Who?"

"Mr. Kunik's first wife?"

"You call him 'mister'?" Ponimirski flared up. "A scoundrel, a cad, not a 'mister'! I am master here, not him! Is this understood?!"

"Understood," Dyzma agreed. "So is she dead?"

"First of all, I don't care, and second of all, she died a long time ago. Give me a cigarette, please."

He lit it and, blowing intricate smoke rings, fell into a reverie.

Dyzma noted that Ponimirski seemed considerably calmer today, so he risked a question:

"And why did they remove Your Excellency from the manor?"

"What?"

"I asked why they removed Your Excellency from the manor?"

Ponimirski didn't answer. Instead, he peered into Dyzma's face for a long time. Finally, he leaned over and whispered, "It seems to me that I will need you . . ."

"Me?" Nicodemus asked, taken aback.

"Quiet!" Ponimirski cast a wary look around him. "I have the feeling someone's eavesdropping on us."

"You're imagining things, Your Excellency. There's nobody here."

"Shh! Brutus! Find the spy, find him!"

The miniature pinscher watched his master with a dopey expression and didn't move an inch.

"Stupid beast!" the count exploded in irritation. "*Sortez!*"

He stood up and circled the bushes on tiptoe. After settling himself on the bench again, he said in an instructive tone: "One cannot be careful enough."

"Your Excellency was saying that you'll need me," Dyzma began.

"Yes, I will use you as a tool, but you must promise me absolute obedience. Of course, not a word to anyone. First of all, you will go to Warsaw, to my aunt, Madam Przełęska. She is a highly respected individual and very stupid. You have probably also noticed that respected individuals are, in most cases, stupid?"

"Indeed . . ."

Ponimirski gave Dyzma an ironic smirk and added, "You, sir, are an exception to this rule because, although you are stupid, you do not inspire respect. But that's a mere trifle. We have more important business here. So, Aunt Przełęska has tremendous connections, and she hates Kunik. That is why she will help you with my case."

"What case?"

"Silence, *sapristi*, when I am speaking! Kunik had me officially declared insane. Me! Can you believe it? And he obtained guardianship of me. So the idea is, my aunt will mobilize I don't know who yet, but someone, to set up some sort of council that will pronounce me completely sane. Do you understand?"

"I understand."

"I will write a letter to my aunt in which I will introduce you as my colleague, even though you look like a shoemaker, but my aunt is so hungry to damage Kunik that she'll be ready to believe it. You will explain everything to her: my ill treatment here, my imprisonment, my letters not being delivered. It needs to be presented in the blackest possible light . . ."

"All right, but . . ."

"Silence! Don't you want to ask me what's in it for you? Then listen and learn—I will give you the honor of my friendship and a lifetime pension. Good enough? I'm going to write the letter now, come here before your trip to Warsaw so I can give you the letter and some detailed instructions. But remember, if you denounce me, I will kill you like a dog. Goodbye."

He whistled for the pinscher and disappeared into the bushes in a single bound.

He's a lunatic, no doubt about it, Dyzma thought. The information the count had shared with him, however, must have contained a healthy dose of truth. Kunicki himself kept saying that he had purchased Koborowo. There was indeed no lack of hostility in his relationship with his wife and daughter. Obviously, it made no sense to take this madman and his projects seriously, but it was worth considering whether it might be possible to extract some benefit from this whole mess.

For now, Dyzma didn't see any opportunities opening up for him, not yet, but he was well aware that knowing other people's secrets certainly never hurt. Especially in his situation.

In any case, he thought, I have to find out somehow if what this crazy count says is true.

It occurred to him that if Ponimirski's allegations were confirmed, he would have the opportunity to threaten Kunicki with exposure. While contemplating this development, he met a servant right in front of the manor house, from whom he learned that the master hadn't returned and had sent back the car, because his business was detaining him an extra day.

This news perked Dyzma right up. One more day of peace of mind! He decided not to postpone his illness though. It would look much better if his rheumatism struck an entire day prior to his conference with Kunicki.

Which is why, during supper, he began wincing as if in terrible pain and grabbing at his shoulder and knee. Both ladies, Nina in particular, sympathetically inquired about the cause of his distress, and when he said it was rheumatism, they both agreed that Koborowo's humidity was indeed conducive to rheumatic attacks. Lady Nina even apologized for not warning him earlier.

As soon as Dyzma swallowed the last drop of his compote, his pain became unendurable. He excused himself to the ladies and was planning to go straight to his room, but Nina told the servant to support him as he walked, and she herself went to the first-aid box to get some medicine.

Dyzma was quite pleased with himself. He'd pulled off the scene perfectly. He even saw it in the face of the servant busily helping him undress and get into bed, and who then brought in the medicine.

Fifteen minutes later somebody knocked on his door. When he said, "Come in," it was Nina's voice he heard.

"How do you feel?"

"Not well, Madam."

"Do you need anything?"

"No, thank you."

"Good night then. I hope you feel better tomorrow."

"Good night, Madam."

Silence fell, and since the supper had been ample, Dyzma grew drowsier and drowsier. As he fell asleep, he thought, That Lady Nina is one hell of a dame. And no wonder! A countess . . .

Chapter 5

Koborowo's climate had a miserable effect on Nicodemus Dyzma's rheumatism. In the morning, it turned out that his pain had increased throughout the night, and he hadn't slept a wink. When a report to this effect reached Nina in her chambers, she called for a new assortment of medicines and asked whether he might wish for a book or two to read.

Dyzma absolutely did not wish for a book to read, but not wanting to betray his lack of enthusiasm for literature, he told the servant it would be too hard for his hands to hold a book.

The result surprised him.

Namely, the sound of Lady Nina's voice outside his door.

"Good morning. I'm worried that you're not any better. Perhaps I should send for a doctor?"

"Oh no, no need," was Nicodemus's firm answer.

"Surely you're very bored. Perhaps someone could read *to* you?"

"Well, there's nobody here to do that."

Outside the door there was silence, and after a moment, Nina's voice:

"May I enter?"

"By all means."

She came in and looked at him with a combination of curiosity and sympathy. With no warning, she suggested that she herself could read to him. There was no way out, and Dyzma, offering his thanks and apologies for the bother, had no choice but to agree.

"Why, it's nothing. It's no trouble at all. It would be my pleasure to read something to you. You only have to tell me which author you'd prefer."

Nicodemus pondered this. He needed to choose someone good, an author who the smarter set used to go for in the Łysków reading room. Now he remembered, there was some English name, it looked different when you saw it printed, but you pronounced it *Dżek London*.

"Maybe something by Jack London?" he said.

She smiled and nodded her head.

"Just a minute, I'll bring a few of his books."

She returned shortly with several handsomely bound editions and said, "I'm not at all surprised that this is the author you prefer."

Dyzma had never read Jack London, but replied, "Indeed, I enjoy this author very much, but how did you figure that out?"

"Oh, please, perhaps I'm just flattering myself, but it seems to me that I'm a fair observer of human nature. It's not hard to guess that your nature is self-contained, you have a rich inner life, a sort of"—here she switched to English—"magnificent isolation . . ."

"Oh yeah?" said Nicodemus.

"Yes. We women, we may not do it scientifically or even systematically, but we are specialists in psychoanalysis, or, I should say, in applied psychology. Our intuition is our scientific method, and our instinct alerts us to our errors."

She just goes on and on! . . . Dyzma thought.

"And that is why," Nina continued, absently flicking through the pages of the book, "that is why it's easier to guess the cipher by reading a closed book than an open one."

"Hmm." Nicodemus considered this. "But why would you have to guess when books are so easy to open?"

He'd thought that Nina, with her talk of closed books, intended to demonstrate for him how to read London through its cover, and added, "Nothing is easier than opening a book."

Lady Nina met his eye and replied, "Oh no. There are some who won't abide it, and those are the ones who are most interesting of all. Those who can only be read through the eyes of the imagination. Don't you agree?"

"I don't know," he answered heedlessly. "I've never come across that type of book. I've even seen very valuable editions, but I was able to open and read each one."

"Ah, that's understandable, I imagine you don't generally reach for books that aren't interesting, while those that do interest you surely open for you as if under some magnetic power. Such are the properties of a strong will."

Dyzma was amused—what kind of baloney was she talking?!—and answered, "Why, even a baby has enough strength to open a book."

"A man such as yourself has an extraordinarily powerful nature . . ."

"Me?" Dyzma was dumbfounded.

"Oh, don't try to mislead me. So much of what I've noticed confirms it"—she smiled triumphantly—"not least of which is your preference for London . . . After all, it's unambiguous evidence of your inclinations. Why not Paul Géraldy, why not Maurois, or Wilde, or Sinclair Lewis, or Żeromski, Mann, or Shaw, but instead London? Why London and his poetry of silent, inspired heroism, with the mighty heathen force of struggle, the glory of hardship!"

Dyzma was silent.

"You see, I could tell right away that you prefer Brahms to Chopin, that you're closer to Matejko than Jacek Malczewski, more Lindbergh than Cyrano de Bergerac, more gothic and skyscrapers than baroque and rococo . . ."

She gazed at him with her huge blue childlike eyes, which seemed to say, "I see you, you rascal, I know what you have in your pocket!"

Dyzma didn't know how to respond, which is why he grimaced and winced with pain. Lady Nina launched a tender volley of questions: Did this conversation bore him? If so, would he prefer . . . Perhaps he'd like to take a nap . . .

"And tell me, be completely honest, have I described your tastes accurately?"

As if I know what the hell you're talking about, he thought, but he shrewdly replied, "Partially yes, partially no."

"Well, all right," she said with a satisfied laugh. "Now we can read. Do you like *The Call of the Wild*?"

"I certainly do."

She began to read. It was a story about some kind of large dog who got stolen. Dyzma kept waiting, page after page, for the police to get involved in this theft, but when the tale took a different turn, his attention waned, until finally he completely lost the thread of the plot and heard only the melodious voice, gentle and warm, of Lady Nina.

He began to contemplate the conversation that had just transpired, and he concluded that there had been something a little strange about it. The expression on this pretty woman's face, as if she weren't talking about actual books . . . Could it be? . . .

He suddenly recalled a small sitting room in the Łysków postmaster's apartment, Mr. Boczek and his two daughters, Miss Walaskówna, the elementary school teacher, Jurczak from the lower court, and the rest of Łysków's golden children. In that little sitting room, shabby indeed compared to this mansion, they were playing a game of Hot Seat, and Miss Lodzia Boczek was sitting in the middle, and she was supposedly a book! . . . Yes, yes, and they were saying different things about her, that her pages were still uncut, and she was a cookbook, and a volume of poems, and she was a book that looked interesting but it was better not to open her . . . Aha!

It must be something like that . . . Something like that, for sure. But was Lady Nina saying something pleasant or unpleasant about him? . . . Probably pleasant . . . Though with these aristocrats, you never could tell.

And if she's falling for me? . . . he thought. Ehh . . . impossible.

Nina's voice rose and fell in gentle waves, sometimes trembling with emotion. Her lowered eyelashes cast long shadows on her snowy cheeks, and the sun penetrating the clusters of leaves outside had formed, on the sofa, a bright, vitalizing patch of light that made the twisted locks of her hair shimmer. The smell of lavender and linden trees hung in the air, various items of furniture flaunted their bronze-plated grandiosity, and, from the arabesque-covered ceiling, there hung a heavy lamp sparkling with ruby-hued crystal.

My God, just last week, who would've thought that I, Nicodemus Dyzma, would be lying here in this magnificent room in a rich person's bed, being read to by a beautiful woman!

He closed his eyes. Suddenly, he shuddered.

And what if it's just a dream, what if it's all some fantasy, what if I open my eyes and I'm back on Łucka Street, staring at Barcik's damp, sooty walls? And this voice? . . . Maybe it's Mańka reading Mrs. Barcik something from the newspaper?

Just then, the voice subsided, and after a moment he heard a hushed question:

"Are you asleep?"

Dyzma opened his eyes and smiled.

"No."

"Has the pain passed? Are you feeling better?"

Again, Dyzma smiled.

"The pain hasn't passed, but I am feeling better."

She was silent.

"You're here, so I'm feeling better."

She gazed at him sorrowfully and didn't say anything. It occurred to Nicodemus that her brother, though utterly deranged, was right: she wasn't happy. Sensing an opportunity to verify the rest of his information, Dyzma said, "Something's troubling you?"

"You might be the only one in this house who can honestly say that he is happy."

"Why the only one?"

"Nothing ties you to this house . . . My God, you could run away from here at any time, run away forever."

Her lips quivered, and the corners of her eyes shone with tears.

"And you will run away, that's for certain . . ."

"No!" Thinking of his salary, he rejected this idea vehemently. "I want to stay here as long as I can."

She flushed.

"Are you being completely honest?"

"Why would I lie? Really, honestly."

"And you're not bothered by the company of such an unhappy creature?"

"No, not at all, but again, why are you so unhappy? You're young and healthy, you're rich, you have a comfortable life—"

"Ugh," she broke in, "if you can call this a life!"

Dyzma gave her an oblique look.

"Is it maybe that your husband doesn't love you?"

"Husband?" An expression of disgust and contempt flashed across her face. "I'd rather my husband hated me. After all, what on earth do we have in common? He's always busy making money and thinking only of himself . . . What interests him is so different from what interests me, his interests are so foreign to me! . . . And what's more, he never gives the slightest thought to how I feel, never tries to understand me."

She bit her lip.

"Anyway, why am I telling any of this to you . . ."

"It's good to get it out."

"But after all, you see everything. Nicodemus, tell me, how can a lonely person, a person who's completely alone, be happy?"

"I know how that is . . . I'm completely alone in the world, too."

"What do you mean? You don't have anyone? Family?"

"No one."

"And that doesn't bother you?"

"Not at all."

"Ah, because you're a man, a strong, firm, self-contained character. You don't know what loneliness is, because you are an entity unto yourself. I don't know if a man with your capabilities can possibly understand the lonely emptiness of a weak little creature like me."

"But you have a stepdaughter."

"Ugh!" she said with distaste. "Kasia . . . She's a woman who . . ."

She bit her lip, staring down at the book laying open on her lap, and began to talk:

"You see, sir, you're the first man in many years with whom I've felt so free and so . . . In your sympathy and your compassion, there's no insulting pity, no extrinsic indifference . . . You see, I actually don't have any friendly companionship at all . . . You are the first with whom I can exchange ideas, with whom I feel I won't be terribly misunderstood."

She was glowing pink and spoke breathlessly. There's no doubt about it, thought Dyzma. Lady Nina was definitely hot for him.

"You're not annoyed with me for dragging you into the sphere of my sorrows?"

"No, God forbid!"

"But what do they matter to you?"

"They matter very much."

"You are so good to me."

"You're good to me, too. Don't worry, everything will work out. The main thing is not to mind too much."

She smiled.

"You treat me as if I were a child, soothing me with a silly joke so I stop crying. But you know, sometimes bluntness is the best medicine."

"You shouldn't give in to your unhappiness. You should think of what to do about it."

Her distress grew.

"Here, there's nothing that can be done!"

"Every man is master of his own fate," he said with conviction.

"But to be a master, one needs strong hands, and you see how weak mine are."

She offered him her hand, from which wafted the scent of perfume.

Dyzma took it and kissed it. She didn't release his hand but squeezed it tighter.

"One needs strong hands," she said. "Such hands . . . Such hands might forge more than one's own fate alone . . . It sometimes seems to me that there is no obstacle such a mighty will can't overcome, that nothing is impossible for a will such as this . . . And if it's not too egotistical, it can even reach out its hand to rescue and redeem others, poor weak creatures in need . . . How poetical is the mysterious potency of a powerful man . . ."

She slowly withdrew her hand and said, "Do you think me too effusive?"

He didn't know what that meant, so he fell back on his old standby: he winced in pain and clutched his elbow.

"Does it hurt?"

"Very much."

"You poor thing. Should I send for a doctor?"

"No, thank you."

"How can I be of help?"

"You have a kind heart."

"For all the good it's done me," she replied sadly.

Mechanically, she picked up the book. "Shall we read?"

"Aren't you maybe too tired?"

"Oh no, I like reading aloud."

There was a knock at the door, and Kasia's voice reverberated in the hall.

"Nina, can I see you for a minute?"

"Excuse me," Nina said, rising to her feet. "I'll be right back."

Traces of Kasia's irritated voice reached Nicodemus's ears, but after a second or two they faded away.

Dyzma turned his mind to the situation at hand. It was clear that Nina had taken a shine to him, that much was certain. So how could he use this to his advantage? Could he, through her patronage, extend his tenure as Koborowo's administrator?

It's doubtful, he thought, that she has any influence over her husband. And the minute the old man notices that I can't actually do anything, he'll fire me on the spot, and after all, I can't be sick forever.

He was a little taken aback by his unexpected success with this refined lady, but it didn't inspire any particular pride or glee. Nicodemus Dyzma's brain was too occupied with its search for ways to stay at Koborowo, and he was not about to be thrown off course by other, more personal feelings. Nina considered him a worthy confidant. He found her attractive, all right, but in the same way he found Kasia attractive, or Mańka, or any other young woman for that matter.

Nicodemus Dyzma's heart had so far been impervious to love. The romantic chapters of his life consisted solely of insignificant passing recollections and totally meaningless encounters of which, at any rate, there were none too many. His current thoughts of Nina had no expectations, made no designs. What's more, his innate sense of caution warned him off anything more decisive, which could make a lot of trouble for him if her husband caught wind of the situation.

A somewhat agitated Nina returned; Nicodemus assumed that her conversation with Kasia must have been unpleasant. She resumed her reading aloud, and they didn't exchange a single word until lunch. After he ate, Nicodemus fell asleep until, at dusk, a loud knocking woke him up. It was Kunicki.

Dyzma's illness had thrown him into a state of extreme concern, and he wanted to wire for a doctor. With difficulty, Dyzma managed to talk him down, assuring him that he was already starting to feel better and he'd be back on his feet tomorrow or the day after that.

"That's very good, very good," Kunicki said heartily, "because that Olszewski is driving me to an early grave. What that man is up to simply defies comprehension. Just imagine, he calls the pinewoods work to a halt just because I supposedly didn't pay the full bid bond. The bid bond, you understand, sir, amounted to forty thousand two hundred zlotys. I forgot about those two hundred. I forgot about those two hundred zlotys, honest to God, I forgot, and that good-for-nothing just stops the entire operation. For two hundred zlotys? Damn that man to hell!"

Indignation had propelled his speech to new heights of speed. He went on for over an hour about his various tribulations with the director of forestry, his tirade culminating in an expression of hope that, thanks to Dyzma, all these unpleasantries would finally be a thing of the past. It was of urgent necessity that Dyzma head to Warsaw with all haste; it was time at last to have a talk with Minister Jaszuński.

Dyzma assured him that he would be on his way to Warsaw at once, just as soon as he was able to stand.

"And what do you think, my dear Mr. Nicodemus, will it be easy to get this deal taken care of? How quickly can you move things forward?"

"It won't be a problem," Dyzma replied. "Relax. There may be some expenses though."

"Expenses? Why, don't be silly! There's always cash on hand, whenever and whatever you need. Well, and how do you like it here? You're not bored?"

Dyzma demurred. It was very nice, very nice indeed.

"Only, please note, sir, just for your information, when you take care of our little errand in Warsaw, please remember that Koborowo is not bequeathed in my name, but rather in my wife's name. I had to do it as a matter of formality."

"Then, in a way," asked Dyzma, recalling his conversation with Ponimirski, "aren't I acting on behalf of your wife?"

"Yes, yes, although you're acting on my behalf as well, since I'm the actual owner, and besides, I have full plenipotentiary powers as regards my wife."

Dyzma was itching to ask if he also had the bills of exchange, but he restrained himself. The old man was liable to get suspicious.

Kunicki was gearing up to probe Dyzma's views on the state of the Koborowo financial situation, but he was forced to abandon this plan when the poor patient was suddenly attacked by rheumatic pain of such intensity that dear Mr. Nicodemus could only hiss, the agony distorting his face into something almost unrecognizable.

After dinner, Kunicki dropped in on Dyzma again, but this time the latter appeared to be asleep; the conversation had been successfully avoided. Long into the evening, though, Dyzma contemplated the inescapable necessity of a trip to the capital, after which he would probably not be welcome to return. But he decided to try to drag it out for as long as he could. In any case, he could seek out Colonel Wareda and ask him about talking with the minister.

He remembered Ponimirski. Who knew? It might be worth it to take that letter from him. If Ponimirski's aunt was well connected, then maybe he could work something out through her. Of course, he didn't for a single second delude himself that he was capable of successfully seeing to Kunicki's business. That would be impossible. But he wanted to create an impression that would keep Kunicki convinced that he, Dyzma, was indeed a friend of the minister's and that, although now wasn't the right time, later on he'd able to wangle a dismissal for Olszewski, or at least get him transferred to another post, plus obtain an allotment from the National Forests that would satisfy Kunicki's insatiable lust for lumber.

Shortly after Kunicki's exit, Nina showed up. She was sadder than usual, and more nervous, but she returned Dyzma's smile. She asked about his health, complained herself of a migraine that had cost her a sleepless night, and finally asked, "I'm told you're going to Warsaw. Will you be long?"

"I'm going for a week, ten days at most."

"Warsaw . . ." she sighed reflectively.

"Do you like Warsaw?"

"Oh, no, no . . . That is, I once was very fond of it . . . Even now I'm fond of it, I'm just not fond of spending time there myself."

"Yes . . . But you don't have any friends there, any family?"

"I don't know . . ." She wavered a moment. "No."

Dyzma decided to nimbly settle the question of Aunt Przełęska's existence.

"But isn't Madam Przełęska a cousin of yours?"

Dismay flashed across Nina's face.

"Ah, so you know Aunt Przełęska? . . . Indeed, yes, but after my marriage, we very much drifted apart. We don't even write anymore."

"Yes," Dyzma said.

"Do you call on her often?"

"Sometimes." He chose his words carefully. "Madam Przełęska, it seems, can't stand Mr. Kunicki, but she does like you."

Nina, disconcerted, quietly asked, "You've talked with her about me? . . . Ah, excuse my indiscretion, but, you see, it's very upsetting to me! But that's hardly a surprise. After all, almost all my memories are bound up in Aunt Przełęska's house, her circle . . . And you go there . . ."

"But why can't you just drop in on her?"

"Ah, but you yourself know why. None other than *him*, my husband . . . They'll never forgive me for that . . ."

She shook her head and added, in almost a whisper, "Just like I'll never forgive myself."

Nicodemus lapsed into silence.

"I ought to be ashamed of myself, carrying on and making confessions . . . I'm so helpless . . . so weak . . . so unhappy . . ."

"Please don't get worked up, everything's going to be fine . . ."

"Please, you don't have to console me. I know—I feel it—I've found in you, in your deep and abundant soul, a sincere reception. We've only known each other for a short time, but I have such faith in you . . . There's no need to console me; there's nothing to be done for my particular tragedy. It's enough that you understand me . . ." She paused, then added, "You alone."

"But why did you say there's nothing to be done? Can't you just get a divorce?"

"I cannot," she replied, staring at the floor.

"Hmm, so you've grown attached to your husband . . ."

Nina's eyes blazed.

"Oh, no, no!" she denied it hotly. "As though you could suspect me of that! Nothing could attach me to that man! He's got the soul of a shop-keeper, that . . . old fossil . . ."

Her voice brimmed with hatred and disgust.

"So why did you say you couldn't divorce him?"

"I wouldn't be able to live . . . in poverty . . . Besides, it's not only me I have to think of."

"You must be joking," Nicodemus began craftily. "After all, Koborowo is big money, millions, and you're the owner."

"You're mistaken, Koborowo actually belongs to my husband."

"But Mr. Kunicki told me himself that . . ."

"Yes, it's in my name, but in the event of a divorce I'd become a pauper."

"Huh?"

"Ah, why are we speaking of such things . . . You see, sir, my husband assumed some obligations of mine, for an amount that exceeds the value of Koborowo."

"He hoodwinked you?"

"Oh, no, he assumed them because they were rightfully his . . . to settle my family's debts to him."

"Aha! . . ."

"Let's not talk about this anymore; it distresses me terribly." She folded her hands and gazed at him with imploring eyes. "And please, don't men-tion me to my aunt, all right?"

"As you wish. But at least—"

"Please! Really, please! That world no longer exists for me, and I won't be going back to it . . . Let's read . . ."

She lifted the book and opened to the bookmarked page. She began to read, but before she managed to complete a single word, her voice began to tremble and her bosom heaved with sobbing.

"Don't cry, there's no reason to cry," Dyzma helplessly attempted to soothe her.

"God, God," she wept, "you're so good to me, so . . . good . . . Forgive me, sir . . . It's my nerves . . ."

She suddenly leapt up and ran from the room.

No question, thought Dyzma. That woman's in love with me.

"She's in love with me," he repeated aloud, with a pleased smile.

On his nightstand, there was a small mirror. He reached for it and peered at his own face for a long time, a little surprised, a little intrigued, and more than a little satisfied with himself.

Chapter 6

Guided by the chauffeur's sure hand, the car glided effortlessly down the road. Here and there, little glassy puddles from yesterday's rain sparkled in the fresh morning sunlight.

Dyzma was heading to Warsaw.

Kunicki had eschewed the train in favor of this car, claiming it would look more impressive.

Indeed, the slender torpedo seemed the very embodiment of impressiveness, so dazzling was its gleaming elegance and luxury, so arresting was the exceptional splendor of all its trimmings. The chauffeur's white livery and the tiger skin rug covering Dyzma's knees rounded out the picture. Which is why, during the few stops they made at little villages along the way, the magnificent automobile was immediately swarmed by clusters of gaping onlookers who admired not only the car but the lordly mien of the passenger sprawled within.

During one of these stops, Dyzma pulled an unsealed envelope from his briefcase. It was Count Ponimirski's letter to Madam Przełęska. He had brought the letter along just in case, and he now began to read. It was as follows:

Dear Aunt!

Seizing the opportunity arising from the general administration of our Koborowo, so plundered by the bandit Kunik, having been entrusted to His Most Honorable Lordship Nicodemus Dyzma (Courlandian nobility), in whom I have total trust—even though his appearance certainly suggests he merits no such thing—as a gentleman and a classmate from Oxford, and who is sympathetic to my cause, which after all is only to be expected, and, equally understandable, unsympathetic to that villain bastard Kunik, I am now penning this missive to my most cherished aunt, in order that you might deign to confer with whomever is needed and, with the help of His Most Honorable Lordship Dyzma's considerable connections, attempt to

liberate me from bondage by way of expert medical opinion, in order
to establish that I am not, in fact, sick in the head and subject to legal
incapacitation, so I can move forward with the case against Kunik
and the misappropriation of Koborowo, and that would go all the
more smoothly if my Beloved Aunt could manage, when you are able,
to compile the most accurate information about that bastard son of
a mangle woman's embezzling ways, that matter you once told me
about, concerning some kind of railway ties, the theft of supplies, and
the brazen appropriation and forgery of the noble name "Kunicki," all
thanks to bribery and corruption, forged documents that an unexpected search might unearth, since Kunik keeps all of his papers in a
curtained-off fireproof safe in his bedroom, which I found out from
the servants, some of whom count themselves among my allies, and
consequently, as a last resort, if nothing else is to be done, I plan to
carry out a coup d'état, at which point I will personally shoot the
vulgarian to death, an act which would afford me no pleasure whatsoever since I, as you know, Aunt, hunt only noble animals, which
that swine Kunik is most definitely not, and he should end up, if not
in a pigsty, then in jail—and on this count I'm relying on you, Beloved
Aunt, since after recouping Koborowo I would immediately repay
every bit of my debt to you, with interest, along with the debt I owe
Zyzio Krzepicki—I would even marry Miss Hulczyńska, although she
is excessively freckled and not exactly young, but I would do it, if only
to please you, dear Aunt, and His Most Honorable Lordship Nicodemus Dyzma is well informed and is au courant with the entire matter,
so please confer with him, since he has vast connections in Warsaw,
particularly in the highest spheres of government, which would not
be unimportant for my case, and, to a certain extent, yours as well,
Aunt, so I'm very much counting on it, and in concluding my letter
I apologize for its length while warmly kissing your hands as your
always loving nephew,

George Ponimirski

The handwriting was so illegible that Dyzma spent a good half hour
hacking his way through it. He was pleased that Ponimirski had given him
a place among the Courlandian nobility but was alarmed by his new affilia-
tion with Oxford University. If, God forbid, someone started talking to him
in English, the jig would be up, no two ways about it.

In fact, he hadn't yet decided whether he would see this Madam
Przełęska. If he was inclined to do so, it certainly wasn't because of that

half-deranged count's letter, which was actually more of a demand, but rather because of his recent conversations with Nina. He had not shared with her his intrigue with her brother, but by piecing together bits of information from both sides, along with a couple of things Kunicki had mentioned, he had reached the conclusion that Ponimirski's claims were not as insane as they might seem.

If he could manage to muster the courage to pay Madam Przełęska a visit, perhaps some light could be shed on the whole affair.

There were other considerations that spoke in favor of the visit, considerations that concerned him personally. Chiefly, this lady's influence and social connections; after all, she did move among society's higher spheres. Connections like those could be instrumental to Dyzma in his undertaking of the Kunicki business, the course of which would determine the fate of his position.

He was musing about this and wondering how he might track down Colonel Wareda when the car rolled into the Warsaw suburbs. It was already well after sunset, and, as if greeting Dyzma personally, a row of streetlamps suddenly lit up.

"Good omen," he said to himself.

"The gentleman wishes to be taken to the Hotel Europejski?" asked the chauffeur.

"To the Hotel Europejski," Dyzma agreed.

After a good night's sleep, he awoke fresh and full of good cheer. He stepped out into the city right away.

From the Ministry of Military Affairs, Dyzma was referred to the information office of the police headquarters, where he learned that Colonel Wacław Wareda always summered at Villa Haiti in Konstancin and typically made it into the city only in the afternoon.

Judging by the extraordinary courtesy with which this information had been relayed, Dyzma surmised that Colonel Wareda must be quite an eminent personage. He even considered inquiring further about Wareda's position but abandoned the idea for fear that his ignorance of state matters might arouse suspicion.

It was not yet ten in the morning, so Dyzma fell upon the idea of going out to Konstancin himself. And so he did. The road was awful, but thanks to the powerful engine and the experienced chauffeur, they made good time and were there in half an hour. It was easy to find Villa Haiti, a beautiful two-story house with an extensive terrace overlooking a garden. On the terrace, which was visible from the road through a wrought iron fence, sat a pajama-clad gentleman reading a newspaper. When the car stopped in front of the gate, the man turned his head and Nicodemus immediately recognized the colonel.

The colonel, though returning Dyzma's bow, squinted nearsightedly at the new arrival, and only after Nicodemus had opened the gate did he spring up and shout, "Why, hello! As I live and breathe, it's the vanquisher of Terkowski! Nicodemus, hello, welcome, where have you been?" He enfolded Dyzma's hand in both of his.

"Colonel, my good man, I was in the country. But I arrived yesterday in Warsaw, and when I learned I could find you here . . ."

"Bravo! Capital idea! Won't you have breakfast with me?"

"I've already eaten."

"Ha, that's right, you country folk like to wake up with the chickens."

The colonel was genuinely happy to see Dyzma. He'd taken an immense liking to the man, and Dyzma's luxury wheels meant he'd be relieved of having to take the disgusting Wilanowska train to the city later that day.

"Did we ever booze it up last night," Wareda said. "You'd think I'd have a massive hangover, but lucky for me I feel great!"

Indeed, he was cheerful and animated; his bloodshot eyes were the only sign of the previous evening's revelry.

"I say 'lucky,'" he explained, "because of course we must drink to your arrival. The story of you and Terkowski has really been making the rounds, did you know that? And as you can imagine, you've done more than a little to cut that idiot down to size!"

"Huh, really?"

"I swear to God. That swine. Becoming chief of the prime minister's cabinet really went to his head. That moron thinks everyone should prostrate themselves before him."

"And what's Minister Jaszuński up to?"

"What do you mean, what's he up to?" asked the colonel, surprised. "He's in Budapest at some convention."

"That's a shame."

"Did you have some business with him?"

"Just a little something."

"Well, then you'll have to stay in Warsaw a few days longer. We can have ourselves some fun, at least. Jaszuński mentions you often . . ."

Dyzma looked at the colonel with naked astonishment. And the colonel added, "I swear to God. What was it he said about you? Wait a minute . . . Aha! That Dyzma has the right approach to life: he grabs it by the balls and doesn't let go! Isn't that terrific? Jaszuński sure has a way with words! I even told him he should publish his sayings in a book."

As the colonel talked with Nicodemus, it further emerged that Jaszuński's position was rather shaky. He faced fierce resistance from both the landed gentry organizations and the small farmers' associations; meanwhile, there was Terkowski and his coterie digging a hole right under him. They were in the grips of a severe agricultural crisis with no solution in sight. And it would be a real pity for Jaszuński, who was a man with a good head and a great guy besides.

The conversation drifted to Dyzma's business affairs, and the colonel asked, "My good Nicodemus, it seems to me that you're a partner or neighbor of this Kunicki?"

"I'm both, actually," said Dyzma, "and his wife's plenipotentiary, too."

"Ah, is that so? Really? That, that . . . Countess Ponimirska? She's that good-looking blonde, right?"

"Yes."

"I've heard she's not so fond of that Kunicki."

"Not so fond at all," Dyzma laughed.

"Just between us, that doesn't surprise me at all; he's an old codger and supposedly quite the shady character. You probably know better than I do."

"Yeah, but what are you gonna do, right?"

"Oh, I get it, I get it," said the colonel, "business is business. You won't mind, my friend, if I dress in front of you?"

"Not at all."

They entered his room, where the colonel was inspired to offer his guest a cocktail of his own invention. Meanwhile, his orderly fetched a uniform, and after half an hour Wareda was ready to go.

They went out to the car and the colonel, enraptured, inspected every detail. It was obvious that he knew a great deal about the subject because, as he chatted with the chauffeur, he tossed out one technical term after the other, all of which were complete gibberish to Dyzma.

"Tremendous, just tremendous," Wareda repeated with delight, settling himself beside Dyzma. "You must have dropped a bundle on this thing. About eight grand, am I right?"

The automobile started up. Taking advantage of the roar of the motor, which muffled his words, Nicodemus replied, "Ha ha, and then some."

On their way into the city, they made plans to have dinner at Oasis that evening.

"It's the best, since we'll see a lot of friends there. Do you know Ulanicki?"

Dyzma did not know him. Fearing that he might be some sort of celebrated figure, however, he assured Wareda that, although they'd never met, he'd heard all about him.

After depositing Wareda at headquarters, Nicodemus returned to the hotel and ordered his chauffeur to pick him up at ten o'clock that evening. That done, he headed to the café, managed with some difficulty to find himself a free table, ordered tea and cakes, and began to wonder what to do with his time. Nothing came to mind. He didn't know anyone in Warsaw, or at least no one he would want to see now that he'd taken this exalted administrator position. He thought of the Barciks and shuddered. Their smoky apartment symbolized the grim reality to which he'd have to return, as did the memory of that dirty, ink-spotted, so-called hall of a post office back in Łysków. He knew his beautiful adventure would soon come to an end, but he preferred not to think about it.

Inactivity, however, drove his mind back to unpleasant reality and, to distract himself, Dyzma went upstairs to his room. There, he recalled Ponimirski's letter. He took it out and read it again.

"Whatever!" He waved his hand dismissively. "I'll just go, what's the worst they can do to me?"

Madam Józefina Przełęska had woken up on the wrong side of the bed that morning. By ten o'clock, this fact had become a universally acknowledged axiom in the kitchen. By eleven, the entire apartment had broken out in such pandemonium and hullabaloo it was as if there was not just one wrong side of the bed but at least two.

By noon, the noble residence of Madam Przełęska was a pitiful scene of chaos and panic, where august antiques fought wildly in single combat, moving from place to place until, amid unrelenting skirmishes, they were cut down in the heat of battle and remained motionless, their fashionably spindly legs sticking straight up into the air. Amid stampeding servants, the lady of the house galloped through the apartment like a Valkyrie on the warpath. Before her resounded the drumbeat of juicy epithets, behind her billowed the flounces of her dressing gown like a burnoose sweeping over the rubble.

The vacuum cleaner growled in the sitting room, salvos of carpets being beaten reverberated in the courtyard, here the windows were thrown open because this stifling air was simply unbearable, there the windows were slammed shut because these drafts could blow your head right off.

On top of everything, the telephone rang without stopping, and the hailstorm of words pelting the mouthpiece slashed the air like a whip.

It was at that very moment the doorbell sounded in the hall. It was the last straw. Madam Przełęska pivoted and darted over to answer the door personally, much to the horror of her servants, who, in their hearts, had already entrusted the welfare of this unfortunate guest to the mercy of God.

The door swung open violently, and the thunderous "WHAT?!" issuing from within was not unlike cannon fire.

Nicodemus was not at all disconcerted by this unpleasant greeting. On the contrary, he felt a surge of confidence; this lady's tone and appearance had put him on more familiar turf.

"I'm here for Madam Przełęska."

"Might I ask why?"

"It's a business matter. Please tell her that a friend of her nephew has arrived."

"What nephew?"

"Count Ponimirski," Dyzma replied haughtily.

This failed to have the effect he'd anticipated. As if defending herself from an assailant, the disheveled lady threw out her arms and cried, "I won't pay! I won't pay a penny on my nephew's behalf! You shouldn't have lent him a thing!"

"What?" Dyzma was startled.

"Let him go to that brother-in-law of his! I'm not giving him a penny, not a single penny! It's outrageous, everyone always comes running to me. It's sheer banditry!"

Dyzma had had enough. Blood rushed to his face.

"What the hell are you yelling at *me* for, goddammit?!" he roared at the top of his voice.

As if struck by lightning, Madam Przełęska went silent. She shrank back, her eyes wide with horror at this interloper.

"Nobody here wants any money from you, and if they want anything at all, it's to pay you back!"

"What?"

"What did I just say? To pay you back."

"Who?" she asked with increasing bewilderment.

"Who do you think? The Shah of Persia? The Sultan of Turkey? . . . My friend, your nephew."

Madam Przełęska clutched her head with both hands.

"Ah, forgive me, please, I have a terrible migraine and the servants are simply driving me up a wall, I do beg your pardon . . . I'm terribly sorry. Please come in."

Dyzma followed her into a small room, where half of the furniture was lying on its side and a polishing brush was resting in the middle of the floor. She led him to a chair by the window, apologizing once again for the state of her attire, and promptly disappeared for a good half hour.

What in the hell? thought Dyzma. She came at me like a chicken with its head cut off! Why the devil did I even come here? The aunt's obviously just as nuts as her nephew. She's supposedly this great lady, and here she is looking just like a charwoman . . .

It took him a while to calm down, and when he finally did, he began to regret that he'd told this old broad about Ponimirski's plan to pay back his debt.

She already thinks he's a fruitcake, he thought. She might take me for one, too.

Finally she reappeared, now clad in a beautiful violet dressing gown. She had done her hair, and her fleshy nose and prominent cheeks were coated in a thick layer of white powder which emphasized the vivid carmine of her lips.

"I'm very, very sorry," she began at once. "My nerves are simply frayed. I am Przełęska . . ."

She extended a long, thin hand, which Dyzma kissed as he offered his name.

She had many questions, but the rate at which she volleyed them at Dyzma was such that, despite his willingness, he was at a loss to respond. Instead, he pulled out Ponimirski's letter and silently handed it to her.

"My God, I've forgotten my lorgnette," she exclaimed as she took the letter in her fingers. "Frania!" she called in a piercing voice. "Frania! Antoni! Frania!"

There was a rapid patter of footsteps, and after a moment a maid appeared with gold-framed glasses.

Madam Przełęska began to study the letter. She soon flushed scarlet and paused several times to offer increasingly effusive apologies to Dyzma.

The letter had made a strong impression on her. She looked it over again and declared that this was a matter of utmost importance, not simply because of George's offer to pay back his debt, but in general.

She inquired at length about the state of affairs in Koborowo, about the state of mind of "that unfortunate Ninette," and about the state of "that thief Kunik's" finances. In conclusion, she asked what her respected guest made of it.

Her respected guest could make nothing at all of it and replied faintly, "Hmm, let's see. It might be good to talk to a lawyer."

"Ah, good thinking, good thinking." Madam Przełęska took up this idea with a note of approval. "You know, it would be best to first consult Mr. Krzepicki. Do you know Mr. Krzepicki?"

"No, I don't. Who is he?"

"Oh, he's a very capable man and, while he himself is young in years, he's a very old family friend. My dear sir, are you staying at a hotel?"

"Yes."

"Would you be so kind as to accept an invitation to dinner tomorrow? Mr. Krzepicki will be here, and we can talk the whole thing over. Would you?"

"What time?"

"At five, if you kindly accept."

"Fine."

"And forgive me that unpleasant reception. You won't hold it against me?"

"It's nothing," he replied. "It happens to everyone."

He took a closer look at her and remarked to himself that she wasn't bad looking at all. She might be in her fifties, but her slim figure and lively gestures made her look younger. She accompanied Dyzma to the entrance hall and saw him off with a grateful smile.

With these aristocratic folks, Nicodemus thought as he walked down the stairs, you never can tell what they're up to.

He stopped off at the nearest bar for dinner. He was more than happy with the lack of company; finally he could behave naturally and not have to be on guard about using a fork with this dish and a spoon with that.

His visit to Madam Przełęska's had left him with the impression that this thing would end up being all talk and no action, and that Count Ponimirski's hopes would come to naught.

Kunicki's not so dumb that he'd let someone pull the wool over his eyes, he thought. That guy's a sharp one! . . .

For a moment, he considered whether it might pay to tell Kunicki everything. But he decided the most practical thing would be to keep his mouth shut. Besides, he didn't want to rat Ponimirski out because he didn't doubt it would upset Nina, and she was such a nice dame . . .

As Dyzma sat in the bar, his eyes were struck by the brilliant glow of a nearby advertisement. A movie theater. When was the last time he'd been to the movies? He looked at his watch; he still had five hours. There was nothing stopping him from going in and buying a ticket.

The movie was incredibly beautiful and exciting. A young bandit falls in love with a lovely little lady who gets kidnapped by another gang, and after multiple death-defying adventures and heroic fights, he gets the girl back and in the big finale they tie the knot; interestingly enough, they're married by the father of the bride, a gray-haired priest with a benevolent smile on his wrinkled face. Nicodemus found this particular detail dubious at first, but he quickly reassured himself that, after all, this was all happening in America, and apparently priests were allowed to have children there.

The movie so enthralled Dyzma that he stayed for two consecutive showings. When he left the theater, the streets were already agleam with thousands of lights. The evening was hot and humid, and passersby thronged the sidewalks. Dyzma strolled back to the hotel, and from some distance away he could recognize Kunicki's glorious automobile parked in front.

"My car," he thought, grinning.

"Well, how's everything?" he asked the chauffeur in response to his bow.

"Nothing new, sir."

"What have you been up to?"

The chauffeur replied that he had been visiting family, as he himself was from Warsaw. They chatted for a moment, and then Dyzma went to his room to change his clothes and put on a fresh collar.

I need to cut a fine figure tonight to get the colonel on my side, he thought. I'll buy him champagne, my treat.

A quarter of an hour later he had already arrived at Oasis. The restaurant was still empty. There were just a few people sitting at the tables.

I came too early, Dyzma noted to himself.

He ordered some vodka and hors d'oeuvres. His waiter, addressing him as "Your Lordship," immediately laid the table with various sauces and seasonings, and two other waiters arrived with platter after platter of all kinds of cold fish, pork, pates, and who knows what else.

Since he was waiting for the colonel to show up, Nicodemus ate at a very leisurely pace. The orchestra played some symphonic pieces. The room slowly began to fill.

At last, around eleven, Colonel Wareda arrived. With him was a stocky brown-haired man in civilian clothes.

"Oh, you're here already!" the colonel called to Dyzma. "Were you waiting long?"

"Nah, just fifteen minutes," Dyzma replied.

"Gentlemen, allow me," the colonel said, making an introductory gesture. "Mr. Dyzma, Director Szumski. And our dear Jaś Ulanicki will be along in a moment."

"Fantastic!" Szumski exclaimed with glee. "That guy's comedy gold!"

"You have no idea what a good one he pulled when we were staying in Krynica in May."

"Go on!"

"Okay, picture this: In our hotel, there's this guy Kurowski or Karkowski or something, you know the type, one hundred percent gentleman, he could play tennis and quote Byron, and Baudelaire, and Wilde, and was all about the Grand Canal this and the Casino de Paris that, and Monte Carlo, and foreign languages, and the vintages of wine, and silks, and friends in high places—a real dandy, in other words. The women were crazy about him, and every night around the dinner table, as sure as anything, here was this know-it-all just holding forth about some new topic. He went on and on, cracking jokes, making puns, tossing around aphorisms in probably ten different languages—just laying on the charm."

"I might know that guy!" Szumski hooted. "If he went around with an umbrella and couldn't say his *r*'s, I bet you anything he was from the Ministry of Foreign Affairs!"

The colonel burst out laughing.

"How did you know? That's exactly right; this fellow would not part with his umbrella."

"So what happened?"

"Just imagine: some five or six days have passed, and as we're heading to dinner, Jaś says to me, 'I swear to God, I can't take it anymore.' And then he's seated, you see, right across from this dandy. And as soon as the soup is served this guy turns on the charm and doesn't let up, even when the roast is served. I'm waiting, but Jaś does nothing. He listens and listens and this fellow, all smiles and elegance, keeps pouring on the charm. I remember, he was just about to enlighten us on this season's most fashionable colors, when suddenly our Jaś puts down his knife and fork, quietly gets up from his chair, leans over the table so he's right in this charmer's face and bellows 'Hooooo!...'"

Dyzma and Szumski could not contain their laughter.

"What do you mean," asked Szumski, "just 'Hoooo'?"

"'Hoooo,' and that was it, but you know that deep voice of Ulanicki's. I can't even tell you what a ruckus it caused. The dandy goes beet red and shuts his mouth like he'd been struck by a bolt of lightning. There's dead silence in the dining room and everyone just looks down at their laps. Until someone can't hold it in anymore and bursts out laughing. And then the floodgates open and the whole table is just shaking with laughter. I swear to God, never in my life have I seen so many people laugh so hard."

"And what about Jaś?"

"Jaś? Well, he just started eating the roast like nothing happened."

"And the dandy?"

"The poor dummy. He didn't know if he should stay or go, and finally he just got up and walked away. He left Krynica that same day."

"And what happened then?" asked Dyzma, who was taking enormous pleasure in this story.

"Nothing, really," the colonel answered, "except that Ulanicki became the most popular person in Krynica."

The restaurant had filled up. The waiters' black tailcoats flashed back and forth between the white tables, and the orchestra played an impassioned tango.

They had just finished supper when Ulanicki arrived. He was an enormously tall man with a face that resembled an escutcheon onto which someone had stuck an enormous pickle and four bunches of coal-black horsehair. His mustache and eyebrows, exceptionally lush, never stopped moving; they stood in marked contrast to his small, sunken eyes, which seemed to be fixed on some point in the far distance.

When he sat down, Nicodemus, flying high on alcohol's wings, said, "The colonel told us about this joke of yours in Krynica. First rate! You really put that guy in his place."

"It was nothing. Your story is better. Wasn't it you, sir, who laid into that idiot Terkowski?"

"He's the one," confirmed Wareda. "Dyzma's a terrific guy. You two are going to get along great!"

There was drinking aplenty. It was long past midnight when, already feeling no pain, they made their way to the second-floor dance hall and ordered champagne. Some extremely frolicsome young ladies showed up at their table. The jazz music so enticed Dyzma that he invited one of them to cut a rug with him. The rest of his comrades looked on with admiration and, when he returned to his seat, they unanimously proclaimed him an ideal companion, and, over yet another drink, they decided it was high time to switch to a first-name basis . . . Facing no opposition, they cemented this milestone with a round of "For He's a Jolly Good Fellow" with, per Colonel Wareda's request, orchestral accompaniment.

The sun was rising when the four men climbed into Kunicki's car. Their first mission was taking the colonel back to Konstancin. The chauffeur had to shake his passengers awake when they arrived, whereupon Szumski, too, bid affectionate farewell to Dyzma because he didn't feel like going back to Warsaw.

"I'll sleep it off here at Wacek's. Bye-bye, Nick old boy, bye-bye."

Dyzma dropped off Ulanicki at his estate and returned to the hotel.

After falling into bed, he attempted a retrospective survey of the night's events, but the fog in his head, not to mention an annoyingly insistent bout of hiccups, so exhausted him that he let his thoughts slide away and surrendered to sleep.

It was well into the afternoon when he woke. His head hurt. Only now did he notice that he'd slept in his clothes, which consequently resembled crumpled-up rags. He was annoyed with himself, but also aware that yesterday's spree with the colonel and the two dignitaries would come in handy in gaining access to the minister.

Then he remembered that he had to be at Madam Przełęska's for dinner, so he had to get his suit pressed.

He sent a telegram to Kunicki, informing him that, owing to the minister's absence, he'd been forced to extend his stay in the capital.

Dyzma took the car to Madam Przełęska's. Since the apartment's windows faced the street, someone might catch a glimpse of him emerging from the vehicle; it would add some additional splendor to the general effect.

He did not in fact know what he would be discussing with Ponimirski's aunt and this Krzepicki guy and didn't see any particular point to this conversation. If he'd agreed to come, it was only out of curiosity and, to a large extent, the appeal of making an appearance in a grand upper-class home.

As he crossed the threshold, he immediately realized that the state in which he'd first found the place did not reflect its usual condition. Today, it was solemn, orderly, and full of dignified silence. Though it was nothing compared to the Koborowo manor, there was nevertheless something elusive about it, which impressed Dyzma even more.

The butler ushered him into the drawing room, and after a long moment Madam Przełęska came in, looking every inch the lady. Behind her was a man of about thirty-five.

"Mr. Krzepicki, Mr. Dyzma," Madam Przełęska said, presenting them to each other.

Krzepicki greeted him gallantly. His excessively expansive gestures, the brazen ease of his manner, and the nasal tone of his voice did little to endear him to Dyzma, though he admitted to himself that the man was indeed handsome, undeniably even more so than Mr. Jurczak, the court secretary in Łysków, who was known far and wide as the most successful lady-killer in the county.

"I'm so pleased to have the privilege of meeting such an honorable gentleman, whom it's been my fortune to have already heard so much about," said Krzepicki, sitting down and adjusting the cuffs of his trousers.

Dyzma resolved to watch his step around this man, who right away struck him as cunning and insincere.

"People are people," he answered evasively. "They like to talk."

"Allow me," Madam Przełęska chimed in, "but it was from Mr. Krzepicki that I learned you are such a distinguished politician. I'm ashamed to admit that we women are quite ignorant when it comes to politics."

"Oh, let's not exaggerate," countered Krzepicki, making further adjustments to his trousers.

Dyzma, at a loss for what to say, simply grunted.

A servant came to his rescue by announcing that dinner was served. At the table, Madam Przełęska and Krzepicki, whom she'd sometimes address by his last name and sometimes by his nickname, "Mr. Zyzio," began to make inquiries about Koborowo. Madam Przełęska was chiefly interested in the relations between "that poor Nina" and her brother and husband, while Mr. Zyzio flooded Nicodemus with questions concerning Kunicki's revenue and the total value of all his assets. Dyzma tried to keep his answers as short as possible to avoid unwittingly betraying how little he actually knew about the matter at hand.

"And can you tell me, sir, whether George's mental illness is so conspicuous that it is impossible to think of restoring his legal competence?"

"I don't really know . . . He's off his rocker, but he might be able to get ahold of himself . . ."

"Apt point," Madam Przełęska agreed. "His condition is caused by the degeneration of the control centers, but I believe that when he recognizes there is a need to hold his tongue, he will be able to keep himself in check, at least for a short time."

"I think so," said Dyzma.

"My one concern," Madam Przełęska continued, "is whether Nina will agree to our plans."

"Meh," Krzepicki shrugged. "Who says she has to know anything about them? Everything can be done very hush-hush. The most important thing is to find the right connections at the Ministry of Justice, but we needn't worry on that front, since fortune has provided us with an ally: the honored gentleman we have before us. Isn't that right, Mr. Dyzma?"

"Ah, it's such a blessing," Madam Przełęska exclaimed, "that you, you, George's friend and colleague, have just now been reunited with him!"

They adjourned to a small sitting room for coffee. Krzepicki took out a notebook and pencil and began forthwith:

"I permitted myself to prepare a little report of sorts. You won't mind? . . . The whole of the matter presents itself as follows: We know that this swindler goes by the name Leon Kunik, sixty-six years old, son of a laundress, Genowefa Kunik, born in Kraków, suspected of dealing in stolen goods, as documented in the files of the Lviv police, then worked as a usurer, and in that capacity ensnared the family Ponimirski and deceitfully deprived them of their estate—"

"Madam Kunicka claims," Nicodemus interrupted, "there wasn't any deception."

"Well, of course, but anything can be fair game for an alternate interpretation. Hee hee hee . . . If our prosecutor receives the right instructions from the beginning, he can get it done. We further know that nine years ago, Kunik obtained new identity papers in which his name was changed to 'Kunicki' and a paternal name was added. That's already a flagrant violation of the law. And then, of course, we all know about the lawsuit over the railway ties. It was never cleared up, unfortunately; at the time it was impossible to prove that the railway ties had ever existed. Kunicki's come up with supposedly authentic documents proving his innocence, but I've no doubt these were obtained fraudulently. After all, the railroad official who issued them has since run off and vanished into thin air. All this can be dug up and dusted off and brought once again to the attention of the court. Sound like a plan?"

"It certainly does!" cried Madam Przełęska.

"Sounds good to me, too," said Dyzma, casting a wary glance at Krzepicki's angular face. The incessant quiver of its muscles and the glitter of its almond-shaped eyes gave the impression of intense alertness and vigilance.

Now Krzepicki licked his upper lip and added, "However, the most important thing is to get back to Koborowo. And this is where the trouble starts. Nina is the nominal owner, after all, and there's no way she'll go along with it."

"She sure won't," Dyzma concurred.

"Just so," Krzepicki went on. "We're left with only one solution. George must file a complaint with the prosecutor against Kunicki. And this in turn should include, among other things, an accusation that Kunicki is forcing the plaintiff's sister to provide false testimony . . ."

"Hmm . . ."

"And George can only file such a complaint if he's restored to legal competence. So we need to start with obtaining a court order to reevaluate George's state of mind. I've consulted an attorney, and he said that such an appeal is, by and large, quite possible, under one condition—the request must come from one of George's relatives."

"Me? It's out of the question!" Madam Przełęska protested. "Absolutely not! I have enough problems already! That's all I need, to have my name dragged through the mud and splashed across every newspaper."

"Well, fine," Krzepicki replied in a slightly irritated tone. "So do you think Nina will do it?"

"Nope," Dyzma shook his head. "Lady Nina won't do a thing."

"And George has no other relatives," Krzepicki said, using his index finger—whose nail was unusually long and glossy—for emphasis.

"No matter what, I refuse to involve myself in this," declared Madame Przełęska. "No matter what!"

Krzepicki's face took on a sour expression.

"Fine," he said coldly. "In that case, we have nothing to talk about. You can say goodbye to the forty thousand that George owes you and me, and goodbye to Biba Hulczyńska's marriage as well."

Silence descended.

"It's just a pity," he added, "that we put our honored guest through the trouble."

"But I cannot, truly I cannot!" Madam Przełęska stubbornly defended her position.

"What's the big rush?" Nicodemus said after a moment. "We can put this off till later . . ."

"And perhaps in the meantime we'll come up with a solution," Madam Przełęska added with relief.

Krzepicki sprang from his chair.

"In the meantime, in the meantime! And in the meantime, I'm dying for money! . . ."

"So then I'll see about finding something for you," Madam Przełęska murmured timidly.

"Ugh," Krzepicki waved his hand dismissively, "another measly five hundred or thousand!"

Madam Przełęska reddened.

"Perhaps we can revisit this issue at a later time. I really don't think it's of any interest to Mr. Dyzma."

"Sorry," Krzepicki muttered indifferently.

"May I offer you more coffee?" She refilled their cups and added, "But perhaps Mr. Dyzma might be able to have some sway over Nina? After all, she can't abide her husband either . . . And you look like a man who can break barriers and bend people to your will . . ."

"Sure, except why would he be the least bit interested in doing that?" Krzepicki shot back cynically.

"Why, Mr. Zyzio," Madam Przełęska protested, "Mr. Dyzma is a friend of George's, isn't that right, sir? And perhaps that's reason enough."

Krzepicki grimaced and flicked his finger.

"Let's be honest . . . I don't believe there's any such thing as a disinterested transaction, forgive me, my dear sir, but I just don't. Accordingly, I think that you, sir, as a man of . . . hmm, a realistic man . . . Let us speak frankly. Has George financially incentivized your participation in this whole affair?"

"What do you mean?" Dyzma asked.

"Well, did he offer an incentive?"

"You mean, did he promise to pay me?"

Madam Przełęska, assuming that Dyzma had been offended, launched into an apology, explaining that Mr. Krzepicki was by no means thinking what Dyzma thought he might be thinking, that there was obviously nothing untoward, etc., etc. The alleged culprit reflected that he had gone too far and clarified that what he had in mind were the expenses the honorable guest might have to incur with regard to George's case.

Noting that this conversation was not going well at all, Madam Przełęska advanced a plan to postpone a decisive conversation, and when she learned that Dyzma would be staying in Warsaw for at least another two weeks, she invited him next Tuesday for bridge. Dyzma graciously declined, saying he didn't know how to play bridge, but when he was told that he would not be required to do so, he agreed to come.

"There will be a few dozen people," Madam Przełęska asked, "and among them you'll meet many friends. General Różanowski frequents us, as does Minister Jaszuński, and Chairman Grodzicki, and Deputy Minister Ulanicki . . ."

"And Colonel Wareda?" Dyzma asked.

"Oh yes, he used to come quite often. Do you know him?"

"Yes, he's a friend," he said breezily.

"Well, in that case I'll make sure that he's there. He's quite a bold man. And, if I'm not mistaken, he's on excellent terms with Prosecutor Paluch. I think Paluch might even have married Wareda's first wife . . ."

"Yes, that's right," Krzepicki confirmed. "Her maiden name was Hamelbein, and Paluch can . . . be a real *pal* when it comes to our case, ha ha . . ."

When Dyzma began to say his goodbyes to Madam Przełęska, Krzepicki also rose, announcing that he, too, had to go; he had some business to take care of in Mokotów.

"Well, let me give you a ride then," Dyzma said. "My car is right outside the gate."

Madam Przełęska made efforts to detain him, but he steadfastly refused.

"I can't. I'll stop by for supper. Bye! . . ."

"Are you a relation of Madam Przełęska's?" Dyzma asked when they were out on the street.

"Nah, she's a very old friend of mine. Her husband and I knew each other well."

"So Madam Przełęska's husband passed away?"

"Oh, he's made his share of passes," Krzepicki replied, winking. "I just don't know how many and at whom. He's gadding about somewhere abroad. Ah, what a machine! First rate! How much gas does that beast guzzle?"

"Ten plus to a gallon," the chauffeur smiled, shutting the door for them.

"It's a fine thing, having a car like this," Krzepicki reflected.

Along the way, he talked a lot about the kind of business opportunities that arise when money becomes available, and Dyzma's silence led him to the conclusion that he was obviously a man of uncommon intelligence and circumspection.

When the young man finally got out near the technical university, the chauffeur turned to Dyzma.

"I know that gentleman. That's Mr. Krzepicki. He had a stable of racing horses, but it didn't work out so well."

"He must be quite a slippery customer!" Nicodemus said.

"Oh ho ho!" The chauffeur just shook his head.

Chapter 7

The spacious office had been done up in the style of Louis-Phillipe, with dark-green wallpaper and tall windows stretching from floor to ceiling.

At the wide desk sat Minister Jaszuński, chin propped in his hands, silently listening to the low, regular voice of the official who, for more than an hour now, had been giving his superior an account of the state of agricultural policy. From time to time, he'd set aside his notebook and pull out a thick file of newspaper clippings; in the many paragraphs he read aloud, certain numbers and words kept repeating themselves, like *export, metric hundredweight, wheat, state of disaster*, and so on.

The content of the report must have been less than encouraging, because the minister's forehead was deeply furrowed and remained that way, even when his mouth smiled and expressed its polite gratitude for such a carefully prepared report.

Upon his return from abroad, Minister Jaszuński had found his department in dire straits. The deplorable state of agriculture and the prospect of an enormous harvest had prompted fierce attacks in the opposition press, and there were even rumbles of discontent from the papers closest to the government.

From the several talks he'd already managed to arrange, Minister Jaszuński was able to conclude that his position had been seriously undermined and that his resignation would be a great relief to the cabinet. They hadn't come right out and said it. Not in the least. But he'd been given to understand that it would be highly desirable to find a scapegoat, someone who would pay for the economic slump and the administration's political blunders. The prime minister had made an unusually sour face and, indeed, had quite unambiguously stated that, in the current situation, it would be virtually impossible to dismiss the entire cabinet, but all that could be avoided with a few replacements. Jaszuński didn't doubt that Terkowski was first and foremost responsible for generating this particular frame of mind; it was his influence to which the prime minister so easily succumbed.

The situation was coming to a head, and he would finally have to make a firm decision. Minister Jaszuński was putting it off, though, until he could run it by his deputy, Vice Minister Ulanicki.

He had been waiting for him since early morning, had even telephoned him several times, but each time he'd been told that the gentleman was asleep.

So when Ulanicki appeared on the threshold of the green office at around two in the afternoon, the minster exploded:

"Are you out of your mind? Living it up all night long while the ground crumbles beneath your feet!"

"You could maybe say hello first," Ulanicki replied from under his large mustache.

"Hello," the minister snapped.

Ulanicki settled himself comfortably in his seat and lit a cigarette. Jaszuński paced his office, hands jammed in his pockets.

"You signed the treaty, and on favorable terms," Ulanicki said in his bass voice. "Congratulations."

"It doesn't matter," the minster replied. "It's probably the second-to-last document I ever sign."

"Why second-to-last?"

"Because the last will be my letter of resignation."

Ulanicki paused. "Do you know Nicodemus Dyzma?"

"I know that he's the one who laid into Terkowski. What does he have to do with anything?"

"I was out drinking with him last night. Well, strictly speaking, I've been out drinking with him for the last few days."

Jaszuński shrugged.

"You're the worse for all that drinking."

"False, I'm the better for it."

"Then spill it! To hell with this! I'm in no mood for guessing games."

"So we were talking about the crisis. And I was saying it was bad and there was no end in sight. 'There's no way to fix it,' I say. And then Nicodemus says, 'There is a way. Stockpile the grain.'"

He broke off and shot a meaningful look at the minister; the latter just shrugged his shoulders.

"So it would be stockpiled by the government?"

"The government."

"What bullshit, there's no money in the treasury."

"Wait, wait, I said the same thing, and he says, 'Money? You don't need any money.'"

"What do you mean?" Jaszuński was astonished.

"Listen! I'm telling you, it's extraordinary, my mouth was just hanging open. Lucky for you and me, the rest of our party was completely pickled and nobody heard a thing!"

"Do tell!"

"So listen. You don't need money, he says, it's a trifling impediment. The state can issue bonds. For a hundred, two hundred million zlotys. Pay with the bonds and that's that. The bonds collect interest at four percent and come to term in six years. In the course of six years, there's bound to be at least one economic boom, so sell the grain then, in country or abroad, whichever, and it's a great deal—"

"Wait, wait," the minister interrupted. "That's not a bad idea."

"Not bad? It's genius!"

"Well, go on!"

"This Dyzma, I'm telling you, what a mind! 'Well,' he says, 'the benefits are enormous. For one, it maintains the value, for another, it increases revenue.' This way, the state puts these new hundred, two hundred million zlotys on the market, because the bonds must be innominate, they replace the cash capital, and so on. Understand? I started to press him on the details, and he said that he wasn't an expert, but he also said he intended to talk to you about it."

"Me?"

"Yes. He's very fond of you."

"So wait, what does he propose?"

Again Ulanicki recounted his conversation with Dyzma, elaborating on the issue and illustrating with sums and figures. He was so inflamed by the plan that he was ready to summon a typist so he could dictate a statement to the press.

Jaszuński, less impulsive, restrained him. The thing must be thoroughly considered, worked out, drawn up. It was his opinion that it wouldn't be out of order to call this idea brilliant. But one shouldn't set out to do it all willy-nilly.

"First of all, this requires absolute secrecy. Secondly, we need to confer with this Dyzma."

"I can telephone him right away."

"He's still in Warsaw?"

"Is he ever! He's staying at the Hotel Europejski. He evidently came to town in the mood to spend a little money."

The minister was surprised.

"What are you talking about? He hardly looks like the life of the party. As I recall, he seems like, you know, the strong, silent type. Men like that usually have the ability to take command, they're organizers . . . Especially good organizers."

"A strong head," Ulanicki added peremptorily.

"Well then, he's our man. Ah, if only this turns out to be real! Terkowski and his crew would be licked once and for all! And as for me? Or, I should say, as for us? Jaś, do you understand how important this is?"

"Bah! . . ."

They decided to have a conference with Dyzma that evening. The minister jotted a few words on a calling card and sent it to the Hotel Europejski.

Dyzma had just woken up when they brought him the letter. He still had enough time to get dressed and eat a leisurely lunch. The ministry was only a few minutes down the street. He looked at his watch and left on foot.

At the bell, a porter opened the door and, casting an unfriendly look at Dyzma, said, "What? The office is closed."

"Move," Dyzma replied haughtily. "I have business with Minister Jaszuński."

The porter bowed.

"Deepest apologies, honorable sir, deepest apologies. The minister is waiting in his office. Vice Minister Ulanicki is also there."

With great solicitude, he removed Dyzma's overcoat.

"If the honorable gentleman would follow me. It's here, on the first floor."

Dyzma could barely grapple with the fact that, in a moment, he was going to be speaking to the minister, and that what had seemed utterly implausible on his journey from Koborowo was now taking real shape. This course of events had swept him along, carried him on its current, he could see and feel these actions, but he was unable to explain to himself the reason for their existence, why this was all happening to *him*, Nicodemus Dyzma.

When he'd received the ministry summons, he immediately guessed that it concerned those grain bonds, which he'd heard about from Kunicki and which had so delighted Ulanicki, and which explained his current fear that the minister wanted detailed answers as to how this project would be carried out. He'd have to be careful. It was critical that he stick to his favored method, the practice of which had yet to fail when it came to getting results: say as little as possible!

Both dignitaries greeted Dyzma effusively.

The fact that Ulanicki was on a first-name basis with him immediately created an atmosphere of intimacy. Minister Jaszuński began with some compliments. He reminded Nicodemus of the July 15 banquet and the incident with Terkowski.

"At the time, I told you that if our country had more men like you, we'd be on better footing. I'm now convinced we'd be on excellent footing, the best footing!"

"You're too kind, Mr. Minister."

"Ehh, Nicodemus!" Ulanicki cried heartily. "Don't pretend to be modest!"

The conversation turned to the issue of grain bonds. Dyzma found himself in the middle of a cross-examination, although both dignitaries had begun by saying that, properly speaking, they themselves did not know much about agriculture; he was very careful not to blurt out anything too stupid. His good memory came in very handy; by releasing little doses of information, drop by drop, he managed to repeat almost everything Kunicki had ever said about it. Just in case, he added what he'd heard about "his" project from Ulanicki.

The minister rubbed his hands with glee. Dusk had just fallen, and Jaszuński, lighting the lamps, called out with good cheer: "Well, my dear Mr. Dyzma, I'd hardly call you an eloquent speaker, but what a head you've got on your shoulders! Well, wonderful. For now, please be so kind as to keep this a complete secret. Till the right time comes. And there's still much to be done. Jaś will prepare a bill, it'll go to the Finance Committee of the Council of Ministers, and I'll have a talk with the prime minister tomorrow. The only hitch I can see in this tremendous project of yours is the matter of the warehouses. There's no question of building new ones; we won't get the loans. Anyway, it's an incidental problem. In any case, Nicodemus, my good man, we won't implement this thing without you; we couldn't do it without you."

"Of course," Ulanicki's bass voice chimed in.

"Surely you'll cooperate, won't you? Can I count on you?"

"Why not? Sure . . ."

"Well then, I offer my sincere thanks. I think that in every matter, the most important thing is who actually gets it done. It's all about the right person for the job!"

Jaszuński shut his desk. Ulanicki called for the porter. It occurred to Dyzma that he might as well strike while the iron was hot and see whether he might be able to finagle that favor for Kunicki.

"Mr. Minister," he began. "I have a request as well."

"Oh? I'm listening." Jaszuński looked at him with interest.

"The thing is, the Grodno District of the National Forests is run by Director Olszewski. This Olszewski is hell-bent on taking down the Koborowo lumber mills. He hates Kunicki, and that's why he keeps hammering away at this, well, this . . . quota of lumber from state forests—"

"Ah, right," the minster broke in. "I remember that. There was even a complaint of some kind. But this Kunicki, evidently he's a pretty shady character. Are you connected with him in some way?"

"God forbid. Just a little business . . ."

"Nicodemus is his neighbor," Ulanicki explained, "and is acting plenipotentiary for his wife, with whom, you realize, Kunicki is currently at odds."

"Nicodemus," said the minister. "I'll be frank. I'm not inclined to change Olszewski's directives. Kunicki's bad news. He's considered quite a crook.

But my faith in you knows no bounds. Is increasing the quota of lumber truly and legitimately in the interest of the treasury? Yes or no?"

"Yes," Dyzma said, nodding his head.

"Is Director Olszewski going after Madam Kunicka's mill for no good reason?"

"For no good reason."

"Then that's that. It's my opinion that the ability to lead lies in the ability to make immediate decisions."

He took out a visiting card, scribbled a few lines, and handed it to Dyzma with a smile.

"At your service," he said. "It's a little note to Olszewski. At any rate, I'll have to send him a proper telegram in the morning. When are you heading back to the countryside?"

"The day after tomorrow."

"That's a shame. But I can't stop you. Just wait for a message from me. But hold on a minute, hold on, Jaś, do you have Mr. Dyzma's address?"

"I've got it. Anyway, we're meeting tomorrow for bridge at Madam Przełęska's. Nicodemus frequents her, too."

"Wonderful. Well, I thank you again and wish you a pleasant journey."

He shook Nicodemus's hand with both of his.

He and Ulanicki put on their coats and together they left with Dyzma. Ulanicki tried to arrange to meet for dinner, but the minister exercised an unequivocal veto.

"You'll get completely sozzled again, and right now, time is of the essence; you can't afford the hangover."

They parted at the corner of Krakowskie Przedmieście, and Nicodemus headed toward the hotel. On the way, he paused in front of one of the brightly lit shop windows, took the minister's card from his pocket, and read:

Mr. Dir. Olszewski—Grodno.

Please favorably and immediately settle the complaint of Mr. Nicodemus Dyzma in the matter of the Koborowo lumber mills.

Jaszuński

He carefully slid the card into his wallet.

"Goddamn, will you look at that!" he said loudly.

His words resounded with satisfaction, delight and surprise, along with no small amount of self-admiration. He felt that the ground was growing more solid beneath his feet, that these people in this strange, once so seemingly inaccessible milieu, these people saw something in him, in Nicodemus

Dyzma, who the hell knew what, but after all, maybe they were on to something . . .

He was pleased with himself.

Another surprise awaited him at the hotel.

There was a thin, dove-gray envelope addressed to him. As he opened it, the fragrance of a familiar perfume wafted up at him. The card had been filled with a profusion of graceful, looping handwriting, and at the bottom there was a signature: Nina Kunicka.

"Look at this! What does it say?"

He lit the lamp beside his bed, took off his shoes, and, arranging himself for maximum comfort, began to read:

My dear sir,

You will be astonished by my letter, and no doubt even more so by the request contained within. However, if I dare to burden you, it is only because the kindness you have shown me permits me to hope that you will not be cross with me.

It concerns a small purchase. That is to say, I am unable to find good tennis balls in Grodno. I would be so grateful if you could buy a dozen in Warsaw . . .

Admittedly, I could write to the store, but I prefer if you select them yourself. Perhaps it's improper that I take up your time, your precious time in Warsaw, when you're so busy with so many amusements, the theater, parties, and, well . . . pretty women, who—as that indiscreet Kasia has repeatedly told me—so enjoy sending gentlemen flowers. Koborowo lacks pretty women, but the flowers are so much more beautiful than in Warsaw. . . . When do you return?

I have, strictly speaking, misused the word "return." After all, "to return" is used to refer to something, or someone, that is considered someone's own, his or her own, to something intimate, something to which our life is bound, our emotions connected . . .

Koborowo is sad and gray these days. One day just follows the next . . . Ah, but you know how capable I am of loving, and how I am forced to hate. I hope you are not put off by the interjection of this somber dissonance into the (certain) bustle and cheer of your Warsaw frame of mind. Oh well—I admit it—I miss your conversation, and I am so alone.

Dear Nicodemus, sir, Koborowo awaits your return—pardon me, again I used that word—awaits your arrival.

Nina Kunicka

Dyzma read the letter twice; what's more, he sniffed the envelope and thought, She's sure got her eye on me . . . Well, she's young still, and her husband's old. Maybe this could work for me?

Again, doubts gathered in his mind: Might Kunicki give him the boot if he started to suspect something? But at the same time, he realized that the balance of power had shifted.

Just try it, you old son of a bitch! he thought. Now I've got you by the short hairs. Just who do you think you're dealing with? Somebody with friends in high places! Got it?

He stood and, in his stocking feet, lit all the lamps and went to the mirror. Chin raised, he took himself in from all sides. He contemplated his image for a long time, until he arrived at the conclusion that until today, he had underestimated himself when it came to the looks department.

Well, he thought, a man looks a certain way since he was a kid, and he gets used to it, he really gets used to it, and just when it seems like he's nothing out of the ordinary . . .

He spent the rest of the evening in a splendid mood. He went to the movies, and later had dinner at some kind of bar. He slept until noon. After breakfast, he tackled the shopping, buying tennis balls for Nina. He ate a voluminous lunch and dozed off until nightfall, when he was roused by his chauffeur. It was time to change into his tails. By the time his car pulled away from the hotel, the city was already sparkling with thousands of electric lights and aglow with snaking neon signs.

At the corner of Marszałkowska and Chmielna, the car came to a stop. The policeman directing traffic was making way for a long line of cars and droshkies on the cross street. Nicodemus idly watched the crowd of passersby. He thought about how terrific it was to sit comfortably on the cushions of this tremendous wagon of his, and how bad it would be out in the crowd, getting jostled around on the jam-packed sidewalk.

All of a sudden, a pair of eyes from the crowd fixed on him. This particular stretch of Marszałkowska was badly lit, so it took a moment for him to recognize them.

Mańka.

He shrank back, hunching his shoulders so the bottom half of his face was hidden in the collar of his coat. But it was too late.

Mańka, making full use of her elbows, pushed her way to the sidewalk's edge. She was close enough to grab him by the shoulders. But she didn't dare; she could only utter, in a low voice, "Nicodemus! Don't you recognize me . . . ?"

He could no longer pretend that he didn't see her. At the same time, he was afraid that the chauffeur would catch sight of this girl in the shawl, and if this little scene grew any louder, the jig would certainly be up. He turned to her and, putting his finger to his lips, hissed, "Shhh!... I'll come see you tomorrow..."

The girl nodded conspiratorially and asked in a whisper, "When?"

But she didn't get an answer. The policeman's baton motioned again, and the car moved forward into the intersection.

Mańka craned her neck, her gaze following him for a long time.

Shit, thought Dyzma. She has the nerve to hook her claws into me. That silly bitch. And she probably thinks I stole this car.

He laughed quietly to himself, but all the same he decided to avoid Marszałkowska in the evenings from now on. Why expose himself to such run-ins and break the spell with reminders...

It was the third time he had seen Madam Przełęska's apartment, and it was the third time it had looked different. All the doors were open wide, and bright light was everywhere. Several rooms were set up with little card tables, their fresh cloths an arrestingly vivid green, and even smaller tables, covered with white napkins, were crammed with trays piled high with cakes and canapes.

No one was here yet. Dyzma wandered through a few rooms and then turned back. He lowered himself onto a couch in the sitting room. From the other end of the apartment, there came the sound of some sort of altercation, which apparently was gathering steam, since the words were becoming more and more distinct.

"So you won't give it to me? You won't?" a male voice exclaimed.

This was followed by a longer tirade in a female voice. Nicodemus could only manage to catch a few epithets, since these words were given particular emphasis.

"Good-for-nothing... scrounger... It's blackmail!... ingrate!..."

"So that's the final say?" the male voice sounded. "Will you give me two hundred?"

"I'll give you nothing!"

A bell reverberated in the hall. The ruckus broke off midsentence, and, after a minute, a smiling Madam Przełęska entered the sitting room. Behind her, his face a mask of courtesy, was Krzepicki. Simultaneously, some old man with an enormous bald spot appeared in the hallway entrance.

Madam Przełęska, welcoming and introducing her guest, began to complain about the lateness of "our gentlemen." The old man, who went by the title Professor, was more than a little hard of hearing, which meant the lady of the house had to repeat her insight about her guests' defective punctuality with extreme volume, four times. And each time, the professor would repeat, "Excuse me, what's that?"

She was reaching her limit when Krzepicki came to her aid. He stood before the professor, smiled politely, and said, "Tara-tara-boom-tick-tock, you old knob!"

The old man nodded his head and said with conviction, "Ah yes, yes, the evening is already quite chilly."

Dyzma burst out laughing.

He was immensely tickled by Krzepicki's joke, and as Madam Przełęska went to greet some new guests, he said, "Wait, I'll say something to him!"

"But not too loud," cautioned Krzepicki.

Nicodemus turned to the professor.

"Why don't you suck an egg, you bald dummy!"

"Excuse me, what's that?"

"An egg!"

"Excuse me, I didn't catch all that, what?"

Dyzma was so helpless with laughter that the old man began to suspect something was amiss. Krzepicki saved the day; he bellowed right in the professor's ear:

"The gentleman wanted to share with you a new joke that's going around!"

"Ah, I'm listening, I'm listening."

Meanwhile, several more people had come into the sitting room, and before he'd managed to meet them, Colonel Wareda appeared in the doorway, freeing Dyzma from his joke.

"Well hello there, Nick! Fancy seeing you here!" called the colonel.

"How's it going, Wacek?"

"So? Did you settle your issue with Jaszuński?"

"Thank you. Everything's good."

Both the sitting room and the room next to it were starting to fill up with a great many gentlemen and perhaps five or six elderly women. At several of the tables games of bridge were already underway.

Nicodemus was chatting with Wareda when Ulanicki arrived. Despite the minister's proviso that everything be kept top secret, it appeared that the colonel was also in the loop about Dyzma's grain project, since Ulanicki spoke freely about the plan's progress, which—in his opinion—was proving to be the very best road to have gone down. Wareda congratulated Nicodemus and wished him a successful fulfillment of his tremendous policy.

As they were talking, Madam Przełęska approached them and asked if they didn't want to play some bridge. The colonel and Ulanicki happily acquiesced.

Every table was already occupied by a game in progress, so their hostess offered herself as a partner. Seeing as Dyzma didn't know how to play, a fourth was invited, some skinny man who—as Dyzma learned later—was one of the police dignitaries.

Dyzma watched the game for a while, but he soon lost interest and eventually, when he spotted Krzepicki among a group of nonplayers, headed that way.

As soon as Dyzma had wandered off, the dignitary of police asked Madam Przełęska, "Who's this Mr. Dyzma?"

"Mr. Dyzma?" she asked with surprise. "You don't know him?"

"Unfortunately not . . ."

"What do you mean you don't know him?" Ulanicki chimed in. "You don't recall his little incident with Terkowski?"

"Aha! Now I know who he is."

"Mr. Dyzma," said Madam Przełęska, "is an admirable, upright man. I know him through my nephew, George Ponimirski—they were at Oxford together. They've been bosom companions ever since."

"He's got land?"

"He certainly does, he's from Courland, and at present he manages my niece's estate."

"Nicodemus's got a good head on his shoulders," Ulanicki added. "Jaszuński says there's a lot more to him than meets the eye."

"He's just an all-around terrific guy," added Wareda.

"He's very nice," assured their hostess.

"Indeed," the dignitary of police agreed, entirely convinced. "He makes a solid impression."

"Two clubs," Ulanicki declared, raising his bushy eyebrows.

"We're playing three clubs," corrected Madam Przełęska, who was partnered with Ulanicki.

Dyzma was bored. He could not for the life of him fathom how anyone could possibly enjoy this game. He'd already drunk several glasses of cognac and polished off an abundance of canapes and cakes. Discussion among the non-bridge-playing crowd was limited to international politics and racing. Both topics were equally alien and tedious, so he began to plan a retreat. He waited for his hostess to get up from the table for a moment, caught up with her in the hall, and said, "I'm very sorry. I have to go."

"What a pity! Are you sure you absolutely must?"

"I absolutely must. I leave very early tomorrow morning. I have to get some sleep."

"But I should have liked to have a longer discussion about the little matter of you-know-what . . ."

"That ship hasn't sailed. I'll be back in Warsaw soon."

Dyzma did not, in fact, intend to get some sleep. As he left Madam Przełęska's, he dismissed his chauffeur, instructing him to bring the car around tomorrow morning at seven and be ready to go. As for himself, he'd head home on foot.

It was already close to midnight, and the street was almost empty. Now and then he saw the odd passerby hurrying home. It was only when he reached Nowy Świat that traffic picked up. The chief cause was the small clusters of women sauntering to and fro, their manner none too subtly revealing their trade.

Dyzma watched them a long time before making his selection, a chubby brunette. They quickly reached an agreement.

By the time he returned to his hotel, the sun was already up. Mańka had crept into his thoughts, and he reflected with a sigh that it was actually a shame he hadn't made that late-night appointment with her instead.

The sky was blanketed with heavy, leaden clouds. Just before seven, it began to rain.

At seven on the dot, he paid up at the hotel. The chauffeur arrived. He'd had to put the top up, and Dyzma, cursing the weather, thrust himself into a corner of the backseat.

They were heading to Grodno. He wanted to return to Koborowo bearing concrete results from his Warsaw excursion, to dazzle Kunicki with an outcome that, after all, he himself found extraordinary.

Dyzma was coming to the realization that he'd gotten this favorable decision from the minister simply by repeating the plan outlined to him by Kunicki. There was an obvious conclusion to be drawn: repeating what he heard from others and passing it on as his own could produce big-time results.

He resolved to apply this method as widely as possible, while keeping in mind, of course, a requisite degree of caution. He was gratified to discover this new possibility of making his way through this strange new world and was beginning to believe that he just might be able to blend in after all. As for Koborowo, he had no doubt: not only would Kunicki not try to get rid of him, he would fight tooth and nail for such an administrator.

"I can use this, too," he said to himself. "That asshole's going to have to give me a raise."

He rubbed his hands together. He felt that he was turning the page on a new chapter in his life, and who the hell was he to question too closely who was writing it and why. He recalled the conversation with Minister Jaszuński and his assurance that he, Dyzma, would not be passed over during the implementation of the grain plan. He didn't know exactly what that meant, but he was inclined to speculate that it might involve a bonus of some sort. Łysków's postmaster, Mr. Boczek, once regaled them with the tale of an official at the District Postal Authority who was given a prize of one thousand złotys for devising a new method of stamping letters. Surely he would be given even more: grain, after all, was considerably more important than a bunch of letters! Remembering Mr. Boczek and Łysków brought a smile to Nicodemus's face.

What would they say if they found out how big my salary is, the kinds of characters I'm rubbing shoulders with, he thought. They'd be completely blown away, those dumb hicks!

Ministers, counts! A lady as grand as this Przełęska inviting him to dinner...

Well, that part wasn't great. He was nagged by the thought that he had embroiled himself unnecessarily in the Ponimirski affair, which was still at loose ends and could only hurt him if—God forbid—Kunicki got a whiff of what was going on. That wily chiseler had enough money to get his revenge. The only way to play this would be to tell Ponimirski that his aunt hadn't wanted to hear it and had written off the debt.

On a wave of such musings, Dyzma was swept into Grodno.

The chauffeur, who knew the town well, immediately located the red barracks that housed the Forestry Administration. Since it was after four, the duty officer was the only person Dyzma saw in the office.

"I'm here for Mr. Olszewski. Is Mr. Olszewski here?"

"He's not here. Please report again during office hours," the duty officer replied disinterestedly.

Dyzma raised his voice:

"Office hours might apply to you, young man, but not to me. And as a rule, you should be more polite when you don't know who you're dealing with."

"I *am* polite," the little official said defensively, "and how would I know who I'm dealing with when you didn't introduce yourself, sir?"

"Well, well, don't get fresh. Now hightail it to your man Olszewski and tell him that Mr. Dyzma has arrived with an order from the minister. And mind that he comes right goddamn now, because I'm short on time."

The official, now fully subdued, bowed several times and declared that, while he wasn't allowed to leave his post, he would telephone the director's apartment right away.

He led Nicodemus to his boss's office and was not surprised when this impertinent guest immediately made himself at home in the director's own desk chair.

Not fifteen minutes had passed when Director Olszewski showed up. He was a little sleepy and demonstrably ill at ease. Every muscle on his square face seemed to twitch, and his close-trimmed reddish-blond pencil mustache stretched above his lips as they formed a courteous smile. He tried to conceal his incredulity at this stranger sitting in his office chair.

"I'm Olszewski, it's tremendously nice to . . ."

"I don't know if it *is* nice for you," Dyzma replied, rising slightly and extending his hand. "I'm Dyzma."

"Why, of course it's nice . . . Just this morning I received a telegram from the ministry."

"You should thank God you didn't get canned."

"Why, my dear man!" Olszewski protested nervously, "I don't deserve this! I've obeyed every law and followed every regulation, always exactly to the letter! Dotted every *i*, crossed every *t* . . ."

"Who cares?" Dyzma sneered. "If those regulations have you selling a measly fixed amount to companies in *our* country, and the rest is sold abroad for chicken feed!"

The official persisted in defending himself, citing dates and paragraphs and clauses, all of which he had right at his fingertips. But then Dyzma pulled out the little notebook containing the whole litany he'd copied from Kunicki and continued the attack. He wrapped it up by fiercely assailing Olszewski for dragging out matters and sweeping everything under the rug, whereupon the accused protested that it was very difficult to come to a decision. Without hesitation, Nicodemus repeated Jaszuński's aphorism: "The ability to lead lies in the ability to make immediate decisions, my dear man!"

He pulled out Jaszuński's calling card and handed it to the official, whose long, trembling fingers groped for his pince-nez. When he'd located it and read the card, his contrition increased tenfold.

He assured Dyzma that he was an old and experienced official, that he always did everything "exactly to the letter," that he had a wife and four children, that the office staff was absolutely useless, that regulations were oftentimes contradictory, so what could he do, he had no choice but to follow them in equally contradictory ways, that Kunicki himself had exacerbated the situation, but that now he really didn't see any impediment to taking care of these quotas.

This interlude drew to a close with the appearance of a typist expressly summoned to draw up suitable documents "exactly to the letter" of Kunicki's notes.

It was already dark outside when they were done, and Olszewski invited Dyzma for dinner. But the latter, thinking that it might be better not to do anything to dispel his Friend of the Minister aura, thanked him and clapped the official on the back, leaving him with, "Well, all right. And don't cross me again, pal, because no good can come of that."

Chapter 8

The quarrel began that evening, when Nina changed out of her dress into a fancier one, and spent longer than normal arranging her hair in front of the mirror. Kasia's powers of observation were keen enough to detect the reason.

"It's a shame," she said lightly, "that you didn't put on a ballgown."

"Kasia!"

"What?"

"Your snide remark is entirely uncalled for."

"So why did you change, then?" Kasia's question dripped with unconcealed irony.

"There's no reason. No particular reason. It's just been a long time since I've worn this dress."

"You know very well," Kasia exploded, "that you look amazing in that dress!"

"I do know that," Nina answered with a smile, and she gave Kasia a smoldering come-hither look.

"Nina!"

Nina was still smiling.

"Nina! Stop!" Kasia threw down the book she had been reading and began to pace around the room.

She stopped short in front of Nina and blew up at her.

"I hate it, do you understand, I despise women who, just to impress a man, make themselves into—"

She searched for an epithet of sufficient strength.

"Make themselves into *courtesans*!"

Nina went white.

"Kasia! You insult me!"

"A woman fawning over a man like this, it makes me think of, forgive me, but frankly speaking, a whore. That's right, a whore! . . ."

Tears sprang to Nina's eyes. She stared at Kasia for a moment, eyes wide and pupils dilated, then buried her face in her arms and began to sob. Her shoulder blades rose and fell to the irregular rhythm of her crying, the skin on her neck glowing pink.

Kasia clenched her small fists, but she was too worked up to rein herself in.

"Can you deny it?" She was shouting now. "Can you deny that ever since this afternoon, since you got that telegram, you've been acting completely different? Can you deny that Dyzma is the reason you got all dressed up?! That you've spent an hour already preening in front of that mirror, all so you can *charm* him?!"

"Oh God, oh God," sobbed Nina.

"It makes me sick, do understand me?!"

Nina leapt from her chair. Her wet eyes burned with rebellion.

"So yes, yes," she whispered vehemently. "It's true, you're right, I *do* want to charm him, I *do* want to make myself look as attractive as possible . . . If that makes you sick, ask yourself: shouldn't it be you and me who make *me* sick?"

Kasia, hands on her hips, burst out laughing. "You've found yourself a little crush," she cried, clutching her sides.

She'd intended to annihilate Nina with her irony, but the latter defiantly lifted her head.

"Yes I have!"

"An uncouth brute!" Kasia shot back passionately. "One of these vulgar 'coming boor' types . . . A gorilla!"

"Yes, yes, fine!" Nina shouted. "And what of it?" Her face was red, and she had worked herself into quite a frenzy. "A brute? Yes! This is a new type of modern man! He's a person of strength! A victor! A winner at life! . . . Aren't you always trying to convince me that I'm a real woman? So I believed you, and now, when I finally find a real man . . ."

"A real *he-man*," Kasia hissed.

Nina bit her lip and caught her breath.

"What are you saying? . . . So, fine, a he-man, a he-man . . . And am I not a she-woman?!"

"He's a pig," Kasia added.

"Not true! Nicodemus is not a pig! I have plenty of proof of his subtlety. If he can be brusque sometimes, it's all intentional. It's all part of his style, his type. I should feel sorry for you, really, your character is too deformed to allow you to appreciate the electrifying effect of such gorgeous strength, this imperious, primal manliness . . . Yes, exactly, *primal*, nature in all its magnificent simplicity . . ."

"How easily you give up the pretension of being cultured."

"You lie, you lie, you're deliberately lying, you said it yourself that living by the laws of nature is the pinnacle of culture—"

"What's with these clichés?" Kasia interrupted with cold irony. "Just admit that you want to go to bed with him, that you're simply quaking with desire to offer up your body to him."

There was more she wanted to say, but seeing that Nina had covered her face with a handkerchief and had started to cry again, she let up.

"You're such a . . . heartless . . . such a . . . heartless . . ." Nina repeated between sobs.

Fire flared in Kasia's eyes.

"Me? Heartless? You're saying that to *me*, Nina? Nina!"

"Maybe all that's left for me," Nina's weeping continued, "is suicide . . . Oh God, oh God, how alone I am . . ."

Kasia poured a glass of water and handed it to Nina.

"Drink this, Nina honey, you have to calm down, go on and drink, sweetie."

"No, no, I don't want to . . . Leave me, just leave . . ."

"Drink, Nina darling," she entreated.

"I don't want to. Go, go, have mercy on me . . ."

She was hiding her face, and tears dribbled down her hands. Kasia embraced her and whispered word after tender word in her ear. Suddenly, Nina flinched. They'd both heard, in the distance, the sound of an automobile. After a moment, the beam from its headlights traced a line through the dimness of the room.

"Don't cry, Nina, your eyes will be all red."

"I'm not going down to dinner anyway," Nina replied with a fresh round of weeping.

Kasia covered her in kisses: her wet eyelids, her eyes, her trembling lips, her hair.

"Don't cry, don't cry, sweetheart, I was being nasty, cruel, forgive me, my dearest . . ."

She squeezed her tightly, as if she thought the stronger the hug, the more likely it would extinguish the next spasm of sobbing.

"Nina honey, my dear little Nina!"

In the doorway, the maid appeared, announcing that dinner was served.

"Tell the master that the lady has a headache and will not be coming down to dinner."

As soon as the maid left, Nina urged Kasia to leave her and go downstairs. Kasia, however, refused to hear a word of it. Nina, sniffling, was wiping her eyes when there was another knock at the door.

A beaming, gesticulating Kunicki flew into the room.

"Come on, let's go," he lisped, "Dyzma's arrived! And with such results, you can't even imagine! That fellow's got the golden touch! I'm telling you, it's everything I asked for, everything I wanted! Let's go! I specifically asked him to wait for you before he tells the story . . ."

He was so absorbed by his excitement that only now did he notice that some kind of spat had occurred.

"What's with you two? Well? Come on, let's go . . ."

He obviously had more to say, but Kasia suddenly leapt to her feet and pointed to the door.

"Get out of here!" she shrieked.

"But . . ."

"Get out of here this minute!"

Kunicki stood motionless. His small eyes glittered with hatred. He emitted a vulgar curse and darted from the room, slamming the door with such force that Nicodemus, sitting on a couch in the foyer downstairs, jumped.

"What was that?" he asked the butler, who smiled knowingly.

"The young lady has presumably just thrown the master out of her room."

He whispered the last few words, since Kunicki was on his way down the stairs, his expression making a lightning-fast transition back to glowing good cheer.

"What a pity, my dear Nicodemus! What do you know, my wife has a terrible migraine and can't come down. And Kasia doesn't want to leave the poor thing by herself. Tough luck, hee hee, we'll have to have dinner without the ladies' company."

He took Dyzma's arm and steered him to the dining room, where the servants had just whisked away two unnecessary place settings.

He wasted no time in asking Dyzma a lot of detailed questions about the course of his mission in Warsaw and Grodno. At each reply, he bounced up and down on his chair, slapping his knees and bellowing ebullient commendations.

"Do you know, my dear Dyzma," he cried in conclusion, "that this will increase Koborowo's revenue by some hundred to hundred forty thousand a year? Which means, according to our agreement, your royalties will amount to over forty thousand a year. Well? Not bad, eh? It paid off, huh?"

"Well, kind of."

"What do you mean, 'kind of?' "

"Necessary expenses have been very high, very high. I had expected that my salary would go up."

"Fine," Kunicki replied coolly. "So I'll add five hundred. That will make an even three thousand."

Dyzma almost said "thank you," but, noting that Kunicki was looking at him with concern, he leaned back in his chair and said, "That's not much. Three thousand five hundred."

"But isn't that a little high?"

"A little high? What are you talking about? Three thousand five hundred seems a little high to you? In that case, make it four."

Kunicki retreated and wanted to turn it all into a joke, but Dyzma held fast:

"Four!"

Kunicki was up against the wall, he had to acquiesce. He justified his capitulation by acknowledging Dyzma's skill in facilitating his business interests.

"I agree," he said, "all the more readily, since a happy beginning makes for an equally happy ending."

"What do you mean?" Dyzma was surprised. "Isn't this a done deal?"

"The matter of quotas, yes. But I was thinking, my dear Mr. Nicodemus, that you could do with some dividends, let's say a hundred, perhaps a hundred and fifty thousand zlotys. Eh?"

"Yeah?"

"There's a way to do it. Well, strictly speaking, there's a way for *you* to do it."

"Me?"

"You, my dear Mr. Nicodemus. Of course, it will require no small amount of effort and exertion. Do you have connections with the Ministry of Transportation?"

"Transportation? Hmm . . . I could make that happen."

"That's right!" Kunicki was delighted. "That's right! And could you get your hands on a bigger cut of the railway ties? . . . Eh? Now that would be a piece of business! You could make real money on that deal!"

"Didn't you already make a deal like that?" asked Dyzma.

"Ach, you're thinking of that lawsuit? I assure you, everything was blown out of proportion. After all, enemies are like weeds . . . The whole thing was exaggerated. Well, and the court found me innocent. I had irrefutable proof at hand."

He looked carefully at Dyzma, and at his silence Kunicki became alarmed.

"Do you think the lawsuit might interfere with getting a supply contract?"

"Well, it sure won't help."

"But what can I do? Well? If anything happens, after all, I have documents, I have them at hand, if anyone has any reservations, I can prove once again . . ."

On and on he went, providing detail upon detail and quoting excerpts of his court defense.

It was closing in on midnight when he noticed his interlocutor's sleepiness.

"But you're tired! Well, anyway, get some sleep. And really, please, my dear Nicodemus, don't trouble yourself too much. Naturally, I would be unbelievably grateful if you could use that eagle eye of yours to take a look at some things for me. Two heads are always better than one, but again, I thank God for my good health and there's no need to burden you with my work. Make yourself at home and get some rest."

"Thank you," Dyzma said, yawning.

"One more thing, though. If you have the time and inclination, maybe look in on my ladies a little bit. Kasia's always riding a horse or doing some sport or another, but my wife, poor creature, she's very bored. She has no one to keep her company. So there's the boredom, the migraines, the melancholy. And I admit: chumming around with Kasia might not have the best effect on her nerves. So I'd be much obliged if you could find a little time for her."

Dyzma promised to undertake the project of amusing Nina, whereupon he headed off to bed. That old sucker, he thought. The woman's throwing herself at me, and even so, he goes and pushes her right on to me!

He propped himself up against his pillows and, taking out his wallet full of money, did a rough count, then began to calculate on a sheet of paper how much more he was going to earn. He was basking in the sum of his dividends when he heard quiet footsteps in the neighboring room. Someone was groping their way through in the dark; several times they had bumped into a chair. Now the someone had made it across the room. His interest piqued, he was about to get up and have a look when the steps stopped right outside his door. The next moment, the knob turned and the door slowly opened.

On the threshold stood Kasia.

Dyzma rubbed his eyes. His mouth hung open in surprise.

She was wearing black silk pajamas with red piping. She peered at him through narrowed eyes. Carefully shutting the door behind her, she approached his bed. Dyzma couldn't detect the slightest trace of embarrassment in her comportment, and he gaped at her with growing bewilderment.

"I'm not disturbing you?" she asked breezily.

"Who, me? But . . . what's this about?"

"I forgot cigarettes," she said off-handedly.

"But I thought . . ."

"What did you think?" She gave each word a haughty emphasis.

He was confused.

"I thought that . . . that you might have some business with me."

She lit a cigarette and nodded.

"I certainly do."

She pulled up a chair and sat, crossing her legs. The gap between her red sateen slipper and the cuff of her pajama pants revealed a slender, swarthy-skinned ankle. Nicodemus had never seen a woman in pants before, and it struck him now as indecent. The silence was broken by Kasia's low, throaty alto:

"I want to have a word with you about something. What are your intentions with Nina?"

"My . . ."

"Please, don't try to sell me a story. I think that you should man up and give me an honest answer. After all, there's no denying that you're trying to win her favor. To what end?"

Dyzma shrugged his shoulders.

"Surely you're not under the delusion that Nina will leave her husband for you. She might be infatuated with you right now, but it doesn't mean a thing."

"How do you know that Nina's infatuated with me?" he asked with interest.

"Never mind about that. I came here to find out what kind of man you are—a gentleman, or someone who's capable of basely exploiting the weakness of an honest woman and an honest wife. I'd consider you the lowest of the low if you took advantage of the situation to make Nina your lover!"

She was agitated, and her voice, which had begun to quaver, was almost a rasp. Her eyes glinted with a dark luster.

"What's your problem with me?" he replied, already more than a little annoyed. "Do I stick my nose in your business?"

"Oh? So am I to take that swinish response as a yes, that's indeed what you're planning to do? Ugh, I could horsewhip you right in your fat face! Nothing would give me more pleasure!"

"You could what?" growled Dyzma. "With what? Me?"

"You! You!" she hissed with loathing, clenching her fists.

Dyzma was furious. Who the hell did this little chit think she was? Showing up in the middle of the night and . . .

All of a sudden, Kasia leapt out of her chair and took hold of his hand.

"Don't you touch her! Do you understand me? Don't you dare touch her!"

Her lips were quivering. Dyzma yanked his hand free.

"I'll do what I want, got it? Who the hell are you to tell me what to do!"

She bit her lip and went to the window.

"This is really something else," Dyzma muttered.

In truth, he was utterly disoriented. Admittedly, he was tickled that Nina was infatuated with him, but he didn't understand why Kasia was so bent out of shape, why she'd come here under cover of night instead of simply sharing her suspicions with her father. He knew that she hated her father, but in that case, why was she so vehemently safeguarding the fidelity of her stepmother? Everything was always topsy-turvy with these upper-class types.

Meanwhile, Kasia had turned around, and Dyzma was once again taken by surprise: she was smiling coquettishly at him.

"Are you mad at me?" she asked in a decidedly sweet voice. "Really?"

"Yes, really."

"But surely you can forgive me? May I sit down?"

"It's time to sleep," he muttered grudgingly.

She flashed him a mischievous smile and, without warning, sat on the edge of his bed.

"Do you always spend your nights so virtuously? So . . . alone?"

He stared at her in amazement. She leaned in a little closer. Her cherry-red lips parted, revealing exceptionally white and even teeth, and above them, her nostrils oddly flared, their color tinged the same tawny peach as the skin of her cheeks. She was downright luscious; how had he not seen this until now? Only her eyes hadn't changed. Under the splendid narrow arch of her knit eyebrows, their gaze was cold and clinical.

"Surely you miss Warsaw, where men are not condemned to lonely nights the way they are here in Koborowo. Oh, I understand . . ."

"What do you understand?" he asked uncertainly.

"I understand why you're stringing Nina along."

"I'm not stringing her along." Dyzma was being honest.

She burst out laughing and suddenly lowered her head and brushed her cheek against his lips.

Ah, so that's what this is about, Dyzma thought. She's jealous! This one's throwing herself at me, too!

"Mr. Dyzma," she began playfully. "I understand your wanting to have a woman out here as well, but I just don't understand why it has to be Nina. Is it because you don't find me attractive?"

The blanket was thin, and he could plainly feel the heat of her body.

"Why, of course I find you attractive."

"I'm younger than Nina . . . She's not any better looking than I am . . . Why don't you take a look . . ."

She undid her pajamas in a few quick motions. The slippery black silk slid down her slender, supple body and dropped to the floor.

Dyzma was utterly flabbergasted. He stared goggle-eyed at this strange young girl standing before him, so shameless, so completely naked. She was close enough that he could have reached out his hand and touched her dusky skin.

"Well? And? How do you like this?"

Kasia dissolved into quiet laughter.

Dyzma sat with his mouth helplessly hanging open.

"I'm quite pretty," she said with a coquettish toss of her head. "Perhaps you'd like to check for yourself how smooth my skin is, how firm my flesh is? Oh, please, don't be shy!"

Not bothering to stifle her laughter, she came right up to the bed.

"Well?"

Something in her laughter frightened Nicodemus. He couldn't bring himself to make a single move.

"But perhaps you think I'm some kind of a floozy? . . . Yes? No, my charming Nicodemus, I assure you, I've preserved my virginity. Perhaps you'd like to see for yourself, if that's more to your taste than an affair with Nina . . . Yes? Okay, then . . ."

She knelt over him, and with one swift motion, pushed her breasts into Nicodemus's face. He felt their cool, supple springiness, his nostrils filled with the fragrance of her tantalizing young body, strangely but subtly spicy.

"Well? . . ."

"God*damn!*" Dyzma groaned through clenched teeth. He lunged at her, greedily seizing her body and pulling it under his.

Kasia felt hot breath on her face. An ineptly shaved mouth began to hungrily seek her lips. Her hands landed on sweaty, hairy skin. She was engulfed by a disgust impossible to overcome. Revulsion rose in her throat.

"Get off, get off! Let me go, please, you disgusting . . . Get off!"

Her slim body thrashed with spasmodic, desperate attempts to free herself from his loutish grip.

No dice.

She realized now that her love for Nina was overrated, she realized that she would not be able to endure this sacrifice, that she'd honestly prefer to die than pay for that affection with these embraces.

But she realized it too late.

When, with trembling hands, she put her pajamas back on, Nicodemus chuckled, "Hee hee hee. . . . You're one first-class gal."

She shot him a look drenched with hatred and contempt, but he didn't seem to notice and continued:

"Was that good for you? Well?"

"You animal!" she hissed through clenched teeth and left his room as fast as she could.

Now Dyzma couldn't figure out what to think—what was going on with this chick?

After all, she herself had come to him, she herself had wanted it, and now . . .

For a long time he couldn't sleep. Musing over the entire event, he arrived at the conclusion that Kasia was not in fact faking her disgust, and that a romance with her was not to be.

"They're all off their rockers here," he decided, remembering Ponimirski.

Only Nina was at breakfast the next morning. She explained that Kasia was still in bed. From Nina's demeanor he deduced that she was none the wiser about Kasia's little stunt.

Kunicki returned that evening and monopolized Dyzma until late into the night.

It wasn't until the following morning that Nicodemus ran into Kasia, in the hallway to the dining room. She answered his bow with a haughty nod of her head. Nina was already at the table. Both women sat in silence. It seemed necessary to start a conversation. At Dyzma's first remark, something about the pleasantness of the weather, Kasia responded with scalding irony:

"Ah, how wonderful it is that you should notice such an extraordinary phenomenon!"

When he rose to reach for the cold cuts, accidentally dipping his sleeve into the butter as he did so, she laughed provokingly.

"Such lovely clothing! What a pity! So beautifully made, and with such taste! Do you have a tailor in London?"

"No," he answered simply, "I buy my clothing off the rack at the store."

He did not sense her derision and was merely amazed that she could find his clothing so impressive. He also failed to register the reproachful look with which Nina attempted to put a stop to Kasia's commentary.

"You see," Nina said, "you've learned a good lesson from Nicodemus. Like I told you before, snobbery is a poor fit for such a man of action."

Kasia crumpled her napkin and stood up.

"Ugh, what do I care? Goodbye."

"You're going to Krupiewo?"

"Yes."

"But you're coming back before lunch?"

"I don't know. We'll see."

"What's she angry about?" Dyzma asked warily, when he was sure she had gone.

Nina nodded. "You're right. She's just angry that . . . Perhaps . . . Do you have a bit of free time?"

"Certainly."

"Shall we perhaps go boating?"

"Great."

She got her shawl and also her parasol, since the sun was beating down mercilessly.

They walked down a narrow path surrounded by stubble fields, toward the glassy and motionless lake. Nina was wearing a white dress of such lightweight material that it was nearly transparent in the sunlight, and Nicodemus, following behind her, could clearly make out the shape of her legs.

In order to reach the boats, they had to traverse a footbridge that spanned a rather wide ditch. Nina hesitated.

"You know, we'd better take the long way."

"Are you scared of crossing the bridge?"

"A little."

"No need for that. It's a strong bridge."

"But I might get dizzy and lose my balance . . ."

"Hmm . . . It's hardly worth going all the way around for that. I'll carry you."

"That's hardly proper!" She smiled almost playfully.

Dyzma smiled, too. He bent down and scooped her up. She made no attempt to ward him off, and when they found themselves on the bridge, she clasped him around the neck and clung to him tightly.

"Oh! Be careful! . . ."

He had deliberately slowed his pace, and he set her on the ground a few steps farther than the length of the crossing necessitated. He wasn't tired, not at all, but he was a little out of breath.

"Am I heavy?" Nina asked. "How long do you think you could carry me?"

Nicodemus looked at her. Her eyes were glowing.

"I could do it for three miles, for five miles . . ."

She turned away quickly, and they walked in silence all the way to the boats. When they had already floated quite far from the shore, Nina said, "Please don't misunderstand what I say. It seems to me that a woman cannot be happy if she doesn't have someone to carry her in his arms. I'm not speaking figuratively. I mean literally carry her in his arms."

Dyzma set his oar down. He was remembering tubby little Mr. Boczek and his wife, who must have weighed at least a hundred kilos. Boczek was surely unable to carry her in his arms—he grinned—but they seemed happy enough.

"Not all women," he replied amenably.

"I agree, but those women who are perfectly happy with no one to carry them, there must be something a little . . . unnatural about them, they're masculinized, deficient in those things that constitute real femininity. For example, Kasia . . ."

There was a note of distaste in her voice.

"What, did you and Kasia have a fight?"

"It's not that," Nina answered. "She's just upset with me."

"But what for?"

She hesitated.

"What for? . . . Well, I don't know . . . Perhaps because I've taken a certain . . . liking to you."

"And Kasia doesn't like me?"

"It's not that."

"But she doesn't like me. This morning at breakfast she was shooting darts at me."

"Well, you certainly didn't let her get away with it. You really do know how to make short work of an adversary with just a few choice words . . ."

Dyzma burst out laughing. He had remembered Wareda's story about Ulanicki's gag in Krynica.

"Sometimes," he said, "it can be done without words at all. When I was in Krynica in May, a certain young upstart was staying in my guest house. You know, one of these guys all gussied up in swanky clothes all the time. He was sitting across from me at the table, and every day he'd talk through the whole dinner, just yammering on and on. Blah blah blah! And in every language! And everyone would listen, especially the ladies. And he'd just sweet-talk them, really lay it on thick."

"I know that type," Nina interjected. "Such ladies' men. I can't abide them."

"I can't abide them either. So one day I just couldn't take it anymore. When he'd already been jabbering on for half an hour, I suddenly leaned toward him, and I just let it out: 'Hoooooooo!' . . ."

Nina burst out laughing.

"What did he do?!"

"Him? He went completely silent, and then we never heard from him again. He went away or something."

"Oh, how marvelous!" Nina cried. "And that's just your style! Even if you hadn't told me, if someone else had told me the story, I would have guessed at once that it was you. Marvelous!"

Dyzma was pleased with the effect.

"You know," Nina continued, "I've never met a man like you. But to me, it seems like we've known each other for years. Right now it seems to me that I'd be able to guess exactly what you would do in any situation, the things you would say. And yet it's puzzling to me that each time we talk, I discover a new revelation in you, a new surprise. After all, you're a monolith."

" A who? . . ."

"A monolith. The structure of your nature is mathematically consistent. For example, your way of relating to women. There's a fascinating straightforwardness. True, perhaps it's a little unpolished, even a little, one might say, crude. But underneath it, one senses a deep well of thought and reflection. It's this very man of action, precisely this type of profound intellectual who must embody this way of being, so untethered from romanticism or lyricism, stripped of such ornamentation and glitz. Oh, you're not one of those people who resemble nothing so much as a storefront, whose every value is on display right in the window. I apologize for the metaphor. Surely a man like yourself can't abide metaphors?"

Nicodemus didn't know what that word meant, so he answered, just in case: "Why . . . certainly . . ."

"You are gracious. But it's not your genre, sir. There's not a hint of the baroque in you. Am I describing you correctly?"

Dyzma's insides were beginning to roil with irritation. He'd never imagined that he could hear someone speaking entirely in Polish and yet not understand a single word.

"Certainly," he mumbled.

"Ah, you don't enjoy talking about yourself."

"No. There's nothing to talk about."

He was quiet for a moment and then, in a different tone, added, "We'll row over to those woods, maybe?" He indicated a rather distant shore overgrown with pines.

"All right. But this time I'll row, and you can be at the helm."

"You won't get too tired?"

"No. There's no harm in a little exercise."

The boat was narrow and none too steady. As they changed positions, they had to hold on to each other to keep from losing their balance.

"Do you know how to swim?" she asked.

"Like a stone," Dyzma replied, laughing.

"Me neither. Which means we must be very careful."

They made it to the woods. The air was heavy with the fragrance of sun-drenched pine needles.

"Shall we get out?" Nina asked.

"Let's. Let's sit in the shade for a little bit."

"Yes, it's awfully hot."

The bow of the boat glided onto the sandy shore. Further up, where the trees began, the ground was covered with dense, woolly moss.

"It's lovely here, isn't it?" Nina asked.

"Not bad at all."

They sat on the moss, and Nicodemus lit a cigarette.

"Were you quite surprised by my letter?"

"Why, I liked it very much," Dyzma answered, reaching into his pocket for the narrow envelope. "I carry it near my heart."

Nina at once started to beg him to destroy the letter, lest it fall into a certain someone's hands.

"You mustn't forget that I'm a married woman. Destroy it, please!"

"No way," Dyzma said, digging in his heels.

"You mustn't suspect me of cowardice. I just want to avoid any unpleasantness."

She put out her hand, but Nicodemus held the letter just out of her reach.

"Oh, please, you must give it back."

"I'm not handing it over," he laughed.

Seeing that Dyzma was flirting, Nina smiled as well, searching for an opportune moment to snatch the letter away from him. She bent toward him so she was leaning against his shoulder. Dyzma seized her and gave her a long kiss. At first she made to push him away, but her resolve only lasted a moment.

In the distance, from the other side of the lake, there was a barely audible whirring.

It was the Kunicki sawmills, hard at work.

Dyzma planted his hands behind his head and stretched out over the moss. Nina sat huddled on the ground. She leaned over him and whispered, "Why, oh why? What have you done to me? Now I'll never be able to forget you . . . I'll be a hundred times unhappier than before . . . God, my God! . . . I can't stand to live this awful life anymore . . . I can't go on without you . . ."

"Why do you have to go on without me?"

"Don't speak! Don't speak of such things, don't speak! I can't take on the role of the wife who betrays her elderly husband. That's atrocious!"

"But after all, you don't love him . . ."

"I hate him! I hate him!"

"So . . . ?"

"Ah, you pretend not to understand me. I couldn't live with such a lie always in my heart. It's beyond my power. It would poison every minute I spent with you. . . . God, God, if only I could break these shackles."

"And what would be so hard about that?" Dyzma shrugged. "Plenty of people get divorced."

She bit her lip.

"I'm base, I'm foolish, and you'd be right to condemn me for it, but I wouldn't know how to make do without luxury, without nice things, without the trappings of wealth. I'm ashamed, but . . . If only you were rich!"

"Maybe I will be. Who can say? . . ."

"My darling!" She folded her hands as if in prayer. "My darling! After all, you're so strong, so clever! You can achieve anything you put your mind to, true?"

"True," he answered uncertainly.

"You see! You see! Take me away from all this! Save me!"

She started to cry.

Dyzma wrapped his arms around her. He didn't know how to calm her down, so he was silent.

"How good you are, how sweet you are, if only you knew how terribly much I love you and . . . I don't want to keep secrets from you, I can't! Perhaps you'll despise me later, but to you, I'll confess everything. Promise that you'll forgive me! Promise! I'm . . . You see, I'm so pitiful, so weak. I truly couldn't defend myself. The effect she had on me, it was positively hypnotic . . ."

"Who's 'she'?"

"Kasia. But I swear to you that never again will I surrender to this hypnosis, never again, I swear! Do you believe me?"

Dyzma had absolutely no idea what she was talking about. So he nodded his head and said that he believed her.

She grabbed hold of his hand and pressed it to her lips.

"How good you are! How good you are! . . . At any rate, it's fortunate that Kasia is leaving for Switzerland."

"When's she leaving?"

"As early as next week. For an entire year!"

"For a year. That must be costing your husband a bundle."

"No. It's not costing him a thing, because Kasia won't take a penny from him."

"What's she going to live on?"

"What do you mean? After all, she has quite a large fortune from her mother in the bank."

"Oh? I didn't know. Mr. Kunicki never said anything about that."

"Ugh, why are you even mentioning him? Let's talk about us."

She was more anxious and discombobulated than usual.

They returned in silence.

They encountered Kunicki on the terrace. He was grinning and, as was his wont, rubbing his small hands together. He greeted them with palpable glee, asking them how they were and whether their excursion had been a success, but even if they'd wanted to answer him, they'd have been hard-pressed to find a chink in his wall of chatter.

"So? What have you heard from on high?" Kunicki inquired.

"You mean Warsaw? Well, nothing in particular. I've been chatting with Jaszuński and Ulanicki about my plan to stockpile grain."

"Do tell! So? How did it go? Is everything right on track?"

"Well, yes. Only . . . well, it's top secret!"

Kunicki put his finger to his lips and whispered, "I understand! Shhh . . . My wife will hear, maybe you can tell me after lunch. I'm beside myself with curiosity."

"I don't mind," said Nicodemus. "After all, Lady Nina won't say anything to anybody. I can tell you in front of her."

"Tell him about what?" Nina asked without looking at them.

"Nina," Kunicki warned, "just be careful. This is top secret. Mr. Dyzma, together with top officials, is preparing a terrific plan to save our country from economic disaster. The people of this country should get down on their knees to thank him for this thing! So please, continue, my dear Nicodemus."

Dyzma gave a brief answer featuring everything he knew concerning grain bonds. Kunicki rubbed his hands and repeated, after every couple of sentences, "Fantastic, fantastic!"

Nina stared at the fantastic project designer, her eyes wide with awed reverence.

"We only have one problem," Dyzma concluded. "Namely, we don't have anywhere to put the grain we buy. We just don't have the cash to build warehouses."

"Ha!" cried Kunicki, "that is a real obstacle . . . But . . . Nicodemus, what do you think of this as a way out of the situation: the government buys the grain, but only on the condition that the sellers commit to storing it themselves. Let's say that not everyone has somewhere to store it. Even then, it would be easier for a landowner to build a granary and sell the grain than to let the grain rot and go bankrupt. It seems to me that this could be a real way out. What do you think?"

Dyzma was positively dumbfounded. The noggin on this old bastard, he thought with admiration. He cleared his throat.

"We touched on that as a possibility," he said slyly, "and we might do something to that effect."

Kunicki began to lay out the details of his idea. Nicodemus was paying as close attention as he could, recalling the words "sly old fox," when the butler appeared.

"Telephone call, sir. The transmission belt in the new mill has broken, and there's been some sort of unfortunate accident."

"What? What are you saying? Quick, the car! Excuse me . . ."

He left the room at a near sprint.

They finished their lunch *à deux*.

"You are a great economist," Nina said, not lifting her eyes. "Did you study abroad?"

"Yes, at Oxford," Dyzma replied, not missing a beat.

Nina's face flushed violently.

"At Oxford? Were...were...you weren't there with George Ponimirski?"

Nicodemus only now realized the extent to which he had really stepped in it. After all, at any minute she could ask her brother and discover that Dyzma was lying. But there was no way out of it. It was necessary to wade further in.

"Of course I knew him," he said. "He was a good friend."

Nina was silent.

"And you know," she asked after a moment, "about the misfortune that befell him?"

"No."

"He suffered a serious nervous collapse. He was leading an impossible lifestyle: he drank, he caroused, he dueled, and it all finally led to madness. Poor George!... Two years in a lunatic asylum... He's slightly better now. He no longer flies into those fits of rage, but a complete recovery, unfortunately, is out of the question... Poor George!... You cannot imagine what terrible suffering he's caused me... All the more so because since his collapse he's become so unkind to me. And we used to love each other so much. He's here, you know, at Koborowo..."

"Oh?..."

"Yes. He lives in the annex, in the park, with an orderly to care for him. You haven't met him because the doctors recommended the rarest possible contact with people, since that seems to aggravate his condition. But I know that perhaps seeing you, a friend from the old days, wouldn't do him any harm. Did you get along well?"

"Of course, we were on very good terms."

Nina was delighted. She seized on this plan and, entreating Dyzma not to say a word about it to Kunicki, proposed that they go to the annex after dinner. A reluctant Nicodemus made a few attempts to weasel out of it, but fearing that this would arouse suspicion, he finally had to agree.

When they were in among the trees, Nina threw her arms around his neck and pressed her entire body against his. Nicodemus, consumed by fears of accidentally giving himself away, gave her a few absentminded pecks.

"It feels so right to be with you," she said. "I feel so calm..."

She slid her arm through Nicodemus's.

"A woman is like ivy," she said, reflecting. "She will grow poorly, just creep across the ground, until she finds a strong tree; then she can climb toward the sun..."

Dyzma thought this was a very clever saying and one worth remembering.

The annex was a small, Renaissance-style villa so overgrown with vines that the white of the wall was only visible here and there. On the closely cropped lawn in front, they could see a deck chair and, sprawled motionlessly upon it, the young count.

The miniature pinscher detected their approach and began to sound the alarm with a round of hysterical yapping that resembled a coughing fit.

Ponimirski turned his head languidly and squinted against the sun as he watched them draw nearer. All of a sudden, he leapt to his feet, straightening his clothing and setting his monocle in his eye.

"Hello, George." Nina reached for his hand. "I brought you an old friend from Oxford. Do you recognize him?"

Ponimirski cast him a look of profound mistrust. Slowly, he kissed his sister's hand. From the expression on his face, it was plain that he feared his plot had been exposed.

"Of course I recognize him, naturally. How pleased I am, my old friend, that you have come to visit me."

Suddenly, he turned to his sister.

"I'm sorry, but leave us alone. You understand, after having parted ways for so long we have so many things to discuss. Perhaps you could sit here a bit while we take a walk?"

Nina did not object. She looked meaningfully into Nicodemus's eyes and entered the annex.

Ponimirski, looking around in all directions, lead Dyzma onto a nearby path and jabbed his index finger into Dyzma's chest.

"What is the meaning of this?" he asked furiously. "You knave! Did you expose me to Nina? And I suppose that scumbag Kunik knows about everything?"

"Why, God forbid! I didn't say a word to anybody!"

"Well, lucky for you. But how does she know that I introduced you to Aunt Przełęska as my friend from Oxford?"

"She doesn't know anything about that. And about Oxford: I told her that myself. It just came up in conversation."

"Not only are you an imposter, you're a moron to boot. After all, you can't speak a word of English, can you!"

"Not a word."

Ponimirski dropped onto a bench and laughed, much to the bewilderment of his pinscher, who was looking at him intently.

"Well, how did it go with Aunt Przełęska and that Krzepicki of hers? She didn't throw you out?"

Dyzma made to sit beside Ponimirski, but the latter stopped the former with a gesture of his hand.

"I can't abide it, people like you sitting down in my presence. Information, please. Briefly, precisely, and without lying. Well?"

Nicodemus knew that the man addressing him was of considerably less than sound mind, but even so, he felt bashful in a way he never did with either ministers or generals, nor with any other of the Warsaw big shots.

He started to tell him that Madam Przełęska had been receptive to his visit, but that both she and Mr. Krzepicki had claimed that right now there was nothing to be done and that the matter should be put aside for a few years.

When he'd finished, Ponimirski hissed, "*Sapristi!* You're not making this up?"

"No."

"You know, in all my life, I've never heard anyone talking about anything in a way so devoid of any degree of intelligence. Did you complete any kind of schooling at all?"

Dyzma was silent.

"As concerns this matter, I'm not such a simpleton that I'd be willing to let it rest at that. So I'll write another letter for you to take to Warsaw. In the meantime, goodbye. You may go. Brutus! To heel!"

"But what about Nina?" Dyzma asked timidly.

"Nina? . . . Ah, right. I forgot about her. In that case, we'll go together. And then you can take her away with you when you go. She frays my nerves."

Nina met them where the paths crossed.

"And so?" she smiled at them. "Did you have a nice stroll down memory lane?"

"Indeed," replied Dyzma.

"My dear," Ponimirski drawled, adjusting his monocle, "it's always nice to reminisce about back when we were young and rich. Isn't that right, my dear fellow?"

He pronounced those last words with special emphasis and laughed shrilly.

"Of course, my dear fellow," Dyzma repeated without conviction, which added to Ponimirski's amusement.

"We were chatting exclusively about Oxford and London, where we had such marvelous fun together," Ponimirski got out through his laughter. "You can't even imagine, my dear, how good it was to at long last hear such fluent English, such as I haven't heard in years . . ."

He clapped Nicodemus on the shoulder and asked, in English, "Wasn't it, old boy?"

Dyzma's veins throbbed in his temples. He racked his memory and—sweet relief!—uttered a word, the one English word that, among the distinguished Łysków society, the son of Notary Winder used from time to time:

"Yes."

This answer propelled Ponimirski's hilarity to new heights; meanwhile Nina, noting Nicodemus's disconcertedness and putting it down to dismay at having to keep company with his insane old friend, announced that they must be going. To her great relief, her brother did not appear to want to further detain Dyzma, and he bid them goodbye without any additional flamboyance.

"Poor George," she intoned when they were in the alley. "Was he very much changed?"

"No, not very . . . Maybe it'll pass . . ."

"Unfortunately . . . I saw what an unpleasant impression his condition made on you. Perhaps I acted wrongly, taking you to George."

"Why?"

"You know, Nicodemus, perhaps it's better you don't visit him, it might even do him harm. The doctors say that other people's presence has a stimulating effect on him, and they've recommended keeping stimulation to a minimum."

"Whatever you want."

"It's not that I *want* it." She snuggled closer against his shoulder. "I'm simply keeping you informed. After all, I know that you'll do whatever is wisest and best."

She began to speak of the springtime—it's what she had in her soul, and that, for the time being, it was best to close one's eyes, to regard it as a kind of unreal dream, which passes, which must pass, which passes quickly. When she demanded a reassuring response from Dyzma, he replied that he felt the same way—it was the answer that would cause the least trouble.

Chapter 9

The days, clear and bright, passed serenely. Dyzma had settled into Koborowo and felt at home there. He was admittedly a little annoyed at the resoluteness with which Nina insisted on remaining faithful to her husband until the moment of liberation arrived, but he did not suffer unduly for this particular reason. By nature, Nicodemus Dyzma had never been one for strong desires, to say nothing of passions.

He ate well, slept well, and generally lounged around.

He felt absolutely great about all of this. He put on a little weight and, since he often wandered around the grounds to kill some of his abundant free time, got a nice tan. Initially he did his roaming on horseback, but after a few trips he concluded that it was an awfully bumpy ride, so he mostly walked. He took another look at the estate, the sawmill, the paper mill, the flour mill, and when something piqued his curiosity, he asked the managers, who doffed their caps whenever they met him. They knew it wasn't just anybody they were dealing with.

Surrounding Dyzma was an atmosphere of profound respect and admiration.

The only clouds in the blue sky of these bright days were the altercations with Kasia.

Although the fusses she kicked up chiefly concerned Nina, they more than once made passing reference to Dyzma. In one particular instance—it was at breakfast—as she was needling him and mercilessly deriding every sentence he spoke, Dyzma snarled, "You forget who you're dealing with!"

"I really don't care," she shrugged, "but you're hardly a Persian shah, are you? Do you perhaps suffer from delusions of grandeur?"

Dyzma did not understand, but from the look on Nina's face, he deduced that it must have been a great insult. He blushed, and suddenly he thumped his fist on the table with all his strength.

"That's enough, you little brat!" he roared. The tableware rattled and clanked, and both ladies froze. Only after a few moments did Kasia, white as a sheet, jump up and run out. Nina didn't say a word, although her expression suggested both approval for Nicodemus's outburst and fear in equal measure.

Applying such radical means got results, but the results were only superficial. True, since that day Kasia had stopped mocking him, but the hatred glowing in her eyes had grown stronger, and was growing all the time, until finally it had to explode. The explosion, when it occurred on Sunday morning, took both sides by surprise.

Kunicki was working in his office. Nina had gone to church. Nicodemus was sitting in her boudoir, leafing through photo albums. That's when Kasia came in.

One glance was all it took for her to realize that the album in Nicodemus's hands was the one that contained countless pictures of Nina in various poses, pictures taken by Kasia herself.

"Give it back, it's mine!" she cried, impetuously yanking the album from him.

"How about some manners?!" Dyzma shouted.

She wanted to leave, but his words stopped her. She turned to face him, and for a moment she was silent, but the way she looked made Nicodemus prepare to shield his face against an anticipated blow while simultaneously kindling the desire to embrace her, press against those tiny, heaving breasts, forcefully kiss those fiery eyes and tremulous full lips, which finally opened to unleashed a torrent of words that cracked like a whip:

"This is villainy, villainy! You're despicable! You've defiled her! You barge into my father's house to seduce his wife! If you don't get out of here right away, at the very first opportunity, I'll beat you like the dog you are! I have zero regard for your social position, zero regard for your connections! Do you understand me? You may impress my father, but not me! I'm telling you for your own good, get out of here, and do it now! . . ."

Her voice was getting louder and louder, and since all the doors in the enfilade were open, it reached Kunicki's ears. Kasia was too worked up to hear his quick little steps. Neither did Nicodemus, stunned by the unbridled eruption of this young lady who had always seemed so composed.

Kunicki stood in the doorway, his face contracted with fury.

"Kasia," he said quietly, "please leave."

She didn't move.

"Please leave," he said even more quietly. "Go to my office and wait for me there."

His voice was calm, but the calmness belied some undeniable force. Kasia shrugged, but she obeyed the order.

"What happened here?" Kunicki asked Dyzma.

"What happened?" he responded. "I'll tell you what happened. Your daughter told me off and ordered me to get out of your house. I don't know what the hell she has against me, but if you kick me out the door, I'm not coming back through the window, if you know what I mean. And as for that . . . that quota and these railroad ties, you can kiss all that goodbye, because I'm . . ."

Kunicki grabbed his arm.

"Nicodemus, I apologize for my daughter, sir. Please forget about everything. Kasia will go abroad, today even. Will that be to your satisfaction?"

"Satisfaction . . . and what about that tongue-lashing she gave me?"

"I'm telling you, my dear Nicodemus, I'm throwing her out of my house today."

The more aggravated the old man was on the inside, the calmer he was on the outside. He reached his hand out to Dyzma and asked, "So are we agreed?"

Nicodemus offered his hand in return.

Kasia left that evening. No one in the house knew what father and daughter had said behind the closed office door. Neither he nor she told anyone a thing. On top of that, Kasia left without saying goodbye even to Nina. The only person in Koborowo she spoke to before her departure was Irenka, her lady's maid. She, however, could only say that the young lady was very angry and had promised to bring her, Irenka, to Switzerland.

After this turbulent and fateful Sunday, no clouds darkened Nicodemus Dyzma's horizon. Kunicki went to great lengths to be affable. Nina didn't once mention the absentee; she herself felt freer and more at ease.

She and Nicodemus took long car rides together. They went sailing on the boat. There was no crack in her resolve, however, that their affair be confined exclusively to conversations—her own monologues, to be exact—as well as a fleeting kiss or two. None of Nicodemus's arguments and persuasions made any headway.

He could not understand the reasons for this insistence. Even more so after he learned from the servants that Nina locked her bedroom door every night, and had supposedly done so almost right from the start of her marriage. The servant who shared this information with Dyzma even made a crack about his master marrying the countess just to make his daughter happy.

It was all so hazy and mysterious to Dyzma. He told himself that someday he'd back Nina into a corner and get a clear explanation of what was what. Meanwhile, he gleaned from her a handful of details about her life and family. When it came to her husband and his finances, Nina displayed complete ignorance.

"After all, it has nothing to do with me," she would say. "That's a matter for men."

In any case, she was aware enough—she constantly repeated it to Dyzma—that their future was entirely in his hands, since she had nothing of her own, not even the proverbial shirt on her back. It filled Nicodemus with unease, because he hadn't the slightest hope of obtaining the fortune it would take to satisfy Nina's current standard of living. Besides, he didn't feel any particular need to marry her. Sure, there was a lot to like, plus she was a great lady, not just anybody—she was Countess Ponimirska . . . But the possibility of marrying her had an air of unreality about it, on par with his other recent successes.

Nina's feelings on the matter, however, were abundantly clear to him. Her love was manifest in every gesture, every look, practically every word.

Kunicki, Dyzma had concluded, was too occupied with business matters and spent too little time with his wife to suspect a thing. Besides, he himself encouraged them to take these excursions together.

Upon returning from one of these trips, Nicodemus found a telegram addressed to him in the hall. He opened it, convinced it was a message from Minister Jaszuński. But something unexpected met his eyes: a short message signed . . . Terkowski!

Nicodemus read it, Nina peering over his shoulder. The message was as follows:

> The Prime Minister requests your presence tomorrow, i.e., Friday, at 7:00 p.m., at the Council of Ministers Finance Committee meeting on a known matter.
>
> Terkowski

Kunicki came in, and Dyzma handed him the telegram. The old man read it in the blink of an eye and, with undisguised awe, asked, "Extraordinary! Is this about that grain business?"

"Yes," said Nicodemus.

"So, it's already happening?"

"As you can see."

"My God, my dear sir," Kunicki spread his arms. "My God, just look at your influence, dear Nicodemus, look how much good you can do for the people!"

"Yes," Nina smiled, "if this influence is used for the public good, and if the needs of the public are properly assessed."

"Oh, excuse me," objected Kunicki, "not just the needs of the public. Shouldn't the needs of the private get a little help? Hee hee! The minister of transportation will certainly be taking part in the finance committee meeting. This will give you a chance to have a word with him about those railway ties. How about it?"

Nicodemus stuffed his hands in his pockets and winced.

"I'd rather not right now. It's not the time."

"Don't get me wrong, my dear Nicodemus! No pressure. I leave it completely to you and your judgment. I'm simply mentioning it in passing because supplying those ties is a business matter worth remembering, hee hee."

To drive that point home, he pulled Nicodemus into his office right after dinner and proceeded to bore him with a lengthy disquisition on the details of the transaction. Then, when Dyzma raised the issue of the previous lawsuit, the old man jumped up and pulled some keys from his pocket.

"I'll show you the documents right now. In my opinion, they should suffice to prove once again that I'm in the clear."

He pushed aside a heavy velvet curtain, and Dyzma saw a safe of enormous size. Kunicki quickly unlocked it, removed a green folder, and began to pull out various files, papers, and forms. He read some of them aloud and handed others to Dyzma, who pretended to read them.

It was already evening by the time he was able to break free of Kunicki. Nina was waiting for him on the terrace, and they went for a walk. She was sad and pensive. The prospect of Nicodemus's unexpected departure, which had interrupted their idyll so abruptly, genuinely distressed her. Hidden among the trees, she flung her arms around his neck and whispered, "But darling, you won't stay in Warsaw too long, will you? Ninette will miss you terribly when you're gone. What shall I do, I've become so used to seeing you every day, talking with you, looking into your eyes . . ."

Nicodemus assured her that he would be back soon. A day or two, three at the most. Nina was very animated during dinner, thanks to her husband's idea that they would both accompany their beloved Mr. Nicodemus to the station. This time Dyzma had to take the train, since the car required a minor repair.

At the station, Nina was highly emotional. Admittedly, she wasn't able to bid Nicodemus farewell in the manner she'd prefer, but the look in her eyes was enough to suggest the most scorching of kisses.

Dyzma was alone in his first-class compartment. Kunicki had greased the conductor's palm, explaining that he should not allow anyone in because the traveler in question was Mr. Dyzma himself, the great figure, personal friend to all ministers.

It had been quite a spree. Nicodemus, three sheets to the wind, was conveyed to the hotel and carried up to his room.

Yes, there had been plenty to drink. Even now, having regained his senses, he still couldn't get over the events of the previous day, which traced chaotic lines through his mind.

First, there had been an official meeting in a large hall with high ceilings, where he, Nicodemus Dyzma, sat at the same table as the prime minister, with the other ministers, on equal footing, thick as thieves.

Then some reports were read, some figures . . . And then there was the moment when everyone started grabbing his hand to shake it because of the grain warehousing concept, the idea of Kunicki's he simply repeated. What were they calling it? . . . Aha, "pawnshop." That was funny! Up until now, he'd thought a pawnshop was only for watches and clothes. And then there was the prime minister's question:

"Would the honorable gentleman agree to assume the directorship of the national grain bank?"

When Dyzma hesitated to respond, and then protested that it was perhaps beyond his capabilities, there was such a flurry of insistence that he had no choice but to agree.

In his hotel room now, he laughed out loud.

"Holy crap! It's fallen right into my lap! President of the National Grain Bank! Mr. President!"

He recalled a cluster of journalists showering him with questions, and the blinding flash of cameras. Aha, he had to see if he had made the papers.

He called the reception desk and asked them to buy a copy of every newspaper. He started to get dressed. When the papers were brought in, he grabbed one off the top of the stack and flushed red.

His photograph had made the first page. There he was, standing with one hand in his pocket and looking thoughtful. And very serious. Well, well! Impressive! Underneath the photograph was a caption:

Dr. Nicodemus Dyzma, architect of the new agricultural policy. He has been awarded the task of establishing the National Grain Bank and has been appointed its president.

Next to the photograph, following a sensational headline, was an extensive article featuring an official government statement, Dyzma's biography, and an interview with him.

The statement concerned the resolution of the Council of Ministers, whose members, at Minister Jaszuński's request, had resolved to wage a decisive battle against the economic crisis through strong intervention in the grain market. A detailed description of the project followed, as well as a preview of the executive regulations that would be issued after the Sejm's adoption of the act.

Dyzma's biography came as a surprise to him. He learned that he had been born on his parents' estate in Courland, that he had graduated from secondary school in Riga, had obtained a degree in economics from

Oxford, had gone on to fight heroically on the Bolshevik front, where he was wounded and awarded the Virtuti Militari and the Cross of Valor, and most recently, had retired from public life to become a gentleman farmer in the Białystok region.

The biography swarmed with adjectives such as "brilliant," "enlightened," "creative" . . . Finally, it was noted that Bank President Nicodemus Dyzma was widely celebrated as a man of uncommon strength of will and character and was known far and wide for his extraordinary organizational capabilities.

The interview left Nicodemus in a state of utter astonishment. He read it again, not believing his eyes. Although he'd gotten completely soused later that evening, he was still more or less sober when he talked to the journalists. He hadn't said a single word of what they put in there! He couldn't make heads or tails of some of the sentences, despite his best effort: there were too many words and phrases he didn't know, too many opinions on various matters that not only had he never expressed but that touched on things he'd never even heard of.

He swore, but not in anger. On the contrary, he was quite pleased, since after reading this interview everyone would regard Mr. Dyzma, Bank President Dyzma, as a man of extraordinary cleverness.

Almost every newspaper ran similar articles and photos of him in assorted poses. He especially liked the one where he was pictured sitting on a couch between the prime minister and Minister Jaszuński, and also the one where he was coming down the stairs, followed by an elderly gentleman with a gray mustache and his hat in his hand while he, Nicodemus, remained hatted. The caption under the photo read,

Bank President Nicodemus Dyzma leaves the Palace of the Council of Ministers in the company of his future associate, the newly appointed Director of the National Grain Bank, Mr. Władysław Wandryszewski, former Deputy Minister of the Treasury.

"Ha!" Nicodemus thought. "Now all of Poland knows who I am."

Suddenly, he was afraid. It had just occurred to him that the news would reach Łysków, that Mr. Boczek, Jurczak, and everyone else who knew him well would be very much aware that this Courland and Riga, this Oxford, was all a bunch of baloney. Shit!

And if one of them gets the idea to spill the beans to some newspaper?

He felt a shiver down his spine. He paced the room, cursing, then went back to reading the papers, and eventually convinced himself that any denunciation by old acquaintances was quite unlikely. His position and connections would surely dazzle and intimidate them. Unless they report anonymously . . . But nobody takes anonymous tips seriously.

He calmed down considerably. But another worry arose as he read all about the many talents attributed to him: how was he going to manage?

Supposedly the most difficult work would fall to this Director Wandryszewski, but after all, he was going to have to actually do things, there would be discussions, signatures, decision-making . . . And all of it would involve matters of terrifying incomprehensibility! No two ways about it, he'd need to find someone smart . . . Kunicki would be ideal, but he'd never agree . . . Considering the situation, he'd have to part with his job at Koborowo. The thought that this would also mean parting with Nina pained him a little, but he said to himself, "It's all right, whatever will be, will be. She's not the only one in the world."

Of far greater concern was finding a guy who would do this job for him . . . He could make this guy, let's say, his secretary . . .

Suddenly he slapped his forehead.

"Krzepicki!"

He jumped for joy. Krzepicki was an honest-to-goodness hustler, he had his ear to the ground and knew which side his bread was buttered on. No one would pull anything over on him, he'd make a good pal, a fellow he could count on, and if Dyzma got in tight with him, Krzepicki could be the brains behind the whole thing.

He was so taken with the idea that he decided to find Krzepicki right away.

He dressed quickly and was at Madam Przełęska's in less than fifteen minutes. They had just gotten up from dinner. Besides the lady of the house, there was Krzepicki and a young woman, the sickly and extremely freckled Miss Hulczyńska.

Dyzma was received with effusive congratulations. Madam Przełęska referred to him as the savior of the landowners, Zyzio Krzepicki called him an economic Napoleon, and Miss Hulczyńska simply looked at him as if he'd hung the moon and all the stars.

The conversation turned to Koborowo, and everyone was sorely grieved when Dyzma announced that he would not have time to take up the matter of George Ponimirski.

"Besides," he added, "he has a screw loose, and nothing can be done about that."

Zyzio swore, the freckled young lady made a sad face, and Madam Przełęska ventured a hope that not all hope was lost.

The climax of Nicodemus Dyzma's visit to Madam Przełęska's, however, occurred when he took a sip of coffee and said, "I came here with a proposal. Mr. Krzepicki, you're currently without a position, correct?"

"Correct."

"And do you want one?"

"Naturally!" Madam Przełęska clapped her plump hands.

"Because now, you see," Nicodemus continued, "I'm in need of a secretary. The secretary of the bank president can't be just anyone, that is to say he must be intelligent, clever, and very responsible indeed. What do you think?"

Krzepicki licked his lips, his face a study of nonchalance.

"Thank you, Mr. Bank President, but I don't know if I have the skills. Besides . . . hmm . . . I'll be honest with you, please don't hold it against me, but I'm really not suited for a clerical job. Fixed office hours, getting up early every day . . ."

Dyzma slapped him on the knee.

"You have nothing to worry about! No fixed hours. You'll only come to work when I come to work, and do you really think that the bank president is supposed to be cooped up in the office all day long? That's the director's responsibility. We'll only deal with the main issues, the most important stuff. So let's shake on it!"

Madam Przełęska was bursting with enthusiasm. Out of sheer excitement, she began calling Krzepicki by his first name, urging him to accept the proposal without delay.

Zyzio smiled and offered his hand.

"Thank you very much, Mr. Bank President. But if I may be permitted to ask, what salary would be allotted to me?"

His use of the title "Mr. Bank President" didn't unduly flatter Nicodemus. Arms akimbo, he asked, "Well, how much would you like?"

"I'm not sure . . ."

"Well, go ahead," Nicodemus encouraged him.

"It's up to you, Mr. Bank President."

Dyzma smiled benevolently.

"Mr. Bank President thinks that the secretary has to decide for himself."

Everyone laughed politely.

"My goodness," intervened Madam Przełęska, "it seems to me that a thousand zlotys . . ."

"One thousand two hundred!" Krzepicki amended quickly.

"That's it? One thousand two hundred? Well, I'll give you one thousand five hundred."

He cast a triumphant gaze around the room, and Krzepicki, amid Madam Przełęska's delighted "oohs," jumped to his feet and emphatically bowed and scraped.

Madam Przełęska declared that this must not be allowed to end on a dry note, and ordered the servant to fetch a bottle of champagne.

"Well," Dyzma said, raising his glass. "Well, Mr. Krzepicki, I have only one condition: loyalty! Do you understand? Loyalty! Loyalty, meaning we have to stick together. And keep your mouth shut about what we discuss . . ."

"Understood, Mr. President."

"And just so you know, if I'm pleased with your work, on holidays and other special occasions I'll kick in another two or three grand."

Krzepicki accompanied Dyzma to the hotel. On the way there, they talked about the bank's organization, and Nicodemus announced he'd introduce Krzepicki to Director Wandryszewski as soon as tomorrow.

"I won't have much time, I'll have other matters to attend to, so this is how we'll arrange it: Wandryszewski will take care of the organizational stuff, and he'll submit the reports to you. Not to me, to you and you alone, get it? And you'll refer everything to me, and we'll talk about it, and then you'll report back to that guy with my decisions."

"That's for the best," Krzepicki kept repeating.

"The ability to lead, Mr. Krzepicki—and make sure you remember this— the ability to lead lies in the ability to make immediate decisions!"

At the hotel, Dyzma found Ulanicki, who greeted him with a booming "Hey there!"

"You know, Nick, my head's still spinning after our bender last night. But never mind about that! Have you already paid your visits?"

"What visits?"

"Well, you know, it's expected. The prime minister, Jaszuński, Brożyński, and then just a few more, since I assume you don't want to visit Terkowski? Although, you know, yesterday I saw that he didn't seem to have any hard feelings."

"Do you think it's absolutely necessary?"

"Well, yes."

"Hmm." Dyzma was disconcerted. "But, you see, on my own . . . If you were to go with me . . ."

"Sure, I'll go . . ."

They made a plan to pay the visits tomorrow, because this evening they needed to hold a meeting regarding the bank's grand opening.

In less than two weeks, the initial organizational work was already in full swing. The bank premises were located in a new building on Wspólna Street, with two floors allotted to the bank's office and an eight-room apartment to its president.

Although the act itself was still being chewed over by committees in the Sejm, it was clear that both chambers would pass the proposal without any major amendments.

Dyzma had no trouble with any of it; every aspect and every step in the process had been taken care of by Wandryszewski and Krzepicki. The latter turned out to be invaluable. He'd set to work with enthusiasm, and since he was by no means short on cunning, he made whatever decisions he wanted, always justifying them with one unassailable sentence: "Mr. President wants it this way."

At first, Wandryszewski and others, less than thrilled with Krzepicki's meddling in even the smallest matters, would ask Dyzma if it was really he who was calling the shots, and not otherwise, but Dyzma, more often than not completely unaware what they were referring to, would invariably reply, "If Krzepicki said it, it means I've already made my decision and there's nothing else to talk about."

Thus, they soon had no choice but to accept his meddling. Krzepicki also made friends with the president, in earnest. Of course, since they met with some frequency, he quickly became aware of his boss's myriad deficiencies. These were, however, quite convenient for Krzepicki, rendering him an indispensable companion to the president. Nevertheless, Dyzma was constantly on guard, even around Krzepicki, who admitted to himself—seeing how his boss was surrounded by respect and general acclaim, and watching his powerful influence and web of relations continue to grow—that Dyzma possessed some inexplicable power as well as a strange and extraordinary mind.

True, he was often surprised by moments that seemed to reveal black holes in Nicodemus's brain, when he seemed ignorant of the simplest matters, but he concluded that the bank president was deliberately playing the chump to catch any scheming on his subordinates' parts. Krzepicki was aware, naturally, that his job depended solely on the bank president and he would end up right back at square one if someone else were to become bank president, so it was in his interest to bolster his boss's position, and he did everything he could to swathe him in a halo of inaccessibility and Olympian dignity. This was all very convenient for Dyzma, too.

The stunning accolades that were showered upon him had admittedly strengthened Dyzma's conviction that he'd rather underestimated himself until now, but that did not diminish his caution in the slightest; he was aware of certain shortcomings with regard to his own intelligence, upbringing, manners, and education. His relationship with Krzepicki was where he felt most free, but even then he always sought to preserve the mystery.

This is how he became known before long as "the least talkative man in Poland." Some chalked it up to a kind of British comportment, while others accepted at face value what he'd said at a party at the prime minister's when the ladies had been nagging him to talk:

"I have nothing to talk about."

Of course, when one has so much to think about, one cannot do much talking.

Because Nicodemus, although he never showed it, was sometimes driven to despair over his lack of familiarity with social rules and his ignorance of a great many words, he resolved to fill in the gaps in his general knowledge.

To that end, he stopped by one of the bookstores on Świętokrzyska Street and purchased three books: *The Dictionary of Foreign Words and Phrases, The Universal Encyclopedia,* and *The Bon Ton Handbook.* The last in particular was extremely useful. On the very first day he found the answer to the question of why Ulanicki had told him to leave in the prime minister's box not one visiting card, but two.

As for the dictionary, he employed it strategically. Whenever he heard a new word, he memorized it and later looked up its meaning. His approach to the encyclopedia, however, was systematic. He started at the very beginning, and by the time he left the city for good, he had managed to reach "F." He did not, in fact, enjoy this book, but he'd seen immediate results during his conversations with various people, and he decided he would read the whole thing.

It was perhaps the primary way Nicodemus occupied himself during that period, except for reading Nina's letters. He received at least one a day. They were long, and Dyzma, although he recognized that they were very beautiful, finally lost his patience and stopped reading them. He would skip all the way to the end; that's where the real information usually was. There he learned that Kunicki did not intend to let go of his genius administrator so quickly and believed that Nicodemus would easily be able to combine the position of bank president with the position of plenipotentiary, since Kunicki demanded absolutely no work from him and left him an entirely free hand.

Nina was very happy, and she begged Dyzma to agree. Nicodemus thought about it for a long time, deciding to accept the offer only when Krzepicki strenuously reminded him that you can't have too much of a good thing.

He didn't inform Nina of this development via post, since they had agreed, at her request, that he wouldn't write to her at all. Every letter to Koborowo passed through Kunicki, and Nina was afraid that he would open them; that had happened a few years ago with Kasia's letters.

Krzepicki had taken to arranging and equipping the bank president's apartment with such zeal that it was ready in two weeks, and Nicodemus moved out of the hotel and into the place on Wspólna Street.

The very next day he went to Koborowo to gather his belongings and talk to Kunicki.

It was Sunday, and since he forgot to call for some horses to meet him at the station, he had to walk. It was less than two kilometers, and the morning was so beautiful that Dyzma even enjoyed himself.

Near the sawmill, he met the elderly foreman of the paper mill, who gave Dyzma a respectful bow. Dyzma stopped and asked, "How are things going in Koborowo?"

"Thanks be to God, nothing new, Mr. Administrator."

"I am no longer an administrator, but the president of a bank. Haven't you read about it in the news?"

"We sure did, and what an honor for us."

"Well then? You should address me as Mr. President. Got it?"

"Got it, Mr. President."

Dyzma put his hands in his pockets, nodded, and moved on. But after a few steps he turned around and called, "Hey, man!"

"Yes, Mr. President?"

"Is Mr. Kunicki in the house?"

"No, Mr. President, the master is in Siwy Borek; they're laying down railroad track."

"But today is Sunday, a day off."

"Oh, around here there's only a day off when the master decides there's no more work to be done, Mr. President," the foreman said with bitter irony.

Dyzma gave him a fierce look.

"As it should be. Work is the foundation for everything! And you would just kick back and loaf around forever. The whole country's like that."

He clasped his hands behind his back and strolled toward the manor house.

The front door was locked, and only after Dyzma had rung the bell several times did the butler open it. He froze when he saw Dyzma's face.

"What the hell, is everybody here dead? You can't even answer the goddamn door?"

"My respected lordship, sir, I sincerely apologize, I was in the pantry . . ."

"So what if you were in the pantry, how dare you?! You idiot! I've been waiting for half an hour and you're in the pantry! You rube, you ox! Well, take my coat, why are you staring at me like a half-wit? Where's the lady of the house?"

"She's not at home, Mr. Administrator, Madam went to church."

"First of all, it's not 'administrator,' it's 'president,' you moron; and second of all, your masters are not at home, and so here you are slacking off. Nothing but a bunch of deadbeats! This isn't Christmas! This isn't a day off! The only day off is when there's no more work to be done, understand?! You all need to shape the hell up! Well, why are you just standing there?"

The butler bowed and slipped out into the hall.

"These rascals need a firm hand," Dyzma muttered to himself, "otherwise they'll walk all over you."

He put his hands in his pockets and began to stroll around the manor. All the rooms had already been cleaned, but someone had left a broom in the middle of Kunicki's bedroom. He rang for a servant and wordlessly pointed to the offending item.

"Ugh, goddamn it!" he growled, as the servant disappeared behind the door.

He made a circuit of the entire ground floor and then headed upstairs. In Nina's sitting room, the windows were open. He has never been in here before, and, out of curiosity, he began to inspect the furniture, the paintings, and photographs.

Most of the photographs were on the desk. Nicodemus lowered himself onto a little seat and looked at them. He casually tried to open one of the drawers, but it was locked. The second one he tried was locked, too, but the one in the middle wasn't.

What's she got in here? he thought, pulling the drawer halfway out. Inside, Nina's things were arranged with the same striking orderliness as everything else on the desk. There were letters banded together with blue and green ribbons. He started flipping through them. They were mostly from Nina's convent school friend, some written in French.

There was a book next to it, bound in canvas. He looked inside. It was a text of some sort, handwritten by Nina. More than half of the pages were blank.

A diary, he thought, his interest kindled.

He took it and moved to the windowsill so he'd able to see the arriving carriage in time.

On the first page, there was an aphorism:

"To understand everything is to forgive everything."

The text began on the reverse page:

I am setting about writing what is so often ridiculed: a diary. No, it will not be my diary. Pitigrilli says that a man who writes a diary is akin to one who looks at a handkerchief after wiping his nose. He is wrong. For is it about recording events? Or even impressions? After all, I, for example, will write only so I can behold my thoughts expressed with precision. It seems to me that, in general, a thought not expressed in words or in writing cannot be truly formulated, is not fully shaped.

And the second falsehood about diaries: I believe it was Oscar Wilde who said that a person who writes a diary does it so consciously, only so that someone, someday, will be able to read it.

My God! Apparently, it did not occur to him that there might exist a human being who has no one in the world, literally no one, in the full terrifying meaning of this word!

For whom could I possibly write? For him? For the man who is entirely synonymous with that terrible emptiness that surrounds me, an emptiness that cannot be filled by anything? For my children? I do not have any and unfortunately never will. So for whom, then? For my family who has turned away from me, or for half-mad George?

For Kasia? Oh, never! We are two opposite poles, she will never understand me. What does it matter that she loves me so much? Without understanding, can one love at all? I do not think so. Anyway, is this love? If so, then it is love of the most shameless, basest degree. More than once, I've wondered if I've become warped due to circumstance . . . Kasia . . . Well, who is she to me, really? Why is it that I, who in the light of day can curse last night, am unable to defend myself against these nights, defend myself, of course, against my own weakness? . . .

Nicodemus shrugged his shoulders.

Blah, blah, blah, that's all this is. What does it all even mean?

He flipped through a few more pages.

The diary didn't include any dates. On one of the following pages, he found a brief mention of a trip abroad, then further reflections on music, and then some twaddle about Bilitis and Mnasidika (probably friends or cousins of Nina's).

He wanted to find something about himself. And indeed, after scanning a few dozen pages, he saw his name.

Well, well, here we go, he thought, intrigued. He began to read:

I met a new man today. He has a strange name: Nicodemus Dyzma. Something about the sound of it strikes my ear as both mysterious and unsettling. He has a reputation as a powerful man. That seems to be true. He would look good with Nietzsche's whip in his hand. He simply exudes masculinity. Perhaps a bit too brutal, too simplistic, but so formidable that he's obviously a force to be reckoned with. Kasia says that he is brusque and crude. She is right about the former. As for the latter, I have not yet made up my mind. I like him.

Nicodemus smiled, pulled out his notebook, and carefully copied down all the words he didn't understand. Well, what's next . . .

There were several pages filled with a description of some dream, and then an argument with Kasia. He paused here, because his name was mentioned again:

> *She does not understand. She hates Nicodemus, for her attitude toward*
> *life is always pathological. What am I besides my femininity? After all,*
> *it's why I exist. It's my intellect and my aesthetic tastes that, in a word,*
> *serve my femininity, not the other way around. Small wonder, then,*
> *that the presence of a man appeals to me—I admit—not only mentally*
> *but also physically. My God, what do I know, perhaps if there were*
> *a different man, an equally healthy and ordinary masculine man, he*
> *would make an equally strong impression on me.*

"There you have it!" Nicodemus shook his head. "Any port in a storm will do."

He glanced out the window to ascertain that it was safe to continue reading. There were now a dozen or so pages that were freshly written, as the ink had not yet turned black.

> *Today he left for Warsaw, summoned by the prime minister. Longing—*
> *what a strange feeling it is. It almost drains the soul of any peace. Will*
> *he be faithful to me? I do not know, I do not know him well enough!*
> *When I think about him, my conviction is strengthened that the essence*
> *of his being is a secret, a mystery that shuts him away like a conch shell.*
> *Who knows if the conch will ever open, even under the warmest rays of*
> *sunlight? And if it opens, will I not be frightened?*
>
> *I do not know. Actually, I know nothing about him, except that I*
> *crave him with every nerve in my body and almost every thought in my*
> *head. He speaks so little, so little and so plainly that one might suspect*
> *him of lacking intelligence, if not for the evidence every single day that,*
> *under that broad forehead, his exceptional brain is constantly at work.*
> *Kasia claimed that he's uncultured.*
>
> *Not true. He is perhaps a bit lacking in sophistication, perhaps he has*
> *some shortcomings in education, some deficiencies, which—I admit—are*
> *puzzling coming from someone who was at Oxford. However, it may*
> *also be a deliberate mannerism. Something like a manifest disregard for*
> *form, to emphasize all the more forcefully the importance of content. It's*
> *also evident in his attire. He is undoubtedly well-built, and it's just his*
> *clothes that make him look ungainly. I wonder if he's handsome or not.*

Probably not. Does his appearance matter to me? He is masculine, I'm in thrall to his masculinity. I'd prefer him to have nicer hands, though. I sent him a long letter today. I miss him.

On the second page, the manuscript began with a long sentence in French, and then Nicodemus read,

A disaster has struck. I thought I would faint when I read the newspapers. I tremble at the very idea that he might not return to Koborowo.

"This chick has fallen for me hard!" Dyzma muttered to himself, and he thought that although it very much tickled his vanity, it might have gotten uncomfortable over time.

Leon sent a congratulatory message to him. My God, if he only accepts Leon's offer and stays with me. I've thought about the possibility of living in Warsaw.

No, that's impossible. I would be afraid to go out and perhaps encounter Aunt Przełęska or some of my old friends.

I wouldn't be able to look them in the eye, but all the same, I wouldn't be able to give up seeing him.

On the next page there was even a shorter note:

I haven't slept all night. God! After all, now he can become rich!!! Does he love me?

When I asked him, his answer was brief: "Yes."

And that can mean so much. It can also mean nothing . . .

Nicodemus turned the page and looked out the window.

He saw a car approaching at the end of the avenue. Kunicki was returning. Dyzma quickly stood up, closed Nina's diary, and slipped it into its place inside the drawer. As quietly as he could, he darted out into the corridor and ran down the stairs.

Just in time—the front door was opening and there was Kunicki, his arms open wide.

Dyzma was pulled into an embrace.

"Dear, dear Nicodemus! At last, at last! Congratulations! Did you get my message? How are you? You've realized this bank on a grand scale! The press is singing your praises to the highest heavens! My heartfelt congratulations! You know very well that I wish you all possible success."

"Thank you."

"Please, sit down, my dear Nicodemus, dear Mr. Bank President! I have a proposal for you."

He sat Dyzma down in the chair.

"But perhaps you'd like a rest?"

"No. I'm not tired."

"Well, thank God. Then listen to me. All I ask of you is that you don't give me an answer right away if you're thinking about saying no. Agreed?"

Nicodemus smiled and narrowed his eyes.

"And what if I could guess what you're about to propose to me? Eh?"

"That would seem impossible," Kunicki said in wonder.

"You would like me to go on working as your administrator. Isn't that right?"

Kunicki sprang up and again pulled Dyzma into his embrace. He launched into an extensive explanation of his plan, refusing to let up until he proved, as clear as two plus two is four, that Nicodemus should agree.

"After all, the president of the bank, dear Nicodemus, is not a civil servant, but the head of a company, and he can use his time as he sees fit . . ."

Nicodemus pretended to hesitate, but after a few minutes agreed—under the condition, however, that Kunicki would not boast to anyone that the President of the Grain Bank also worked as the administrator of his estate.

This condition, of course, was accepted with full understanding of its necessity.

They were discussing this plan when Nina came home.

She didn't say a word of greeting, but the look in her wide-open eyes was so eloquent that, if Kunicki didn't notice it, his powers of observation must have equaled those of a plank of wood from his mill.

It was possible, however, that the joy coursing through him due to Dyzma's unexpected assent blinded him to anything except the happy turn the matter had taken, because he immediately and loudly announced to his wife how pleased he was that Nicodemus would not abandon Koborowo to its own fate, and yes, he would watch over the business and had promised to visit often.

"And I'm very pleased as well," Nina said shortly, then excused herself and went up to change for lunch, which was served at two on Sundays.

They spent the rest of the day together, all three of them, Nina struggling to hide her discontent at this arrangement. Kunicki was keenly interested in the bank and the starting date of operations. He talked at length about the general crisis, complained about the ridiculously high taxes and the burden of social welfare payments, but he was no longer worried about the crops, which happened to be coming along great this year.

After dinner, they all went for a drive. The evening was exceptionally beautiful, and the road through the forest, illuminated by the silver moon, was bathed in some mysterious charm. Nina snuggled dreamily into the car's soft cushions, and even Nicodemus felt that there was something extraordinary about this ride. Only Kunicki kept talking.

It was after ten when they returned home. Nina dashed upstairs, and her husband escorted Dyzma to his room, wishing him a very good night.

Nicodemus began to undress.

Only now did he have the peace and quiet to reflect on what he had read in Nina's diary. It was difficult for him to form a straightforward opinion about it. But one thing was crystal clear: she was head-over-heels in love with him and wanted him to marry her.

He was highly gratified that she hadn't caught on to either this Oxford thing or his intelligence in general. Apparently his system was foolproof. But as for this marriage . . .

It was actually the first time he had given it serious thought. Okay, sure, he liked her, and marrying a countess—that wasn't exactly nothing. None of these great dignitaries had an aristocrat for a wife . . . On the other hand, though, marrying a woman who has no money of her own but so many expenses . . . All those dresses! . . . She changes her outfit three times a day, she travels abroad, constantly putting on another ring, another bracelet . . . And if she divorced Kunicki, he wouldn't leave her one red cent . . .

Although his bank salary was large, it wasn't enough. Besides, who knows, they could always fire him, he'd lose the presidency, and then what would he do with this woman breathing down his neck . . . If Kunicki kept him on as administrator despite the divorce? . . . But no, there was absolutely no way.

And another thing: What would they do with this crazy brother of hers? That nut job was part of the deal . . .

He switched off the light and wrapped himself in a quilt up to his chin. The Ponimirski thing had made up his mind.

"I'm not an idiot," he said and rolled over. He was drifting off to sleep when he suddenly heard quiet footsteps on the gravel path.

"Who the hell is wandering around out there at night?" he thought, raising his head.

He froze.

In the fantastical interlacing of shadowed branches and pale patches of moonlight, he clearly saw a figure standing by the glass door leading to the park . . .

"A burglar!" flashed through his mind.

The figure stood motionless for a moment, then suddenly raised its hand, and he heard a knock.

A shiver went down Nicodemus's spine, and a sudden thought occurred to him:

Ponimirski! He's completely lost it and has come to kill me.

There was more knocking, louder this time. Dyzma didn't move a muscle; he was simply too afraid. Only when he saw that, although the knob was jiggling, the door remained shut (so it was locked!), did he calm down.

Emboldened, he quietly stood up and walked to the door, positioning his body against the wall. He carefully bent his head so he couldn't be seen.

He nearly shouted in surprise.

Standing behind the door was Nina.

He quickly put on his pajama bottoms and opened the door. Noiselessly, she slipped into the room and flung her arms around his neck.

He steered her in the direction of the bed.

"No, no." Her resistance was firm. "I implore you, not . . . Let's sit here . . . I love you so much for being able to understand me, what might even be my oversensitivity on this particular point. Do you love me?"

"I do."

"My sweetest . . ."

And there began a long story about longing, about hope, about joy, a story frequently interrupted by kisses.

"I had to come, you see, I wouldn't be able to sleep if the day had ended without me holding you, telling you how good and right I feel when you're here with me, when I'm certain that no other woman is stealing you away from me. Tell me, have you cheated on me?"

"No."

"You really haven't?"

"Not so far, no."

"Tell me," she insisted, "in Warsaw, do you have some old lover?"

He assured her he didn't, and he was rewarded with more kisses.

He was angry at himself for lacking firmness and was afraid that, after leaving his bedroom, even Nina would think of him as some kind of namby-pamby who didn't know what to do with a woman when he had her.

Meanwhile, she started talking about his new position and whether that meant they could now get married.

It was necessary to be diplomatic about this. After thinking it over for a moment, he replied that they would have to wait for now, since his income wasn't high enough.

"And second, you yourself said that you don't want to live in Warsaw, and that's where I have to be."

Nina was worried. That was true . . . unless they lived somewhere *near* Warsaw. Nicodemus could commute by car. She began to make plans for their future together.

Nicodemus's eyes were getting heavy. He was afraid he was going to fall asleep, so he lit a cigarette.

"Oh," she said, "and we'll have children together! What a delight, what a blessing, to have children. Tell me, darling, do you like children?"

Dyzma hated children. He said, "I really do."

"Oh, how wonderful! We'll have so many children—"

"Listen," he interrupted her, "won't your husband notice that you're not in your bedroom?"

She became uneasy. Indeed, she had spent too much time here. She was ultimately indifferent to her husband, but she did like to avoid arguments.

She wished him an affectionate goodnight and left.

Dyzma got back into bed, pulled the cover over his head, and muttered, "Ehh . . . to hell with all this love shit."

Chapter 10

The National Grain Bank prospered. The economic experiment surpassed every expectation. This drew the attention of other European countries, and the foreign press, particularly in countries dependent on agriculture, began to demand that their governments likewise implement "the Dyzma method."

The bank president himself became a veritable star in government spheres; even the opposition treated him with respect and, incredibly, sometimes paid him the odd compliment.

And no wonder.

The National Grain Bank, thanks to his iron-fisted resolve, served as a model of efficient organization, cost-effective and wise management, and vigorous action.

Moreover, Bank President Dyzma's industriousness had become legendary.

Here was a man characterized not only by astounding creativity, but by unparalleled diligence. His office was an impregnable sanctuary to which clients were very rarely admitted. Only Krzepicki, his personal secretary, had unlimited access. It was he who submitted the daily reports of the individual heads of departments to the bank president, and it was he who briefed him on all correspondence, press reports, and current affairs.

Director Wandryszewski showed up every day at eleven o'clock for a brief meeting. The meetings always followed the same pattern: the director would present an issue whose complexity would normally have required lengthy and thorough consideration, and President Dyzma would invariably issue an immediate and final decision:

"Reject this offer."

Or,

"Settle favorably."

At first, Director Wandryszewski had extremely serious doubts; over time, however, and to his utter amazement, he found that the president's decisions were always the right call, every single time.

Of course, it didn't cross his mind for a second that the president's consultations with Krzepicki played any role in the decision-making.

At the same time, the dish for visiting cards in President Dyzma's private apartment began filling up with cards bearing the names not only of every big fish in the political and financial world, but also those of the aristocracy. Whenever other cards covered that of Prince Tomasz Roztocki, Nicodemus himself took it out and placed it on the very top.

He rarely received visitors, explaining that his mountains of work prevented him from doing so. Nevertheless, he did return all visits, making sure to adhere strictly to the rules outlined in the *Bon Ton Handbook*.

Nicodemus's connection to Madam Przełęska, as well as the magical word "Oxford," opened all the doors to both the pluto- and the aristocracy. Prince Tomasz trumpeted him as a modern Wokulski, and the multimillionaire Zbigniew Szwarcnagel declared him the Necker of the twentieth century.

Therefore, it was only natural that, when a sharp conflict arose between the government on one side and the oil industry on the other, both parties confidently turned to Bank President Dyzma for arbitration. He settled the dispute like King Solomon. First he delayed the decision, which guaranteed him the gratitude of the industrialists, and then he decided that tariff relief payments for crude oil should not be implemented, which satisfied the government.

Due to the arbitration's success, Nicodemus's picture was once again in the papers, which he wouldn't have enjoyed nearly so much if he could have predicted the result, and the speed with which it would come about.

He was in his office one day, absorbed in reading the crime chronicles in the daily tabloids, when he heard agitated voices coming from the adjoining room, which was Krzepicki's office.

Someone evidently wanted an audience with the president and, far from agreeing to Krzepicki's demand that this person leave the office, was daring to make a scene.

Dyzma was highly irritated. He jumped up and threw open the door.

"What the hell is all this racket?!"

Krzepicki, who was standing by the door, reported:

"Mr. President, there's some Bączek or Boczek who wants very much to—" He didn't finish, because a short, fat man cut in front of him and cried, "Hey, Nicodemus, it's me."

Dyzma reddened. There stood the head of the Łysków post office, with his beefy hand outstretched in greeting. Dyzma paused for a moment to regain control of himself.

"Oh, good morning," he said, "please come in."

He closed the door, and, taking into account the fact that Krzepicki might overhear them, he led his guest to the furthest corner of the room. He sat down on the couch and offered Boczek a chair.

"What do you want, Mr. Boczek?"

Only now did Boczek feel intimidated.

"You see, we go way back, Nicodemus—"

"Mr. Boczek," Dyzma interrupted, "the prime minister may address me as Nicodemus, but you can make the effort to call me Mr. President."

"Sorry, it slipped out of my mouth, just like old times, a friend to a friend . . . Mr. President."

"Well, forget about old times. What do you want, Mr. Boczek?"

"Oh, just, I'm coming to you, Mr. President, as an old acquaintance with a humble request."

"Yeah, yeah, and?"

"I need you to stick up for me. I've been out of work for a month and my wife, my children . . ."

"You were fired?"

"I was let go, uh . . . Nic . . . Mr. President, those jerks sicced some agency on us, there was this Skowronek from the district—a real weasel, this guy—and he checked the books for irregularities regarding valuable shipments, the same books that, you know, you yourself once worked on—"

"Quiet, goddammit, why are you yelling?"

Boczek's heavy eyelids lifted and his small eyes widened in surprise. He was nowhere close to speaking loudly, so . . . Was Dyzma, his former subordinate, afraid someone would overhear that . . . ? Boczek was clever enough to see what was going on.

"Well then? What do you want?"

"I would like to ask you for a job, Mr. President, because—"

"I don't have any openings. Everything's taken."

"Mr. President, you're joking. If you, the illustrious president, just lift a finger . . ."

"But I wouldn't even think of lifting a finger, do you understand, Mr. Boczek? Not for a second! Why should I lift anything, huh? Give me one goddamn reason. Remember, pal of mine, when I worked under you, the way you treated me, the way you spoke to me, and now you come crawling on your hands and knees? You're not getting squat from me, that's for sure!"

Boczek sat there grimly.

"No way are you getting a job! Look at this guy! Always the big shot, but see how the mighty have fallen."

Nicodemus, agitated, stood up and stamped his foot.

"Do you know who you're dealing with? With the president of the bank, a friend of government ministers! You idiot! Get up when I stand!"

Boczek reluctantly got up.

"I could have you thrown right down these stairs! And no one would bat an eye! You've got some nerve. Now get the hell out, and keep your mouth shut, got it?! Not a word to anybody about your fu- . . . your post office, or about knowing me! Not a word. Now scram!"

Boczek did not move, and after a while, without raising his eyes from the floor, he said, "Okay, I'll go . . . I just want to say that, as for throwing me down the stairs, it's not so easy . . . There's still some justice in the world . . . And if there should be a story in some newspaper about how a certain bank president treated his former supervisor . . ."

"What?" Dyzma roared.

"What are you yelling for, Mr. President, you think that's going to make me hold my tongue? You won this round, but we'll see what happens. I'm leaving . . . Goodbye . . ."

He bowed and headed for the door.

"Wait!" Dyzma called.

Boczek stopped and scowled at Dyzma.

"I'm waiting, Mr. President."

"What exactly were you planning to do?"

"What on earth could I be planning to do?"

"Ugh . . . you rat!" Nicodemus spat on the carpet.

He wiped it away with a brush of his shoe, sat down at his desk, and grabbed the telephone receiver. He dictated a phone number and after a moment he said, "This is Dyzma, the president of the Grain Bank. Good morning, Director, sir."

" . . . "

"Thank you. I'm okay. By the way, my good man, would you be able to stick another guy in your factory?"

" . . . "

"Yeah, he's fine, capable . . . yes . . . yes . . . His name is Boczek, Józef Boczek."

" . . . "

"So, it's done . . . Thank you very much . . . it's important to me, yes . . . goodbye."

He turned to a smiling Boczek and said, "Fine, goddamn it. You've got your job."

"Thank you kindly, Mr. President."

"Just be careful, Mr. Boczek." Dyzma walked up to him and held his clenched fist in front of his former boss's nose. "Just see that you keep your dirty mouth shut!"

"I understand, Mr. President, not a word to anyone." He bowed, bumping his nose on Dyzma's still raised fist.

Nicodemus returned to the desk and wrote the address on a sheet from his notebook.

"You should be there tomorrow at one."

"Thank you, Mr. President."

He extended his hand to Dyzma and then withdrew it, as Nicodemus had stuffed both hands in his pockets.

He made another low bow and left.

"Shit!" Dyzma swore.

He'd seen the hatred in Boczek's eyes, and although Dyzma was sure that he'd changed his plan to fink on him, he decided he'd need to come up with something to ward off the danger. Meanwhile, Krzepicki entered the room with some mail and the latest gossip, which concerned a bookkeeper who was writing love letters to a typist from the Department of Correspondence.

"Which one?" Nicodemus asked.

"That pretty brunette. She sits by the window."

"And what's the director doing?"

"He doesn't know anything about it."

"Should we just fire the bookkeeper?"

Krzepicki shrugged.

"Ehh . . . what for? It'd be a pity, he's married, he's got kids . . ."

"What a swine! Tell him I know about everything and that he needs to cool it with these little romances."

Krzepicki nodded and began to summarize the papers he'd brought. Nicodemus listened absentmindedly and finally interrupted:

"Is she pretty?"

"Who?"

"You know, that brunette."

"Very pretty."

Dyzma grinned.

"And how is she in terms of . . . ?"

Krzepicki sat himself on the edge of the desk.

"Mr. President, is it possible to know anything about any woman?" He chuckled.

Nicodemus patted him on the knee.

"You're a real piece of work yourself! But if you knew the kind of woman I've been dealing with, you would fall over dead!"

"I assume you're not talking about Mrs. Jaszuńska?"

"Pfth, that fat pig!"

"Do I know her?"

"You know her, no, you *knew* her before she got married. Any guesses?"

"I have no clue."

Nicodemus raised a proclamatory finger and announced, "Madam Kunicka."

"Nina? . . . Nina? . . . Impossible!"

"I give you my word of honor."

"Impossible . . ."

Dyzma rubbed his hands together.

"A first-class dame! I'm telling you, top-notch . . . !"

"Mr. President, please don't take offence, but I would never believe that Nina runs around with everyone."

"And who said anything about everyone? 'With me' is not the same as 'with everyone.'"

"Even with you," Krzepicki insisted. "I took a shot at her once, but nothing doing. And now that she has a husband . . ."

"To hell with that husband of hers," Nicodemus was getting exasperated. "That old geezer, that old bucket of bolts, good for nothing! And she's in love with me, you understand, she fell for me in no time flat . . . !"

Krzepicki looked incredulously at his superior. He was familiar with Nina's subtle disposition and could not imagine how she . . .

"So you don't believe me?"

"I believe that, with women, nothing's unexpected."

In fact, he was thinking that this news confirmed all the more that President Dyzma wielded some mysterious force, a force that he, Krzepicki, could neither see nor comprehend but whose power was manifest at every turn.

"She would follow me to the ends of the earth," Dyzma added boastfully.

"Perhaps you'll marry her, Mr. President?"

Dyzma shrugged.

"She's broke."

"And Koborowo? Surely she has some share of it?"

"On paper, the entire Koborowo estate is her property. But only on paper."

"Hold on, I've forgotten, why is that?"

Dyzma briefly explained the situation. Krzepicki shook his head.

"Hmm, interesting . . ."

The phone rang, bringing the conversation to an abrupt close. Director Wandryszewski asked Krzepicki to stop by his office for a moment to discuss an important matter.

That evening, Dyzma was invited for five o'clock cocktails at the Prince and Princess Roztocki's, the top salon not only in the capital, but in the whole country. For this reason, Nicodemus wanted to wear a tailcoat to make the occasion even grander and more elegant. Since *Bon Ton* clearly prescribed a tuxedo, he called Krzepicki just in case, and, at his recommendation, abandoned his tailcoat idea.

Ignacy, the bank steward, who also worked as the president's footman, opened the door for him and declared, "Mr. President, you look like Valentino!"

"That's good, right?"

"Every woman will faint away!" Ignacy confirmed, thumping his chest with emphasis. It gave Dyzma a little more confidence. In fact, he was rather frightened. The ministers, or even Madam Przełęska, that was all fine and good, but the true aristocracy was a different story. Once upon a time, in Łysków, he had imagined princes and counts the way he pictured them in the most beautiful novel in the world, *The Leper*. He had even once had a dream that he himself was Michorowski, and as such, he'd won the favor of the younger Miss Boczek, that bastard Boczek's daughter.

But ever since staying at Koborowo and making the acquaintance of that lunatic count, he'd been anxious that all members of the nobility would treat him the way Ponimirski did.

It held him back from visiting the aristocratic houses to which he'd been invited for quite some time. He'd simply continued to leave visiting cards; this evening was his first attempt.

He consoled himself with the thought that, as soon as he arrived at Prince Roztocki's salon, he would find Jaszuński and Wareda and could lean on them for support. In fact, he saw the latter right there in the entrance hall, handing his coat to a servant.

They exchanged warm greetings and together ascended the wide marble staircase to the second floor, where there were already a dozen or so people.

Right beside the door stood Prince Tomasz, a tall man with dark, slightly graying hair. He was speaking in German with two gentlemen.

"You'll observe, Nick," Wareda informed him, "that mousy little guy is Baron Reintz, a diplomat from Berlin, and a champion race car driver, see?"

"Okay, and the other one?"

"Count Hieronim Koniecpolski. He looks like some Volga River clodhopper, and it's said that his mother . . ."

He didn't get a chance to finish, since at that moment Prince Tomasz noticed Dyzma and, apologizing to his companions, hurried over to greet the newly arrived guests.

"Hello, hello, finally the bank president does us the honor. And when, Colonel, will we see you in the rank of general? . . . Please, gentlemen, allow me . . ."

With a wave of his hand he directed them to the right and introduced Dyzma to both men; the colonel had already known them for a long time.

They spoke German. The prince praised Dyzma's economic genius to the heavens and frequently referred to him as the Napoleon of the economy, to which the diplomat nodded politely, while Count Koniecpolski did so fervently.

Suddenly, a tall and extremely slim lady rose from the couch. The prince stopped his monologue and took Dyzma by the arm.

"Mr. President, permit me to introduce you to my wife. She has long desired to meet you."

He led him toward the skinny lady, who could be twenty-five as easily as forty. Her grin was visible even from a distance, and before Dyzma's name had escaped the prince's lips, she called, "Oh, I know, I know, I've already been told. Welcome, Mr. President. I am so happy that I have, at last, the opportunity to shake the hand of the man responsible for saving the very heart and soul of the nation: the landed gentry."

She gave Dyzma a wide, ugly hand with a small, unassuming ring.

"Agriculture, my dear, agriculture," the prince said, in a lightly corrective tone.

"Isn't that just a synonym?" the princess asked, smiling at Nicodemus.

"Excuse me, please," her husband bowed, "but I have obligations to my guests."

"Will you let me introduce you to Countess Koniecpolska? She's an admirer of yours. Although she was raised in Vienna and her Polish is poor, she has a keen interest in our country's affairs. By the way, do you prefer speaking German or English?"

"I prefer Polish."

"Ah, how very patriotic. I know just what you mean. One learns foreign languages to become familiar with the great works in the original, but one's own language is of the highest value. For example, Jean Ogiński . . . do you know Ogiński? . . ."

"Very little . . ."

"Well, I admit he is a bit of an odd duck, but who knows whether he might just become one of the most commendable people in this country thanks to those theories of his. Namely, his endorsement of the slogan "Only Polish" when speaking with foreigners! It's nice, isn't it? Because, indeed, why in Paris or London must we use *their* languages? Let them use ours when they're making merry in our country."

"That's true, only they don't know how . . ."

"Ah, I understand, what's good in theory is not so good in practice. And you're right, Mr. President, Jean Ogiński is a bit of an odd duck."

They approached the corner, where seven or eight people, mostly ladies, were in the midst of a lively conversation.

"Allow me," said the princess in French, "to introduce President Dyzma."

The gentlemen stood up and gave their names while firmly shaking Nicodemus's hand. Madam Lala Koniecpolska twittered a few pleasantries in German, a stiff man in a monocle said a sentence in English, crisply enunciating each word, and all Nicodemus understood was his own name, which they'd said twice.

He was flustered and longed to escape, but the princess had already disappeared, and he had been offered a chair.

He sat down—there was no other way out—and smiled helplessly. A silence had fallen, and Dyzma understood that he was supposed to say something. There was a desperate emptiness inside his head and anger that he had been assailed by three completely incomprehensible languages. He wanted to say something and couldn't.

Salvation arrived via a stout bald man sitting beside Countess Koniecpolska, who said, "So we have the opportunity to see for ourselves that the bank president's famed taciturnity is no mere legend."

"Finally something in Polish!" The words slipped out. The hopelessness of the situation had made him so nervous that his reaction was entirely involuntary, and it struck him as probably the last nail in the coffin of his reputation.

The company erupted with peals of laughter, and Dyzma realized, to his astonishment, that not only had he not committed a gaffe but had actually said something witty.

"Are you, Mr. President, an enemy of foreign languages?" asked a young lady with narrow lips and eyebrows plucked so thin they looked like strands of thread.

"No, not at all!" Dyzma said, regaining his composure. "I just think that Mr. Ogiński is right. One must know foreign languages to read the great works in the original and to travel abroad, but one should speak Polish."

"Ah," said Countess Koniecpolska, "und ven zomeone is not able to do zis?"

Dyzma thought about it and replied: "Then he should learn."

"Bravo, bravo!" several voices rang out.

"This is how you cut a Gordian knot," a stocky dark-haired man with a gold pince-nez said with conviction. "This bears upon our national dignity."

The stiff, monocled gentleman leaned toward a silver-haired lady and remarked in a stage whisper, "The Chamberlain of His Holiness will once again render us a great world power. The future Hetman of the Crown Lands!"

Everyone smiled, but the stocky brown-haired man persisted:

"Earl, you cannot wave these issues away with jokes. I will always maintain that there are two paths that lead to the development of our beloved fatherland as a player on the world stage: elevating our dignity and intermarrying with the great families of Europe. Therefore, I am heartened that today we have in our midst a great statesman and a man of action, whom I take to be a supporter of mine. For . . ."

He continued on in this vein; meanwhile, Nicodemus used the monocled gentleman's offer of a cigarette to ask, ""Why did you call that man the future Hetman of the Crown Lands?"

"What do you mean? You don't know him, Mr. Bank President? Why, it's Deputy Laskownicki, a landowner from Kraków. Oh, it's just harmless snobbery . . . He considers himself quite the magnate because his wife is Baroness von Lidemark . . ."

". . . this idea of being a world power," Laskownicki was continuing, "people in our sphere have been cultivating it for centuries. Let us not forget that Czarniecki crossed the sea, that Żółkiewski seized Moscow, that Jan of Varna conquered Vienna—"

"All this is true," the bald count interrupted, "but, my dear friend, today we live in different times."

"What difference does that make? In the past, our noble upper classes shed their blue blood on the battlegrounds of the borderlands, whereas today, we, in our fatherland, are the inheritors of their dream of Poland as a world power, we are the invincible stronghold, the treasury where the idea continues to reside!"

"It would seem, unfortunately," the silver-haired lady said dryly, "that the dream is the *only* thing that resides in our treasury."

The monocled gentleman, who had just been referred to as "Earl," responded, with a half-bow to Nicodemus, "Here's hoping that before long it will be filled with something much more substantial."

Countess Koniecpolska turned to Dyzma with a charming smile:

"Ah, *sagen Sie, bitte, Herr Praesident* . . . ach, pardon . . . Can you tell me how one zinks up such ein gut idea?"

"What idea?"

"*Bien*, zis *génial* idea viz zese *céréale* bonds? I've never met people . . . so . . . so . . ."

"Resourceful?" the earl suggested.

"*Mais non*, peoples in die *Oekonomie*, zuch as *par example* Stravinsky in muzik . . ."

"Ah," said the bald man. "Madam Lala is referring to innovators, creators of new trends!"

"Yes, yes," she confirmed, "I am curiously, how do you zink it up?"
Nicodemus shrugged his shoulders.

"It's very simple. A man sits down, he thinks, and he gets an idea." To
illustrate this concept, he rested his head on his hand for a moment, which
caused the entire group to howl with laughter. A lady in a gray dress, who
had been silently observing Dyzma through a lorgnette, nodded.

"Mr. President, you really are extraordinary. Your sense of humor
reminds me of Buster Keaton, the motionless mask of your face perfectly
underscoring the joke."

"You're vicked," Countess Lala said, with a slightly piqued expression. "I
asked, is it *difficile* to zink up somezing, such ein idea?"

"No," Dyzma replied, "it's quite easy. When it comes to thinking, you
just need to have a little . . ."

He could not recall whether the *Dictionary of Foreign Words* called it
"invention" or "intention." In any case, he needed to finish the sentence:
"A little . . . intention."

There was another round of laughter, and the silver-haired lady exclaimed
to their hostess, who was heading their way, "Jeanette! Your bank president
is charming!"

"And such an *esprit d'à-propos*," said the young lady with abrogated
eyebrows.

The princess was overjoyed. Although Dyzma had not made as big a
splash as the supposedly real cousin of Alain Gerbault, whom she'd invited
to their previous five o'clock party, everyone nevertheless found this current attraction more than satisfying. The steadily growing crowd of people
surrounding Nicodemus was proof enough.

Among others, Dyzma said hello to a skinny old lady he had met back
at Madam Przełęska's bridge party. It was Baroness Lesner, with whom
Madam Przełęska apparently shared no secrets, since the first thing
she asked Dyzma was if he knew how "that poor George Ponimirski is
doing."

"Not bad, thank you."

"Oh, you know Ponimirski?" said the lady with no eyebrows, interested.

"We go way back," he said. "He's a friend from Oxford." There began a
discussion about the Ponimirski family; everyone here knew them well.
At some point, Deputy Laskownicki piped up, "What a dreadful tragedy
with that house! They gave their daughter away to some usurer, what was
he called?"

"Kunicki," Nicodemus said.

"Awful, just awful," the deputy continued, "these unbefitting marriages
robbing our sphere of—"

"Sir," the princess said, "please excuse my interruption, but I would like to ask . . ." and when he got closer, she added in a whisper: "Be careful, it seems that President Dyzma is related by blood to the Ponimirskis."

Meanwhile, they were discussing Madam Przełęska. The baroness claimed that Madam Przełęska was definitely over fifty, while the earl asserted that she had not yet hit forty-five.

Nicodemus considered it his duty to correct them:

"Madam Przełęska is thirty-two."

Everyone looked at him with astonishment, and the bald count asked, "How do you know, Mr. President? Isn't that rather low?"

"Not at all," Dyzma said, taken aback. "Madam Przełęska told me herself."

He'd said it in good faith, so he was surprised when everyone exploded in laughter once again, and Madam Koniecpolska, for the tenth time, reiterated how "vicked" he was.

Despite the progress he was making in getting the hang of these people, Dyzma felt enormous relief when he caught sight of Jaszuński. He excused himself and headed toward his friend. Before long, they both stood against the door frame, Jaszuński regaling him with an anecdote.

"An extraordinary man," Deputy Laskownicki said.

"Who is he talking to?" the silver-haired lady asked.

"Ah yes. This Bank President Dyzma . . . You can tell that even in the midst of a light conversation, inside his head he's considering matters of great seriousness. A very interesting type."

"A statesman type," the deputy said peremptorily.

"Quite interesting," said the lady without eyebrows.

"Does he really come from Courland nobility?" asked the silver-haired lady.

"Oh, yes," confirmed Laskownicki, who was renowned for his heraldic ambitions. "With certainty."

"Entirely *comme il faut*," the princess said.

Nicodemus was home early and immediately climbed into bed. Right away he began to analyze his success at Prince and Princess Roztocki's party.

He'd been introduced to all the members of the highest aristocracy, and he'd met with their approval. He'd received several invitations for later dates. He wrote them down in his notepad, because he'd decided to visit as many houses as possible. It couldn't hurt, and it just might help.

In fact, his opinion of the aristocracy was not high.

What a bunch of chumps, he thought. Anything you say to them, they fall all over themselves like you discovered America.

But that didn't mean he was planning to change his famous Man of Few Words routine.

Ruminating on these topics thwarted any chance of sleep. He tossed and turned, smoked one cigarette after another, and finally turned on the light.

He could always look through Nina's letters . . .

He had three large bundles, nearly all of them unopened. He lay down again and began to read. There were recurring topics: love, longing, hopes, requests for his return, plus no shortage of long psychological allocutions.

The letters were so boring that after a few minutes he tossed them on the floor and turned off the light again.

He thought about the women he had met in his life. There weren't many of them, and he had to admit that none of them required as much time and consideration as Nina did. He recalled Mańka from Łucka Street. She'd probably gone completely to the dogs, but maybe she'd finally gotten herself her working papers . . . Actually, he felt sorry for the girl . . . What would she say if she found out what a big deal their former tenant was these days . . . Her mouth would fall right open . . .

And what about these ladies he'd met at Prince Roztocki's salon . . .

"Sure, they were hot for me, but seriously, I wouldn't know what to do with that type . . . They're all the same, though . . . Any healthy guy would fit the bill, and they're up for anything . . ."

Chapter 11

President Dyzma called the meeting of the bank supervisory board to order, after which Secretary Krzepicki read the agenda and Director Wandryszewski took the floor.

The dozen men assembled there listened intently to the report; it appeared that the first quarter of the Grain Bank's activity had more than lived up to their hopes and dreams—the proof was an increase in agricultural revenue, mass purchasing of synthetic fertilizer, farm machinery and dairy installations, and so on and so forth. Raising the price of grain, the document attested, had had a phenomenal stimulative effect on the overall economic life of the country and was making great strides toward alleviating the financial crisis, all thanks to the brilliant experiment of our distinguished president and his vigorous leadership on agricultural policy.

There was rapturous applause. The bank president, rising to his feet, bowed in all directions, at every member of the advisory board.

They were just about to delve into the details of the report when the porter tiptoed in to summon Secretary Krzepicki. After a moment, Krzepicki returned and bent toward the president's ear.

"Mr. President, Countess Koniecpolska has arrived."

"Koniecpolska? What the hell does she want now?"

"She wants a few words with you. Quite a girl, that one. Ask if Department Director Marczewski can fill in for you, and then you can leave."

"I can do that?"

"Sure. Nothing important's going on here, and the motions will all be approved without discussion."

"All right. But what do I tell them?"

"You can say there's some émigré who needs to see you."

"Who?"

"It doesn't matter, they won't ask. An émigré."

Nicodemus raised his hand, interrupting the official's recitation.

"I beg your pardon, gentlemen, but I have an important client, a Mr. Émigré. Can Mr. Marczewski fill in for me?"

"But of course, of course."

Dyzma bowed and left.

A stout man with black-framed glasses leaned toward his neighbor and, in a low voice, said, "That Dyzma, always so much going on inside his head. He's got the mind of a chancellor!"

"The guy's inexhaustible!"

In the little sitting room that served as a waiting area, Dyzma beheld Countess Koniecpolska, but in such a getup that he hardly recognized her.

Clad in a waxed driving jumpsuit and leather helmet, gleaming goggles pushed up over her forehead, she offered Nicodemus a zesty greeting and, mercilessly butchering her Polish, announced that she had come specifically for him, in order to steal him away to the countryside.

He was taken aback. He didn't have the slightest desire to go to the countryside with her, even less so because he'd arranged to meet Wareda later that night. But Madam Lala did not belong to the world of the meek. She hinted at a delicious surprise, and when that failed to have the intended effect, she announced point-blank that her husband was out of town, whereupon she gave Dyzma an encouraging and unmistakable look.

There was no getting out of it. He was instructed to stop by his apartment to change and, at Lala's behest, pack his pajamas. He ordered Ignacy to inform Krzepicki of his departure and headed down the stairs.

Madam Koniecpolska was already sitting behind the wheel of a convertible sports car. There were no doors, a detail that did nothing to increase Dyzma's enthusiasm for the journey.

She peeled out into the street at lunatic speed, nearly running down a policeman at the intersection, and grinned at her slightly terrified passenger as she stepped on the gas. In a few minutes, they had reached the city limits. A new road started here, straight as an arrow and freshly paved, which inspired Madam Lala to increase her speed to 120.

"Does you like zis?" she asked.

"No," he answered bluntly.

"Vy not?"

"Too fast, hard to breathe . . ."

She slowed down.

"You don't likes it fast?"

"I don't."

"I'm crazy for it. Last year in Munich at automobiles rally, I von for speed second prize, und zen I reached—"

She was interrupted by a loud bang. She pressed the brake and brought the car to a stop at the edge of the road.

"What happened?"

"Vee blew a tire," she laughed, leaping out of the car. "So, give me eine hand, give me eine hand . . ."

He helped her unscrew the spare tire and position the jack under the axle. When they were ready to set off again, she cried, "Rats! Zere's a eyebrow in mein eye!"

Dyzma burst out laughing.

"An eyelash, you mean?"

"Oh, be quiet, it's all same," she scolded him. "Can you see it and fix it? Meine hands are dirty."

He peered at her. Indeed, one very long eyelash had been bent back and was poking her eyelid.

His hand was just reaching over to remove the offending hair when it received a light slap.

"Not your hand, it's dirty, too . . ."

"How then?" he asked, surprised.

"Ach, such a smart man, but such fool, too! Your lips!"

He laughed.

Yes, so much the better.

His lips made several passes over the fluttering eyelid.

"Better now?"

She nodded.

"Zis eye's fine, and now zee other."

"How come? Is there something in the other one?"

"Not yet," she smiled, "but zere might be later."

She presented her other eye, and when he began to kiss it, she pressed her mouth to his lips.

"Do you like it?" she asked.

"Yes," he replied.

"Well, zen let's go!"

And then, with a single bound, she was back in the automobile.

"Sit! Sit!"

She stepped on the gas and the machine roared to life.

Hell's bells! thought Dyzma. These fillies are going to eat me alive!

They had just emerged from the woods when they caught up with another car. Lala screamed something in French. Two young ladies gave a cheerful shout in response. For a while, the two cars drove side by side while the ladies peered at Dyzma and he at them. They seemed good-looking, although it was hard to tell for sure, since both were wearing driving goggles that covered up almost half their faces.

"Who are they?" he asked Lala.

"Miss X and Miss Y," was her amused answer.

"I don't get it."

"You don't need to. You need to understand everyzing? I take you to Borowo."

"Are they headed to your place too?"

"Aha!"

"Are there going to be more people there?"

"Oh no, so curious! You'll see. I already said: eine surprise."

Dyzma sat and stewed. He'd thought Countess Koniecpolska had bundled him out of town only because her husband was away, an assumption made all the stronger by that business with the eyelash, and now he finds out they won't be alone . . .

Sure enough, when they turned into a lane bordered by carefully manicured hedges, he saw several automobiles already parked in the forecourt.

On the terrace, some six or seven women were lounging in wicker lawn chairs. As soon as Lala's car rolled to a stop, they all came running down the stairs, raucously greeting the lady of the house and directing curious gazes at Dyzma, who was utterly disconcerted by the single-sex company in which he found himself.

"Ah, so this is what a strong man looks like!" gushed a peroxided lady with heavily lined eyes.

Dyzma bristled and silently bowed. Madam Koniecpolska begged her company's pardon and ran off to change. Meanwhile, the remaining ladies closed in on Nicodemus.

"Are you, Nicodemus, sir, an adherent of the Western Order?" asked an undeniably squat little brunette.

He looked at her with surprise.

"I don't understand what you're talking about."

"You needn't be embarrassed," reassured a pale, slender young woman with dreamy eyes. "All of us here are initiates."

This is no good, thought Dyzma They're making a fool out of me.

"Yes," the brunette continued, "only we don't know if you belong to the church of lightness or the church of darkness."

"I'm a Catholic," Dyzma answered after a moment's hesitation.

The unanimous laughter prompted by his response increased his bewilderment. He silently cursed himself for agreeing to this trip.

"Why, Mr. President," the peroxide blonde smiled, "you're unparalleled! Is it that a strong man such as yourself must consider women too trifling to engage in conversation regarding matters of a higher nature?"

"The bank president is mysterious."

"No, I just don't know what all this is about."

"Well, fine," said the brunette. "Just give us your opinion—would young Miss Rena make a suitable conductor within the astral plane?"

Nicodemus glanced at Miss Rena and shrugged.

"How should I know?"

"Understood, but what do you suppose?"

"If she knows the way, sure."

Silence fell. The ladies grew more serious.

"Are you referring to the Esoteric Path?" the brunette asked.

"Yes," Nicodemus replied. He resolved to consult a dictionary as soon as he went home to find out exactly where this esoteric path went.

Meanwhile, another car had pulled up. It was the two young ladies whom they had passed on the highway.

There was another round of welcomes and introductions. He learned that they were Miss Iwona (the older) and Miss Marietta (the younger) Czarska. They immediately went off to change.

"Very pleasant young ladies," remarked the peroxide blonde. "And at the same time, I think that Marietta has all the makings of an excellent medium. Her openness, combined with a subtle tension, give her an unusual sensitivity, don't you think, Mr. President?"

"Certainly, why—"

"You wouldn't refuse me, sir," she continued the attack, "an experiment with her? I have the distinct impression that your powerful will could easily break the spiral reaction of self-consciousness. The Order's imperative is the ability to activate potential stratifications of higher forces, the existence of which, the subject or, if you prefer, the object, has hitherto not manifested itself in the fourth degree. And intuitive conflagration . . ."

Luckily, Madam Koniecpolska returned, and Dyzma wiped the sweat from his forehead.

"Just be on guard, ladies!" she called from the doorway, "because zee guest can't bear it ven foreign languages is spoken! Good morning . . . Good morning . . ."

She merrily greeted everyone. A moment later, servants appeared and invited them all to brunch.

Fortunately for Dyzma, the volubility of his company freed him from the threat of longer orations. It sufficed simply to issue a few monosyllables now and then. The conversation mainly concerned fashion and looking ahead to the fall season. It was just the no-nonsense brunette who kept returning to that weird business, which Dyzma at first took for a hoax before he settled on the idea that it must have something to do with calling on spirits to levitate tables.

It was already four when they left the dining room. Since the ladies had all drunk more than a little wine and brandy, the mood was one of exceptional exuberance, verging almost on sauciness; against this backdrop, the dignity and pensive solemnity of Nicodemus Dyzma were thrown into sharp relief.

They went back outside to the terrace. The cars out front had vanished, evidently moved to the garage for the evening. Some of the company dispersed to the park or elsewhere on the grounds; meanwhile, the lady of the house took Dyzma by the hand and, beckoning to the squat brunette, who was named Stella, led him to a little sitting room. Nicodemus supposed that now he'd finally find out why he'd been hauled out here.

Indeed, Madam Koniecpolska had assumed a very serious expression, and while Miss Stella crossed her legs and matter-of-factly lit a cigarette, she began to speak, inflicting grave injuries upon the Polish language and throwing in a multitude of various foreign expressions.

She was talking about some revelation, which—as far as Dyzma understood—called for the construction of a lodge in Poland, because such lodges existed in many other countries but not, to date, here. The lodge was supposed to have twelve ladies and one man. The ladies would be called Pilgrims of the Thrice-Rayed Star, and he would be called the Great Thirteenth. He was to rule over the lodge with three principles: life, love, and death. In which forest this lodge was supposed to be built, Madam Koniecpolska didn't say.

At that point, it was Miss Stella's turn. Her speech was so immediately incomprehensible that Nicodemus understood virtually nothing. It seemed to him that they had established some kind of nunnery, but then again, maybe it was a gang of blackmailers or traders in white slavery; there was talk of "strategies to recruit young girls" and "forced spiritualism" and "the eternal law of bondage" and so on. The one thing he managed to work out was that, as far as this whole business was concerned, the countess was small potatoes compared with Miss Stella.

Now it was Madam Koniecpolska's turn again.

She explained that they'd decided to honor Nicodemus with the request that he become the Great Thirteenth. They had concluded that he—a man of might, of unbending will, of profound ideas—he alone was worthy to rule. Only he could justly reign over their lodge, wielding the principles of life, love, and death, these three rays that constituted the secret Universal Order of Happiness.

Dyzma was furious. He sat with his hands in his pockets and seethed. He swore to himself that he wanted not even the slightest part of this affair. Why the hell would he? Had he finally landed himself a job like this, a cash flow like this, only to end up in jail? Oh, hell no!

Which is why, when both ladies rose, and Miss Stella, in a sepulchral voice, asked, "Master, do you accept the honor of the Great Thirteenth?" he answered shortly:

"No, I don't accept."

Surprise and disappointment swept across their faces.

"But why?"

"I can't."

"Is there some hermetic reason?" the brunette asked enigmatically.

"I have my own reasons."

Countess Koniecpolska wrung her hands.

"But zat is only silly trifles. Zink of our revelation!"

"Nah," he made a dismissive gesture. "I don't know about these kinds of things."

The brunette was indignant.

"You? You don't know? Please, Master, don't tease us like this! After all, it was revealed to Lala that only you can be our Great Thirteenth."

"I don't even have the time!" Dyzma was becoming irritated.

"Master, it takes so little time. Besides, the Mysteries will only be held once a month."

"I don't want to."

The two women exchanged a despairing look.

Suddenly, the brunette raised her hands to the sky and intoned in a tragic whisper, "In the name of the Almighty Order, I implore you to open your heart to the Eternal Three Rays!"

Lala folded her arms over her considerable bust and reverently bowed her head.

Nicodemus was a little scared. He wasn't superstitious in general, but just to be safe, he preferred not to entirely rule out the existence of women with "the evil eye" who might cast a spell on him.

The stubby Miss Stella had such uncanny eyes, and they were glued to him with such determination that he started to feel physically ill.

He scratched his head.

"Just like that, with such short notice, I can't . . . I need to give it some thought . . ."

The brunette shot a triumphant look at Lala.

"But of course!" she cried. "As the Master commands! Even though we know from Mr. Terkowski, who experienced it firsthand, that you possess a mysterious power, and therefore—"

"What does Terkowski know?" Dyzma broke in, frustrated that he had not yet managed to weasel out of this. "I don't know myself what this is all about, what exactly is supposed to be going on—"

"And now, Master!" the brunette stopped him and reached into her handbag. "And now, Master, I present to you the Lodge Decree and the Creed of the Three Principles of Knowledge."

She drew from her bag a small pamphlet and several sheets of paper covered in typescript and handed them all to Nicodemus.

"Excellent. Look these over, Master. Two hours should be enough, right, Lala? In that case, we'll say goodbye for now and give you some time alone. At seven, before dinner, we will gather to receive the final decision from the mouth of the Master himself. May the Wisdom of the Stars light your way along the path of contemplation."

Both women bowed and left in silence.

"These dames are nuts! Damn!" cursed Dyzma, crumpling up the papers in his hand and hurling them into the corner.

He was in real trouble. They had sprung this on him so unexpectedly, this thing that seemed to be somewhere on the scale between crude scam and shady communion with the spirit world.

The things that filled these people's heads! They have money, piles and piles of money, and yet this is what they cook up! Did these birds have a screw loose or what?

Anger welled up in him as he considered the trick they'd played, luring him all the way out here. If he were still in Warsaw, he would have already gone home.

But maybe he should see what it said in those papers.

He picked up the pamphlet and swore: it was printed in French. He would have thrown it to the ground a second time if not for the heading, or rather the drawing next to it. That certainly piqued his interest.

It depicted a large room with no windows. In the middle, seated on a throne, was a skinny guy with a black beard and closed eyes. Above his head shone a three-rayed star and three flaming torches. All around him, lying flat on their backs, were naked women.

He used the end of a matchstick to count them.

Twelve! . . . Aha, these are apparently the pilgrims . . . And I'm supposed to be this guy . . . What in the hell?!

He flipped through the booklet. On the last page there was another drawing, the sight of which made him flinch: a depiction of a goat with twelve horns, a goat with a man's face.

Dyzma had no doubt about it: Satan.

He didn't count himself among the faithful, either in belief or in practice, but he now saw fit to cross himself and, just in case, grab a button and give it a squeeze.

"Pthu!" he spat. "Swine!"

Then he transferred his attention to the manuscript and noted with relief that it was written in Polish.

He gave it his careful attention, rereading some sections two or three times. Nevertheless, there was much he didn't understand, chiefly because so many of the expressions made no sense whatsoever.

What he could piece together concerned the creation of a "sororal society," the purpose of which was to bring them closer to the perfection of the three laws: life, love, and death, and that the heights of wisdom could be attained through pleasure—of the soul, the body, and the mind. With this goal in mind, the twelve pilgrims must embrace the Grace of Servitude and select a Virgin Disciple, who searches for the Man of Will, Master of Stars, Giver of Understanding, whom they would call the Great Thirteenth.

Here he learned that the chosen one must distinguish himself through outstanding talent, must be a man of intellect, creativity, and fecundity. Above all, he must possess exceptional will and be in perfect physical health.

The Great Thirteenth was to serve for three years, after which a replacement would be chosen. This paragraph contained an addendum noting that the Great Thirteenth had the right of absolute authority over the pilgrims, and that any disobedience could be punished at his discretion. Betrayal of the Secrets of the Lodge, however, had one punishment only: death.

There followed descriptions of various rites and some talk of combining soul and body, as well as some items about wine, prayers, and conversations with the deceased. At the end was an admonition to anyone who even thought about comparing the Order to black cults or white magic.

Nicodemus put the manuscript down and fell into a pensive mood.

They were unquestionably all part of some coterie that trucked with the devil. What he would give to have known this before his departure from Warsaw! Ho ho, then he'd like to see those countesses try to drag him out here, but now? Now here he was . . . Who knows what these "pilgrims" would do to him if he refused? . . . Now that they'd let him in on their secret, were they ready to do him harm so he wouldn't be able to spill the beans? After all, it said right there in the booklet that the punishment for betrayal is getting bumped off.

Ooh, they'd really gotten their hooks in him!

He stuffed his hands in his pockets and paced around the room. It occurred to him that maybe, on second thought, the situation might not be so dreadful after all; if he was going to be the one giving the orders . . . Would it hurt to try?

At any rate, it was better than them slipping him some poison or making some kind of deal with the devil at his expense.

If, with every passing minute, he inched closer to accepting this bizarre proposition, it was because a certain curiosity also played a role: What would it be like? His trepidation at fulfilling the whole "thirteenth" and "great" part was tempered by a paragraph in the manuscript emphasizing that, while the Master was the spiritual leader of the Lodge, official responsibility for directing the rites and rituals lay with the designated Disciple.

When the clock struck seven and someone knocked at his door, Dyzma was ready with his decision.

He was alarmed to see Miss Stella only. The presence of Countess Koniecpolska, with her lively gestures and laughing eyes, lent an earthiness to the entire proceedings, whereas there was something downright demonic about this brunette; even worse, she carried with her an air of schoolmarmish severity.

She closed the door behind her, and Nicodemus suddenly felt like a man in a dark alley facing off against an opponent armed with a heavy club.

"It's already seven." Her voice was almost a baritone.

"Seven?" said Dyzma, smiling. "Really, how time flies . . ."

"What have you decided? I trust you're not refusing the dictates of the revelation?"

"No, I'm not refusing," Nicodemus assured her.

"Which means I stand before the Great Thirteenth, before my lord and commander."

She performed a low bow, so low that her broad hips, along with her generously equipped haunches, were propelled upward and closely resembled a Byzantine dome. She suddenly straightened and, in a grandiloquent voice, asked Dyzma a question in Latin. She looked fixedly at him, awaiting an answer.

His insides knotted in despair. What's this vixen want from me? he thought.

Miss Stella waited a moment and then repeated her Latin query. There was no way out. He needed to say something in response. Nicodemus feverishly racked his brains for any shred of Latin he might have picked up in church or school. Suddenly, relief flooded his body, and he answered: "Terra est rotunda."

He didn't remember what it meant, let alone if it had anything to do with the question put to him, but despite his film of cold sweat, he was pleased he had at least managed to produce some Latin. And evidently it wasn't even entirely meaningless, since the brunette once again bowed deeply and, crossing her arms over her chest, replied, "Your will, Master."

Then she opened the door and, in a completely normal voice, announced that dinner was ready.

Dinner was a sumptuous and elegant affair. Dyzma was starting to wonder, however, why not even wine had been brought to the table, and when one of the Czarska countesses petulantly demanded "a drop of something stronger to give us a little encouragement," Madam Koniecpolska smiled, but said firmly, "No, my darling, not yet. Don't rush it."

As a matter of fact, the general mood had become more serious. Faces had grown flushed, and many of the ladies were nervously picking at their food. There were flashes of anxiety in the involuntary glances they kept shooting at Nicodemus.

When they moved to the boudoir for black coffee and the servants were dismissed, Lala peeked into the neighboring room to make sure no one was listening in and then signaled to the brunette. Miss Stella stood and, surrounded by a silent audience, began to speak.

"My dear ladies, whom I will soon be able to call my sisters, my dear ladies and you, sir"—she bowed deeply in Dyzma's direction—"now we adjourn to our rooms and give ourselves over to silent contemplation, to prepare our bodies and souls for the great Mystery, which will start promptly at midnight. You must purify your minds, cleanse your thoughts of all mundane matters, you must remove your commonplace clothes and don robes of white, which you will find ready for you. When you are finished, wait for me. I will come for each of you. Adjourn to your rooms and await my signal."

Her speech finished, she turned to make her exit. At the doorway, she stopped to proffer another bow to Dyzma, and then she was gone. Behind her, the other women filed out in similar fashion. Madam Koniecpolska led Dyzma to his designated room and bid him farewell with a silent nod of her head.

Goddammit, he thought. They're probably going to try to summon a ghost or something.

He looked around. He had expected to find something extraordinary in this room, but he was disappointed. There was nothing particularly special about the furnishings. The only item of possible interest was a flat black valise on the desk.

Nicodemus's thoughts were chugging away at half-speed after that lavish dinner, but he stretched himself out on the sofa and nevertheless attempted a calm assessment of his situation. There was no getting away from his sense of displeasure and unease in the face of this midnight ceremony. He had no idea what sort of role he was going to have to play in all this. What would they make him do? True, he was the main guy, but who knows what these dames would require the main guy to do . . . Besides, anything was possible: what if they ordered him to call up the devil?

Pthu! He spat on the rug.

The thought occurred to him that he could, after all, play sick. Rheumatism, for example. It had served him very well that time at Koborowo . . .

The memory of Koborowo filled him with longing. How quiet it was! Calm, plenty of grub, no work . . . And Nina . . . That one certainly liked to kiss!

He'd found Koborowo to be the best place on Earth, especially after Kasia left. What a pain this whole project of Kunicki's was, landing him this bank president job . . .

He chuckled to himself.

Hey, brother, don't complain, don't complain. Really, everything's just fine. Thoughts were flitting through his head more and more aimlessly; the heaping plate he'd had at dinner was taking its tranquilizing effect.

So sound asleep was he that he didn't hear the knocking at the door, didn't hear Miss Stella's footsteps or the click of the black valise's lock. It wasn't until she was violently shaking his shoulders that he opened his eyes.

It immediately came back to him where he was. The brunette stood before him, holding something out, a sort of white silk dressing gown with red lining.

He leapt to his feet and rubbed his eyes.

"It's time, Master," Miss Stella whispered.

"Already?"

"Yes. Everyone is waiting. Please change into your habit, quickly."

"What do you mean?" He was surprised. "Right in front of you?"

"No, I'm leaving. Just please take everything off and put on the habit and the sandals." She pointed to a pair of soft red slippers with gold stars embroidered on the toes, then tiptoed out of the room.

Dyzma swore, but he nevertheless made haste. He was ready in a few minutes. The housecoat and slippers turned out to be more than a little big on him, but the cool touch of silk on his bare skin was invigorating.

He looked at himself in the mirror and couldn't help but laugh. The robe hung down to the floor, and the slotted sleeves and low neckline created a bizarre impression.

The brunette appeared again. She took him by the hand and led him silently down a dark corridor. There was utter silence all around them. They proceeded for a few moments, then up some stairs and down another corridor. At the end of it, Miss Stella stopped and knocked three times on a door, which opened slowly. They entered a dark room, and the doors behind him closed as if on their own. Dyzma heard the sound of a key turning in the lock and, after a moment, the voice of Madam Koniecpolska.

"Everyzing is in place. All zee doors are locked, and I have forbidden zee servants to entering zee palace until noon tomorrow."

"Good," the brunette replied without releasing Nicodemus's hand. "Go and take your place."

When Lala lifted a thick curtain to leave, a shaft of purplish light fell upon her, and Dyzma noticed that she was dressed in a white robe too.

Next, Miss Stella disappeared down the corridor, leaving him to wait by himself. He heard the murmur of voices from behind the curtain. Time was dragging on, and he was inching closer to try and peek inside when suddenly the curtain swept open and there, on the threshold, stood the brunette in a white robe. She lowered herself in a deep bow.

The room was very large and devoid of furniture. The floor was completely covered with rugs, and mounds of decorative cushions were scattered everywhere. Right in the middle stood a gilded chair upholstered in red satin, flanked with three tall candlesticks with burning candles. What's more, a pendant lamp hanging from the ceiling bathed everything in purple light.

On both sides of the chair, Dyzma saw all the women, every one of them clad in identical white robes.

A large bedsheet was stretched across the opposite wall. Someone had stuck a three-rayed star onto it, under which they'd pasted an inscription cut from red paper.

"Terra est rotunda," it proclaimed.

"Enter!" Miss Stella cried, stepping aside to make room for him. She led him to his designated throne.

When he sat, the ladies made a half-circle around the chair. Miss Stella stepped forward into the middle and began:

"Initiates! You, the Pilgrims of the Thrice-Rayed Star, and you, Master, on whose breast will shortly shine the symbol of knowledge, of power, of happiness. It is I, your sister Disciple, whose unworthy lips declare that the hour is upon us! We open the thirty-third Lodge of the Order of the Thrice-Rayed Star, whose watchword, at the Great Thirteenth's will, is a dictum of utter profundity: 'Terra est rotunda!' Bound up in this dictum is the faith that our Order will hold dominion over the entire world, the hope that our Lodge will become one of the strongest links in this chain, and the indication that we, the living beings of planet Earth, shall remain in the sealed circle of the Order. I must emphasize here that, in accordance with the law of the Order, each of us must fulfill the second imperative, the exchanging of the sacred watchword while touching the left hand to the forehead, the heart, and the womb. Before we enter into the rite, I wish to remind you of the hermetic principles . . ."

Dyzma had stopped listening. He was too fascinated by the singularity of the situation to be able to focus for long on any particular point. He looked around at all the young ladies surrounding him. Some of them looked quite fetching indeed in their strange robes. The naked shoulders emerging from the white folds of shimmering silk, the plunging necklines, not to mention the fact that here he was, the sole man among all these women—it had a highly stimulating effect.

Gone were the thoughts of how and why. Only two thoughts remained: if and when.

Meanwhile, Miss Stella had finished her speech and had opened a little red box and taken out a small gold star on some kind of chain. In reverent silence, she approached Nicodemus and hung the star around his neck, then took three steps back and prostrated herself on the rug. All the other ladies did the same—all except Lala, who went to the door and flipped a light switch.

The purple lamp went out. Nicodemus shuddered. The room submerged in darkness, the faint flicker of the three candles above him, the motionless white figures spread around him—the impression was deeply uncanny.

Suddenly, Miss Stella groaned. "We welcome you, welcome, Lord of life, love, and death."

"Welcome, welcome," trembling voices chanted over and over again.

"Welcome, we welcome you, giver of will!"

"Welcome, welcome," the other voices repeated.

"Welcome, dispenser of knowledge!"

"Welcome . . . welcome . . ."

"Welcome, master of life!"

"Welcome . . . welcome . . ."

"Welcome, creator of pleasure!"

"Welcome . . . welcome . . ."

Dyzma, listening to this litany, thought, These chicks are out of their minds! . . .

And then, suddenly, Miss Stella was done. She came toward Dyzma and, before he was able to get his bearings, kissed him on the mouth. To his astonishment, Lala came forward and did the same, and then it was the Czarska countesses and all the others.

"Now light the incense," Miss Stella commanded.

After a moment, bluish smoke began to rise from the four corners of the room, its fragrance strange and sweet and intoxicating.

Again, the women gathered around Dyzma.

At Miss Stella's signal, they took hold of each other's hands, forming a semicircle. She herself raised her hands toward the sky and chanted, "Appear before us, appear, O Lord!"

"Appear before us," everyone repeated.

"Show us your mercy!" Miss Stella cried.

"Show . . ."

"Descend upon us!"

"Descend . . ."

"Enter the soul of your surrogate!"

"Enter . . ."

"Enter the body of our Master! . . ."

"Enter . . ."

"Kindle the flame within him! . . ."

"Kindle . . ."

"Ignite him with your immeasurable power! . . ."

"Ignite . . ."

"Penetrate him with the heat of your breath!"

"Penetrate . . . !"

A chill passed through Nicodemus.

"Who are you calling to?" he squawked in a strangled-sounding voice, his throat clenched tight with fear.

His question was met with screams of terror, some so piercing they turned his blood to ice.

"He spoke, it's . . . It's Him . . . !" a voice rang out.

"Who? . . ." asked Dyzma, trembling from head to toe. "Who are you calling?"

Then, as if right in his ear, he heard a distinct growling noise. He wanted to leap up, but he'd been sapped of his strength; amid the intoxicating smoke filling the room, he could almost see little wisps of flame, glimmering multicolored flames.

"On your knees!" howled Miss Stella. "He has come! We praise thee, we praise thee, Lord of love, life, and death, we praise thee, we praise thee. Prince of Darkness! . . ."

The young Czarska ladies erupted in spasmodic laughter; another girl sprang up and, clutching Lala, shrieked, "I see Him, I see!"

"Who?!" Dyzma's voice was ragged with desperation.

"Him, Him, Satan! . . ."

It suddenly seemed to Dyzma that cold hands were squeezing him around the neck. A shrill, inarticulate sound escaped his throat, and then the Great Thirteenth was slumped and inert upon his chair. He had fainted.

His first impression, as he slowly came to, was something sweet flowing into his mouth. He opened his eyes. Right in front of him were the black pupils of Miss Stella's eyes. Before he could completely regain consciousness, her mouth had attached itself to his, and again he tasted that sweet, fragrant liquid on his tongue. Wine. He needed air and pushed Stella away.

All around him, amid the smoke, he could see white-robed figures. They were bringing in tables from the neighboring room. Each was laid with bottles and glasses. Madam Koniecpolska, a little vial in her hand, was administering a few drops of something to each of the glasses, then filling them up with wine.

Once all the glasses were ready, each of the ladies took one, and Miss Stella passed the largest to Dyzma.

Now the room was thrumming with muffled conversation. Nicodemus took a long swig and smacked his lips.

"Weird wine," he remarked.

"We partake of the peyote's blessings!" Miss Stella intoned emphatically. Already everyone's glasses were empty. They were refilled.

"What's *in* this wine?" Dyzma asked.

One of the Czarska ladies was standing near him. She lowered herself onto the arm of his chair and, brushing her lips against Nicodemus's ear, replied in a dreamy voice, "The divine poison peyote, divine . . . Do you feel the flush, the heat in your veins, my lord? Is it not true? And what marvelous music, and such colors! . . . Is it not true?"

"It's true," he agreed, and downed the rest of his glass in one gulp.

He felt something extraordinary happening inside of him. He was suddenly overcome with joy, everything around him had become so beautiful, so colorful, even dumpy little Miss Stella was infused with charm and allure.

In fact, the mood around him had changed beyond recognition. Dyzma was surrounded by giggling clusters of ladies, the room was filled with a hubbub of merry squeals and snatches of coquettish songs. Someone flourished her empty glass and smashed it down to the floor, gave a cry of "*Evoe!*" and, in one swift motion, slipped out of her robe and began to dance.

"Bravo! Bravo!" someone else cried.

In no time, the rug was covered in slippery white patches of silk . . .

Bright-green drops of magical liquid from the little vial continued to flow into brimming wine glasses.

Someone knocked into the candlestick and it went out, plunging the room into darkness, steamy, red-blooded darkness, full of passionate whispers and spasmodic, crazed laughter.

. . . .
. . . .
. . . .
. . . .

Chapter 12

A red streak of light from the rising sun broke through a gap in the heavy curtains. Nicodemus sluggishly reached for his watch.

It was six o'clock.

Strange. Absent were the headache and disgusting taste in his mouth that customarily greeted him the morning after a major spree. He just felt terribly weak.

Every move, even lifting an eyelid, seemed a task of extreme onerousness.

And yet he had to get up. He had to head into Warsaw, after all. What would they think at the bank . . .

He rang for assistance.

A stiff butler appeared and announced that his bath was ready.

Dyzma listlessly pulled on his pajama bottoms and headed to the bath-room. Glancing at the mirror, he gave a start: his face was white as a sheet, save for two large blue circles under his eyes.

"Goddammit," he cursed, "they messed me up good!"

He dressed and dragged himself downstairs.

Madam Koniecpolska was waiting for him there. She greeted him with a languid wave of her hand.

"Are you hungry?"

"Oh, no, thank you."

He looked at her out of the corner of his eye and was met, as usual, with a mischievous twinkle. He blushed up to his ears.

Damn her, he thought, She's not even embarrassed. Because it's not like she forgot, did she?

"I'd like to leave," he said after a moment.

"Of course, ze auto is at your disposal."

There was nothing particularly special about their goodbye, which put Nicodemus off even more. As the car turned onto the main road, he looked back.

"Pervs!" he said with conviction.

"Yes, sir?" the chauffeur turned his head.

"Drive, just drive, I'm not talking to you."

"My apologies."

His thoughts were focused on last night. He was perturbed. What troubled him most was his recollection that everything that had transpired last night may or may not have involved the devil. Although he did enjoy the discovery that, within these exalted spheres of society, he had the same rights as any count or prince. More, come to think of it. They had to obey him; just one word from him and they all came running like common street tarts.

How differently had he imagined them, these proud and elegant ladies . . .

He chuckled with satisfaction. Krzepicki was right; they're all the same kind of whore . . .

It started to drizzle. By the time the car stopped at Wspólna Street, it was raining cats and dogs. He hurried across the pavement and entered through the gate. The stairs were worse. He climbed them as if dragging a heavy load.

"Goddammit, they messed me up good!"

Ignacy said hello and informed him that about ten people had come by yesterday and today, the secretary several times, and there was a constant stream of telephone calls about whether or not the bank president was back yet. The worst had been a pushy little man who'd thrown a fit and insisted on nosing around the apartment, since he'd refused to believe that the president wasn't in his office. He was going on about the president hiding from him . . .

"What did he look like?" Dyzma asked.

"A short, fat guy."

"Did he say his name?"

"Baczek, he said, or something like that . . ."

"Shit!" said the president. "What does that bastard want now?"

"If he shows up again, Mr. President, I can throw him down the stairs," offered Ignacy.

"No, no need."

The phone rang. It was Krzepicki. There were some very important matters to discuss; could he come over right now?

"What happened?"

"Nothing, nothing special."

"Well then, I'll be waiting for you."

He ordered Ignacy to get him a black coffee and then collapsed on the couch. He wondered whether to tell Krzepicki what his visit to Countess Koniecpolska's had entailed . . . But he concluded that it could be perceived as a betrayal, and he didn't want to risk it.

Ignacy brought his letters. It was just private correspondence, which hadn't been opened by his secretary, and consisted of three new letters from Nina and an extremely long telegram from Kunicki, who asked Dyzma to hurry up with the railway ties thing, because the matter had become particularly timely.

Dyzma was reading this message when Krzepicki arrived. He opened with a few wisecracks about the trip with Countess Lala, relayed a few anecdotes, casually mentioned that everything was fine at the bank, and then posed a nonchalant question:

"Who's this Boczek, Mr. President?"

Nicodemus tried and failed to remain unfazed.

"Boczek?"

"Yes, that fat guy. Every day he stops by the bank and demands an audience with the president, and he's so bold about it, like he's sure you'll wave him in. Is this a friend of yours, Mr. President?

"Yes indeed . . ."

"Because, I'll be honest, I thought he was some kind of crank."

"Why?"

"Well, because when I told him that Friday is the day you receive visitors, he blew a fuse: 'What do mean, Fridays?' he says, 'on Fridays your great president can receive whoever he wants to receive, and then you'll see, you'll get your ears boxed for not letting me in. This great president of yours,' he says, 'isn't such a bigwig to me . . .'"

Dyzma's face was red as a beet.

"And did he say anything else?"

Krzepicki lit a cigarette and added, "He called you a brawler and a boor . . . He even allowed himself to make some idiotic threat against you, 'I'll show him' and blah blah blah . . ."

Nicodemus frowned and muttered, "Yes . . . Mr. Krzepicki, if he comes again, let him in to my office . . . He's a crackpot . . . He's always been like that . . ."

"Absolutely, Mr. President."

He said it quite simply, but Dyzma had no doubt that Krzepicki either knew something or wanted to know something. He resolved to keep Boczek quiet at any cost.

Krzepicki stayed for dinner. The conversation moved to Koborowo, and Dyzma said, sighing, "Living in the countryside is so nice, so peaceful . . ."

"You have good memories of Koborowo, Mr. President," Krzepicki observed. "And what a property! Well, have Nina divorce Kunicki and marry you instead."

"Bah!" Dyzma nodded, "if Koborowo belonged to her, I'd do it in a second flat!"

"But, after all, isn't she nominally the owner?"

"So what? Kunicki has unlimited power of attorney."

"Power of attorney can be withdrawn."

Nicodemus shrugged.

"But promissory notes can't."

Krzepicki pondered this and began to whistle a little tune.

"You see," Dyzma added, "there's squat that can be done about it!"

Krzepicki's whistling did not stop.

"Well, what do we have tomorrow?" Nicodemus asked.

"For tomorrow . . . nothing special. But yes, there is an invitation to the circus. It's supposed to be quite a sensation. The world's greatest strongman will be there, I forgot his name, but he's fighting the Polish champion, Wielaga. Do you enjoy wrestling, Mr. President?"

"I sure do. So, we're going? What time?"

"It's at eight."

Dyzma dismissed his secretary and went to bed. Putting on his pajamas, he noticed that the golden star was still around his neck. He took it off, shoved it into a matchbox, hid it in his desk, and, as he switched off the light, he made the sign of the cross just in case.

The following day went as he expected it would. Sure enough, Boczek showed up at one o'clock. And indeed, he projected enormous self-assurance. Vodka fumes wafted from him.

Dyzma changed tactics.

He shook Boczek's hand, offered him a chair, and asked with extreme politeness whether he could be of any help, whereas Boczek, feeling ever more confident, felt no need to restrain himself in either word or gesture, even going so far as to give the president a pat on the shoulder.

For Dyzma, that was going too far. He jumped up and shouted, "Get the hell out of here, goddammit! Beat it!"

Boczek shot Dyzma a baleful look and stood up.

"You're going to be sorry you said that. Think you're a big shot, huh?"

"What do you want from me? Money, is that it, you son of a bitch?" Dyzma snarled.

Boczek shrugged.

"Money could also come in handy."

"Ugh . . . you scumbag! . . ."

Nicodemus took twenty zlotys from his pocket, and after a moment of thought added an additional twenty.

"What are you so mad about, Mr. Dyzma?" Boczek began in a conciliatory tone. "After all, I don't want to cause you any harm—"

" 'I don't want, I don't want. . . .' Then how come you're running your mouth around my secretary, huh?"

Boczek sat down.

"Shh, Mr. Dyzma. Isn't it better just to live in peace with each other? You help me, and I don't cause you any harm—"

"Didn't I give you a job already?"

"You call that a job?" Boczek shrugged. "Eight hours of slaving away for a lousy four hundred zlotys. And the noise in that factory! All the banging and crashing, my nerves can't handle it. It's really not for me . . ."

"Maybe I should make you a minister, how about that?" Dyzma sneered.

"Are you kidding me, Mr. Dyzma? Why do you think they made you a bank president?"

"Because I've got the brains for it, you hear me?"

"Everyone has brains of their own. And I'm thinking that if you can be a bank president, it would be a real travesty if I, your former superior, didn't have a salary of at least eight hundred zlotys."

"Have you lost your mind, Mr. Boczek? Eight hundred zlotys? Who's going to give you that?"

"Let's not kid ourselves, Mr. Dyzma, I know that if you really put your mind to it, you can dig up more than a few who will."

Dyzma's eyes flashed with hatred. He made a sudden decision.

"Well, okay, Mr. Boczek, I see I have to . . . Hmm . . . I could make you the deputy director of the State Alcohol Agency . . . How's that?"

"That would be a definite step up. Can it include accommodations? Then I could bring my family."

"Sure, there's an apartment that comes with it, a nice one, four rooms, a kitchen and free firewood, electricity."

"And the salary?"

"The salary will be one thousand zlotys."

Boczek was deeply moved. He stood up and wrapped his arms around Dyzma.

"Well, you see, Nicodemus? We're just two guys from the old neighborhood, we have to look out for each other."

"Sure," Nicodemus confirmed.

"I've always been your friend. Others may have turned their backs on you, called you a bastard, a foundling, supposedly born out of wedlock—"

"Knock it off, goddammit!"

"Others, I say, all the others in Łysków, but not me. I even allowed you to come into my house—"

"Big deal," Dyzma said with contempt.

"Back then it was a big deal," Boczek said phlegmatically, "but we don't need to argue about that now."

Nicodemus's mood was black as night. His memories of being a found-ling had him twisted up inside. He suddenly realized that there wasn't enough room in Warsaw for both of them, for Boczek and him . . . And not just in Warsaw.

The bright look on Boczek's face would have vanished without a trace if he had been able to read his former subordinate's mind just then.

"I'll tell you what, Mr. Boczek," Dyzma began. "Come tomorrow and bring your papers, all your papers, because getting you a job like this is hardly a piece of cake. I'll have to talk to the right people and explain that you're capable of being the deputy director."

"My heartfelt thanks, Mr. Dyzma. You won't regret this."

"I know I won't regret it," Dyzma muttered. "One more thing now: not a word to anyone, because there are about a hundred other candidates inter-ested in this position, do you understand?"

"Sure I do."

"Well, we're done, then. Tomorrow at eleven."

Somebody knocked on the door, and Krzepicki appeared in the door-way. Boczek gave Dyzma a sly wink and bowed as low as his corpulent figure would allow him to.

"My highest regards to you, Mr. President, everything will be arranged according to your command, Mr. President."

"Goodbye. You can go now."

Nicodemus saw that Krzepicki, pretending to be absorbed by the papers he was holding, was discreetly watching Boczek disappear behind the door.

"Well, what's new, Mr. Krzepicki?"

"Everything's in order. Here's the invitation to the circus."

"Yes, right, we're going."

"And Countess Czarska called, but I told her that you were busy."

"Well, that's a shame."

"Hee hee hee! I understand you, Mr. President. Those Czarska girls are *fin-fin* . . . Last year—"

He didn't finish, because Colonel Wareda had barreled into the office without closing the door behind him.

"Nick! Hello! Where have you been!"

"How are you, Wacek?"

Krzepicki bowed and left.

"You know, brother," boomed the colonel, "I dropped by because it crossed my mind that you might like to go to the circus. This Tracco fellow is arriving today, you know, the world's strongest man, and he's going up against our champion, Wielaga."

"I know, I'm planning on going."

"That's fantastic!" He slapped Dyzma on the knee. "The whole gang'll be there, Uszycki, Ulanicki, Romanowicz and his wife . . ."

The telephone rang.

"Hello?"

Krzepicki announced that it was Miss Czarska calling again. Should he put her through?

"Give her to me . . . Hello! . . . Yes, it's me, good morning, Mademoiselle . . ."

He held his hand over the receiver and whispered to Wareda: "It's Countess Czarska!"

"Whew! . . ." He shook his head.

"No, you're not interrupting. No, the opposite, I'm very pleased . . ."

He cradled the telephone against his shoulder and lit the cigarette the colonel had offered him.

"But, Mademoiselle, I'm no expert in literature . . . Word of honor . . . And when is that? . . . Well, okay, okay . . . And how is your sister's health? Hmm, you know what, me too, but it's better not to discuss that over the phone . . . What, to the theater? Ehh . . . you know what, wouldn't you rather go with me to the circus? . . . Oh no, today the world's strongest man is fighting . . . What? . . . Wacek, what's his name?"

"An Italian, Tracco . . ."

"No, my friend Wareda is here . . ."

"Nick, tell her that I send my regards."

"He sends his regards . . . He will be, yes . . . Well, what a nice coincidence. I'll pick you up in my car . . . See you."

He put the phone down and smiled.

"Ah, these dames, all these dames! . . ."

"Are they coming?" the colonel asked.

"They wouldn't miss it!"

"Then let's go, we're having dinner."

"We'll be taking Krzepicki as well."

"Whatever you want," Wareda agreed.

They met Ulanicki at the restaurant, and, right away, things got entertaining.

"Do you already know the one about the bulldog and the pinscher? Tell me, have you heard it?" he asked as coffee was being served.

"Watch out!" Wareda warned him. "Don't forget that whoever tells an old joke, a bottle of cognac is on him."

"Wacek, you wisenheimer," Ulanicki scolded, pulling a serious face. "I myself was the very Lycurgus who established this legal principle. But listen. Well, a pointer is lying on the corner of Marszałkowska—"

"You said it was a bulldog."

"Pipe down. A pointer is sitting there, and suddenly he sees a bulldog, this huge bulldog is scampering out of the Saxon Garden . . ."

Dyzma stood up and muttered, "Excuse me for a moment."

"Do you know this joke?" Wareda asked.

Nicodemus did not, but he replied, "I do."

He threw on his coat and ran out through the door the concierge had pulled aside for him.

His driver started the engine and opened the car door.

"You can go home," Dyzma told him.

He stood for a moment on the pavement, watching his car drive away, then went in the direction of Bielańska Street. He got into a taxi.

"The corner of Karolkowa and Wolska."

When he was still a mandolinist at Bar Under the Sun, he often spent time in this district with casual companions and guys from around the way. Sometimes visitors to the bar, when they were feeling particularly festive, took the band with them. There were several that played on long, narrow Karolkowa Street.

When the car stopped, Nicodemus paid and waited for the taxi driver to leave. Then he turned onto Karolkowa.

On both sides of the street, crowded together like tenements, were dull-red brick factories. Here and there, the monotony was broken by a wooden fence or a small wooden house in whose windows little light bulbs glowed from behind yellowed curtains. These were workers' pubs, and there was so little difference between them that one would be hard-pressed to tell them apart.

Nicodemus walked confidently until he found the narrow door he was looking for and pushed it open. He was immediately engulfed by the smell of beer and sauerkraut. A wide glass counter covered in white lace took up half the small room, and a layer of fresh sawdust covered the stone floor. Loud accordion and violin noises were coming from behind a green curtain. A grim, ruddy-faced man and two aging women stood behind the counter. In the sitting area, only two tables were occupied.

Nicodemus went up to the bar.

"A double?" asked the owner.

"You know it," Dyzma responded. He drank and reached for a piece of herring.

"Well, Mr. Malinowski," said Dyzma, "how goes it?"

"It's going."

"Does Ambroziak play here, Ambroziak the accordion player?"

"Who's asking?" the owner replied with suspicion.

"Pour me another," said Dyzma, and he drank. He popped a marinated mushroom in his mouth.

"You don't remember me, do you, Mr. Malinowski?"

"A lot of people come around here," he said indifferently.

"I'm Pyzdraj. I played at Under the Sun on Pańska."

"On Pańska?"

"Yes. Mandolinist. They call me Pyzdraj."

Without a word, the owner poured him another.

"Yeah, good . . . So how are things around here?"

"It is what it is . . ."

Dyzma drank his vodka and asked, "Is Ambroziak playing there," he used his chin to gesture at the curtain, "right now? Tell me, he's a friend of mine . . ."

"He is," the owner said shortly.

Nicodemus lodged a toothpick in his teeth and went over and parted the green cretonne. Here there were more people, and the orchestra was playing a long song, evidently by request. The accordionist locked eyes with Dyzma, and as soon as they were done with the tango, he came over.

"Good evening, Pyzdraj."

"Good evening," Dyzma called, with something that resembled cheer. "To celebrate the occasion, give us two tall ones, Mr. Malinowski."

"Well, since the old comrade's in town," the accordionist added, "give us a couple shots, too, the special blend."

They drank.

"This a business matter?" Ambroziak asked.

Nicodemus nodded.

"And are you working somewhere these days?"

"Me?" After a moment of hesitation, Dyzma continued, "Ehh, in the countryside."

"How's life?"

"It's life."

"Well, if you want to talk business, let's sit over there."

They picked up their glasses and went toward the window.

"Ambroziak," Dyzma began, "I'm asking as an old friend, there's a thing I need you to do for me . . ."

"What sort of thing?"

"I need three, maybe four guys, the kind of guys who don't get cold feet, to make a problem go away."

"Wet work?" the accordionist asked in a low tone.

In his chair, Nicodemus nodded.

"There's this guy who's really gotten under my skin."

"Political guy?" Ambroziak was curious.

"No, what are you talking about, he's just . . . an asshole . . ."

"And what, he needs to be bumped off?"

Nicodemus scratched his shoulder.

"No, no need for that, just shut up him so he'll stop talking . . ."

The accordionist drained his glass and spat.

"It can be done, why not, you'll just have to shell out a hundred zlotys or so . . . maybe a hundred twenty . . ."

"I'll manage," said Dyzma.

Ambroziak nodded, stood up, and disappeared behind the curtain. Dyzma waited. After a while, the accordionist returned, accompanied by a short blond man with smiling eyes.

"Allow me. Pyzdraj, this is Franek Lewandowski."

The blond man extended an unbelievably large and gnarled hand.

"So who's dead?" he asked cheerfully.

"Well," Dyzma replied with deliberation, "it's just a little business matter."

"If we're talking business, how about a crumb and a drop?"

Nicodemus nodded to the owner.

"Mr. Malinowski, a bottle of vodka and a pork cutlet."

Ambroziak leaned closer to the blond man.

"Franek, who will you take with you?"

"I think Tony Klawisz'll go, and Cuz too, that'll do it."

"Will three be enough?" Nicodemus was dubious.

"Why? Is he so strong? . . . What is he, a shyster or a sucker?"

"Sucker. From the sticks . . . Fat like a barrel."

"Done," Franek nodded. "Now excuse me for asking, but who are you?"

"What's it to you, Franek?" Ambroziak said. "He's my friend, that's all. Why stick your nose in?"

"I'm not, just asking. Okay, let's talk."

Nicodemus leaned over the little table and began to explain.

Both Lewandowski and the accordionist continued to drink, shot after shot, while Dyzma kept them company. Hence the empty bottle at their table, which the owner soon removed and replaced with a new one. Without waiting to be asked, he also brought them a new cold cutlet with pickles.

He knew that if someone was having "a talk" with Lewandowski, plenty of sustenance was required to seal the deal.

Ambroziak got up several times, heeding the call of his orchestra duties, and then returned to the table. The owner lit a gas lamp. Again and again the door swung open and new guests arrived at the pub.

Almost every newcomer directed a bow at Lewandowski, who returned them all with a careless nod.

Dyzma had heard a lot about him. He never would have imagined, however, that this notorious roughneck, whose knife inspired fear and respect throughout the Wola and Czyste districts, would have such a boyish and gentle appearance. In any case, he knew that the matter had been entrusted to good hands.

It was nearly eight o'clock when he paid the bill and discreetly handed Franek a hundred zlotys.

"And the main thing is to search his pockets so there's no record," he said, shaking Lewandowski's gnarled hand goodbye.

Ambroziak walked Dyzma to the door and, after assuring him that Franek was a real brick, asked if he could borrow ten zlotys. Stuffing the money in his pocket, he said, not without irony, "You must make quite a living out there in the country. You're rolling in dough!"

"Yeah, it's going well."

The street was empty. When he reached the corner of Wolska, he stopped to wait for the tram. The number 9 soon arrived.

The circus was full. The piercing cries of the boys circulating among the crowd cut through the general hubbub:

"Chocolate, lemonade, wafers!"

When Nicodemus entered with the Czarska sisters on his arm, the band had just played a march, and the athletes were approaching the arena in single file. There were about ten of them: men of enormous size, with grotesquely overdeveloped muscles and bull-like shoulders, in skimpy leotards that exposed folds of skin sprouting patches of bristly hair.

They circled the arena, keeping a rhythmic pace.

When Dyzma and company got to their box, Colonel Wareda was already there, and Marietta Czarska laughed:

"What impressive mountains of flesh!"

They exchanged greetings.

"That one's Mike," Wareda said. "He's built like a boy, but he's stronger than most of these other hippos."

The showcase was starting.

The athletes stood in line, and the referee at the jury table listed their names. He gave a title to each: English champion, Brazilian champion, European champion, and so on. When he called two names in particular, the galleries resounded with applause. Greeted thusly were Wielaga, the Polish champion, and Tracco, the enormous Italian.

Then the arena emptied. Only two contestants remained: a hulking German with long arms like a monkey and slender Mulatto Mike, who looked, in comparison to his opponent, like an antelope soon to be trampled by a rhinoceros.

There was a whistle, and the opponents went at it.

"He's already got him!" cried Dyzma, seeing how Mulatto Mike, under the German's bulk, had dropped to the mat.

"No way, brother," Wareda grinned, "you'll be good and tired before you pin that slippery little eel to the ground."

Indeed, Mike proceeded to slip out of his opponent's hands in one clever move. When the German, wheezing with strain, lifted him up to slam him back onto the mat, Mike unexpectedly bounced off the mat with one foot, which—so it seemed—actually helped the German to maneuver, though there was a surprise in store for him. Namely, Mulatto Mike's swarthy form springing up and arching over his opponent's head. The German, since he was holding his opponent under his arms, lost his balance and toppled over onto his back. At that very moment, Mike jumped squarely onto his chest.

The referee, a whistle in his mouth, rushed in just in time to catch the second when both German shoulders touched the mat. And it was literally just a second, because the defeated man jumped up with a barbaric howl and slammed his conqueror to the ground with the ease of a horse tossing an unskilled rider from his saddle.

The fight was over, however, and the chairman of the jury announced the win for Mulatto Mike, who bowed with a smile of gratitude amid thunderous applause. And the defeated man, cursing, left the arena to the sound of jeering whistles from the gallery.

"Ah, he is so beautiful, this mulatto," Marietta Czarska marveled. "Like a bronze statue! Mr. President, would there be a great scandal if we were to take him with us to dinner?"

"Why, Marietta!" her sister cried.

"It might not be appropriate," Dyzma said, but the rest of the company was of the opinion that it would be as good an attraction as any, and if they sat in one of the private dining rooms, everything would be fine.

Meanwhile, the second pair was taking the arena. Dyzma was enthralled, his rapt gaze never leaving the fighters. During moments of tense action, he clenched his hands with such fervor that his joints cracked. Again and again, words of exhortation and encouragement burst through his clenched teeth:

"Harder! Pound him! . . ."

Sweaty bodies tumbled and rolled upon the mats as groans and roars were ripped from battered throats.

Again and again, salvoes of shouts, whistles, and applause issued from the gallery.

Several matches had already been decided.

And now came the evening's main attraction.

The two strongest rivals stood opposite each other.

The Polish champion, Wielaga, with his monstrous arms and herculean shoulders, his short, squashed-looking nose and shaved head, looked not unlike a gorilla. Opposite him was Tracco, taller and thinner, great knots of muscle pulsing under his gleaming skin, standing with his legs splayed like two knotty oak trunks.

A whistle shattered the silence. The rivals, unhurried, exchanging appraising looks, approached each other. They were equally serious about the competition, but it was clear from the start that each had chosen a different tactic. The Pole wanted a lightning-fast fight. The Italian, however, was electing to drag out the action for as long as possible, counting on his opponent to wear himself out. So he put up minimal resistance and, after a few moves, got caught in a kind of pirouette and ended up flat on his stomach.

Wielaga stood over him and tried to roll him onto his back. This attempt lasted several minutes. When he realized it wasn't going to work, he began furiously rubbing his rival's neck.

"What's he doing?" Marietta asked.

Wareda leaned toward her and, without taking his eyes off the fight, explained:

"It's called a massage. Hitting isn't allowed, you see, but a massage is acceptable. This way, it crushes his neck muscles and weakens them considerably."

"Yeah, it must hurt his skin, too."

The Italian apparently thought the same thing, because he suddenly sprang up and, slipping out of his opponent's grip, grabbed him around the waist from behind. However, his arms were too short for Wielaga's massive form. The Pole took a deep breath and tensed his stomach muscles, and Tracco's clasped hands immediately broke apart.

The gallery rewarded this trick with a deafening roar of applause. Since the start of the match, there had been no question that the audience's hearts were with the Polish wrestler.

Meanwhile, the fight was thus far still a draw, which had provoked Wielaga's undisguised fury. Cheers from the gallery inflamed him:

"Wielaga, don't give in!"

"Finish that wop!"

"Bravo, Wielaga!"

The athlete's eyes were flecked with blood, and a dull rattle was coming from his chest. The fight was getting more and more violent. The wrestlers' bodies were bathed in sweat.

Wielaga ferociously attacked his opponent, who defended himself fiercely, but always with proper form and in accordance with the rules, whereas Wielaga showed no interest in suppressing his brutal urge to destroy the Italian, and the referee even had to intervene several times due to illegal maneuvers. Suddenly, Wielaga managed to catch Tracco in a terrible hold called the full nelson. His enormous hands passed right under the Italian's arms and locked behind his neck. The circus froze in anticipation.

The wrestlers stood motionless as stone, but it was a motionlessness so strenuous that clusters of rigid muscles seemed ready to split the skin.

Wielaga held on. The Italian's face first turned purple, then blue. His eyes bulged with unbearable torment, and saliva dripped from his open mouth and outstretched tongue.

"Disgusting!" Marietta said, covering her eyes.

"He's going to kill him!" Her sister was terrified. "Mr. President, it's horrible . . ."

"Let him break his neck!" Dyzma replied.

"Shame on you, Mr. President!" Marietta was upset.

The colonel shrugged. "After all, he could always surrender."

But the Italian did not think of capitulating. He bore the hellish pain, and it was clear that he wasn't planning on giving in.

Wielaga had also reached this conclusion, and knowing that any minute the whistle would announce the break, he decided to end the fight once and for all. In one rapid motion, he shifted his opponent to the side and, tripping him slightly, threw his body to the ground and slammed his own body against it, driving both shoulders into the mat.

The circus shook to its foundations. A huge roar, a storm of applause, and the stamping of thousands of feet merged into a single deafening sound that eclipsed both the referee's whistle and the chairman's bell.

"Bravo, bravo, Wielaga!" Dyzma bellowed so loudly that beads of sweat popped out on his forehead.

Meanwhile, the wrestlers had risen from the mat. Wielaga was bowing to the crowd, while Tracco was at the jury table, rubbing his neck and telling them something.

At last, the noise subsided. The referee walked to the center of the arena and announced, "The wrestling match between the Polish champion, Wielaga, and the Italian champion, Tracco, remains undecided, because Wielaga tripped him, which is an illegal move. The jury has concluded . . ."

Any further words were drowned in the roar of protest.

"Lies!"

"He didn't trip him!"

"The ref's a jackass!"

"Down with that greasy wop!"

Finally, the chairman of the jury was allowed to speak.

"Gentlemen! The fight is undecided because Wielaga tripped his opponent. The referee saw it and so did I."

"You're a liar, he didn't trip him!" Dyzma shouted.

"You, sir, are the one who's lying," the chairman huffed.

"What?!" Dyzma shouted. "What? If I, the president of the National Grain Bank, say that he didn't trip him, who are you going to believe, me or some loser with a whistle?"

The circus shook with applause.

"Bravo, bravo!"

"He's right!"

The chairman rose from his seat and called out, "In wrestling, the jury decides the results, not the public. This fight is undecided."

With that, Nicodemus completely lost all control and screamed, over the entire circus, "I don't give a fuck!!!"

The effect was colossal. A maelstrom of applause, laughter, and cheering rose from the gallery, and the word Dyzma had just used rang out again and again.

Nicodemus put his hands in his pockets and said, "We need to get out of this dump, it's killing me."

They left, every one of them laughing.

"Well," Colonel Wareda said, "after this, you'll be quite a celebrity!"

"Ehh . . ."

"Not 'ehh' . . . a bonafide celebrity. Tomorrow, all of Warsaw will be talking about this. You'll see. People like strong words."

The next day, they weren't just talking about it, they were also writing about it. Nearly every paper gave a detailed and piquant account of the scandal, and some even ran a photograph of the hero of the event.

Nicodemus was angry at himself.

"I was right to tell them off," he told Krzepicki, "but now people are going to take me for some kind of yokel."

"It's nothing, a trifle," Krzepicki assured him.

"Those assholes just made me so mad!"

Chapter 13

Krochmalna Street was completely empty. And no wonder, since it was after midnight, and the people who lived in this neighborhood had to get up at six to go to work. Red-brick tenements drowsed in the dim light of gas streetlamps. Every now and then there was the echo of footsteps, a passerby hurrying home.

But in one doorway there stood three men. They stood in silence, leaning against the wall. They were waiting. One might have thought they were dozing, if not for the glowing ends of three cigarettes.

Suddenly, the sound of heavy footsteps reached their ears. Someone was coming from the direction of Żelazna Street. One of the men waiting at the gate crouched and bent his head near the ground, then drew back and whispered, "It's him."

The steps came nearer, and after a moment they spied a short, fat man in a black coat. When he passed the gate, they slipped out after him.

He looked behind him.

"Sir," called the skinny one with blond hair. "Do you have a light?"

"Sure," replied the fat man, reaching into his pocket.

"Is your name Boczek?" the blond man asked abruptly.

Fatso looked at him.

"How come you know who I am?"

"How come? How come you're an asshole who can't keep his mouth shut?"

"When—"

He didn't finish. A heavy fist smashed into his nose and upper lip. At the same time, he received a blow to the head from behind and a powerful kick in the stomach.

"Jesus!" he yelped, and he rolled into the gutter. There was a buzzing inside his skull and he could taste blood in his mouth.

But his assailants did not consider the job done. One bent over the fallen man and bashed him again and again in the stomach and chest. Another came running into the street and, with the heel of his boot, delivered two terrible blows to the face.

The excruciating pain seemed to rouse the laid-out man. With unbelievable—considering his corpulence—speed, he staggered to his feet and, in a desperate voice, howled, "Help! Help!..."

"Shut him up!" the blond man growled, out of breath.

His associate grabbed the victim's hat from the ground where it had fallen and crammed it against his battered face.

"Help!... Help!..." he screamed without a second's pause.

At the far corner of the street, someone stopped.

"Hey Franek, somebody's coming."

"Help! Help!..."

"It's no use, we're gonna have to deep-six this guy."

A switchblade flicked open, and its long, wide business end noiselessly entered Boczek's body and sank to the hilt. One, two, three...

"Kaput."

He wiped the knife off on Boczek's jacket. The other two quickly rifled through his pockets. A watch, a passport, a wallet...

A moment later, Krochmalna Street was empty once again.

Dawn was already starting to break when two policemen turned their bikes onto Krochmalna. Night patrol.

"Look at this," one called out. "Someone's lying over there."

"Probably a drunk."

They hopped off their bikes. When they saw the pool of blood, they immediately knew what they were dealing with.

"Gutted like a hog."

"Check for a pulse."

"He's already cold."

"What the hell's the matter with these people? We need to head to the station."

"This is the third one this week."

It began to drizzle. A fine, cold autumn rain.

At roughly five o'clock this morning, during their bicycle patrol of Krochmalna Street, officers from the Eighth Precinct came upon the body of a man.

According to the doctor who arrived with the ambulance, the cause of death was blood loss resulting from a puncture of the pericardium with a sharp object, as well as a skull fracture. Due to the extent of his facial injuries, the identity of the victim has been impossible to determine. No documents or personal objects that might facilitate the investigation were found. The corpse was taken to the morgue. There is speculation that this death may be connected to feuding among political parties.

Bank President Nicodemus Dyzma set the newspaper down and started to drum his fingers on the baize surface of his desk.

"Well, can I help it if that's what happened?"

He shrugged his shoulders.

At first, he was horrified by the news of Boczek's death. He figured that an investigation could eventually lead to him. He was also afraid that the murdered man's ghost might keep him up at night. On the other hand, the awareness of the eradication of this highly dangerous man, the awareness of his safety, his escape from the threat that had been hanging over him all this time—it was a feeling stronger than fear, a fear that was dwindling to zero. Who would suspect him, a bank president, of inciting some thugs to murder?

Besides, was he really to blame for Boczek's death? After all, he hadn't explicitly demanded it.

It's his own fault, Dyzma thought. Stupid chump . . . He got what was coming to him . . .

Into the office came Krzepicki. He closed the door behind him, and with a mysterious smile, said, "Mr. President, would you be willing to receive a certain inquirer? A most interesting inquirer?"

"Who?"

"An old acquaintance of yours."

Dyzma went white as a sheet. He leapt from his chair, trembling from head to toe, and asked in a voice not quite his own, "Who?! . . ."

He was overcome by an unearthly fear that waiting behind those doors was Boczek himself, drenched in blood, his face smashed in . . .

"What is it, Mr. President?" Krzepicki asked with alarm.

Dyzma was supporting himself against the desk.

"Are you ill?"

"No, no . . . So who is it?"

"Kunicki."

"Ugh, Kunicki . . . Fine . . ."

"You'll see him?"

"Fine."

A moment later, Kunicki flew into the office, red-cheeked and full of beans as usual. He'd set his greetings in motion even before crossing the threshold, firing out lispy verbiage with ungodly speed.

For a few minutes, Dyzma gaped at him, unable to concentrate enough to understand a word he was saying.

"Well it's the man himself, my dear Nicodemus, time marches on but the man doesn't age. But indeed, sir, you're looking marvelous! What's going on politics-wise? Well? How's business? Everybody's complaining about stagnation, about taxes, my dear sir, after all, this sales tax is bleeding our citizens dry! To say nothing of benefits! Believe me. You've got a nice office, some style, some class. Perhaps you can do me a favor, my dear Nicodemus, well, my dear friend, you wouldn't say no to breakfast with me, I haven't had a bite to eat since this morning . . . Nice office. You wouldn't come back with me to Koborowo, would you? True, this weather's for the birds, but such peace, such quiet. A salve for the old nerves, and it would make Nina happy, poor thing, so lonely . . . Come out for a few days, how about it?"

"Of course, maybe next week."

"Hot damn! Thank you, thank you! So let's have some breakfast. Maybe Bacchus, how about it?"

"Thanks, but I can't. I'm having breakfast this morning with Prince Roztocki."

This wasn't true, but it had achieved the desired effect. Kunicki nearly slavered with rapturous enthusiasm as he began to enumerate all the possibilities that might open to him with such towering connections as were possessed by his beloved Nicodemus.

Now he came out with the real reason for the visit: railway ties. Fawning and preening, the old man laid it on thick. He showered Dyzma with profit figures, all of which would be theirs to share if only Koborowo was the supplier of these railway materials, explaining that, ultimately, if they didn't want to give it to him because of that lawsuit, they could, after all, always give it to Nina Kunicka.

"I don't know," Dyzma said, trying to fend him off.

"Hee hee, but I know that you wouldn't mind putting your thumb on the scale . . . Listen, just have a little chat with the minister of transportation!"

He kept sawing away at Nicodemus until he finally agreed.

"Just don't go anywhere," he warned Kunicki, "because if we need to make our case, you know more about this than I do."

Kunicki, overjoyed, assured the dear president that of course he wouldn't go anywhere if there was a chance he'd be needed to flesh out the details, even though he was convinced that a man with such a brilliant head for business wouldn't have any need for him.

The entrance of Krzepicki with the mail interrupted Kunicki's torrent of speech. He said goodbye to Dyzma and, assuring him he'd see him tomorrow, left.

"He's a crafty old schemer," Krzepicki remarked. "Everyone knows it."

"Oh ho, and how!" Nicodemus agreed. "It'd be hard to pull one over on *him*."

Krzepicki's long face widened with a contemptuous smile.

"In my opinion, Mr. President, there's no schemer so great that he couldn't be taken in by someone even greater."

Dyzma's laughter was totally sincere. He considered himself to be just such a schemer. And the confidential smile on Krzepicki's face suggested that he'd had the same thought.

"Well, so what do you reckon?" asked Dyzma.

"I reckon," replied Krzepicki, lowering his eyes, "that these times belong to those who know how to seize an opportunity."

"An opportunity such as? . . ."

Krzepicki lifted his head, ran a hand over his protruding Adam's apple, and remarked, almost off-handedly, "Koborowo is worth a pretty penny."

"Bah! . . ."

"It doesn't come along for just anyone . . ."

Dyzma nodded his head.

"But it came along for Kunicki."

"But maybe it'll come along . . . for you, too."

Nicodemus gave him a wary look.

"Me?"

"The world belongs to those who are capable of tossing scruples out the window."

"You mean, not be scrupulous?"

Instead of answering, Krzepicki just gazed intently at Dyzma.

"Mr. President," he finally said, carefully enunciating each word, "you must know that, for you, I'm more than obliging."

"I know," Dyzma replied.

"So I want to speak frankly. For your benefit and, I won't deny it, for my benefit as well. Right now, only a fool would squander his big chance."

He paused to reflect, and an impatient Dyzma cried, "Well, get on with it, goddammit!"

"You're not angry with me, Mr. President, are you?"

"What is this? Are you calling me a fool?"

"Not at all, that's why I'm telling you . . ."

He pulled his chair forward and grew more serious.

"Mr. President, is Kunicki's wife still in love with you?"

"Is she ever! Every day I get one of these letters."

"That's very good."

He leaned in toward Nicodemus and began to speak.

It was already after three when they both left the bank and climbed into the car.

"Oasis!" Dyzma shouted to his chauffeur, and he clapped his secretary on the back. "What a head you have on your shoulders! If only it all works!"

"Why shouldn't it work? So, you're in?" He held out his hand.

"It's a deal." Dyzma grabbed his hand and squeezed hard.

That evening, Nicodemus Dyzma paid a visit to Roman Pilchen, the minister of transportation.

He was a slight, brown-haired man, always smiling and pleasant, renowned for his passion for corny expressions. He and his wife, a graying brunette of a highly Semitic type, gave Dyzma a rapturous reception.

"Ah, Mr. Bank President, old buddy, old pal!" Pilchen cried at the first sight of Dyzma.

"That little word of yours at the circus made quite a splash! Color me tickled pink! Why, I caught a case of the giggles that lasted so long I thought I might keel over and die! Now that's what I call the right word for the right time, am I right?"

"It was none too courteous, perhaps," his wife drawled in confirmation, "but very masculine."

"You sure are right about that, yes siree, our little old country is stuffed to the gills with too many spineless fraidy cats and capital-L losers, too many softies and sweetie-pies! A strong word now and then is like a great big bucket of cold water over the old noggin."

Dyzma laughed and, exculpating himself, explained that he'd gotten so worked up that he'd just had to "fire a few shots."

After dinner, they got down to business.

Dyzma had no idea it would be so easy.

True, Pilchen explained that he wouldn't be able to offer a final decision until he spoke with the relevant department at his ministry, but, by and large, he was prepared to do anything "for the tip-top, top-notch Mr. President." And besides, railway ties would always come in handy one way or another.

"And you have my pinky promise that we'll take care of all this lickety-split, by hook or by crook, and it'll be quick like a bunny, that's my tried-and-true method."

Dyzma scratched his head.

"Actually, if it were up to me, I wouldn't mind if this matter got dragged out for a while . . ."

"Dragged out, buddy of mine?" The minister was surprised.

Nicodemus chuckled. "Let's just say I'm in no big hurry."

Pilchen laughed and opined that, in that case, he must consider Dyzma a most unprecedented petitioner, one of a kind and in a class all by his lonesome.

Dyzma asked if he could drop by the ministry tomorrow and, receiving an affirmative answer, began to say his goodbyes.

"That's one smart cookie," the minister remarked after the doors had closed behind Dyzma, "and believe it, honeybunch, every teeny favor we do for him means plenty of moolah for us—he's a doozy of an investment."

"Oh, I don't know," Mrs. Pilchen answered. "I don't know much about all your political machinations, but I have to admit that Mr. Dyzma makes an extremely good impression. Perhaps it's a mark of his English education."

Nicodemus went home and immediately telephoned Krzepicki to announce that everything was proceeding according to plan. Next, he got down to reading a pile of letters from Nina that had sat unopened for a long time. He was looking for confirmation that her feelings for him were still going strong.

Her words left him with not even the slightest shred of a doubt on this account. Gushing forth from every letter was love and agonies of longing, tender memories of moments spent together and fantasies of their future happiness when they would finally be united as one. In one letter, he found mention of her sorrow at the idea of abandoning Koborowo, where she had been born and that spoke to her of the bright, unfettered years of her childhood.

Grinning and rubbing his hands, Dyzma opened his desk. He took a printed form from a bundle of papers and began to read it carefully. It was a document of plenipotentiary powers, granting Dyzma full financial and legal rights in the name of Nina Kunicka. It had been given to him by Kunicki right after his arrival in Koborowo.

Dyzma neatly folded the sheet of paper and slid it into his wallet.

He whistled a cheerful tune as he took off his clothes and, with a spring in his step, hopped into bed. His thoughts were entirely consumed by this tremendous game he'd begun, and his head was almost bursting with joy and excitement.

And then, from out of nowhere, at the very moment he switched off his bedside lamp and the room fell into darkness, it slammed into his consciousness like the butt end of a rifle:

"Boczek murdered."

He froze.

"Murdered at my command . . . On account of my money . . . I murdered Boczek . . . Shit!"

His brain was gripped by one stubborn thought. Was there indeed life beyond the grave, was it true what they said about ghosts? . . .

Suddenly, on the opposite wall, he discerned some kind of movement in the darkness . . . Some kind of shape forming . . .

The hair on the back of his neck stood up, and, with a trembling hand, he groped around for the light switch. But his pajama sleeve knocked against the lampshade and the entire lamp clattered to the floor.

He stiffened. The shape advanced toward the bed. All the blood rushed to his heart, and a long, piercing shriek escaped his throat. Then a second shriek, a third and a fourth . . .

The seconds seemed like hours.

He heard the sudden patter of slippers. Through the gap in the adjacent doors came a streak of light, and there was Ignacy, standing on the threshold with a revolver in his hand.

"What happened?"

"Turn the light on, quick!"

He felt around until he found the switch. With a quiet click, the room was flooded with light—dazzling, blissful, life-preserving light.

"What happened, Mr. President?"

Dyzma sat up in bed.

"Nothing. A dream. I dreamt that . . . that this . . . this thief . . ."

"You gave me a scare! Well, thank God."

"It's my nerves. You know what, Ignacy? Take your sheets and come sleep here on the divan."

"As you wish."

"Ah, and go to the credenza and pour me a glass of vodka and bring it here. It'll do me good."

By the time he had gulped down two vodkas and had a few hard rolls for a snack, Ignacy had finished setting himself up on the divan, and Nicodemus had completely regained his peace of mind.

"Pthu, get a grip," he told himself. He turned over and fell fast asleep.

Chapter 14

Krzepicki looked at the plenipotentiary agreement and, returning it to Dyzma, said, "Looks good, everything's in order."

"Did you find out who in the ministry is going to be handling this hoo-ha?"

"Yeah, I did. Some Scoopak, he's the head of the department."

"Scoopak, huh? Funny name. But that's not the point. The point is, who is this guy?"

"I don't know him, but supposedly he's a reasonable man. Anyway, the fact that Minister Pilchen personally handed the case to this Scoopak means he's smoothed the way for us."

Kunicki came at eleven. He opened with some words about the weather and then the story of yesterday's visit to the theater, but anxiety was written all over his face. Had Dyzma done that thing for him or not?

Finally, he made a cautious inquiry. Nicodemus nodded.

"Yes, I met with the minister yesterday . . ."

"My dear man! Well? And?"

"It was difficult, but he promised to take care of it . . ."

"Hot damn! My very dear Nicodemus, you are a gift from heaven."

"I do what I can."

He explained to Kunicki that the matter might drag on for a few days, perhaps even a week, that it would necessitate a series of conferences and discussions, and that, for the time being, while the case was under review, it would be best if Kunicki maybe didn't show himself at the ministry. When it was time to finalize the contract, however, he would have to discuss the specific details in person.

"Wonderful, wonderful!" Kunicki was delighted. "But, Nicodemus, sir, what about the expenses? . . . I'm at your service."

He took out his wallet while waiting for an answer. Nicodemus leaned back in this chair.

"I think," he said slowly, "I think five thousand should be enough . . ."

"Ehh . . . let's call it six! We'll make it all up anyway with a nice percentage, hee hee. If it's speed you're after, you need to grease the axles! Don't skimp on the grease! This, Nicodemus, my good sir, is the first rule in business. If you want to make a lot of money, don't be afraid to spend it!"

He counted out twelve brand-new banknotes, which Dyzma carelessly slipped into his pocket. He'd become so used to such big amounts that the shock they'd caused him at the beginning of his new life now seemed part of his distant past.

This time he accepted Kunicki's invitation to breakfast, during which he was subjected to an entire dissertation about supply in general, and the supply of railway ties in particular.

At three o'clock Dyzma went to the ministry. Pilchen had already put on his coat and hat, but when he saw Dyzma, he immediately expressed his willingness to stay.

He'd already familiarized himself with the case and declared that he was basically in agreement. The "one and only Mr. President" could go over the question of the quota and the conditions of the transaction with the department head, Mr. Scoopak, at his leisure.

"Naturally," he added, "we'll nail down this little matter for you because we know you're as honest as the day is long, and I know deep down in my heart that when a good egg like you gives us his Scout's honor, everything's sure to be on the up and up, the old straight and narrow."

"You bet your boots," Dyzma said.

That evening he had a party to go to at Countess Czarska's. She was the widow of Maurycy, the heir of the Kaszowicki estate, who had left behind an insubstantial inheritance and an even less substantial body of literature in the form of fourteen novels, self-published by the author, and six historical dramas, none of which, unfortunately, had ever been staged.

As a result, Countess Czarska considered it her sacred duty to surround herself with writers, and there was not a single big name in the Warsaw literary world who had not appeared on her salon's guest list.

Most of them appeared frequently, arriving with their stomachs empty and leaving with them completely full, carrying under their arms at least two volumes of works by the deceased Maurycy Czarski so as to facilitate, at their next dinner on Szuch Avenue, their praise for their late colleague's talent and the expression of their sincere indignation that such a brilliant writer was so underappreciated.

Only two people at the salon yawned conspicuously during the very loud reading of the six historical dramas; they were Misses Iwona and Marietta, the nieces of the lady of the house. Those two were the reason why, aside from the writers, quite a few young people from the aristocracy frequently stopped by.

As soon as Nicodemus stepped through the sitting room door, he saw a number of people he'd already met at Madam Przełęska's or at Prince and

Princess Roztocki's, as well as—and this rattled him a little—almost every lady from that diabolical night. His only consolation was the absence of Miss Stella, whom he found downright scary.

He was greeted with joy and respect.

The greeting he received from the ladies of the Thrice-Rayed Star Lodge, Madam Lala Koniecpolska at the fore, made him feel particularly uneasy. There was something in their faces that reminded him too much of the devilish evening they'd passed together. Their eyes sought his eyes, their movements seemed to retain traces of a hidden licentiousness.

Nicodemus would have gladly made his escape, if not for his confidence that his presence at Countess Czarska's would expand his network of con-nections and help him find some new contacts that he could use in the future.

Countess Czarska, as soon as she caught sight of him, fired a barrage of questions at Dyzma concerning the epic works of her late husband.

Nicodemus evaded as much as he could, claiming that he read both *Flowers of Feelings* and *The Nightingale Song* several times.

Fortunately, the Misses Czarska and Madam Lala Koniecpolska came to his rescue, relieving him from having to listen to quotes from the epic works of the late Maurycy Czarski.

Instead, Miss Marietta invited Dyzma to meet a supposedly extremely interesting writer named Zenon Liczkowski. Liczkowski at once began try-ing to convince Nicodemus that he, Nicodemus, should participate in the activities supporting the arrangements that would lead to the creation of a literary academy.

"I have no doubt, Mr. President, that you fully recognize the need to establish an institution that would finally set about to rationalize literature under the banner of compiling select literary names and making available to these chosen few the possibility of exploratory study . . ."

"Indeed," Nicodemus said, not knowing what any of it was about, but aware that it was important to agree with Liczkowski.

That thin gentleman in horn-rimmed glasses grabbed Dyzma unceremo-niously by the lapels and, with rare zeal, began to expound on the principles of organizing the literary academy, and reiterated his conviction that the bank president, as a supporter of the formation of a Polish literary axis, would surely be more than happy to promote the project not only to the minister of education but also to the president of the republic. Several oth-ers had joined them by now and, sparing no eloquent turn of phrase, they united to persuade Nicodemus to support the entire action. Dyzma prom-ised them he would do everything in his power to support this program of the Liczkowski literary circle.

Countess Czarska, perpetually flitting from guest to guest, had already found enough time to deprive Nicodemus of two hundred zlotys for some charitable institution. So when two extremely aged ladies joined the conversation, Nicodemus took advantage of the situation to excuse himself and disappear without a trace.

At home, he found a new letter from Nina in which, apart from the usual confession of her feelings, there was a long paragraph detailing her need for him at Koborowo.

Nicodemus called Krzepicki, and they spent a long time going over their entire plan in detail. Both were satisfied with its current course. Krzepicki reminded Dyzma how imperative it was to win Kunicki's complete trust.

"He must believe you, Mr. President, otherwise it'll all go to hell."

"Why wouldn't he believe me? . . ." Nicodemus shrugged.

"If only Lady Nina doesn't ruin everything at the last minute."

"Don't worry, we'll manage."

Kunicki came at around one o'clock. He was in an excellent mood and overflowing with optimism.

When Dyzma informed him of the minister's decision and the imminent settlement of the supply contract, Kunicki threw himself into his arms and assured him that nowhere else on Earth could there be found such a dear, dear man as his dearest Nicodemus.

It was about four o'clock when Nicodemus called the head of the department, Mr. Scoopak, and invited him to dinner.

Krzepicki did not accompany his boss that evening.

Scoopak was forty years old, a restless man with no aspirations other than to abandon his job for something that would make him a lot more money. Nicodemus sensed this immediately. Which is why, without further ado, he offered Scoopak the position of managing the Koborowo sawmills.

Only now did he understand that, thanks to Minister Pilchen's favor, he could get the strongest objections—the ones related to the old lawsuit— removed entirely from the picture.

The department director had apparently never met a problem that he couldn't make go away, as long as adequate compensation was involved.

Scoopak, without digging too deeply into the bank president's intentions, promised to follow his instructions faithfully.

"Mr. Scoopak, in two days you will summon Mr. Kunicki to your office."

"Yes, sir."

"You will start to go over the whole thing with him, point by point, and do it so he gets the impression that it's a done deal, only there are a lot of formalities that still need to be worked out."

"I understand, Mr. President, I'll wear him down."

"After three days of talks you'll tell him that on Friday morning he'll be seen by Minister Pilchen, who has to ask him about a couple of things in person, and he can only do it then because he's leaving the very next day to go abroad for a month. Are you following?"

"Yes, sir."

"Good. So tell him that on Thursday morning. Remember, Thursday morning! At about . . . let's say eleven o'clock, you'll say goodbye, and then at one you'll call me at the bank. Kunicki will be there with me. Well, you'll ask me to put him on the phone, and you'll tell him that a big obstacle has come up, that the minister has found out about some old lawsuit against Kunicki, and he says that it's a no-go if Kunicki doesn't immediately present documents regarding his innocence in that case."

"And was there such a case?"

"There was. Kunicki will tell you that he has the documents, but they're in Koborowo, and that he'll go there right away to get them and will be back in time the following day to give them to the minister before he departs. That's what he'll say. Well, your job is to tell him that's impossible, because the minister is hell bent on discussing the trade aspect in person, and this meeting is scheduled for Friday morning. Do you understand?"

"Yes, Mr. President."

"It needs to be done in a way so that Kunicki has no choice but to send someone else to get these documents, since he, Kunicki, can't leave Warsaw. You, Mr. Scoopak, can make that happen."

"For you, Mr. President, hee hee hee, I can make anything happen."

"You won't regret it," said Dyzma, getting up.

The next two days went by in a hectic blur. Dyzma had endless conversations with his secretary, who had drawn up a plan of astounding meticulousness, accounting for everything down to the smallest detail; he had frequent meetings with Kunicki, whose sunny cheer rivaled that of the finest May morning, a long visit with Madam Przełęska, an even longer visit with her friend, the commissioner of the Office of Investigations, as well as a flurry of phone calls, letters, and conferences, not to mention frequent calls to and from Scoopak.

Nicodemus admired Krzepicki's cunning from the bottom of his heart. He felt completely at home in his company and knew that Krzepicki felt the same about him.

The plan was gradually and systematically coming to fruition. Kunicki hadn't noticed a thing, but the net was tightening. After each conversation with Scoopak, he showed up at the bank to give Dyzma a comprehensive report, not bothering to hide his joy and adoring appreciation for the brotherly goodwill his beloved Nicodemus had shown him. The beloved

Nicodemus, by the way, gave flattery as good as he got, and assured Kunicki of his eternal friendship.

And then the fateful Thursday arrived. At one o'clock on the dot, the phone rang in the office of the president of the Grain Bank.

"Goddammit!" Nicodemus exclaimed with expertly faked irritation. "Excuse me, Mr. Kunicki, let me see what people want from me this time."

"Of course, my dear Nicodemus, of course," said Kunicki.

"Hello . . ."

" . . ."

"What? . . . With who?"

" . . ."

"Oh, good day to you too, sir, certainly . . . Well sir, it just so happens that Mr. Kunicki is here with me right now."

He handed the phone to Kunicki.

"It's the head of the department, Mr. Scoopak. He's been looking for you all over the city."

Kunicki grabbed the receiver.

"Hello! . . . My respects to you, sir, my respects. What can I do for you, sir?"

Dyzma got up and walked to the window. He listened. He was so excited he literally drove his fingers into the windowsill. He listened. Little by little, he started to relax. The conversation was going exactly according to plan.

Kunicki's tone slowly underwent a transition from anxiety to horror, then a moaned request, and at last, when he hung up the receiver, a howl of unadulterated despair:

"What am I going to do? What do I do?"

"What happened?" Dyzma asked sympathetically.

Kunicki threw himself into a chair and wiped the sweat from his forehead. Lisping even harder than usual, he began to tell Nicodemus that they were demanding documents from the trial, that he must deliver them by eight tomorrow evening, that it was impossible for him to leave, since he had an appointment at eleven o'clock in the morning because the minister had to catch a train in the evening and was leaving for a whole month.

"Save me, dear Nicodemus, sir, tell me what to do! What should I do?"

"Hmm . . . It's simple: wire Koborowo and have them send you the documents."

"Bah!" Kunicki exclaimed. "As if that were possible! The documents are in the safe, and obviously the keys are with me."

"Well then, you'll have to send someone there. After all, you have your car with you. Maybe the chauffeur?"

"Chauffeur?! Dear Lord! How could I give the chauffeur the keys to my safe? There's cash in there, and papers, and jewelry, and various documents of enormous significance . . . Oh God, God, what to do, what to do . . ."

Dyzma pondered.

"Well, do you trust anyone in Warsaw?"

"No one, no one, not a living soul!"

"Well, then we'll have to kiss the supply deal goodbye."

"Good God, but millions are at stake, millions!" Kunicki was incensed. "I've been dreaming about this for years! And now suddenly . . . Argh, I'm such an idiot, why didn't I bring it?! . . ."

"Bring what?"

"Well, that file that I showed you . . . Don't you remember? . . ."

Suddenly, Kunicki struck his forehead. He almost said something but bit his lip.

"Yes, I remember," Dyzma said calmly. "A green folder."

"There is one way," Kunicki said hesitantly, after a long pause. "There is one way out of this . . . but . . ."

Dyzma lowered his eyes so Kunicki wouldn't see the anticipation dancing in them.

"What way?"

"Well . . . I wouldn't even dare to ask . . . But you know how important this is to me . . . To me and to you, too . . ."

"Of course, a million isn't exactly small potatoes."

"My dear Nicodemus!" Kunicki burst out. "You are the only man who can save this thing."

"Me?" Dyzma faked a look of surprise.

"*You*, sir, because you're the only man I can trust. Dear Nicodemus, dear sir, do not refuse me!"

"Refuse what?"

"It will be a bit tiring, true, but that hardly matters at your young age! Dear Nicodemus, sir, hightail it to Koborowo!"

He took a leather pouch from his pocket, keys clanking within.

"Save me! You're my only hope!"

Nicodemus shrugged.

"I don't like the idea of rummaging through somebody else's safe."

"Hell's bells, c'mon!" Kunicki folded his hands in a gesture of entreaty.

Nicodemus pretended to give it some thought.

"I'd have to rush like crazy, there and back . . . And I wouldn't get any sleep . . ."

"So what am I going to do, what am I going to do?" Kunicki lisped desperately. Dyzma drummed the desk with his fingers, then waved his hand.

"Ok, all right. Fine, I'll go."

The old man immediately began to lisp his gratitude, shaking Nicodemus's hand again and again, but Nicodemus could see flickers of obvious fear and distrust in his small, restless eyes.

"Which key is it?"

"This one, this one, and it's very simple to open, the top rosette just has to be set to nine and the bottom rosette to seven."

Dyzma took a pencil and wrote down both numbers.

"Well then, I'll have a bite to eat and then I'll get going. Please call for the car."

An hour later, after a short conversation with his secretary, Nicodemus went downstairs.

Kunicki was waiting for him at the gate. He was so nervous that it was no longer possible for him to hide it. He couldn't help but cast a suspicious eye at Dyzma as he gave him the last bits of information, explaining that the file folder was on the right side at the very top, and that absolutely all the documents regarding the lawsuit were there in the file, "so no need to look for them anywhere else—"

"Okay, okay." Dyzma cut him off and opened the car door.

"And, my dear Nicodemus, don't forget to relock the safe. And turn the rosettes."

"Done. See you later. Drive!"

The engine started. Fifteen minutes later, they had already left the city behind.

Nicodemus pulled a long, narrow steel key from his pocket and examined it with interest.

"Funny how something so damn small," he murmured to himself, "can do something so big."

The car sped down the familiar road. Soon it began to rain, and tiny droplets covered the windows. The early autumn twilight was closing in. Nicodemus adjusted his collar and, reflecting on the plan, dropped off to sleep. They stopped only once—to change the tire, since they'd run over a nail. By the time they saw the lights of Koborowo ahead of them, it was already completely dark. Dyzma hopped out when they reached the forecourt and gave the chauffeur instructions. The front door opened, and the servants ran out to greet him.

"Is Madam home?" Dyzma asked, not returning their bows.

"Yes, sir, she is. Madam is in the library, sir."

"Fine."

"Should I announce you, sir?"

"No need. You can go, I'll do it myself." He crossed the dark sitting room and opened the door.

Nina was sitting at the table, bent over a book. She didn't look up.

Nicodemus closed the door behind him and cleared his throat.

Only now did she look up at him, and a muffled cry escaped her lips. She jumped up and ran to him, flinging her arms around his neck.

"Nicky, Nicky, Nicky! . . ."

She squeezed him tight, her face shining with happiness.

"You came, you came! My sweet, my only!"

"How are you, Nee Nee?"

"My God, I've missed you so much!"

"You think I didn't?"

"Sit down! Tell me, how long can you stay?"

"Sadly, only a couple of hours."

"Oh, don't tell me such things! That's terrible."

"It's how it has to be."

She stroked his face with the tips of her fingers. Nicodemus briefly explained the purpose of his visit and added that he'd undertaken the trip so eagerly because it meant he'd be able to spend at least a few hours with her. She sat on his lap and, interrupting herself now and then to kiss his face, spoke of her longing, her love, the hope with which she awaited that happy moment when she would finally become his wife.

"If nothing unexpected happens," Dyzma interjected, "we'll be married sooner than you think."

"How's that possible? And the divorce? After all, divorce trials can last months."

"Fear not, we can do it without a divorce. I consulted a lawyer. Your marriage can be annulled."

"I don't know about that." Nina was dubious. "But anyway, you're very good to think about it."

Dinner was served. They went to the dining room. She asked Nicodemus about how he was spending his days. She was thrilled that he frequented the Czarskas and Roztockis, that he was a patron of the Literary Academy Project Development Committee, that he already had several tens of thousands of zlotys in the bank.

They rose from the table when the servant announced that the chauffeur was ready to go.

"Good. Tell him to wait."

He glanced at his watch and told Nina he had to hurry. She wanted to go with him to her husband's office, but Nicodemus asked her to wait for him in the dining room.

"But why?" She was surprised.

"Well . . . You see, I have to read over some papers and notes in there . . . And if you come with me, hee hee, I'll hardly be in the mood for work . . . Wait for me, I'll be back soon."

He turned on the lights and pushed aside the heavy velvet curtain.

There was a large, green fireproof safe in the recessed wall. Nicodemus gazed upon it with satisfaction. It occurred to him that a burglar would have to work extremely hard to get at the contents of this steel box, whereas he would be able to open it in less than a minute, with zero effort.

"If you have the brains," he muttered, "you don't need a skeleton key . . . True, it's not *my* scheme, it's Krzepicki's, but I'm reaping the benefits . . ."

The key slid silently into the lock, and with one turn of the handle, the safe stood open.

Inside, everything was in exemplary order. Books and paper-filled folders were carefully arranged on the shelves on the right, and stacks of banknotes were piled on the left. Two shelves held nothing but boxes, and Dyzma looked inside those first: jewelry. A huge quantity of gold rings, necklaces, brooches, diamonds, rubies. It was like a jewelry store in here.

But he had to hurry. Nicodemus took out all the files, books, and notepads. They made quite a stack. He brought everything over to the desk and, after setting the green folder aside, opened the first book. Flipping through the pages filled with dates and digits, he quickly realized that it was a book of Kunicki's debtors from the old days, back when he made a living as a usurer. This was made abundantly clear by the amount of interest collected. Among others, the name of Nina's father popped up frequently: "Count Ponimirski $12,000," "Count Ponimirski 10,000 zlotys," and so on and so forth.

Dyzma picked up the second book. It contained the records of Koborowo's income and revenue. The third, fourth, and fifth books were also filled with numbers.

These failed to hold Nicodemus's interest. He turned to the files. In the first, he found what he was looking for right away: the promissory notes. Actually, not the promissory notes, but blank bills of exchange. An entire file of them, all signed: Nina Kunicka, Nina Kunicka, Nina Kunicka . . . Beneath the promissory notes was the plenipotentiary power of attorney, issued by Nina in the name of her husband, and the notarized deed of sale of Koborowo to Nina. Dyzma folded the latter and put it into his pocket, then neatly tied up the file and put it on top of the green folder.

That was not, however, the end of his search. And the result was his crowning joy. He found two envelopes in the next file. There was an inscription on the small one: "My last will and testament"; and on the second one: "In the event of my death, burn without opening."

"In the event of his death," Nicodemus laughed. "But since he hasn't died, I'm free to open it."

He broke the wax seal and removed the contents. It was the Austrian passport that caught his attention first.

"I got you now, pal."

The passport was issued in the name of Leon Kunik, son of Genowefa Kunik and Father Unknown. Under the heading "Profession," there it was, in black and white: waiter.

The next document was the verdict of a Kraków court sentencing Leon Kunik to three months in jail for stealing silver cutlery. Beneath this was a bundle of letters and, again, a notebook, entirely filled, and another verdict of another court, this one in Warsaw, sentencing Kunicki to two years in prison for his complicity in a counterfeiting operation.

Nicodemus glanced at his watch and swore. It was already past midnight. He quickly gathered the scattered papers and put them in his pocket. He returned the rest of the items to the safe, locked it, and, with both files under his arm, he went to say goodbye to Nina.

She was waiting for him in the boudoir, a bit miffed by his long absence. However, she smiled up at him and asked, "Must you leave, dearest?"

"I have to. I can't help it." He sat down beside her and took her hand.

"Dearest Nee Nee," he began, reminding himself of the plan laid out by Krzepicki. "Dear Nee Nee, do you trust me, I mean truly?"

"How can you even ask that?" she said in a tone of reproach.

"Because, you see, you see . . . Let's just say that there are things on the horizon that will settle everything . . ."

"I don't understand."

"Everything will be settled. Either it goes on like before, which means you'll be with Kunicki until one of you dies, or we get married, and Kunicki can go to hell. The choice is yours."

"Nicky! It's obvious, isn't it?"

"I think so, too. So I'm asking you, Nee Nee, I'm asking you to trust me on this, agree to everything, don't contradict anything, and I'll do the rest."

"Yes, but why are you being so mysterious? Isn't it obvious?"

"Not everything is buttoned up quite yet," he said hesitantly, "but soon it'll be clear. He's an old man, and we have our entire lives ahead of us . . . Do you understand? . . ."

She felt a little uneasy, but she preferred not to ask too many questions. She simply said, "I trust you unconditionally."

"Everything's fine then!" He slapped his knees and stood up. "And now I have to go. See you, Nee Nee, see you soon . . ."

He put his arms around her and started kissing her.

"Goodbye, my sweet, and don't take me for a bad guy. Whatever I do, I do it because I love you more than anything."

"I know . . . ," she answered between kisses. "I know . . ."

Nicodemus gave her one more kiss on her forehead, then picked up his briefcase and left. In the hall, as a servant was helping him with his coat, she bade him an official farewell:

"Goodbye, sir. I wish you a safe trip. And as for the matter discussed, do whatever you consider correct . . . I have to believe you that it's necessary . . . I have to believe someone, after all . . . Goodbye . . ."

"Goodbye, Madam. Everything will be fine."

"Please visit us soon."

"I'll come as soon as I can get away."

He kissed her hand. The servant opened the door, and Nicodemus, in the pouring rain, ran the few steps it took to reach the car.

"This goddamn weather," he swore as he closed the door.

"It'll be coming down all night long, you can be sure of that," the chauffeur said.

Indeed, the rain did not stop until morning, and the car, when it arrived in Warsaw, was caked in mud.

It was not even eight o'clock when Dyzma opened the door to his apartment. Despite the early hour, Krzepicki was already there. They closed the door to the neighboring rooms to prevent any servants from eavesdropping and began poring over the documents Nicodemus had brought back to Warsaw.

Krzepicki was ecstatic. He rubbed his hands with glee, and when they found, in a bundle of letters, the evidence of his bribing an official regarding the old lawsuit, he leapt up and cried, "Well, what are we waiting for? Let's go to the Office of Investigations right now!"

"And the promissory notes?" Dyzma asked.

"Promissory notes . . . hmm . . . You could always keep them in case there's any change in Lady Nina's feelings or intentions, but it's really safer to burn them. That is, of course, if you're sure that Lady Nina will marry you."

"I've got that nailed down nice and tight."

"Great. Then let's go."

Detective Chief Inspector Reich, head of the Office of Investigations, belonged to that class of people who are uncompromising in their fight for survival. Cold, brilliant, analytical, and razor-sharp, he immediately sussed out President Dyzma's intentions. In spite of Krzepicki's lush eloquence, which attempted to weave a story of selflessness on the part of his boss, Inspector Reich finally asked, "Mr. President, do you mean to marry Madam Kunicka?"

Dyzma had no choice but to admit that, indeed, he had given it some thought.

"Do not assume, Mr. President, that I wish to interfere in your personal affairs. Far from it. However, I believe that putting Kunicki in prison will result in a court trial, purely as a natural consequence."

"Right," Krzepicki confirmed.

"Well," the commissioner continued, "such a trial would naturally cause a sensation, and perhaps it would not be an entirely pleasant state of affairs for your future wife or, for that matter, Mr. President, for you."

"Hmm . . . so what can we do?"

Chief Inspector Reich sat in silence for a moment.

"Mr. President," he began thoughtfully, "there is a way to solve this problem . . ."

"What is it?"

"Let us assume that Kunicki is facing ten or at the very least six years of hard time. This is beyond a doubt. The evidence is ironclad, there's no getting around it. Well, what would you say, Mr. President, if we try to make some kind of arrangement with Kunicki? . . ."

"Arrangement?"

"Well, yes. I think that the prospect of ten years in the clink might put him in the right frame of mind to accept a proposal from us. How's this: he waives any claims on property belonging to his wife and you, and in exchange you give him a set amount of money and a foreign passport. Let him go wherever he wants, we'll just throw him there head-first."

"But he could always come back later on."

"Well, we can prevent that. Here's what we'll do: I'll arrest him, interrogate him, maybe rough him up a little, I'll show him all the scribbling in those books and lock him up for, let's say, three days. That'll soften him up some. After that, I'll interrogate him again, and that's when I'll make our offer. If he doesn't accept, so much the worse for him. If he does accept, I'll give him a passport and allow him to escape somewhere abroad. Escape! Do you understand, gentlemen? Escaping means not being able to come back, because then I'd have to issue a warrant for him. What do you say to that, Mr. President?"

"Very smart," Krzepicki nodded.

"I think so, too," Dyzma added.

"It is indeed," Reich continued, "a perfect plan, but I don't know if I'll be able to carry it out. Consider my situation, gentlemen. If this plot were to be discovered, I would be the one to take the fall. My dismissal would be a certainty, and I might even face jail time. So it's a risk—"

"Chief Inspector," Krzepicki interjected, "it seems to me that these fears have no basis. Consider the president's connections within the government.

Nowhere in Warsaw can you find a man who is more capable of making things happen than Bank President Dyzma."

Chief Inspector Reich bowed.

"Oh, I'm well aware of that. It would be my pleasure to do such a small favor for such an estimable person, all the more so because I have no doubt that President Dyzma will keep me in his grateful memory."

"Naturally," Dyzma nodded.

"My heartfelt thanks, Mr. President. To prove how highly I value your support, Mr. President, I was just thinking that one of these days I'm going to pay you a visit with a small request."

"I'll be happy to do whatever I can."

"To you, Mr. President, it's a mere trifle, but to me it's very important. That is, the deputy chief of police is leaving his post at the beginning of the year. If I had the support of such a distinguished personage as yourself, Mr. President, I could certainly count on the nomination . . ."

"And who does it depend on?" Nicodemus asked.

"The minister of internal affairs."

"Well, in that case," said Dyzma, "it's a done deal, no need to worry. He's a friend of mine."

"My heartfelt, heartfelt thanks."

He jumped up to shake Nicodemus's hand.

They began to go over the details of the case. Reich and Krzepicki didn't neglect even the smallest detail, and Dyzma listened with awe, acknowledging to himself that there was no way he would ever have been able to do this on his own.

When they returned to the bank, Kunicki was already there. Every movement, every expression on his face and in his eyes—it all betrayed his enormous disquiet. Krzepicki gave him an ironic look as he passed, but Kunicki didn't notice. He skittered up to Dyzma and lisped, "You came back! I'm so happy. Did you bring the file?"

"Good morning. Yes, I did."

"Nicodemus, sir, I really don't understand what it all means!"

"What?"

"This meeting with the minister! Scoopak told me it was postponed. The minister's not leaving after all. Nicodemus, he never had any intention of leaving. What's the meaning of all this?"

"Let's go to my apartment," Dyzma said, starting to flush. "I'll explain it to you there."

"I really, truly don't understand," he lisped relentlessly, trotting after Nicodemus.

"Ignacy, you can leave," Dyzma said to the servant. "Take the rest of the day off."

When Ignacy had left, he turned to Kunicki.

"Mr. Kunicki . . . hmm . . . Well, your wife has decided to divorce you."

"What?!" Kunicki jumped up.

"You heard me. She's divorcing you and marrying me instead."

Kunicki shot Dyzma a black look.

"Oh, really . . . Perhaps she came here with you?"

"No, she stayed in Koborowo."

The old man bit his lip.

"Just when did my wife make this decision? After all, it's impossible! She didn't mention anything like that to me! Is this a passing fancy, perhaps? A fancy resulting from your dastardly machinations . . ."

"What machinations are those? She just fell in love with me. She was fed up with being married to an old geezer."

"But this old geezer," Kunicki hissed, "has millions."

"He's got zip. Both the millions and the estate belong to Nina."

"On paper, only on paper, my dear sir! Not much there to covet!"

"Or is there?" Dyzma replied philosophically.

"Unfortunately, I'm very sorry to inform you," Kunicki laughed viciously, "there's the little matter of my wife's promissory notes, which I have in my possession and which are issued for an amount that covers the estate's entire value and more."

Nicodemus stuck his hands in his pockets and puckered his lips.

"As for the promissory notes, Mr. Kunicki, there were indeed promissory notes, that's true. At least there used to be, but not anymore."

Kunicki turned deathly pale. Trembling from head to toe and struggling to catch his breath, he moaned, "What? What? . . . What do you mean?"

"I mean just what I said."

"You stole them?! You stole those notes from me?! The key, give me back the key to the safe right now!"

"I'm not giving you the key."

"This is a robbery! You're a thief, a bandit! I'll make sure you end up in prison!"

"Shut up, you old crook!" Dyzma roared.

"Robbery! Give me the key!"

"No, because the key isn't yours. Don't you get it, you dum-dum? It's not yours, it's Nina's. *Her* fortune, *her* safe, and *her* key."

"Oh, no you don't! You villain, don't think that old Kunicki will let you pull the wool over his eyes. There's still justice in Poland, there are courts!

There are witnesses who will testify that I gave you the key. Don't get ahead of yourself, pal! Nina, too, will have to swear an oath that she signed the promissory notes over to me."

"Don't worry, I'll take care of that."

"There are still courts!" Kunicki fumed.

The doorbell sounded from the hall.

"You bastard, where do you get off, trying to scare me with the courts, pthu!" Dyzma spat on the floor and went to open the door.

"Scoundrel! Scoundrel!" Kunicki was running around the room like a fox in a cage. "I need to go to the prosecutor, the police, right away . . ."

But he didn't need to go there after all: the door opened and a sergeant and two plainclothes detectives entered the room.

"Are you Leon Kunicki, aka Leon Kunik?" the sergeant asked in a hoarse voice.

"Yes, I'm Kunicki."

"You're under arrest. Put on your coat and come with us."

"Me? Under arrest? But for what? It must be a mistake."

"There's no mistake. Here's the warrant."

"But what for?"

"That's not my business," the sergeant shrugged. "They'll tell you at the Office of Investigations. Well, move! Got a weapon?"

"No."

"Search him!"

The detectives searched his pockets. There was no weapon.

"Well, move! Our respects, Mr. President. I'm sorry for disturbing you, but I had my orders."

"Orders are orders," Dyzma said. "Goodbye."

Kunicki turned his head, wanting to say something, but the intelligence officer gave him a shove, and he staggered and then found himself all at once on the other side of the door.

Nicodemus stood in the empty hall for a long time. Finally, he went to the mirror and smoothed his hair, then headed into the dining room. His breakfast was waiting on the table; he hadn't thought about it until now. He felt a sharp pang of hunger. The coffee was already cold, and the sugar wouldn't dissolve in it. He took a carafe of vodka from the sideboard, loaded his plate with heaps of ham, sausage, and veal, and fell on his food.

"Apparently, I was destined to be a great man," he said, slurping his third glass. "To your health, Mr. Bank President!"

A fine, stinging rain lashed against the windows, and outside it was gray.

Chapter 15

Dyzma did not like General Jarzynowski for several reasons: because of his perpetually derisive expression, because of his chilly reserve, but mostly because the general's closest friend was Terkowski. Accordingly, despite multiple invitations, Dyzma had steered clear of calling on Jarzynowski. But this evening he was finally going to have to put in an appearance, since the general had announced that "the bank president's absence would be considered a personal insult." Anyway, Dyzma knew that Terkowski was taking the waters at Żegiestów, so he was guaranteed not to see him there.

In fact, he didn't have any real reasons for avoiding Terkowski. He had no personal antipathy for him, but rumor universally had it they were bitter enemies. This rumor was so ubiquitous that Nicodemus ended up believing it himself, and he was just smart enough to note Terkowski's obvious reserve and use it as evidence of their mutual enmity. Fortunately, Dyzma was too powerful to necessitate giving this fact undue consideration. He did prefer, however, to bypass any contact with Terkowski, and for another reason altogether: he had guessed from the hints the "pilgrim" ladies dropped that the prime minister's fat chief of staff had some connection with "the initiated," which frankly gave him the willies.

The Jarzynowskis lived on Wilcza Street, and Dyzma set off on foot. It looked to be quite a gathering, since more than a dozen cars were parked at the gate. The entrance hall was literally overflowing with coats, and from the neighboring rooms came a steady roar of laughter and conversation.

The general and his wife met Dyzma with deferential greetings and led him to a drawing room where a hush had just fallen and some heavyset woman with arms that called to mind great slabs of ham was settling herself at the piano. Out of social necessity, he stopped before the doors and acknowledged the nods of various acquaintances with many silent nods of his own, not realizing at first to whom he was sending his mute greetings. The first person he recognized among the sea of black tailcoats was Terkowski.

"God damn it to hell," he muttered to himself as the first crashing piano chords resounded throughout the room.

He resolved to maneuver around Terkowski so as not to meet him face-to-face, a plan that was, given how many people were there, completely feasible, all the more so because Dyzma assumed that Terkowski himself had no great desire for an encounter.

So Dyzma was astonished when, a few minutes later, Fatso made a bee-line for him. Terkowski pressed his hand and lightly clapped him on the shoulder, whispering, "Let's have a smoke."

Every eye followed them as they left the salon and disappeared behind some curtains into the general's study.

Terkowski drew from his pocket a huge gold cigarette case and offered one to Nicodemus.

"The honorable president of the Grain Bank!" he began cordially. "It's been ages since I've seen you."

Dyzma, surprised and mistrustful, didn't say anything.

"How's your health?" Fatty continued. "As for me, I feel great, thanks to six weeks of rest and relaxation. Would you believe that I lost seven kilos? Not too shabby, huh?"

"Pretty good," Dyzma replied.

"There's nothing like it, Mr. President, nothing like a good rest. A change of scenery, right? New people, new activities, new lifestyle, new scenery . . ."

"You were in Żegiestów?" Nicodemus asked, in order to have something to say.

"Yes. I found it thoroughly refreshing."

Dyzma could hear the distant banging of the piano from the salon, and fragments of bridge players' bids drifted from the neighboring room. Terkowski continued to drone away in a dull, heavy voice that seemed to emanate from somewhere under his enormous white dickey. His small, fishy eyes swam beneath their thick eyelids, and his stubby little fingers caressed his big cigarette case.

What does this jerk want from me? Dyzma thought, struggling to figure it out.

"Do you know, Mr. President," Terkowski continued, not changing his tone, "I had the pleasure of meeting an old friend of yours, a very nice fellow, a certain notary named Winder."

Terkowski suddenly fell silent, his eyes searching Nicodemus's face.

Dyzma truly hadn't heard him, and asked, "What did you say?"

"I met an old friend of yours."

Nicodemus's jaw clenched.

"Who might that be?"

"Mr. Winder. Very nice fellow."

"What? Winder? . . . I don't recall him."

It took every ounce of his will to master his outward appearance. He forced himself to look Terkowski straight in the eye.

"What do you mean? Are you telling me you don't recall knowing a notary named Winder? . . ."

"A notary? . . . No. I don't know him."

Terkowski chuckled with explicit irony.

"Well, he remembers *you* very well. We were riding in the same compartment, and that lovely old man told me all about you and all about Łysków . . ."

Dyzma's head was spinning. Was this the end? Catastrophe? Was he finally exposed? In his pockets, his fists were clenched so tightly they hurt. The thought flashed through his mind of simply pouncing on Terkowski, grabbing him by the neck, that fat neck of his with its folds spilling over his collar, seizing his neck and squeezing until his disgusting face turned blue.

"Deepest apologies." This sudden voice, of a lady who had accidentally jostled him while passing, yanked him out of his reverie and back to the present moment.

"What's this about Łysków? What are you talking about?" He shrugged his shoulders. "It must be some kind of hoax. I don't know any Winder."

Terkowski raised his eyebrows and coolly flicked the ash from his cigarette.

"Ah, of course," he said smoothly. "Perhaps it's merely a misunderstanding."

"I'm sure it's just a misunderstanding," Nicodemus said with relief.

"These things can happen. All the better, then, that we'll soon be able to clear it all up. Notary Winder will be arriving in Warsaw next week. I invited him myself—after all, he's a very, very nice fellow. Evidently, he's been talking about someone who has the honor of sharing your name, or perhaps it's even some relation of yours . . . Hee hee!"

Dyzma didn't have time to respond. The concert in the salon had ended, and, amid thunderous applause, dozens of people poured into the study, surrounding them in a dense circle.

The remainder of the evening felt like walking over hot coals, until finally, at around midnight, Dyzma quietly slipped out.

A fine, sharp rain lashed his face. Not even bothering to fasten his coat, he trudged home. Once there, he threw himself onto the couch without getting undressed.

It was an open-and-shut case.

The ball was in Terkowski's court. And Terkowski wasn't one for letting things slide. He was a vengeful son of a bitch. And dealing with him wasn't like dealing with Boczek . . .

A shudder ran through him.

He stood, turned on every light, took off his overcoat, hat, and tailcoat, and began to pace around the room. Inside his skull, his thoughts whirled like a spinning wheel until his forehead was glazed with sweat.

So let's say Winder turns up dead . . . Would it be possible to make that happen? . . . Case closed, problem solved?

Now that Terkowski had picked up the trail of Łysków, he wouldn't let himself be thrown off the scent. And if Winder disappeared, well! Right away he'd know I had something to do with it . . . I wouldn't just get fired. They'd put me away . . .

Ask him nicely? Sure, like that would accomplish a goddamned thing.

He knew all too well what Terkowski was.

There was a buzzing in his head. It was a long, sleepless night. He felt terribly helpless and alone. He had no one to confide in, not even Krzepicki. What to do . . . What to do . . .

He didn't eat his breakfast and ordered Ignacy to phone the bank and tell them he was feeling ill and wouldn't be coming in. But half an hour later it occurred to him that word of his absence might get back to Terkowski. He was flooded with ire. He gave Ignacy a baseless dressing down and headed to the bank. Here he made an ostentatious inspection of every office; he looked in on Wandryszewski and picked a fight with him about the lateness of some balance sheet, even though the previous day he had approved a three-day delay. He grunted a hello to Krzepicki and then closed and locked his office door.

He spent a long time speculating about whether Terkowski might have already gone to someone with this tidbit of information and his attendant suspicions, but he concluded that a cunning man in possession of such an advantage would not be inclined to share it with anybody. As for its use? Dyzma didn't delude himself. Terkowski was itching for a scandal to topple him—him and Jaszuński, and Pilchen . . .

Which meant there was only one way out: hand in his resignation immediately, gather up what cash he could, not forgetting about the safe in Koborowo, grab his passport, and flee before Notary Winder arrived in Warsaw. Of course, the marriage to Nina was a bust. Kunicki would have to be released and some reconciliation would have to be made . . . So he wouldn't sue . . .

"Shit . . ."

The telephone rang. It was Krzepicki announcing the arrival of Countess Koniecpolska along with another woman. They insisted on seeing him.

"Tell them I'm sick."

"That's what I did tell them," explained Krzepicki, "and they told me to announce them anyway, because 'Mr. President will surely accept.'"

In a black gloom, he set down the receiver and opened the door.

"Please," he said brusquely.

Madam Koniecpolska's companion was that demonic Miss Stella. His mood grew blacker still.

They began to make tender inquiries about his health and offer suggestions about various doctors.

Finally, they expressed their conviction that this indisposition would by no means interfere with the Master's timely appearance at the Mystery of the Lodge. That time, incidentally, was tomorrow; unfortunately, Madam Koniecpolska's husband was *not* out of town, and the Mystery would have to be held at the Great Thirteenth's apartment instead.

And with that, Dyzma's irritation was complete.

"Just give me some peace and quiet! I can't think about this right now!"

"The Master will recover by tomorrow," Miss Stella declared peremptorily. "And the obligation to the Thrice-Rayed Star must be fulfilled."

"What's this 'recover,' I don't need to 'recover,'" Dyzma snapped. "My health is fine, I just don't have the head for this right now. I have my hands full with more important matters!"

Silence fell. Dyzma, chin in hand, turned his face to the window.

"Mein master," Madam Koniecpolska said quietly, "are you in zome kind of troubles?"

Dyzma laughed ironically.

"Trouble, trouble . . . ha ha, trouble . . . Some shithead has shown up to give me a hard time . . ."

"Oh, but Master, surely you can handle anyone," Miss Stella said confidently.

Dyzma gave her a serious look.

"Not everyone. How about a guy who digs up dirt like a pig, a slanderer who lies like a dog . . . Who wants to drag a man's name through the mud, to drive him out . . ."

Miss Stella's eyes narrowed.

"Whoever could such a man be?"

Dyzma waved his hand dismissively and said nothing.

"Tell us, Master, who it is who opposes you."

"What am I even saying . . ."

"You must tell us," cried Madam Koniecpolska, her voice rising. "You must! Perhaps zere is a somezing we can zink of, some way."

"The Order of the Thrice-Rayed Star is powerful," Miss Stella added gravely.

Nicodemus lifted his head from his hunched shoulders and, surprising even himself, responded, "Terkowski."

Surprise flashed across both women's faces. Dyzma silently cursed himself: What had he told these dames for? Idiot!

Miss Stella stood and solemnly approached Dyzma.

"Master! You have the right to command it. Must this man *disappear*?"

Dyzma was alarmed. This chick was nuts.

"Master!" Miss Stella persisted. "Must he be removed once and for all, or only for a certain amount of time? Command it."

Nicodemus burst out laughing. It seemed such childish nonsense—this squat lady ape, in all seriousness, with a voice like she was delivering a sermon, was asking what should be done with such an influential tycoon as Terkowski. At the same time, however, the thought occurred to him that Winder's arrival was only a few short days away. And then that would be that. It would all come to an end. Terkowski would team up with Winder . . . Unless Terkowski wasn't in Warsaw when Winder got there.

"Let them send Terkowski up a tree in Africa or somewhere else in the middle of goddamn nowhere!" he spat with a bitter sneer.

"When?" Miss Stella asked resolutely.

"Let's make it today, ha ha ha . . . You're a real cutup, aren't you? But c'mon, let's not bother ourselves with fairy tales. So what about this Mystery?"

The ladies insisted that the Mystery deadline be met. Afraid that some indefinite misfortune might befall him if his part in the ritual remained unfulfilled, Dyzma capitulated and agreed that the second gathering of the Lodge of the Thrice-Rayed Star would be held at his place.

That evening, he went out to Oasis with Wareda to drown his sorrows and, returning home, collapsed into bed and was dead to the world.

The next morning began with Miss Stella and Madam Koniecpolska turning his entire apartment—which he had left to their mercy—upside down. Dyzma wanted to keep this whole Mystery business under wraps, so good old Ignacy had been given a three-day vacation. It was for this reason that all the heavy lifting, all the moving of furniture and rolling up of rugs, fell on him alone.

Part of him didn't mind at all, since it left him less time to dwell on Terkowski and the threat of Winder's arrival. The ladies made no mention of Terkowski. Apparently they'd forgotten. So much the better, he thought. I shouldn't have spilled my guts to them in the first place. With renewed fury, he attacked the furniture and rugs.

Which is why, when evening fell, he was so worn out that he would gladly have shut himself in his room and locked the door. Unfortunately, his bedroom—along with three other rooms and the bathroom to boot—had been designated a dressing room for the pilgrims.

Around eleven, they hit quite an obstacle; it turned out that, because her husband had come home ahead of schedule, one of the ladies was unable to attend. Since the rules were firm about the need for twelve pilgrims, the other ladies were plunged into despair.

Nicodemus, meanwhile, proposed they put off the Mystery until the following week, but Miss Stella indignantly declared that this would be a violation of the principles and that she, for one, never followed the path of least resistance. There had to be some way to do this. Then one of the ladies, Baroness Wehlberg, suddenly and surprisingly came to the rescue. She knew a girl whom they could, without fear of betrayal, rent for the night. She was nice and young, a *fille* from one of the cabarets. The baroness knew her well; before her marriage, she herself had performed in that very same cabaret and was aware that this little Władzia could be entrusted with many a secret.

There were no other options, so it was agreed that little Władzia should be telephoned at once. At first, she refused, on account of the chagrin it would cause for the friend with whom she'd agreed to dance at the cabaret that night, but she eventually allowed herself to be persuaded through eloquent argument and reason, otherwise known as a hundred in cash. Thanks to her, the Mystery was able to commence at the stroke of midnight with the entire ritual intact.

At one o'clock, during the Satan summoning, there was a bit of an incident with Władzia. Already more than a little dazed, she burst out crying and screamed that she wanted to go home. They barely managed to convince her to stay, but after a glass of wine with peyote, she calmed down completely.

By two o'clock, President Nicodemus Dyzma's living room did not resemble a living room in the slightest, and especially not the living room of a bank president. It rather called to mind a smokehouse with a touch of the Roman baths, but most of all the type of "house" that might be preceded by "cat" or followed by "of ill repute."

The pale light of late December daybreak was peeping through the slits of the curtains when the assembled company adjourned to their separate rooms. Only the Great Thirteenth remained on the field of action. He sat propped against the wall, his snoring nearly enough to rattle the windowpanes.

It was well into the afternoon when he finally woke up. He was infernally exhausted, and his head spun and throbbed. He got dressed and poked his head into his bedroom. The pilgrims were beginning to rouse themselves. In the bathroom, there was a crowd. One after the other, they said their goodbyes to Dyzma and left, barely managing to stay on their feet.

At last he was alone. He opened all the windows and lumbered to and fro in an attempt to bring the apartment back into some kind of order.

He had just moved the piano back to its old position when, in the hallway, the doorbell rang. In came Krzepicki.

"Oh ho ho, Nicodemus, sir!" he hailed. "You must have had quite a night."

Ever since Kunicki's arrest, the intimacy between them had increased to the point where he no longer addressed his boss as "Mr. President."

"To hell with all of this," Dyzma said grimly.

"Just look at you!" Krzepicki was impressed. "I didn't know you liked that sort of thing."

"Who the hell said anything about liking it?!"

"Ah, so it's for the purposes of self-mortification?"

"Why don't you go to hell," Dyzma bristled. "You could always offer to help."

"But why are you doing it all yourself? Where did Ignacy go?"

Dyzma, panting, didn't answer. Finally, he swore and threw himself onto the couch. Krzepicki lit a cigarette.

"I've come from Reich."

"And?"

"Kunik finally caved. A night in a dark cell with no heat did the trick. He was quite adamant about seeing his wife—that was his only demand. He only gave in after Reich read him and then showed him that letter from Nina, the most recent one she sent you. He agreed on a hundred thousand, but on the condition that the compromising documents are handed over to him."

"And?

"Of course, Reich was too smart to take him up on it. He promised him one thing, that the documents would remain at his home, not in the files of the Office of Investigations."

"Did he end up going for it?"

"He said that he needed another day to think. Don't worry. He's going to have to agree to it."

He rose, flicked the ash from his cigarette, and added, "And while we're on the subject, you should let Lady Nina know that her husband has been released and, of his own will, is going abroad . . . Hmm . . . Maybe you can even write that he's taking half his assets in cash and securities. It'll allay her curiosity, so to speak."

"Yes," Dyzma remarked after a moment of thought. "Finessing it a little wouldn't hurt. I just think it's better not to put it in writing. A letter like that might fall into the wrong hands or something."

Nicodemus suddenly thought of Terkowski and shuddered. No, no . . . He resolved to put it out of his head, no matter what. What would be, would be. Just don't think about it . . . at least, not now. Koborowo . . . He should head out there . . . None of his limbs would obey him. He grimaced and said, "Just not today."

Indeed, Dyzma was thoroughly enfeebled. He spent the entire day lying frailly on the couch. He didn't even pick up the phone, which rang several dozen times.

His thoughts were concentrated on how he might safely retire from the Lodge of the Thrice-Rayed Star. This second all-night orgy, which had both frightened him and reduced him to an exhausted shell of a man, had definitely affected his stance toward the honorable role of the Great Thirteenth.

Besides, it was logical to assume that, thanks to the Lodge, he had established an extremely special acquaintance with these ladies from the very highest society, and that their doors had been opened to him, and if he now managed somehow to wriggle out of the Order, it wouldn't necessarily diminish these relations he had worked so hard to earn.

But how to wriggle out? His best bet would be to consult Krzepicki, who always had a ready solution. But this he couldn't do. Cemented in his memory was the penalty of death for betraying the Secrets of the Lodge.

Then, after much contemplation, an idea came to him: Might it not work best to tell those crazy dames that, this very evening, the devil had forbidden him from continuing the whole "thirteenth" thing? . . . He doesn't like me much, and he announced that he won't appear anymore as long as I'm there . . . He resolved to go to Countess Koniecpolska's first thing tomorrow and put the matter to rest.

Let them wear someone else out. He chuckled to himself: Wareda had popped into his head. He'd stick Wareda with this mess! He'd tell them the devil urgently wanted Wareda instead.

Ignacy brought dinner and laid out the evening newspapers. Dyzma pushed them aside with distaste and was just about to take a bite of food when the phone rang.

It was Wareda. After a brief hello, he asked, "Well, have you read?"

"Read what?" Dyzma mumbled.

"What you do mean, 'what'? Are you playing dumb? How can you not know?"

"So tell me!"

"Well, Terkowski's gone."

Dyzma staggered to his feet.

"If . . . so . . . huh?"

"Yep, he left this evening for Peking as an envoy to the new post. You haven't read the evening papers?"

He was saying something else, but Dyzma had stopped listening. He threw the receiver into its cradle and ran back to the dining room.

He quickly unfolded the newspapers.

Indeed, all of them were reporting that, in connection with the newly established government in China, the former head of the cabinet of the prime minister, Undersecretary of State Jan Terkowski, had been appointed envoy and minister plenipotentiary to the Chinese government and was leaving today for Peking.

Dyzma lifted his eyes from the paper. Inside his chest, his heart was beating like a hammer.

He sprang from his seat and began to shout, " Hooray! Hooray! Hooray!"

A bewildered Ignacy rushed in, stopping in the doorway.

"Did you call, sir?"

"Ignacy! Bring vodka. We must raise a toast!"

The servant fetched a carafe and a glass and poured Dyzma a drink.

"Pour one for yourself, too!" cried Dyzma. "To sons of bitches twisting in the wind!"

They drank. One, another, a third, a fourth . . .

Nicodemus sat down.

"You know what, Ignacy?"

"What, Mr. President?"

"Listen up. Whoever gets in my way, whoever crosses me, Nicodemus goddamn Dyzma, better watch his step. Understood?"

He knocked back his drink, and his eyes involuntarily went to the black crack between the doors of his office—round, glowing eyes seemed to stare out at him from the darkness. He spat and made the sign of the cross.

"Let's drink, Ignacy!"

It was long past midnight when, crawling into bed, Dyzma said to his servant, "Listen, Ignacy, women can turn the whole world upside down, because they have the devil on their side."

"That's for sure," Ignacy agreed.

Chapter 16

On Tuesday, Nicodemus and Krzepicki went to see Mr. Licuński, an attorney specializing in divorce cases. On Wednesday, they paid a final visit to Commissioner Reich, leaving his office one hundred thousand zlotys lighter.

On Thursday, over at the main railway station, two trains were set to depart in two opposite directions. In one sat a hunched old man, trembling all over. In the other sat the president of the National Grain Bank, cheerfully saying goodbye to a group of friends who had accompanied him to the station with best wishes and congratulations.

But the old man on the first train was not alone either. A stocky, red-faced fellow sat in the other corner of the compartment, his right hand hidden in his coat pocket in a particular way, which, in this case, was the result of professional habit and not necessity.

The Warsaw-Berlin train left first. The other one, the Białystok-Grodno, left less than ten minutes later.

Hopping off the steps of one of the passenger cars at the last minute was Krzepicki who, in a few brief sentences, gave his boss a hurried report of his conversation with Kunicki at the Office of Investigations before his departure. The secretary reported that Kunicki was not making any difficulties, that he was completely resigned—nay, broken inside—and that he'd handed over the information and explanations regarding Koborowo's interests to the new administrator, who, by order of the owner's fiancé and plenipotentiary, was now Krzepicki.

Dyzma was fully satisfied.

He made himself comfortable in the empty compartment and started to think about his next steps.

That he'd renounce the bank presidency was beyond question. Because what would he need this whole bank rigmarole for? Koborowo's colossal income, a life of comfort and peace, no need to watch his every word, no constant fear of saying something inappropriate—everything pointed to quitting the bank.

Of course, he was aware that he would not be able to administer the Koborowo estate himself.

Fortunately, he had Krzepicki, and Krzepicki could do anything. Dyzma didn't doubt it was unwise to place excessive trust in his secretary when it came to finances. But he comforted himself with the thought that Krzepicki wouldn't do anything to put such a lucrative position in jeopardy.

Dyzma gazed out the window of his compartment. Vast plains covered with thick snow stretched as far as the eye could see.

Terkowski popped into his head, and he clenched his jaw. By now he was well aware that he owed his freedom from Terkowski's persecution to the ladies from the Lodge. What methods they used, what web of connections they had at their disposal, he didn't know and didn't want to know. He was afraid of them. He was even more afraid than he'd been before, when he'd trembled at these dames' familiarity with ghosts. After all, the living are more dangerous than the dead.

So he did not abandon his resolution to leave the Lodge as soon as possible. Of course, he'd maintain the closest possible relationship with these ladies; he'd just install Wareda as his replacement.

He chuckled to himself as he imagined the solemn faces of Madam Koniecpolska and Miss Stella as he grimly broke the news about "the will of Satan." Now it would be the colonel's turn to deal with that dog and pony show!

The train dipped into a forest corridor.

Evening was approaching, a foggy winter evening, when the railroad switches of Koborowo thudded under the train's wheels. On the platform stood a few railway workers and Nina. She spotted Nicodemus in the window, and a smile lit up her face.

She threw out her arms to greet him, so he had to put his suitcase in the snow.

"At last, at last . . ."

They crossed through the empty station and got into the car. The motor growled, the wheels slipped and spun in the snow, and finally they pulled away.

"Tell me, tell me, did he . . . did he . . . agree right away?"

Her voice quavered with anxiety. Dyzma laughed.

"He had to."

"What do you mean, 'he had to'?" she asked apprehensively.

"Nee Nee," he said shortly, "you said it yourself: love conquers all."

The lanterns lit up just as they were passing the sawmills. The few people standing along the road took off their hats.

"But what . . . what will he do now?"

"What do we care?" Nicodemus shrugged. "He took everything that was in the bank. It was worth almost as much as Koborowo. He's not going to die of hunger."

"Did he go abroad?"

"Yes."

"Then won't he come back at some point?"

"No way. I guarantee it."

She was thinking.

"Nicky, you said that he *had* to agree. Were . . . were there any reasons of another nature? . . ."

"Don't you have anything else to worry about, Nee Nee? It's over and done with. Why do you care?"

"He was my husband, after all . . ."

"And I'm telling you that he never *was* your husband."

She was surprised.

"What do you mean he wasn't?"

He began to explain, at least to the best of his abilities, the complex procedure for annulling a marriage, repeating the attorney's arguments.

"In two months, if all goes well, you'll once again be Miss Ponimirska, and in three months, if you still want to, you'll be my wife."

She was silent.

Dyzma was somewhat troubled. Maybe now she was changing her mind . . . Maybe, having tasted freedom, she wouldn't be so excited about tying herself to him.

"Why are you so quiet, dear Nee Nee?" he asked as sweetly as he could.

"Ah, it's nothing, nothing." She shook off her reverie. "I was thinking about what you just told me. But there's no need to think about it, right? . . . It's passed, it's over . . . This is apparently the way it had to be . . ."

She hugged him.

"That's life," he said with conviction.

"I'm afraid of life. Life is dangerous."

"I'm not afraid of it."

"Oh, I know, because you're strong, so terribly strong."

Every window in Koborowo glowed with light. Nina explained that she had recently ordered that every evening be illuminated so thoroughly; she was afraid of the dark.

All the servants were gathered in the hall.

They admittedly had no concrete information, but based on the fragmentary observations of the chauffeur who'd returned from Warsaw without the master, they had drawn a few conclusions. These were confirmed by Madam's unprecedented trip to the station.

They sensed something was afoot. Nina's term was "intuition," whereas Nicodemus called it "sniffing something out." At any rate, he saw no sign of surprise on the maid's face when he ordered her to make up a bed for him in Kunicki's master bedroom.

Nina was fretting that she would be alone once again when he went back to Warsaw.

"You can come too, Nee Nee. I'll take you with me."

"Ah," she smiled, "if only that were possible."

"And why not?" He was confused.

"What do you mean? It wouldn't be proper! Don't you understand what a scandal it would cause?"

"Pff," he shrugged, "no big deal. After all, we're getting married. Anyway, you could stay at a hotel, and we could see each other every day."

She clapped her hands together.

"I know, I know! Auntie Przełęska! I will stay at Aunt Przełęska's!"

"See, there you go!"

"But I'd rather not prolong my stay in Warsaw too much. I don't like cities. I feel my best in Koborowo. We will live permanently in Koborowo, won't we, Nicky?"

"Music to my ears. I've been up to my eyeballs in Warsaw, I've had enough."

"You're so good. Come, I'll play you something I always play when I'm thinking about you."

They went to a small sitting room. Nina opened the piano.

"Do you play?" she asked.

"Only the mandolin."

She laughed.

"You're joking, right?"

"I swear to God."

"That's hilarious, you playing the mandolin."

"Why?"

"I don't know, it just seems so terribly funny to me. Such a serious man, a president, a statesman, and all of a sudden—the mandolin."

"I regret that I left it in Warsaw. I'd play something for you, too."

She kissed him on the lips, but when he moved to embrace her, she slipped out of his arms, laughing, and began to play.

"Do you like it?" she asked, closing the lid.

"Yes. Very much. How do the words go?"

"Words?" She was surprised. "Oh, you thought it was from an opera! No, this is a sonata, do you know by whom?"

"By whom?"

"Tchaikovsky."

"Well, it's a nice piece. What's it called?"

"C-sharp Minor."

"See a sharp miner? Silly. Why a miner? And what's so sharp about him?" Nina, amused, wrapped her arms around his neck.

"My master is in a playful mood today. Oh . . . now I get it, this mandolin of yours was also a joke. Naughty boy! Teasing your little Nee Nee like that. Nee Nee! Do you know that no one has ever called me that before? . . . Nee Nee . . . You know, perhaps it's not the most beautiful name in the world, but it is my favorite, so say it again . . ."

"Nee Nee," Dyzma said, thinking, What's so damn funny about my mandolin?

"Yes, I like it, I like it more than any other name. You say it so, so . . . hard. There's such a roughness in your voice, a strength. No, more of a command, sort of. I don't know why, but it strikes me as the kind of voice that a sailor might have, a rugged sailor with a salt-soaked throat."

"Salt? Do sailors have to gargle with salt that often?"

She laughed.

"You're really in a wonderful mood today. You know, you really do have a true talent for comedy. Your delivery is always so serious when you tell jokes, it magnifies their comic power. You have no idea how happy I am whenever I'm with you. Right now I feel so light, so free and full of joy, so safe. Your little Nee Nee will sleep so sweetly, so safe and sound, for the first time in many, many days, and sad thoughts won't give me any trouble . . ."

Nicodemus winked.

"But something else might give you some trouble instead."

She blushed and squeezed him tighter.

"Oh, no," she countered without conviction. "Little Nee Nee will sleep sweetly upstairs, and Nicky with sleep sweetly downstairs."

"Out of the question. This time, out of the question. You're wasting your breath."

"Nicky! . . ."

"Nope! . . . it's settled, it's decided. The discussion has ended. As soon as the servants leave, my Nee Nee's coming down to me."

"I'm not coming down," she teased him.

"Then I'll go up."

"And you'll find the door locked." She laughed, brushing her cheek against his lips.

"The door? The door means nothing to me! I'll break it down in nothing flat."

"Ooh, my dearest, dearest strongman! Lean in, darling, I want to whisper something in your ear."

She put her lips close to Nicodemus's ear and whispered, "Nee Nee will come to her master."

"Now that's what I'm talking about! . . ."

It was past eleven when they parted and Dyzma headed to Kunicki's former quarters. He turned on the light in the office and opened the safe. He gazed at the stacks of banknotes piled on the shelves. He removed one bundle of cash and gently swung it back and forth, as if to test its weight.

"Mine . . . All mine. This cash, the safe, the house, the factories . . . I'm sitting on millions."

While he undressed, he tried to imagine how he was going to use this enormous wealth. First of all, he decided to inspect the estate and summon the managers for some kind of a briefing. He was thinking about the speech he would make to them when the door creaked.

Nina had come.

Nicodemus was not destined to sleep that night.

At seven o'clock, the servants came in from the service wing to begin their chores, and Nina had to dash upstairs to make it back before they did.

Dyzma lit a cigarette and adjusted the pillows.

"If this is the way it's going to be," he thought, "I'm not going to make it to old age."

He tried to fall asleep, but he couldn't.

"I guess I'm getting up," he muttered and called for the servants.

He ordered them to prepare a bath and make him breakfast right away: ten scrambled eggs, plus ham.

"And make sure there's plenty of fat on it!"

When he dressed and went to the dining room, he saw that the table was not set and the scrambled eggs had not been served. He reprimanded his servant—"You idiot!"—and when said idiot began to explain that the scrambled eggs would've gotten cold had they been put out earlier, he roared, "Shut your mouth, you dummy, they wouldn't get cold if you made them on time. You could see I was out of the bathroom already. You riffraff, I'll teach you how to maintain order around here! Now give me my scrambled eggs and tell them to saddle a horse for me . . . Wait! No, tell them I want a sleigh."

"Yes, sir."

After breakfast, he got into a smart little sleigh pulled by several pairs of horses and demanded to be taken to the paper mill. When he entered the office, he was provoked by the sight of the clerks drinking tea.

"What the hell is this!" he shouted. "Is this a factory or a pub?"

The clerks leapt to their feet.

"Is this how it goes these days?! Am I paying you to stuff your face? Where's the foreman?"

"Here I am, Mr. President."

"Get these glasses out of here, goddammit! And no giving them anything to eat in here. You can stuff your faces at home, gentlemen. Got it?"

He strode through the office and yanked open the door to the mill director's room. It was empty.

"Where is the director?"

"The director comes in at nine," one of the clerks explained, his voice trembling.

"Whaaat? . . . At nine? Parasites, goddammit!"

He entered the factory. There the work was in full swing. The workers each greeted Dyzma with a characteristic nod of their heads, a nod that somehow manifested all the distrust, fear, and insolence they felt toward their employer.

A young engineer scurried toward Dyzma and greeted him with respect.

"Well, everything in order?" Nicodemus asked.

"Everything is fine, Mr. President."

"Tell your director he needs to be here at seven o'clock every morning. A superior should set an example for his subordinates."

He offered him his hand and left.

The paper mill, sawmills, stables, cowsheds, the distillery, all this kept him busy until noon. He swept through Koborowo like a great storm, leaving panic in his wake.

As he was driving back toward the manor, he saw Nina in the window. She was grinning and stood with her arms raised, waving them in greeting. She was still in her dressing gown, but she ran to the hall to meet him.

"Where's my master coming from?" she asked in a low voice, because a servant was setting the table in the room next door.

"I was walking the grounds. I made an inspection."

"And how is everything?"

"Too many loafers around here. I need to whip them into shape."

"Darling, I don't want you to spend all your time taking care of the estate. After our wedding you must hire a new administrator. Think—it takes up so much time! You'll be gone all day, and I don't want to be left all alone. Will you do that, Nicky?"

"I've already done it," he laughed.

"I don't understand."

"I hired an administrator."

"Really? That's marvelous."

"Well, since we have to be in Warsaw for a few months, somebody has to look over Koborowo, otherwise everything will be stolen out from under us."

"And whom did my master hire?"

"That Krzepicki. I believe you know him?"

"Really? Zyzio? Zyzio Krzepicki, Auntie Przełęska's companion?

"Uh-huh. That's the one."

"He always was a funny boy. He used to court me. But back then he didn't have the best reputation."

"I haven't heard a single bad thing about him, to be honest. He's been my secretary since the bank launched."

"And you're happy with him?"

"Why wouldn't I be? Don't you want him as administrator?"

"What? No! My dear, I'm not very interested as far as these matters are concerned; I know very little at all about them, really."

A servant reported to Dyzma that the Koborowo management staff had begun to gather. When Nicodemus entered the spacious office, located just behind his quarters, a dozen or so gentlemen were speaking in low voices. They rose to greet him.

He nodded to them and took a seat at the desk, not inviting them to sit down.

"I summoned you," he began, drumming his fingers on the desk cloth, "to inform you that the owner of Koborowo, Madam Nina Kunicka, is divorcing her husband and has taken plenipotentiary power away from him. Now *I* am her plenipotentiary. And I'm telling you right now that the gloves are off. You know from the newspapers that the Grain Bank runs like clockwork, and that's because of me, because *I* hold the reins. So I repeat, the gloves are off, as far as I'm concerned."

His own words were stirring him up, and his voice grew louder and louder.

"I'll be brief: work is not fun. I'm in charge now, which means you're going to have to work your ass off, because I will not pay for loafing! Got it? If you slack off, you get fired. And if, God forbid, I catch you at some scheme, if I find out that one of you is trying to rip me off? Well! I'll put you behind bars so fast your head will spin! No playing games with me! Got it?"

He pounded his fist on the table.

The administrators stood in stunned silence.

"Mr. Krzepicki will be coming to take over the position of head administrator. What he says is law. But these days, one can't trust even his own brother. So here's what I'm thinking: if one of you notices that somebody's involved in any kind of con, if you know what I mean, if you come to me and tell me, you'll get yourself an easy five thousand zlotys, plus a raise. I'm not here to do any harm, I'll be like a father to you, but I don't take shit from anyone. That's all. You can go back to your duties."

One of the assembled, the gray, hunched manager of the distillery, took a few steps forward and said, "Mr. Bank President . . ."

"Well, what else do you need?"

"From what you said, Mr. President . . ."

"Did you understand what I said?"

"I did, yes, but . . ."

"Did you understand everything?"

"Everything, and that's why . . ."

"Then we have nothing to talk about. I didn't bring you all here to have a chitchat. If you don't like it, leave. Hit the road, make a fresh start somewhere else. I'm not keeping anyone here by force. But think about it, really give it some thought. It's not so easy to find a job nowadays. And getting a recommendation from me, good luck with that! And I have connections all over the place too! Personally, I wouldn't advise anybody in this country to become my enemy! Goodbye, gentlemen!"

He left, slamming the door behind him.

For a moment, there was complete silence.

"Well, here's a pretty business," one of them said.

"It's outrageous," said the manager of the distillery. "He wants us to spy on each other."

"And his tone!"

"I will resign."

"He treated us like punk kids."

"And the language he uses! It's disgraceful! Speaking that kind of slang to us, as if he thought we weren't capable of understanding intelligent speech!"

"He spoke as if he meant to offend us!"

"There's one choice: we should all resign!"

"All in solidarity!"

Not everyone, however, shared this view. A young agronomist in his early thirties, Taniewski, disagreed.

"I'll say this right now: count me out, gentlemen."

"Me too," added the veterinarian.

There followed a hail of indignant questions. Taniewski shrugged.

"What's the matter? If you're objecting to the style of his briefing, I consider that trivial. President Dyzma is a great man, the country owes him so much, his head is filled with so many important state issues that it's no wonder he doesn't exactly follow the Versailles rules of etiquette. And anyway, it's not a social gathering, it's a matter of—"

"A matter of snitching!" The chief accountant was irate. "Shame on you, Mr. Taniewski, I thought your ethical principles were a little less flexible."

"I'm sorry, but he's not forcing anyone to snitch."

"He isn't? So what about those rewards for reporting on each other?"

"And who's forcing you to claim the reward?" Taniewski was getting irritated. "And besides, the way I see it, if someone's stealing, I'm duty bound to bring it to the attention of the one getting robbed. No? You don't think so? I don't see anything wrong with it: the president wants to provide himself—not even himself, but the rightful owner—a guarantee against misconduct. It's smart business, and that's that! Only losers let themselves be robbed. Do you think that if he looked the other way as his own bank got robbed, he'd still be world-famous? Would he have been able to fix our economy in a few short months? And if he demands a conscientious and diligent workforce, is that so wrong? Well? . . ."

He stopped and waited for objections. But everyone was silent.

"Life is not a song! We Poles and our prickly pride, we're always getting our feathers ruffled, always up in arms about something or other, and then we're given the boot and have to go sniffing around for another job, any job that will have us, that's what our pride gets us. I've seen it too many times, and I can't take it anymore. Besides, honestly, I don't see any reason to be insulted. What is there to say? He's a great statesman, an economic genius, and we—and my apologies, gentlemen—we're just small fry, little specks. Those of you with your heads in the clouds, feel free to 'take appropriate measures,' but as for me? I'm staying, and I'm telling you that the president's a great guy: he knows what he wants and he can afford to tell it like it is, that's all."

There was silence.

"No doubt you're right," a voice was heard. Then a second, a third, a tenth . . .

"I know I am," said Taniewski, taking his fur coat from the hanger.

The distillery manager spread his hands.

"Hmm. Do what you want, gentlemen. I, however, am bowing out."

Everyone began to urge him to accept the situation, to assure him that everything would work out somehow, to remind him that it would be difficult to find another job.

The old man, however, only nodded.

"No, gentlemen. I know it will be difficult, but I'm not accustomed to this way of running things. It's not for me. You might even be right, but I've lived too long, the old principles mean too much to me. I cannot."

They slowly went their separate ways. The door closed behind the last of them. A multitude of footprints were left on the unpainted floorboards, for the snow outside was extremely slushy that day.

Chapter 17

Madam Przełęska had given the two most beautiful rooms in her apartment to her beloved Ninette to use at her disposal. The rooms resembled two giant flowerbeds, and each night, both the footman and the chambermaid put in considerable work taking these baskets and flowerpots down to the scullery, to save her ladyship (such was the title they were required to use) from certain asphyxiation.

Every day, starting at noon, there was a steady stream of lords and ladies on a high-society pilgrimage to see the unequivocal sensation of the season for themselves.

After a week of rationing out these individual visits, the matter was sealed with a great ball so Madam Przełęska could present her beloved niece to everyone at once.

Even Prince and Princess Roztocki deigned to make an appearance at the ball, and when a flushed Madam Przełęska greeted them, they declared how nice it was to visit a house that President Nicodemus Dyzma held in such esteem.

In these circles, Nicodemus's engagement was an open secret; the official announcement would have to wait until Nina obtained an annulment.

The issue that fascinated all the ladies, that was causing particularly the ones famous for always being in the know about this sort of thing to nearly perish of curiosity, was the question of what had happened with that Kunicki.

It was known only that he had gone abroad and had agreed to the annulment. But why? And beyond that, why had he left Nina his entire fortune?

Only a few people could say for sure, but Krzepicki brushed aside any questions with a smile, and Madam Przełęska was not a woman from whom you could wring a single word against her will. It would be unseemly to ask Nina herself, and, well, no one would dare ask President Dyzma.

Madam Koniecpolska alone tried to do so, reasoning that their recent fellowship in the Thrice-Rayed Star entitled her—so she thought—to a little familiarity, and later complained, "Just imagine, he asks me if zere are better zings for me to worry about!"

The ball went off without a hitch, although its heroine was unable to hide a certain sheepishness that arose from her present situation and the fact she was making a return to her former position.

In Warsaw, she was surrounded by an atmosphere of interested friendliness and respect, for which—she soon realized—she had Nicodemus's enormous popularity to thank.

Every person who came near her considered it his sacred duty to say a few sentences about Dyzma using nothing but superlatives. She listened to all of it with unabating pleasure, but with a tinge of something like surprise. Although she'd known for a long time that Nicodemus was a celebrity, a powerful statesman, and a man of great wisdom and talent, back in Koborowo, he'd seemed less so. And now, as she was bombarded with words of admiration and reverence from all sides, as she became convinced that she had underestimated his value, her attitude toward him was increasingly one of bashful awe.

Despite her new life's attractions—or rather, thanks to its unceasing attractions—there was a pleasant monotony to Nina's days.

In the morning, she went out with her aunt for a stroll or to make the rounds at the shops. At one she returned home, always finding someone who had dropped by to see her. Then there was lunch either at home or at an acquaintance's, or sometimes, at Nicodemus's invitation, at a restaurant. At seven, the man himself showed up, and they went to the theater or a movie. In the event of the former, Nicodemus would escort her home, and they would say their goodbyes at the gate, whereas after movies—the cinema closed much earlier than the theater—he went upstairs with her and they had their dinner together.

Nicodemus kept insisting that she come over to his place, and she kept putting him off from one night to the next.

They were fresh from another of these bawdy farces when Dyzma resolved to outmaneuver her obstinacy. After the car deposited them in front of Madam Przełęska's house, he sent it away.

"I'll go on foot," he told his chauffeur. "It's not far."

When Nina went to press the doorbell, he stayed her hand.

"No, Nee Nee, tonight we're going to my place."

"Oh no, I'm going upstairs."

"You absolutely must!"

"But it's impossible! What would my aunt think of me?"

"Let her think what she wants. What do you care?"

"No, no, no." She dug in her heels.

"Just for a minute or two, for a tiny little half hour," he pleaded. "You don't love me anymore?"

She pressed her body to his and whispered,

"Okay then, just not right now."

"Yes, now!"

"No. Tomorrow. We'll say we're going to the cinema."

He scowled and began a new round of wheedling, but Nina had rung the bell, and they could hear the footsteps of the night watchman heading for the gate.

She gave him one last quick kiss and then disappeared inside.

The chill was enough to make Nicodemus turn up his fur collar. He took a few steps toward home, then came to an abrupt halt and turned back toward Krucza. There was still quite a lot happening on Jerozolimskie Avenue, and he could see that Nowy Świat was jam-packed with people.

He dropped into a bar, downed a few vodkas, and devoured a big plate of pork knuckle with peas. Behind the counter stood a stout girl in a white apron.

"Not the worst-looking girl," he thought, and it suddenly occurred to him that, come to think of it, all he had to do was go out to the street and point a finger at any girl he wanted.

He paid, not even bothering with his usual practice of suspiciously scrutinizing the bill, and headed outside.

Indeed, there was a wide range from which to choose. After a few moments, he made his selection. He didn't want to take her to his apartment, opting instead to pay for a room at a nearby hotel. She led him to some filthy hole on Chmielna Street.

It was already after three when he began to put his clothes back on. He took out twenty zlotys, laid them on the table, and, mumbling "goodnight," stepped out into the dark corridor. Just then, someone at the very end switched on a light bulb.

It was a fat old lady, the proprietress of the hotel, ushering in a new pair. At the other end of the hall, a door opened—someone was leaving.

Nicodemus, through force of habit, reached for his cigarette case and found it missing. He quickly turned and stormed back into the room without even closing the door behind him.

The girl was squatting on the bed, running a chipped comb through her tousled hair.

"Gimme my *porte-cigare*, goddammit!"

"What *porte-cigare*?"

"'What *porte-cigare*?'! Oh, I'll show you 'what'! Give it here right now, because if I have to find it myself, I'm going to smash your face in!"

"What are you yelling for? You trying to draw a crowd? You can't even shut the door?!"

He looked over his shoulder. Sure enough, someone was standing in the dark corridor. When he swung around and the light fell on his face, he heard a quiet yelp and footsteps scurrying away.

He slammed the door shut, turning the key and shoving it into his pocket. He went to the bed. The girl was still phlegmatically combing her hair. In a flash, he ripped her comb from her hands and hurled it to the floor.

"Come on, are you serious?!" she said, her voice almost a baritone. "Why'd you do that for, you loser?!"

"Give me my *porte-cigare*, do you hear me?!"

"I don't have it," she said, shrugging her shoulders.

He drew back his fist and struck her face so hard she toppled over, her head knocking against the wall.

"Give it, goddammit!" He took another swing at her.

She shielded her face with her elbow. He grabbed her handbag. Inside were a few pathetic trinkets, a pair of crumpled banknotes, and a dirty handkerchief.

She silently glared at him.

"Ooh . . . you vermin!" he snarled.

In one swift motion, he yanked the pillow from under her and threw it to the floor. The cigarette case fell with a clank along with it. He picked it up, examined it, and put it back in his pocket.

"Thief," he growled. "Scum."

"You put it there yourself, loser."

"You lie!" he roared.

She didn't answer. He opened the door and left. Outside, the streetlamps shone with a thin, watery light.

There was no trace of any cab. He'd have to go on foot. The chill had gotten worse, the snow crunched beneath his feet. There were almost no passersby. He hurried along. When he turned onto Marszałkowska, he looked around. On the other side of the street, a few buildings down, some girl was also hurrying along.

"And here's another one," he said to himself. "I'm no fool."

He began to walk so quickly that the girl was forced to almost run to keep up with him, but she'd evidently elected not to give up the chase because when he turned around at Nowogrodzka, he caught sight of her again. He stopped, and to his surprise, she stopped too, in front of some unlit shop window. A slight girl in a black hat and shabby dress.

He spat and continued on his way. He turned onto Wspóla Street. In a few minutes, he was at his own gate. The night watchman opened it with a deep bow.

"What time did the chauffeur get back?" Dyzma asked, since he enjoyed checking up on his subordinates.

"If you please, Honorable Sir, around eleven."

"And the garage roof has been repaired?"

"To be sure, Honorable Sir."

He nodded and headed up the stairs. Neither Nicodemus nor the night watchman took any notice of the silhouette of a girl watching them through the bars of the gate. Her heart was hammering. She lifted her eyes to the building's façade. At the second-floor level she could see a black inscription:

NATIONAL GRAIN BANK

Bank! . . .

And suddenly everything was clear. Entirely clear. Nicodemus, her Nico-demus, who'd tossed her aside even though she'd loved him, even though she loved him still and couldn't put him out of her mind, her Nicodemus was gearing up for a big job. A tunnel, maybe, or cracking the safe open . . . In any case, the night watchman was in on it. After all, she'd seen how they'd quietly spoken, and how he'd let him in.

The National Grain Bank.

Maybe he was palming himself off as a janitor? Or maybe not, because why would he be coming by at night?

Her heart was hammering.

She crossed to the other side and waited.

Maybe the alarm would go off, maybe police would appear at the end of the street? Oh, she knew very well what she'd have to do then: ring the bell and warn the watchman . . . True, Nicodemus had lied to her, had forgotten her, true, he hadn't come back for her, but he still *might* come back . . . He'd done well for himself, he had a fur coat . . . And he'd been going around in an expensive car that time . . . When he'd lived with them on Łucka, she'd thought he was just some shady guy from the sticks; she never dreamed that this Dyzma was such a heavy hitter . . .

Dawn was just beginning to filter through the thick layer of clouds when she decided to call it a night. It was cold. When she got to Łucka Street, the gate was already open—twenty cents saved.

The next morning she went to Wspólna, anxious that she might arrive to find the bank surrounded by police, and Nicodemus arrested, unless he'd managed to make a run for it.

She sighed with relief. The revolving door spun ceaselessly as usual. Clients came and went, one after another cars pulled up and pulled away.

Maybe it was a tunnel or a breach in the wall . . . Maybe he was playing the long game . . .

She'd found him at last. Oh, he wouldn't slip away from her this time. She was certain she wouldn't see him here during daylight hours, but she'd come back that night, she'd keep vigil and finally see him face-to-face . . . And she did come.

Ten, eleven . . . With nervous footsteps she made her way down the opposite sidewalk. A gentle snow was drifting down, the big flakes glowing white under the streetlamps and then fading to black.

Twice she was stopped by potential customers. One of the guys was young and even looked like he had some money, but she shook her head no.

She began to worry: maybe tonight he wouldn't come? . . . But—she would wait! She had to . . . Men were always like that—out of sight, out of mind. But after all, Zosia's red-haired Władek had come back to Zosia . . .

She anxiously peered up and down Marszałkowska, and it was only when the gate banged shut that she turned her attention back to the bank building.

Nicodemus was leaving with some elegant lady alongside him.

They were laughing together.

The girl hid herself behind a pillar in the wall. They were going to walk right past her, the sidewalk so narrow she could reach out her hand and touch them as they went by. She could distinctly hear Nicodemus's voice.

"As you wish, Nee Nee, my love, it's . . ."

The words that followed were drowned out by the honking horn of a passing cab. She could see, however, that they were holding hands.

"So that's how it is! . . ." she said to herself, falling into a pensive mood.

She drifted after them.

The existence of a rival didn't surprise her. After all, she hadn't supposed he'd sworn off women. Nevertheless, she was alarmed by this lady's beauty.

He loves her . . . He loves her for sure . . . But why—here a little flame of hope flickered—why, in that case, had he been with that other woman at the hotel? . . .

Something mysterious was going on here. If not for that, she could catch up with them right now and throw it right in this woman's face—it was *she* who had a previous claim on Nicodemus, it was *her* that he loved . . .

He'll come back to me, he will . . . I'll tell him how I've cried my eyes out, how every girl like me has a man of her own, but I don't, even though top-shelf guys keep asking . . . He has to come back . . .

Nicodemus saw Nina to her door and started toward home. He had just been reflecting on Jurczak—regarded as Łysków's leading connoisseur of women—and how wrong he'd been when he'd maintained that only brunettes were capable of true passion, when he heard his own name.

He turned around. Standing before him was Mańka.

"Nicodemus," she whispered softly.

"Ugh, it's you," he said, not hiding his displeasure.

"Do you remember me? . . ."

"What do you want?"

She looked at him, her eyes wide. She didn't know what to say.

"So, what do you want?" he asked again with irritation.

"This is how you say hello to me?" she said reproachfully. "What did I do wrong, Nicodemus?"

"Enough of this bullshit. It's not about wrong, it's not about right: what is it that you want?"

She was silent.

"Speak, goddammit!"

The girl remained silent.

He swore and made to leave, but she grabbed him by the sleeve.

"Let go!"

"I won't let go. You have to listen to me."

"So say something, for Christ's sake. What the hell is this about?"

"You see, Nicodemus, you probably have no idea, but I've missed you so much, and because, you know, I don't even have a fella, I've been waiting for you . . . I've been looking all over for you, I kept thinking that you'd come back, that you wouldn't forget."

He shrugged his shoulders.

"What exactly was there to remember or forget?"

"But you said you'd come back!"

"People say a lot of things. It's not like we tied the knot."

"You see . . . I love you."

He chuckled. "Big deal. You love somebody every night."

"That's how you speak to me?! Do you suppose that I'm one of 'those girls' for fun? Should I just starve to death? I do what I have to do, but every time it makes me want to puke."

"Yeah yeah, enough kidding around."

"I'm telling you the truth. There's nobody on Earth who'd be jealous of me. It's a life for dogs."

"Fine, but what do I care?"

"Come back to me!"

"No. No way."

"You could live with us for free. I'd pay your share."

He burst out laughing.

She stared at him, deeply discomfited.

"What are you laughing for?"

"I'm laughing because you're so dumb. I'm not coming back, so get that idea out of your head."

"Why don't you want me? Don't I do it for you anymore?"

"Knock it off, Mańka, you've got some nerve."

"But back then you told me you would come back."

"To hell with what I said! Got it? I'm getting married, and you need to get it through that thick skull of yours that I'm not going to bother with trash like you. Not now that I've had a taste of genuine class."

"You're marrying that one you were walking with?"

"This one, that one, it's none of your business."

"I know it's her." Her voice was shaking with hatred.

"What do you care?"

"Because I love you!" she screamed.

"Quiet! What are you yelling for! Love me then, go ahead, I don't give a shit. Now leave me alone. I don't have time for this."

Again she grabbed his sleeve.

"Just wait a minute."

"Yeah?"

"Spend the night with me . . ."

She clung to the hope that she could still manage to persuade him, entice him away from that other woman.

He gave her a little shove.

"Scram."

"Nicodemus! . . ."

Her eyes glittered with tears.

"And now here come the waterworks. Well I'm telling you, I can't. I can't right now. Even if I wanted to."

"Why?"

"I have a job."

"Ah! . . ." she nodded solemnly.

She understood, of course, that "doing" a bank was no small thing and that she, Mańka, paled in significance.

"But later," she began, "later . . ."

"Maybe later. Bye."

He again made to leave, but again she restrained him.

"Nicodemus, you're not going to kiss me?"

"Jesus H. Christ! You're killing me."

He bent down and gave her a peck on the cheek. Mańka, however, refusing to be fobbed off like that, threw her arms around Dyzma's neck and pressed herself against his mouth.

Her lips were moist, firm, and cold from the freezing weather.

"Enough!" He backed away from her.

"Come back!" she whispered. "Come back to me!"

"What a pain in the ass you are. We'll see, maybe later. Goodbye."

She nodded her head silently.

For a long time she just stood in place, watching him go. When he disappeared at the intersection, she wiped her eyes with her handkerchief and went off in the opposite direction.

Nicodemus was fuming. This Mańka, who suddenly shows up out of nowhere . . . He'd forgotten her a long time ago . . . And what claim, if any, did she possibly have on him?! Well, sure, she was in love and, sure, she was basically a decent girl, but that was still no reason to go looking for him . . .

But what if she compromises me? Or blabs about it to Nina? Shit!

He resolved that, if she got hold of him again, he'd tear her a new one, and that would be the last time she dared have anything to do with him.

Back in his apartment, Nina's perfume still hung in the air. He got undressed and was about to climb into bed when he remembered that tomorrow morning Krzepicki was driving out to Koborowo and he needed to get all sorts of papers together.

He toiled for a good half hour and was just wrapping up when the telephone rang. He picked up the receiver.

It was Wareda. The whole gang was at the bar and had decided to give Nicodemus a call.

"Ever since Nina arrived," the colonel complained, "we never see you anymore. You absolutely must come out."

Dyzma, however, refused to budge. He was sleepy and simply worn out.

He generally didn't care for bars. Sure, he liked a bottle from time to time, but sitting at a table for hours on end, drinking himself into a stupor? No thanks. If on previous occasions he'd gone out boozing with Wareda, Ulanicki, and the others, it was mainly in the interest of making connections.

Now his dream, to which his thoughts constantly turned, was of a calm, uneventful life in Koborowo.

The matter of Nina's annulment was moving along briskly. The fact that her husband had falsified his surname gave her case a big boost—the rest of it simply required money, and these days Dyzma had no shortage of that.

The days flowed one after another, bringing with them nothing of particular importance. With every step he took at the bank, however, Dyzma keenly felt Krzepicki's absence. Although he'd already established a routine and knew what should be done in this case or that, issues would arise that he didn't know how to handle. Then his only recourse would be an acute attack of rheumatism.

If, after all, despite moving ahead with maximum caution, he committed a blunder or three, it was put down to the absentmindedness of a bank president in the throes of true love, which had been discussed at great length around the office. The chief source of information on that account was Ignacy, who carried daily baskets of flowers to the apartment of the president's bride-to-be.

Meanwhile, Nina was going over to Dyzma's place several times a week.

Madam Przełęska, unaware of this, offered loud, enthusiastic commentary on the remarkable change in her niece's mood and appearance.

"To love and be loved," she told her. "That, my dear, is better than any cosmetics a woman can buy. Why, you've blossomed practically overnight!"

Later, telling this to Nicodemus, Nina laughed and laughed.

She gave almost no thought at all to her husband. Besides, she didn't have the time. The merry-go-round of her social life absorbed her completely. And she enjoyed herself all the more because she was immensely popular. Men young and old determinedly paid court to her, and she was thronged by admirers at every salon.

There was a particular one among them, though, upon whom Dyzma began to look with unease.

His unease was justified not so much by this fellow's merits as by Nina's behavior. It was only too obvious that she was singling him out. It was with him that she danced and chatted most often.

He was a man of nearly forty, tall, slim, with sun-kissed flaxen hair. He'd arrived on the scene suddenly, from the-devil-knew-where, maybe from the entire world, since he referred to Australia, Peru, or Greenland as casually as one would Konstancin or Milanówek. His name was Hell, Oskar Hell. He said he had been born in Russia and, after hearing that Dyzma had studied at Oxford, referred to him as a colleague. He himself was a Cambridge man. In any case, he spoke Polish extremely well, in addition to at least ten other languages. When asked about his nationality, he threw up his hands in amusement.

He'd made quite an impression on Nina right from the start. That much was easy for Nicodemus to see, all the more so because she made no effort at all to hide her fondness for this interloper.

You couldn't yet call the situation unsafe, but Dyzma's concern was growing. To top it off, he didn't have Krzepicki—who always knew how to fix everything—at his beck and call. He wrote to him about it, but he never heard back.

Meanwhile, Oskar Hell had settled in Warsaw for good. He had connections everywhere and popped up at every ball, open house, and nightclub. And since he never conducted any business but always had money, he became renowned for his fortune and even for being a desirable match. He'd been brought to Poland by a Count Pomiałowski, who'd invited him to hunt wild boar. The count himself could say little about Hell, since they'd only met recently, on the deck of an Italian ship during an excursion to the Canary Islands.

Nicodemus poured the entire stock of his wits into separating Nina from this globetrotter, but he was afraid to put the issue before her too directly, since it might make matters worse.

God only knows how long this state of affairs would have lasted if, during a conversation between Hell and Nina, the name "Kasia Kunicka" had not just happened to come up.

It turned out that Hell knew her well, that he saw her often in Davos, in Cannes, *and* in Geneva, that they even wrote each other from time to time, since they shared an interest in telepathy and would exchange new insights and information on the subject.

Nina was extremely excited by this news. Until now, she'd had no idea what was happening with Kasia, and after all, she liked her so much. In any case, she was too deeply bound up in memories of Kasia to be able to handle this surprise with nonchalance.

Naturally, she told Nicodemus at the first opportunity.

"Just imagine, Mr. Hell knows Kasia very well! He met her abroad, and they even send each other letters! Poor Kasia, so alone . . . I feel so sorry for her."

"Ehh . . . Maybe this Hell is just telling lies."

"Nicky! How can you say that!" Nina was indignant. "Oskar is a true gentleman."

That did it.

Dyzma decided to act. This was urgent. He decided to seek Wareda's advice and asked him to dinner that very night.

After the first vodka, he got right down to business.

"Well, you see, Wacek . . . Do you know this Hell?"

"I know him. Pleasant fellow."

"Pleasant, unpleasant, I don't give a damn what he is. He's sniffing around my turf, see."

"What do you mean?"

"He's horning in on my fiancée."

"Well, give the punk a smack across the mouth. If he gives you a hard time, pistols at dawn and that's that."

"A duel?" Dyzma winced.

"Well, sure. I'm telling you, Nick, in cases like these it's best to get it done wham-bam, without a lot of chitchat."

"But, you see . . . It's not about me. It's about the lady. And the lady would be even more ready to go if I hurt him or something."

"So what do you think we should do?"

Dyzma scratched his chin.

"Maybe he can be arrested? . . . The devil knows what gives with this scoundrel, this globetrotter, this bum . . ."

"Hmm . . . Just between you and me, there's not a single reason to arrest him."

"A spy, maybe?" Dyzma said uncertainly.

"And if he isn't? Why exactly would we suspect him of being a spy?"

"Maybe we can, maybe we can't. No one knows him. Where does all that cash come from? From what? Who does he live with?"

"Hmm."

"A stray, a foreign alien."

"Well, it figures." Wareda was giving it some thought. "It's possible. His documents could be checked. If necessary, a search of his hotel could be done, but if it turns out that everything is shipshape, it'd be a fiasco. That's not the way . . ."

He downed a glass of vodka and suddenly slammed his palm on the table.

"It *is* the way! Don't you see, it's the way . . ."

"Oh yeah?"

"After all, you don't want to *put* him away, you just want to *get* him away. "

"What do you mean get him away?"

"Get him away from Miss Nina."

"Well, sure."

"So, this is the way to do it. Arrest him, do a search, run a paragraph in the newspapers, then, afterwards, beg his pardon and let him go."

"And how will *that* help anything?"

"What do you mean? Don't you get it?"

"No."

"Why, it's simple. Do you really think Miss Nina wants to be associated with someone suspected of spying?"

Dyzma gave it some thought and, after a long pause, replied, "I don't think so."

"Do you think that high society in general will take a thing like this in stride? . . . No, brother, after a bit of mischief like that, he'll have to pack his bags and go."

"Hmm . . . But . . . after all, if he explains it was all a mistake, maybe—" Nicodemus considered.

"—while we," Wareda said, "we give it to be understood that he was released because he was wily enough to get rid of the evidence in time."

Dyzma could admit that the colonel had a point. A plan was drawn up and set into motion without delay. Wareda called up his pal Colonel Jarc, the chief of the Second Division headquarters.

The three of them had a meeting that evening. They were less than thorough in laying the case before Jarc, since Dyzma felt no need to acquaint him with his anxiety concerning his affianced. At any rate, Jarc wasn't interested. It completely sufficed that President Dyzma suspected this foreigner; it didn't matter one way or the other to Jarc if Dyzma wanted to discredit this Hell, and besides, the dinner really *was* exquisite.

The thing was carried out early the following morning.

Dyzma had been in a state of high excitement since he'd arrived at the bank. He couldn't wait for the afternoon newspapers and, every few minutes, dispatched the porter to the street to ascertain whether they had come out yet.

At last, the porter returned with three newspapers. Dyzma began a feverish inspection of them. In the first two, there wasn't a single word about Hell. On the front page of the third, however, there was a notice in small, black print under the headline: "On the Trail of New Communist Cell: Arrest of Gentleman Spy at Luxury Hotel."

This mention did not, as had been decided, give Hell's complete name. It appeared as "H." However, the series of details presented about "H" left no doubt in the mind of anyone who knew Hell that he was the very man in question.

Dyzma rubbed his hands.

His internal equilibrium restored, he shuffled through some papers, ordered his correspondence to be fetched and brought to him for his signature, cracked a few jokes with his secretary, made an expedition to the bank offices, where he met each bow with a smile, then settled down to read some letters. Among them he found a letter from Krzepicki. He'd written:

Dear Mr. President,

First of all, I hasten to report that, to date, everything is in order. I have met with neither opposition nor sabotage. I have already familiarized myself with the business to some extent. Koborowo is the land of milk and honey—my congratulations! In a month, I'll know every pebble and pinch of sawdust. Everyone here is scared stiff of you! Even more so than at the bank. I've twice been to the Department of Treasury in Grodno. Rabinowiecz will give 700 zlotys apiece. He wants to take 30 heifers, but he wants to pay with six-month notes supplied by "Natan Golder & Company" and endorsed by Kugel

Countinghouse in Białystok. Sir, please telegram whether I should accept. Kasperski tells me they are reliable.

I don't know this Hell of whom you write and have heard nothing about him. If it were up to me, I would advise you not to worry too much about him. But caution never hurts. To that end, I think that it would be best to tell Miss Nina that this Hell suffers from an incurable venereal disease. That should scare her off.

I went twice to George Ponimirski's annex, since he's gravely ill. The doctor says that it's pneumonia. Very high fever, delirious, doesn't recognize me at all. So I think that he's going to go belly up. When he found out that Kunicki had taken off like a bat out of hell, he went completely crazy with joy and ran out into the park without a coat. He gave himself a cold, of course. He was flying all over the park and screaming at the top of his lungs. When it comes down to it, I feel sorry for him. Poor guy.

Krzepicki then gave an account of revenues and expenditures, asked Nicodemus about expediting the matter of the railway ties, and announced that he'd soon drop in on him in Warsaw for a day or two.

Nicodemus was pleased. He dictated a telegram to the typist, recommending that the notes payable be accepted, if Krzepicki trusted the source, and phoned Madam Przełęska to announce himself for dinner.

When he arrived, he found, apart from the ladies of the house, the younger Countess Czarska and two young men whom he recognized, but whose names he could not remember.

Immediately after greetings were exchanged, he asked, "Have you already heard about this arrest?"

"Which one?"

"No, we haven't heard."

"Who did they arrest?"

"You see," Dyzma shook his head, "nowadays you can never be sure. And he seemed like such a nice guy."

"But who?!" Madam Przełęska couldn't take it.

"Who? Why, that Oskar Hell."

"Who?" Nina asked fretfully.

"Hell," he replied, carefully observing the expression on her face.

"That's not possible! Oskar?!"

Nicodemus reached coolly into his pocket and handed a newspaper to Madam Przełęska, pointing out the spot that had been circled in red pencil.

She read it aloud and, upon finishing, sighed, "What a pretty story *this* is! My God!"

Nina took the paper and read the notice herself. She became all the more dejected.

"One cannot trust anyone these days," Madam Przełęska said with an aphoristic air.

"Disgusting!" Nina blurted. "People are disgusting. It's all one great swamp!"

"Hey, no need to go overboard," Dyzma said shortly.

There began a conversation about Hell, during which everyone recalled all sorts of details about his behavior, which had appeared highly suspicious from the very beginning.

Nina wasn't listening. Instead, she was thinking about how awful and false the world was, and how terribly alone she was in it, how unprepared for the sudden blows that might rain down upon her from every direction.

She watched Dyzma. The shaggy hair, the blocky forehead and stubby nose, the thin mouth and that enormous, powerful jaw. His torso, perhaps a little on the longish side, and his wide-legged stance.

"One would think he's just an ordinary man," she thought, "and yet underneath that commonplace exterior throbs a kind of concentrated, secret strength, a kind of dormant power, but he deliberately conceals it . . . Nicky . . . my Nicky . . ."

It struck her anew that this powerful man with the wise half-smile on his face, who was listening in silence to the prattle of these people, that this statesman, the great economist, this man so . . . alien—well, perhaps not alien, but remote, at least—that this was her Nicky! Yes! Her fiancé, and soon her husband, who would henceforth be in charge of steering her fate, her life, who would assure her safety, shield her from everything bad in the world . . . Oh, how capable he was, like no one else! He was like a pyramid in the desert that no gale could budge. Mr. Hell was also a real man, but . . .

She would prefer not to give *him* another moment's thought.

Dinner was served. There was the normal flow of conversation about nothing.

When, after dinner, they found themselves alone for a moment, she whispered to Dyzma, "I love you. I love you so much."

He took her hand and kissed it.

"Nicky . . . today let's go to your place?"

"Oh, you'd like that?" he asked playfully.

"She bit her lip and, looking him full in the face, her pupils dilated, whispered, "Very, very much . . . very . . ."

She'd gone a little pale, a sign that Dyzma already knew quite well.

"Three days," she said, "three days since the last time we were together . . ."

"All right," he nodded, thinking, Oh ho, she's really going to put me to work.

When they left just before eight, Nina announced that they were going to the opera. Later, with a grin, she explained to Nicodemus that she had chosen the opera because they were currently performing *African*, which didn't finish until after midnight.

"Your Nee Nee is clever, isn't she?" she said.

"Oh ho!"

He waited at the gate until Nina's steps had faded away and then looked at his watch. It was one o'clock. He started toward home.

He was only a few meters away from the bank building when he saw Mańka. She was leaning against a lamppost. Evidently she'd been waiting for him.

He bristled. He wanted to just pass by and pretend he didn't notice her, but she was already coming toward him.

"What?!" he snarled at her.

"Nicodemus . . ."

"What?!"

"Nicodemus . . . Don't be mad . . . But I can't go on living without you . . ."

"Get lost! I spit on you! You better get out of here before I smash your face in."

She gazed at him in horror.

"But how come? How come, Nicodemus?"

"You're a pain in my ass, that's all."

"But I love you, and you promised me."

"I spit on what I promised, and I spit on you! Understood? A common slut, a worn-out bag like you, clamping onto me and giving me trouble, you're nothing but gutter trash!"

"Nicodemus! . . ."

"Scram, goddammit!"

He shoved her so hard she staggered and fell onto a mound of dirty snow. She didn't get up. Her eyes followed the man now striding away.

"So that's it?"

She buried her face in her frozen hands and sobbed.

The words echoed inside her head: Trash . . . whore . . . slut . . .

Suddenly, she sprang up and shook her fist in the bank's direction.

"Ooh, just you wait!"

She brushed the snow from her thin coat and started to walk as fast as she could in the direction of Marszałkowska.

"You'll remember *me*, all right, you won't forget me this time! . . . If I can't have you, then neither can she! I'll fix you good, you'll see."

The thirst for revenge, for immediate revenge, had completely consumed her. She was nearly running. She didn't hesitate at all when the policeman standing at the entrance asked her what she wanted.

"I want to rat on somebody," she said.

"Rat? . . . Fine, go tell the officer on duty. That door."

In a large room divided by a balustrade, she stood in front of the desk.

"What?" asked the officer, who was busy writing something. He didn't lift his eyes.

She looked around. They were alone.

"I want to rat on someone."

"Yeah?" he asked impassively.

"Back in May he bumped off some Jew. He raked in a bunch of cash. He showed it to me himself, he was bragging about it. And now he's gearing up to clean out a bank on Wspólna."

The officer put down his pen and raised his eyes to look at her.

"A bank? Who's this?"

"The name is Dyzma. Nicodemus Dyzma."

"And you know this how?"

"I just know."

"What's your name?"

"Mańka Barcik."

"Address?"

"36 Łucka."

"Your profession?"

She hesitated for a moment before answering. "Working girl."

"And why are you informing on him?"

"That's my business."

The officer wrote down her name and address.

"You're telling me he's gearing up to do the bank on Wspólna?"

"Yes."

"And you know this is no place for joking around? If you're lying, you're going to jail."

"I know."

He gave her a long look. She was calm. From the determined expression on her face, he concluded she was telling the truth.

"Where is this Dyzma right now?"

"Inside the bank."

"What?!"

"I saw him go in myself. He's friends with the night watchman."

The officer grabbed the telephone receiver and requested a number.

"Is the commissioner there? . . . Then wake him up, please. It's an urgent matter. Duty Officer Kasparski here."

After a long moment, he heard the commissioner's voice. The officer relayed this doozy of a report.

"Detain her," the commissioner ordered. "I'll be right there, and I'll question her myself."

The officer replaced the receiver. He gestured to a bench against the wall.

"Wait there."

"Fine."

She sat. Ooh, he'd never forget *her*!

Nicodemus was lying in bed reading the newspaper when the telephone rang.

"What the hell?!"

He jumped out of bed without even putting on his slippers, stumbling over a chair in the dark room.

"Hello!"

"May I speak with Bank President Dyzma?"

"That's me. Who's this?"

"Commissioner Jaskólski speaking. My respects to you, sir."

"Good evening. What's this about?"

"My apologies, Mr. President, for calling so late, but this is a very important matter."

"What kind of matter?"

"A prostitute by the name of Barcik showed up at the police station, testifying that you are digging a tunnel under the Grain Bank, sir."

"What?! . . ."

The commissioner burst out laughing.

"She doesn't look like a nut job, but she's not letting go of the story I just told you. Do you know her, sir?"

"How the hell would I know her?"

"Sure, of course. I ordered her to be detained. At first I thought she might be drunk, but no. She didn't know that you're the president of the Grain Bank. And even when I told her, she still didn't want to retract her statement. She must have some bone to pick with you. Did you really once live on Łucka Street?"

"Why, God forbid! I've never even been there."

"I was sure of that," the commissioner replied. "What a scammer! You'll have a good laugh over this, Mr. President, but she claimed that in May you killed and fleeced some Jew. She even named the hotel where you showed her the stolen money!"

"She's a goddamn liar!"

"Well, clearly, Mr. President. But I don't know what to do with her."

"Kick her ass back out on the street!"

"Meanwhile, she's digging in her heels over her testimony and is demanding that we write a report. In any case, the rules dictate that I have to follow protocol."

"But what for?" Dyzma asked hurriedly. "There's no need for any protocol."

"I understand, Mr. President, but it might be necessary if we're to bring her up for making a false accusation."

"Nah, what for?"

"She'll get three months' time for that."

"Not worth it. It'd be better if the commissioner could just give her a little advice on how to keep her mouth shut."

"Bah! She won't agree. She's a stubborn little thing."

"Well, that depends on what kind of advice you give her."

"I don't understand, Mr. President."

"I'm just saying that you, the police, you have your own methods."

"Aha!" The commissioner caught his drift. "It'll be taken care of, Mr. President. My highest regards. Once again, I apologize for disturbing you."

"It's no bother. Thank you very much. And I'll be sure to remember your help at my next opportunity, Commissioner."

The commissioner, overflowing with gratitude, put down the receiver. Simultaneously, he pressed a button that sounded a bell. A policeman appeared in the doorway.

"Bring her here . . ."

"Well, so you see, your testimony is false. You're going to jail."

He waited for an answer, but the girl was silent.

"But I feel sorry for you. You're young and stupid. So I'm telling you again, for your own good, take back your testimony."

"I'm not taking it back," she said stubbornly. "Let them throw me in jail."

The commissioner leapt to his feet and began to shout and bang his fists on the table.

"Argh, you silly bitch! Take it back! I'm telling you, take it back! Retract your statement and run away with your tail between your legs!"

He stormed around the room. Finally, he stopped in front of Mańka.

"Well? Do you take it back?"

"No," she answered shortly, and bit her lip.

"Walasek!" he called. A policeman entered. "Take her to the room at the end and explain to her that that lodging false accusations against eminent gentlemen doesn't pay off."

"Yes sir, Commissioner."

He took the girl by the elbow and led her down the corridor.

"Am I going to jail?" she asked.

"No, you're going dancing at Oasis."

In the small room there were a few policemen playing cards. They greeted the girl's entrance with ironic exclamations. They set down their cards, and one of them called, "Well, since we have such pleasant company, maybe we can play a round of pass the ball?"

Mańka's eyes widened. She'd guessed that they were mocking her. She wanted to say something, but then the policeman standing behind her gave her a little shove, straight into the policeman standing directly in front of her. He, in turn, passed her to Walasek in the same manner. Walasek, to the next person. Again and again, she was thrown, reeling, into different hands. At first, it didn't seem like this would be too unbearable, but then they started to speed up. The impact of hands on her chest and back was becoming more and more violent. She was dizzy and it hurt to breathe. Her hat fell from her head, her little handbag slipped from her grasp and knocked against the floor, spilling its contents.

Mańka realized that her only hope was to cling to one of the policemen so hard that he wouldn't be able to push her away. But her attempts failed. She wanted to collapse, but that too, became impossible. She began to scream. That put a stop to the game. One of the policemen covered her mouth.

"Quit singing, angel, this isn't the opera!"

"What are you hitting me for? What for?" she groaned, trying to catch her breath.

"Come on, take off your clothes," Walasek called out.

"How come?" Mańka asked.

"We're going to make love," Walasek laughed, "so be quick about it!"

She didn't obey, so he grabbed her by the hair and threw her to the ground.

"When I tell you to take your clothes off you do it!"

She started to cry. They grabbed her arms and stripped off her coat, her cretonne blouse, and her worn woolen skirt. The rest she took off herself.

At the same time, one of the policemen brought a bucket of water in which a second policeman plunged a sheet he'd taken from a cabinet. Mańka, thin and cowering, huddled in the corner, eyeing their preparations with horror. She knew what was coming. Dirty water streamed from the twisted sheet. She shook from the cold, yet the touch of the frozen sheet burned her skin like fire.

"Don't hit me, have mercy, don't hit me," she whimpered.

"Gag her!"

. . . .
. . . .
. . . .
. . . .

She'd been dragging herself along the street for a long, long time. The sun was already up, and there were more and more people. She stumbled and staggered. Passersby were staring at her. Some old woman passing her said, with contempt, "Pthu, shameless drunkard!"

Mańka said nothing.

Chapter 18

The attorney's office was splendidly appointed, combining seriousness with chic, austerity of form with elegant good taste; in brief, it had the same characteristics as its owner, a gray-haired gentleman with a small, square-trimmed beard, a celebrity in the world of divorce cases, a city councilor, a trustee of the Society for the Protection of the Family, and chamberlain to His Holiness.

On the other side of the desk from him was Dyzma, watching him with respect and listening attentively to his quiet, calm voice, the flow of his mild, distinctly enunciated words like a wide, gentle river.

A large portrait of the pope hung in a heavy gilded frame above the attorney's head.

Without pausing his oration, the attorney opened the desk and pulled out a folder, from which he withdrew a large parchment document folded twice over. He held it up to unfold it.

Two huge wax seals hung from white silk strings. The attorney kissed one of them with reverence, then handed the document over to Dyzma.

It was written in Latin. Nevertheless, Nicodemus knew exactly what it contained. It was the annulment of Nina's marriage.

Now that he had it in his hand, it crossed his mind that this was really going to cost him.

It'll be interesting to see how much this lawyer tacks on for himself, he thought.

As if in answer to his unspoken question, the attorney took out a small piece of paper from the folder, made some calculations with a golden pencil, and said, "My fee is four thousand two hundred zlotys."

Dyzma jumped up from his chair.

"How much?"

"Four thousand two hundred, sir."

"You've got to be kidding me! I thought it would be a thousand, two at the most! . . ."

"Mr. President, I informed you at the outset of the process that I would take the case only on the condition that you accept my usual fees and other incidentals."

"But four thousand! That makes almost sixty thousand total!"

"Mr. President, kindly take into account that no other attorney could have had this marriage annulled under these circumstances. I had to spend a significant sum merely preparing additional witness testimonies . . ."

"But the witnesses aren't even alive anymore."

The attorney smiled wanly.

"Indeed, Mr. President, I don't assume that you imagine it could possibly take any less to obtain testimonies from beyond the grave . . ."

Nicodemus understood.

"Which means? . . ." he asked.

"Which means," the attorney replied, rising from behind the desk, "that it takes what it takes."

Nicodemus reached into his pocket, took out a wad of cash, calculated the amount due, and stood up himself.

Following Dyzma into the hall, the attorney explained how to finalize the remaining details—namely, how to make the appropriate changes to certain critical records and so on.

Finally, he gave Dyzma an extremely solemn and dignified nod. Nicodemus went straight home to Nina.

He was in a terrific mood. Things had been going exceptionally well the past few days. Mańka had completely dropped out of sight. He'd spent three days riddled with anxiety over whether she would repeat her accusation to the police or the prosecutor. But lucky for him, she seemed to have calmed down.

And now he was holding in his hands the document that would allow him to marry Nina and leave Warsaw behind.

That wasn't all: this morning, he'd received a telegram from Krzepicki announcing his arrival in the city.

This was immeasurably important for Dyzma, because the meeting of the Finance Committee of the Council of Ministers was supposed to take place on Wednesday. Hugely important issues were at stake. The Ministry of the Treasury was requesting the export sale of grain stockpiled in the bank. Nicodemus would be forced to speak and take a position for or against the project and he had no idea what he was going to say. That's why Krzepicki's arrival was going to come in so handy.

Recently, he'd often found himself mustering the courage to articulate opinions on various issues that were being bandied about in the press. At times such as those, he'd choose the opinion he regarded as most suitable and pass it off as his own. In the case of this meeting, however, everything was happening in strictest secrecy.

At Madam Przełęska's, there was excitement in the air. Madam Przełęska was flushed pink, and Nina was pale.

"What happened?" he asked, surprised.

"Ah, Mr. President, Mr. President," Madam Przełęska said breathlessly. "Can you imagine? Mr. Hell has been released from prison!"

"He was arrested by mistake," Nina added quickly. "They've just apologized to him. He's completely innocent."

Dyzma frowned, his mood darkening.

"Ahhh," Madam Przełęska said, gesticulating energetically, "I thought I would have a heart attack! Can you believe that half an hour ago I received a call from Janek Karczewski—you know, that tennis player—and he told me that Hell had called him and had explained that it was all a huge mistake, and he asked him to let us know, and to let the Czarska sisters know, and just to let everyone know in general! And to make matters worse, he told Janek that he would call on us to explain the situation in person. What should I do? I don't have even the slightest idea what to do! Can I really receive such a person?! After all, he was in prison. He was accused of espionage!"

"Yes, but," Nina interrupted shyly, "the accusation was withdrawn."

"What should I do? Mr. President, what do you think? Have you heard about any of this?"

Nicodemus arranged his face into a grave expression.

"Not only did I hear it, but I have the most accurate information. This Hell was released from prison only because he was clever enough to destroy the evidence of his guilt in time."

"What are you saying?!"

"I'm telling you what I know. The chief of the Second Division headquarters told me about it. Hell is the ringleader of a Bolshevik espionage gang, and he's been under surveillance for a long time. And when they searched his place, instead of the incriminating documents, all they found was a pile of ash. At the time, it was necessary to apologize to him and let him go. The hope is that they'll catch him at the right moment somewhere down the line. The chief specifically called me and other people who are in the know about state secrets, to warn us to be careful with this rogue."

"Well, if that's the case, the situation is perfectly clear." Madam Przełęska had delivered her verdict.

Nina was silent.

They were sitting in the living room near an open door that led to the hall. So when the doorbell rang, Madam Przełęska hurried over to push the door closed, just in case.

After a few minutes, a servant entered and announced, "Mr. Oskar Hell."

Whereupon Madam Przełęska said loudly, so that each word could be clearly heard in the hall, "Tell that man we are not at home, nor will we *ever* be at home for *certain* people."

The sound of a slammed door resonated down the hallway.

"People are so awful," Nina sighed.

Nicodemus turned his back and pretended to be looking at the trinkets in the china cabinet. He glimpsed the contours of his smiling face in the pane of glass, and he smiled wider still.

Krzepicki carefully read the six pages of the typed letter containing the Ministry of the Treasury's proposal, then made a quick review of the foreign and domestic exchange rates for grain. He shrugged.

"Hmm . . . So what is your opinion, Mr. President?"

Nicodemus frowned.

"Mine? . . . What do I think? . . . Well, I think it's maybe not the best deal."

"It's the worst deal ever! It's suicide! What are they thinking?! Now, when the stock market hits bottom, now they want to sell the grain! Now, when they know in advance that they'll lose thirty to forty percent! It's madness! To say nothing of the fact that dumping such a large amount of grain on the international market will lower prices even more, which means our markets will take a hit as well. And that's not all! Grain bonds will sink like a stone."

Nicodemus nodded.

"That's what I told Jaszuński yesterday," he said. "I warned him that I would stand in strong opposition to the treasury's proposal."

"Well, obviously! You are absolutely right, Mr. President."

"I wanted to hear your opinion, though, and I'm glad we agree. All right, Mr. Krzepicki, get a typist to dictate my response to the proposal. I'll give them a piece of my mind."

The response was ready within two hours. The meeting of the finance committee was to take place at seven o'clock, so they had an hour to spare.

They spent it talking about Koborowo, and specifically about Nicodemus's marriage.

The biggest problem was the question of what to do with George Ponimirski after the wedding. He knew that Nina would insist on transferring him from the pavilion to the manor house. She'd mentioned it many times. Dyzma didn't actually have anything against it. George was not such a loon that he needed to be sent off to Tworki. Dyzma was just concerned that he'd let slip about the whole Oxford thing.

Of course, he did not share fears of this nature with Krzepicki, who thought it would be prudent for Dyzma to try to satisfy Nina's request. If it turned out that life with George was intolerable, they could stick him in some asylum. The conversation ended there. Krzepicki drove Dyzma to the Council of Ministers building and headed to Madam Przełęska's.

Nicodemus was sitting silent and obdurate at the large table, glowering at the prime minister, the minister of the treasury, who was midspeech, and the remaining dozen or so dignitaries. There were two stenographers sitting at a little table nearby.

In a dry voice, and with frequent long pauses, the treasury minister was justifying his proposal. He explained that the only way to cover budget deficits was to sell the grain. At the same time, the international situation might improve, enabling us to borrow from foreign countries. In conclusion, he added that he was a philologist, that what he knew about the economy was as much he could pick up from his experience the last couple of years, that he'd held the office under protest, but that he did not intend to be the treasury minister in name only, so if his proposal were rejected, he would resolutely proffer his resignation.

In turn, the prime minister assured the preceding speaker that his merits were highly valued and that the proposal should be accepted. He received a general nodding of heads in response.

All eyes, however, were fastened on a stubbornly silent Dyzma. There was a sense of anticipation that he'd come out with something unexpected, and he did not disappoint. When the prime minister turned to him with a smile, asking for his opinion, Nicodemus stood up.

"Gentlemen, I'm not a fan of chitchat, so I'll be brief. This is not about us, it's about the good of the state, and this is no time for mumbo jumbo or gobbledygook. This plan you're talking about here? It's horrible. I will limit myself to reading my declaration."

He unfolded the response Krzepicki had prepared and read it.

Dyzma was still reading when the audience began to stir. When he finished, the agitated treasury minister leapt up, gesticulating and sputtering in protest. The room was buzzing, there were sharp exchanges of opinions and even a scuffle, which gradually, as a result of the prime minister's persuasion, assumed the form of a discussion.

At some point, Minister Jaszuński turned to Dyzma with an irritated question: "How is it, Mr. President, that your opposition to this project is so unyielding when the day before yesterday you assured me that you were in general agreement with this plan?"

Dyzma reddened.

"I never said that!"

"Yes you did, you said it might be good."

"That's not true!"

"*You're* the one who's saying things that aren't true!" Jaszuński shouted. "Maybe you didn't use those exact words, but you more or less told me that you supported the project!"

"But, sir," the treasury minister said in a scathing tone, "don't you understand? This was President Dyzma's strategy, to ambush us with his opposition."

Nicodemus stood up.

"I have nothing more to talk about. I said what I had to say. And you gentleman can do as you wish."

The treasury minister's proposal was approved.

"I don't really care," Nicodemus said to Krzepicki that evening when they were returning together from Madam Przełęska's, "since I'm going to resign anyway."

"But the bank! Such a pity!"

Dyzma shrugged.

"But it was your idea, sir, your baby!"

"The hell with it!"

"There'll be quite a furor tomorrow!"

"What furor?" Nicodemus asked cluelessly.

"Well, in the papers. After all, they're like flies to manure. But surely a significant part of the press will be on your side."

"So what good does that do me?"

"Well, of course, the profit is purely platonic, but you know, Mr. President, I have a thought!"

"Yeah?"

"What we have here is a superb opportunity for you. In other words, submit your resignation tomorrow."

"Ehh . . . not worth it. I was planning to resign right before the wedding. What's the point of losing out on a couple thousand zlotys?"

"And you'd be right, Mr. President, if not for the fact that they won't have a successor lined up. And anyway, they certainly won't be eager to let go of a man like you. So, it'll get dragged out, but for you, there's a big moral profit."

"What profit?"

"Well, it's simple. You'll submit your resignation without giving a reason. It will then become clear that you don't want to bear any responsibility for the bloodbath at the Grain Bank, which is what approving this proposal will lead to."

"Aha." Dyzma was catching on.

"You know I'm right, Mr. President. And public opinion will be entirely on your side."

Nicodemus laughed and slapped Krzepicki on his shoulder.

"You're quite the smooth operator, Mr. Krzepicki."

"I'm at your service, Mr. President."

Chapter 19

Krzepicki's prediction came true insofar as, the following day, most of the papers published stories, albeit very cautious and somewhat vague, concerning the finance committee's resolution, as well as a communiqué issued by the finance committee in which the opposition press found much to decry.

That same day, Nicodemus—together with Krzepicki, who accompanied his boss to underscore the moment's solemnity—paid a visit to the prime minister and submitted his resignation. The prime minister, surprised and disoriented, pleaded at length for Dyzma to withdraw his resignation and not make an already bad situation worse. The man in question, however, emphatically declared that his decision was irrevocable. He agreed to fulfill the duties of his post until a successor was nominated but stressed that under no circumstance, nor with any amount of persuasion, would he change his mind.

As he left the Palace of the Council of Ministers, Nicodemus was repeatedly photographed by reporters from three different papers, since Krzepicki had tipped them off about the resignation beforehand.

That was just before one o'clock; by two, Minister Jaszuński had arrived at the bank. His nerves were completely unstrung, his hands shook like jelly. Every few sentences, he repeated, "For the love of God, don't do this!"

He explained, established, elucidated, urged, this was unpatriotic, this resignation would trigger a panic in economic spheres, it would set off political shock waves that would endanger the state, it might lead to a rift that would bring down the cabinet. He appealed to Dyzma, furthermore, as a friend who had no business hamstringing him, Jaszuński, and all the rest.

Dyzma had not managed to say a single word when the treasury minister was announced, and right behind him were MP Lewandowski, Colonel Wareda, Vice Minister Ulanicki, Chairman Hirszman, and Prince Roztocki. Meanwhile, the telephone was ringing off the hook: Bank President Dyzma had been summoned to the Castle at five o'clock.

Everyone had mobilized to put Dyzma off his intention to resign. To this end, it was agreed that they would annul the finance committee's resolution, but Dyzma was unmoved.

"I never change my mind."

A crowd of reporters had gathered in the waiting room. He came out to them for a moment.

"You want to know, gentlemen, what's going on?" he said. "So yes, I handed in my resignation."

"For what reason, Mr. Bank President?"

"For personal reasons. That's all I can tell you."

"And your decision is final, sir?"

"Set in stone, in iron, in concrete!"

He nodded and left.

"There's a man with a true iron will," one of the reporters said.

"And a *smart* politician," added a second. "He knows what he's doing."

The morning papers were ablaze with sensational headlines. Political spheres buzzed. Predictions were made that the minister of the treasury would step down, and the entire cabinet with him. Of course, as Krzepicki foretold, a direct link was drawn between the fracas at the finance committee meeting and Bank President Dyzma's resignation. Somehow or other his formal declaration was released. It made a colossal impression. With the exception of the official state news, everyone was in Dyzma's corner, sparing no superlative in appraising his wisdom, his intellect, the virtues of his character. His epithet at the circus was fondly recalled, and his curriculum vitae was republished, along with photographs with captions along the lines of,

The brilliant economist, Bank President Nicodemus Dyzma, who pulled our country out of economic crisis, leaves the Palace of the Council of Ministers accompanied by his personal secretary, Z. Krzepicki, after tendering his resignation, the protest of an eminent statesman against the cabinet's suicidal policy.

Even the opposition press, which until recently had been more than happy to attack him, now sung his praises, using his name as a cudgel against the government.

Nina read through the piles of newspapers, her cheeks flushed. Her breath caught from sheer emotion. My God! After all, this towering figure was her Nicodemus! She pitied herself for her inability to truly grasp his greatness. She was proud.

She herself had asked him to quit the bank. After all, she had wanted him all to herself. But now, as she realized what an enormous blow this would be to the state, her beloved fatherland, she was ashamed of her egotistical desires, and she resolved to ask her fiancé to withdraw his resignation.

She ran out into the hallway. She expected Nicodemus to be somber from the difficulty of the decision, overcome with worry for the fate of the nation, battle worn from the struggle between the statesman bearing the burden of responsibility and the private man in love.

Which is why the cheerful expression on Dyzma's face filled her with an astonishment that didn't subside until she explained to herself that Nicodemus was masking his sadness with a smile so as not to upset her.

She greeted him with passionate kisses and led him to her bedroom. Here, in the full feeling of the greatness of her sacrifice, she announced to Nicodemus that she was prepared to relinquish Koborowo and settle in Warsaw, since he was needed for the good of the country. Perhaps in a year, someone might be found who could take over Nicodemus's chairmanship, and then—

"There's nothing to discuss," Nicodemus broke in. "I've been to the Castle, and my resignation was accepted."

"But they'll be so happy when, despite that, you stay!"

"Of course!"

"And the country will gain!"

"I'm sure that it would gain."

"So?"

"You don't know politics, Nee Nee. I did what I must. And for another thing, I love you too much and I want to be with you in Koborowo. Can you blame me for that?"

Nina threw her arms around his neck.

"Darling, darling, if only . . ."

There was a knock at the door.

It was Madam Przełęska. An outpouring of rapturous admiration followed, culminating in a grandiloquent sigh.

"You don't even know, my dear Ninette, you don't even realize how lucky you are that your path in life has led to such a man!"

The conversation turned to the subject of weddings.

Nina announced her desire for a modest, quiet ceremony in Koborowo's parish church, and afterward they would spend the entire spring in Algeria or Egypt.

Madam Przełęska accepted the second part of this proposal. She objected, however, to the first.

"But Ninette, it's sheer nonsense to hide this wedding away! More than nonsense, it's tactless!"

"What do you want, Auntie? Daddy always said that seventy percent of women don't have an ounce of tact. I'm only a woman."

"It's my belief," Madam Przełęska was not giving up, "that your president will by no means agree to your plan. How could he?! The ceremony simply must be held in Warsaw, with great fanfare, with a full retinue. So your friends, and the president's friends, can be there! *Mon Dieu*! Countess Ponimirska marrying a brilliant man of state! What is there to hide?! I would simply be ill if you decided otherwise. Well, Mr. President, I appeal to your judgment!"

Nicodemus jutted out his lower lip and raised his eyebrows.

"Here's my thinking: Why not have the wedding in Warsaw?"

"Bravo, bravo!" Madam Przełęska was gratified. "Wise words. You see, Ninette, I knew that's what he would decide. Followed by a grand reception . . . I know it's hard for you, Ninette, but you must take into account that your fiancé is not a private citizen—"

"He is now," Nina cut in.

"Ach, 'now,' 'now,' what do you mean, 'now'? All over the city they're saying he'll be a minister before you can blink an eye!"

"Nah . . . take it easy," Dyzma waved his hand. "No need to exaggerate. But you're not wrong, Madam. We'll have a party."

Nina meekly agreed. Since this was what he wanted, there was clearly some hidden logic he didn't wish to divulge, and she had long since abandoned her attempts to penetrate this locked-away soul, whose depths she could not plumb, and whose steadfastness she could sense only with her womanly instinct.

"And as for this trip," Nicodemus began, "I'm thinking that it's better not to go."

Nicodemus furrowed his brow and rubbed his hands. The very thought of traveling abroad, where his unfamiliarity with foreign languages would be exposed, made his blood run cold. The few snatches of German he could scrape together—for want of anything better—would not be enough to manage.

"Do you," Madam Przełęska asked in a sugary tone, "perhaps consider it unpatriotic, in times like these, to spend money in foreign lands? But everyone does it!"

"Exactly! It's exactly the wrong thing to do! Every penny taken abroad is a robbery of one's fatherland." Dyzma recited the slogan he'd read on some propaganda poster not long ago. "It's the wrong thing to do."

"Well, but you render such service to your fatherland . . ."

"All the more reason! I have to set a good example for others. No, we're not going abroad. We can tour the country."

"You're right, Nicky, I was being foolish when I said that. We can go to Zakopane, Krynica, the Beskid Mountains . . ."

A servant appeared in the doorway and addressed Nina, "Please, Your Ladyship, a lady has arrived for Your Ladyship."

"For me? Who?"

"She didn't want to give her name. She's in the sitting room."

"Excuse me," said Nina. "I will see who it is."

She went through the dining room and the boudoir and then opened the door to the sitting room. Her scream was involuntary.

Kasia was standing before her. In her short, ash-gray fur coat and her high-crowned fur cap, a cigarette hanging from her mouth, she looked like a slender young boy who had just put on a skirt.

"Hello, Nina," she said in that familiar, metallic alto.

The blood rushed to Nina's face. She didn't know what to do. Kasia's surprise arrival put her in a state of utter perplexity because, after all, it brought her such joy. She'd kept convincing herself, and others as well, that she had forgotten, but now she knew that she'd remembered everything. As if she could ever forget! That first spring, the first intoxicating discovery of that delicious secret that nature had locked up inside her . . .

"You're not going to say hello to me?" Kasia took a few steps and stood right in front of Nina. "Maybe you're angry that I'm here?"

Nina came to her senses.

"But no, Kasia, not at all! I'm very glad to see you."

Kasia took hold of her hand and gently but firmly drew Nina to her.

"No, a formal greeting like that from you, that won't do at all."

She encircled Nina's neck with her arms and kissed her on the mouth.

It happened so unexpectedly that Nina didn't have time to move away. Not until a long moment had passed did she break free from the embrace and whisper reproachfully, "Kasia! . . ."

Kasia looked into her eyes. "Forgive me," she replied. "Your mouth is even fresher and more succulent than before . . . You're not inviting me to sit down? . . ."

"Why, of course, Kasia!" She gestured to a chair and sat down herself. Kasia reached into the pocket of her fur and pulled out a large gold cigarette case, lit a new cigarette, and gazed at Nina in silence.

"You're smoking a lot," Nina murmured.

"You're not going to ask me how I got here?"

"Did they give you my address at Koborowo?"

"No, it was given to me by Oskar Hell, whom you know."

"Ah! Poor man."

" 'Poor man'?" Kasia was surprised. "As far as I know, he's rich and completely self-satisfied."

"I don't know if you heard," said Nina. "He was arrested and charged with espionage."

Kasia shrugged.

"It's possible. I really don't care. I'm very grateful to him, seeing as he gave me a little tidbit of information about you . . . You're divorcing that old bastard?"

"Kasia, how can you speak that way about your own father?"

"Let's let that lie. So? You're divorcing him?"

"Yes, and as a matter of fact, it's already done. I got an annulment."

"Very wisely done. Hell wrote me that my venerable father left you Koborowo. I really couldn't understand it. Where he managed to find the honor to do it, I'll never know. But enough about that. I came here to take you away. You must come with me, it'll do you good. It's spring right now in Sicily . . ."

Nina gave her a wan smile.

"No, Kasia, I can't . . ."

"Here in Warsaw, the sky hangs over your head like the grave, but there it glows like a smile . . ."

"I'm getting married in a month," Nina said quietly.

Kasia leapt up from her seat and crushed her cigarette in the ashtray.

"Aha, so it's true!"

Nina was silent.

"Oh, I pity slave women like you! You just can't live without the yoke, without the grindstone! And I suppose you're getting married to that Dyzma?"

"I love him."

"What bullshit!" Kasia swore.

She crumpled up her gloves.

"Nina, Nina!" she suddenly exploded. "You can't do this! Nina, don't you realize what it's doing to me? Don't you have the smallest glimmer of feeling for me? Think, stop and think! . . ."

"Don't torture me, Kasia, you know how much I love you. But I'm telling you . . . I consider it my duty to tell you, I want to be honest with you . . . I swore to him, and to myself, that I'd never go back to you . . ."

"Nina, I'm begging you, put off the wedding, have mercy on me! . . . Just for half a year, for three months . . . Some time to reflect on it, maybe you'll come to the conclusion that you're making a mistake. Nina, I'm begging you, if you could only see the light and realize he's not worthy of you . . . I'm not asking for much, just a delay, a short delay! . . ."

Nina, gently smiling, shook her head.

"You're mistaken. *I'm* not worthy of *him*. You know so little about him and anyway, you're still living abroad, you don't realize what he is to our country, to our society, what it—"

"Ugh, what does that matter to me?" Kasia interrupted her. "I only care about you, about your happiness and my happiness! Nina, Nina, I'm begging you . . . Nina . . . Nina . . ."

She fell to her knees, taking both of Nina's hands and covering them with kisses.

"A short delay . . . I'm begging you . . ."

"Kasia, calm down, what are you doing? Kasia, get ahold of yourself!"

There were steps coming from the adjacent room. Kasia picked herself up heavily from the floor. Dully, she put on her gloves.

"I'll go now."

"Be well," said Nina. "And don't think ill of me . . ."

Kasia nodded silently. She stood still for a moment and was gazing at Nina when the door opened and in walked Nicodemus. After a moment of astonished speechlessness, he quickly regained his equilibrium. He jammed both hands in his pockets and curtly asked, "What are you doing here?"

Kasia took his measure with a look of pure loathing.

Dyzma noted Nina's pallor. He guessed that there must have been some kind of incident, and ire swept through him.

"I'm asking you, what do you want with my fiancée? What?"

"Oh, Nicky!" Nina attempted to pacify him.

"Why the hell did you come back here? I don't want to see you—"

He didn't finish, for Kasia burst into harsh, ironic laughter and spun on her heel.

The door slammed shut behind her.

"What did she want from you?" Dyzma asked after a pause.

Nina began to cry. He was unable to get a single word out of her, and he stomped angrily around the room, shaking the furniture.

Madam Przełęska came in but beat a hasty retreat, assuming she had chanced upon a jealous quarrel or some serious couple's argument.

It took a while for Nina to calm down, and afterward there was nothing she wanted to say. She only assured Nicodemus that he could be certain of her faithfulness and that Kasia would never come back.

"How does that make any kind of sense?" Dyzma puzzled it over. "Dames really do have feathers and sawdust where their brains should be."

Chapter 20

It was a poignant moment. The entire staff of the National Grain Bank was gathered in the boardroom, which had been cleared of tables and chairs.

At the front stood the director, his two deputies behind him, then there were the signatories, and finally all the clerks. There was a hum of hushed conversation. The door swung open, and the bank president strode in.

A hundred pairs of curious eyes fixed themselves to his face, straining to read their boss's thoughts, but the stone mask of his features was as mysterious and impenetrable as always.

He stood before them, cleared his throat, and began to speak:

"Ladies and gentleman. I invited you here to say goodbye. Despite their urgent desire for me to continue in this position, I'm stepping down. Maybe you know why, or maybe you don't, it's all the same to me. In leaving, I want to thank you for your hard work and service, and thank you for assisting me, the creator of this bank, in my exemplary leadership.

"I think I'm leaving you with good memories of me, because I was a true father to you and—not to brag—many of you learned a lot from me. I don't know yet who my successor will be. But I'll say this: you should give him the respect you gave me, because you should always respect your superiors, although I can tell you I'm sure he won't be a great statesman, and he'll probably even screw up all the good work I did here, but after all, a boss is a boss. Continue to work for the good of our precious country, so the state may benefit, since they're the ones writing your paychecks. It pains me to leave you, and maybe I haven't been so delicate with you sometimes, but that's just me, that's who I am, and in my heart I've become attached to you."

He took out a handkerchief and loudly blew his nose.

After these words, the director took over. In his long speech, he extolled the many virtues of Bank President Nicodemus Dyzma, emphasizing his excellent organizational skills and benevolent attitude toward his subordinates. He concluded by expressing his grief, on behalf of himself and everyone gathered, that they were losing such a wise leader, and then, amid loud cheers, he handed the president a magnificent desk pad bound in gilded leather.

On its cover was a large silver panel with the image of Nicodemus's face at the top, a picture of the bank building at the bottom, and the following dedication in the middle:

To the venerable Nicodemus Dyzma, economist extraordinaire: creator, founder, organizer, and first President of the National Grain Bank—

Your grateful employees

Numerous signatures followed.

The bank president's personal secretary had taken copious notes throughout the entire ceremony, especially during the speeches, and now he quickly transcribed the dedication and instructed one of the clerks to make the appropriate number of copies and get them out to the press.

He was in a hurry himself, because they still had to change into tailcoats to make it to the farewell banquet the chairman of the Council of Ministers was giving in honor of Nicodemus.

Meanwhile, Dyzma was saying his goodbyes to the staff, offering everyone his hand.

Upon his arrival at the Palace of the Council of Ministers, Nicodemus was informed that a big surprise was awaiting him: before the banquet, he was to be given a medal of honor.

At the table, innumerable toasts were made, all characterized by an overt cordiality, so as to mitigate the negative effect his resignation had made on public opinion.

At the end of the banquet, Ulanicki rose and, grinning broadly, delivered a convivial speech in which he announced that the culprit who had necessitated today's ceremony had authorized him to report that very soon he would marry Countess Nina Ponimirska, and it was his great pleasure to invite everyone present to both celebrate their nuptials and consume great quantities of alcohol.

His words were greeted with playful shouts and joking questions, since the news was no surprise to anyone.

After the banquet, there was a soiree attended by several dozen people. A common theme of conversation among partygoers was the possible consequences of Dyzma's resignation. The lion's share of attention was drawn to the alarming fact that the Grain Bank had taken a big hit on the stock market. The optimists were claiming it was a blip of distress caused by Dyzma's resignation and that the bonds would go up again, while the pessimists warned that a market meltdown was coming. When Nicodemus was asked for his thoughts on the matter, he shrugged.

"The government did as they wanted, and we'll see what comes of it."

Of course, this statement was taken as a prediction of a crisis, and since the recent months had ushered in a series of fresh political tensions and economic failures, it was generally expected that the current cabinet was not long for this world. Under these circumstances, the decision of President Dyzma, he of outstanding organizational acumen and incredible strength, to withdraw from public service because of a difference of opinion, naturally attracted a great deal of attention.

When a journalist attempted to investigate whether Dyzma might be casting about for a new government portfolio in the event that the cabinet fell, his answer was one of categorical denial:

"No, I'm going to the country and tending to my estate."

The news immediately swept the salons, but of course no one believed it was true.

Chapter 21

There were twenty-two carriages and over a hundred automobiles. Crowds blanketed the square in front of the church and the adjacent streets; the trams had been stopped. Two long police cordons maintained order. A red carpet ran from the pavement all the way to the top of the sanctuary steps. Policemen checked invitations at the entrance. Through the open doors, one could see the church's interior, ablaze with a thousand lights and bursting with flowers.

The automobiles and carriages stopped at the red carpet, and passengers were emerging to the crowd's immediate recognition, their murmured names rippling through the assembled throng.

"Prince Roztocki . . . The Italian ambassador . . . Minister Jaszuński . . ."

Ladies in sumptuous gowns, gentlemen in gleaming uniforms or tailcoats. The fragrance of perfume, flowers, gasoline.

The church was filled to the brim, and still automobiles kept coming.

A magnificent limousine had just arrived, and out of it stepped President Nicodemus Dyzma.

"That young man, you see, you see, it's President Dyzma! . . ."

They knew him well from the many photographs in the papers. From somewhere deep in the crowd, someone yelled, "Long live President Dyzma!"

"Long live Dyzma! Long live Dyzma!" shouted the crowd.

Every hat was waved up high.

"Long live Dyzma! Long live Dyzma!"

Nicodemus paused at the steps and, in his top hat, offered bows to all sides. On his solemn face, a kindhearted smile appeared.

The crowd roared with enthusiasm; Nina's carriage had just pulled up. At the sight of the crowd's ovation for her fiancé, she almost burst into tears from sheer emotion.

"Look," Madam Przełęska said in her ear. "Poles know how to appreciate the achievements of their great men."

Nicodemus went down to meet them and, amid the nonstop screaming of the crowd, escorted Nina into the church. There was a blast of organ music.

It had been a long time since anyone had seen such a splendid wedding.

After the ceremony had concluded, the newlyweds stepped out of the church to a fresh volley of cheers and then were taken by carriage on the traditional ride through the city.

Meanwhile, a seemingly infinite line of vehicles was bringing guests to the Hotel Europejski, where a wedding feast had been prepared for two hundred forty people.

Here, too, in front of the hotel, a crowd of onlookers had gathered and was waiting.

And here, too, Dyzma was met with cries:

"Long live Dyzma!"

Nicodemus beamed with joy. Nina's smiling face glowed.

They accepted best wishes from a never-ending procession of guests. Before dinner, the toasts were equally endless. Reading out the congratulatory telegrams took an entire hour, so it wasn't until eleven that the ball began. The young groom nearly danced till he dropped, and with such panache that the guests, unaware of his exploits in Łysków, shared observations along the lines of, "Who would have thought that President Dyzma had such a good sense of humor?"

Or:

"The new husband's gotten himself tipsy, look how he's clowning around."

"Bah, why not have some fun? A wife like that, and Koborowo supposedly a king's fortune!"

The morning sun was already shining when Krzepicki, who was in charge of everything, gave the word that the ball was over. The train that would take the newlyweds to Koborowo was departing at eight twenty. Most of their guests accompanied them to the train station. Their parlor car, lent to them at no charge by the transportation minister, was literally stuffed with flowers. There were final well-wishes and goodbyes, then the locomotive blew its whistle and the train was off.

Nina and Nicodemus stood at an open window, bowing toward the profusion of handkerchiefs and hats waving at them from the receding platform. The train picked up speed, and the platform disappeared in the gray haze of the city.

Nina threw her arms around her husband's neck.

"My God! How happy I am! Nicky, tell me, how is it possible to be so happy, what did I do to deserve you?"

"What? . . . um . . . to deserve? . . ."

"Yes, Nicky, what did I do to deserve you, my great, wise, beloved *you*, to have you as my husband? What? . . ."

Dyzma, scratching his chin, thought about it. He had absolutely no answer for this question, and it irritated him.

"Ehh," he grunted, "don't you have anything bigger to worry about?!" They drew together in a passionate kiss.

The road from the station to the manor was flanked with two rows of green birches and dotted with dense clusters of calamus. The station building itself was festooned with wreaths of greenery, the platform crowded with Koborowo laborers and officials, as well as a great many local gawkers. Many of them had heard yesterday's radio broadcast—the "Veni Creator" sung by famous soloists, the choirs, the organ, the cheers in honor of the bride and groom.

Accordingly, interest was running extremely high.

When the train appeared in the distance, the hubbub of conversation ceased instantly, as if severed by a knife. At once, the amateur orchestra struck up a march and a ceremonial mood fell upon the crowd. The main officials stood at the front of the platform, along with the little daughter of the director of the steam mill, who wore a white dress and was carrying a bouquet of wildflowers.

Unfortunately, owing to the train conductor's inattention, the parlor car stopped considerably wide of the platform's center, coming to a halt between a grain warehouse and a ladies' and gentlemen's restroom kiosk. Which meant that the entire assembled elite, along with the mill director's little daughter, had to trot along the track in order to make it there by the time the newlyweds disembarked. They came running up just in time, and the daughter handed Nina the flowers. At this point she was supposed to declaim a verse, but she was struck by stage fright and, despite prompting, was unable to open her mouth. Nina kissed the little girl, while Dyzma stood on the steps of the parlor car and received well-wishers.

Finally, he saw fit to say a few words:

"We thank you very much. And I, and my wife, we'll make sure that none of you ever regrets greeting us so warmly. For now, in honor of our wedding day, I hereby decree that all employees, without exception, get a bonus. Even though it'll cost me."

At these words, a tsunami of cheers crashed over them, and the orchestra banged out a fanfare. Passengers from the neighboring cars were watching with interest, and some of them, swept up in the mood, were shouting out too. Particularly invested in the scene was a skinny little Yid in a third-class car, who, God knows why, kept yelling in a thick accent at the top of his lungs, "Huzzah! Huzzah!"

At the threshold of the manor, the steward and the housekeeper, surrounded by the entire staff, met the newlyweds with bread and salt.

Nicodemus placed two five-hundred-zloty bills on the tray and said, "To divide among yourselves."

Inside the manor, Krzepicki had already made some fundamental changes. Upstairs, Nina's former apartment had been turned into guest rooms, whereas her bedroom had been moved to the room directly next door to Nicodemus's bedroom, with a bathroom on either side. The entire left wing had been redone as living quarters for George, while the annex in the park would be taken up by Krzepicki.

After the ball and their journey home, the bride and groom were tired and went to bed at a reasonable hour. Earlier that evening they made a plan: tomorrow they would go together to the annex to have a talk with George and propose that he be transferred to the manor.

But Dyzma had mulled that over for a long time before he fell asleep and had reached the conclusion that visiting Ponimirski together with Nina might not be the best idea in light of Ponimirski's unpredictability.

What if he goes nuts and everything starts to fall apart?

That's why he ordered that he be awakened at eight.

It worked. He peeped into his wife's bedroom and was reassured that she was still asleep. After all, she never got up early.

Nicodemus got dressed quickly, told the servants he would eat breakfast when the lady awoke, and headed to the park.

He had planned in advance for his conversation with George, but as he neared the annex, he felt a sudden loss of self-confidence. Ponimirski was the only person whose presence elicited in him a kind of fear. And it was understandable, considering George's abnormal state of mind and his proclivity for unexpected mischief.

Dyzma found him still in bed. He had just eaten porridge with milk and was whistling a little tune. The miniature pinscher was sitting on the duvet, from time to time giving his master's porridge dish a casual lick.

The footman closed the door behind Dyzma, and it was only then that Ponimirski became aware of his presence.

"Good morning," said Nicodemus.

"Ah!" The count burst out laughing. "My distinguished friend! Well, my friend, get rid of this lousy porridge."

Dyzma obediently carried out this order and then sat himself in a chair right next to the bed. Ponimirski gave him a rancorous smile. His huge eyes, set against his bloodless, sickly little boy's face, his sharp nose, and his thin, twitching lips, evinced great satisfaction.

"How's your health, sir?" Nicodemus began. "They say you were seriously ill?"

"Thank you. Don't let my health worry you, my friend."

"I'm not worried about your health as a friend." Dyzma pulled the trigger. "Only as a brother-in-law."

"Whaaat? . . ."

"As a brother-in-law," Nicodemus repeated, with extra volume to bolster his courage.

"What's the meaning of this?" the count shouted.

"What it means is, it means that you're my brother-in-law. I married your sister."

In one swift movement, Ponimirski threw off the duvet and stood atop the bed in his pink silk pajamas, looming over Dyzma.

"Liar! You shameless deceiver, you idiot!"

Dyzma was seized with fury. He, the great Bank President Dyzma, venerated by cheering crowds, cozy with members of the highest spheres—who did Ponimirski think he was, speaking so insultingly to him? . . . He sprang from his chair, grabbed George by the wrist and flung him down on the bed.

Ponimirski hissed in pain as he fell onto the bedsheets. The miniature pinscher began to yap violently.

"Uuugh . . . shit," Dyzma muttered.

At the door, the footman appeared, along with the nurse.

"Is the count worse?" she asked. "Am I needed?"

"Go to hell!" Dyzma roared, and they both immediately disappeared.

He lit a cigarette and offered one to Ponimirski, who, after a moment of hesitation, took it.

"You see, Count, I'm not kidding around. I'm telling you, I married your sister. The ceremony was the day before yesterday. What do you think about that?"

"I think it's a scandal!"

"Why a scandal?!"

"How could Countess Ponimirska marry such a boor, such a peasant, how could she take for a husband a man as coarse as you? Mr. . . . . Mr. . . . . what are you called?"

"Dyzma," answered Nicodemus.

"An amusing name," Ponimirski said, shrugging.

"So you wanted her to stay married to Kunik, the criminal? Is that it?"

"Well, no. In any case . . . I suppose that you, even though you are a highly sleazy character, can't be any more of a bastard than Kunik was. After all, you're too stupid to—"

"Count," Dyzma interrupted menacingly. "I suggest that you watch what you're saying!"

Ponimirski went quiet.

"Instead of insulting me, you should thank God."

"What?!"

"That's right, thank God. Because I won't mistreat you the way your first brother-in-law did. You'll move into the house and have complete freedom for yourself. We'll live together, the three of us, eating together, paying and receiving visits . . ."

Ponimirski's spirits improved markedly.

"Are you serious?"

"Completely serious."

"And they'll give me saddle horses to ride?"

"Everything. Generally speaking, you'll be free. I'll even give you a small allowance. I've already paid off your debts. But I have my own conditions."

"Such as?" Ponimirski became alarmed.

"First of all, keep your trap shut. Don't you dare tell anyone that what they're saying about Courland and about this Oxford isn't true."

George laughed.

"So people actually believe that absurdity?"

"Why shouldn't they believe it?"

"Well, taking a single look at you would suffice!"

Dyzma glared at him.

"That's not your business. Just keep quiet. And second of all, very hush-hush, so nobody finds out, you have to teach me a little English."

"Me?" Ponimirski was indignant. "I'm to teach boors? Insolent boors?"

"Quiet, you stupid ape!" Dyzma bellowed. "It's your choice. Either you do what I tell you, or I'll ship you off to Tworki in seconds flat."

Ponimirski bit his lip and burst out crying.

"Brutus, Brutus," he said through tears, stroking the miniature pinscher. "Are you hearing this? They want to lock up your master in a madhouse again . . . Brutus! . . ."

The profusion of tears dripping down his pale, round face astounded Dyzma.

"So," he asked, "which one will it be, George?"

"Please be so kind as to be more formal when addressing me," Ponimirski replied haughtily, his tears drying up immediately.

"And why should I? Seeing as now we're basically brothers . . . We should be on a first-name basis with each other. What would people think? That old friends and brothers-in-law should be calling each other 'mister'? . . ."

"Hilarious," smirked Ponimirski. "Do you not realize the vast distance that lies between us?"

"What kind of distance? It looks to me that I'm normal and you're nutty as a fruitcake. Simply put, it's your choice. And I'll say this to you again:

remember, no funny business. If you even think of opening your trap, I'll knock every one of your teeth out."

He brandished a clenched fist under Ponimirski's nose, but, contrary to expectation, Ponimirski looked pleased.

"Really? That's interesting. I've heard tell of such powerful blows, but I've never actually seen one. Do you know what? I'm going to call Antoni, and you can demonstrate this sort of punch on him. All right?"

He was already reaching for the bell, but Dyzma restrained him.

"What kind of crazy shit is that? I don't want to smash Antoni's face in, just yours. Just you try me. So then? Do we have an agreement?"

Ponimirski wrung his hands in despair and sighed heavily.

"Ugh, what a humiliation, what a disgrace! I have this simpleton, this yokel who wants to call me by my first name as if we're equals, and to top it all off, now I'm supposed to cram some English into his thick skull. Just look at the skull in question, it's right out of Lombroso."

Dyzma stood up and looked at his watch.

"Well, I guess this means farewell."

"You're leaving? Stay a while, it'll be boring all alone."

"You won't be all alone. I'm sending you to Tworki right now."

Ponimirski leaped out of bed, his entire body quaking, and ran to Dyzma: "No! No! I agree to everything!"

"You agree?"

"Yes."

"And you won't run your mouth?"

"No."

"You're going to teach me?"

"I will."

"Okay, super, and you'll call me by my first name?"

"But I don't remember your name. It's something idiotic."

"Nicodemus."

"Now I know . . . Nicodemus."

"So we're good?"

"What?"

"Well, so we're agreed?"

"We're agreed."

"Put 'er there, George. Bye!"

They shook hands and Dyzma left.

Ponimirski sat down on the rug and laughed for a long time—at what, he himself didn't even know. Finally, he began to shout, "Antoni! Antoni! Antoni!"

When his manservant opened the door, Ponimirski flew at him, fists flying.

"You kept this from me!"

"What did I keep from you?"

"That my sister got married! Old jackass! . . . Well, pack up my things, and be quick about it!"

"Pack? What for, sir?"

"We're moving."

"Where to?"

"To the house!"

Chapter 22

Two days after the newlyweds' arrival, Krzepicki, who had liquidated his boss's interests in Warsaw, also returned to Koborowo.

He immediately got down to work, since the delivery of railway ties was already underway and the regular springtime tasks required constant supervision. For this reason, he wasn't able to spend much time with Nicodemus and his wife, which didn't trouble those two in the least. They passed their days and weeks amusing themselves with excursions over water and land, by boat, motorcar, and horse. They also played billiards.

Nina felt entirely happy. Admittedly, certain doubts arose in her mind every now and then, but she pushed aside any marks against him; such peculiarities and prejudices could be forgiven in such a remarkable man and such a singular individual. Besides, she had so many reasons to be wholeheartedly grateful for him! If, during the day, any doubts and suspicions cropped up, the night brought a bliss that blurred everything. Nina's senses—so long had they withered on the vine, and now they'd found a natural outlet for their exuberant growth—were a decisive element in this.

Therefore, the marriage felt good and promised to last.

They planned to wait a few months before calling on the neighboring estates and accepting local visitors of their own, particularly because they were expecting Madam Przełęska for the summer, along with a multitude of guests from Warsaw.

Nicodemus spent a lot of time studying. He'd lock himself in the library, either with Ponimirski or on his own, and read. He took no pleasure in it, but he had wits enough to understand the benefits a book or a foreign language could bring him.

Over dinner in the evening, he would often make casual reference to things he'd read, citing freshly memorized opinions of various writers and noting the impression he made on those at the table. Not only Nina, but Krzepicki too, listened to his recitations with respect. Before long, a term for Nicodemus's hours in the library became widespread among the people of Koborowo: they called it "the master's academic work."

Only rarely did Dyzma visit the farms and industrial plants. The entire estate was in Krzepicki's hands, and its steadily increasing income was proof positive that the new administrator was managing beautifully.

George Ponimirski quickly adapted to his new role and behaved in a way that gave Nicodemus no reason for obvious dissatisfaction. True, there were incidents when he'd come out with some ambiguous word or a sarcastic laugh, but an ominous look from his brother-in-law was enough for him to regain control and pipe down. He hardly spoke with his sister. He nursed a chronic resentment toward her, and besides, he had a pathological inability to see women as beings capable of thought and reason.

At any rate, he was enjoying a kind of freedom he hadn't had for a long time, riding horses and even driving a car. Dyzma had given him permission to do so, harboring a quiet hope that one day he would break his neck.

George, however, although no stranger to practical jokes, brawls, scenes, and many other kinds of mischief, was particularly careful when it came to preserving his own neck. His mild insanity, harmless to those around him, soon became the area's favorite topic of amusing anecdotes.

Krzepicki he treated with imperious haughtiness. When forced to shake his hand, he barely offered two fingers and, as a rule, ignored his questions if they did not include the words "Your Excellency." Krzepicki laughed at this and didn't take George's airs personally.

"The old madman's pretty funny," he said. "I always find his antics amusing. It's an invaluable thing in the countryside. Now I understand why kings used to have jesters."

"He can go to hell," Dyzma responded.

Meanwhile, the letters and messages from old friends in Warsaw were less than reassuring.

The economic crisis deepened from day to day, and it was becoming apparent in Koborowo as well. His paper mills and sawmills were operating only thanks to government contracts. Mounting bankruptcies scuttled Dyzma's business interests again and again. Luckily, Krzepicki's resourcefulness and his supply arrangement with the government continued to guarantee him plenty of income. In any case, he was a veritable Croesus compared to the local landed gentry. They were doing worse and worse. It reached the point that, in the surrounding area alone, thirty estates had been put up for auction.

News from the country at large was no better. Farmers stopped using artificial fertilizers, reducing their own expenses to the bare minimum. What's more, rumors began to swirl that there was widespread selling of the grain owned and stockpiled by the National Bank. As a result, and combined with other economic complications, the bank bonds plummeted.

Bondholders started panicking. The stagnation in trade, the falling stock market, the severe crisis in industry, and the insolvency of banks—it all painted a picture of impending catastrophe. The newspapers were filled with bankruptcies, lockouts, strikes, and the many suicides of those who had lost fortunes or any hope of finding a job.

A murmur of dissatisfaction was growing in the country, aimed straight at the government. The call for a powerful man, who would take the helm of state in his strong and capable hands and navigate them through the crisis, was getting louder and louder.

Meanwhile, the harvest was approaching, and the prospect of a high-yield disaster loomed over the country again.

Nicodemus read the news and shook his head.

"Damn! What can come of this? . . ."

Chapter 23

It had been a long time since the harvest festival had been celebrated with as much fanfare as it was this year. The new squire liked to have fun and had money to burn. Guests came in droves. The first to arrive was Madam Przełęska with an endless caravan of chests and trunks, and that same evening Colonel Wareda drove out with both Countesses Czarska. The next day, the Koborowo cars and both carriages were kept busy all day long.

Provincial Governor Szejmont came with his wife and son, as did District Governor Ciszko, Minister Jaszuński and his wife, Baron and Baroness Rehlf, Uszycki with his sister in tow, General Czakowicz, the commandant of the district corps, along with two adjutants, Ulanicki, Holszycki, and Earl Korzecki's wife, as well as a dozen or so local personages.

The manor was swarming with guests, full of noise and bustling activity. Nina was so happy. She loved society life. For a week, she, with Krzepicki's help, had been planning a program of excursions, and games, and entertainment, had conducted an inspection of the pantries and an inventory of the cellars, had added more servants to the ranks, had readied the guest rooms, and had seen to the million other matters deemed necessary for a worthy gathering of family, acquaintances, and friends.

George was electrified. He whirled from guest to guest, playing the lord, showing off the stables to the gentlemen and trying in general to cut a fine figure. He felt like a great master again and nearly forgot that it wasn't he who owned Koborowo. Guests, discreetly forewarned of his mental illness by Krzepicki and Madam Przełęska, indulged him and didn't contradict a word he said.

Nicodemus greeted everyone politely, but with a reserve that bolstered the air of respect and esteem around him. Despite the presence of all these people, he didn't break with his custom of shutting himself away in the library. This contributed to his guests' incredible regard.

In the evenings, an orchestra imported from Warsaw played in the park, and the entire company frolicked in the fresh air, strolling the grounds or dancing on lawns illuminated by strings of colored lights. Sometimes they ventured into the forest with horses or carriages. Nina was extremely fond of these moonlight trips.

There were nonstop games of tennis from the moment the sun came up. Both courts were busy until noon, when lunch was served. Actually, everyone did exactly what they pleased all day long. The more aged subset of their company eagerly toured the industrial facilities and farm buildings, while the younger ones took their pleasure in riding horses, swimming in the river, and organizing races with motorboats and rowboats alike.

"Your estate is wonderful," everyone said to Nina and Nicodemus. "Koborowo is a real jewel."

And truly, everyone felt fantastic. The smoking room had been commandeered by bridge players who scarcely got up from their tables. The breakfast room was laid, from morning to night, with various snacks and tidbits, and the drinks flowed freely.

On the third day, a great ball was held. It was a wonderful thing. Of the one hundred forty who had been invited, one hundred sixty-three came.

The ball commenced at ten in the evening and staggered to a close, with a riotous mazurka, at one in the afternoon. More than a few strong drinks had been imbibed, which meant that the servants had their work cut out for them, searching through the bushes and various nooks and crannies for "corpses" to cart off to their beds. At any rate, everyone eventually got some sleep, since the harvest festival was to take place that evening.

Tar barrels were set up around the lawn in front of the manor, as well as long tables for the peasants; the ones on the veranda were for the guests. The provincial governor joked that the harvest leader with whom Dyzma was planning to have the first dance, the true harvest leader, would be none other than the automatic reaping machine.

"It's funny," he added, "the exceptional speed with which mechanization upsets every tradition. Such as, for example, the harvest festival, which nowadays has lost its raison d'être."

"It's sad," Nina said.

"Yes, I agree, but it's true nevertheless."

"And how will it all end?" sighed gray-haired Mr. Rojczyński, a neighbor of Koborowo. "It's utterly insane: these machines not only vulgarize our existence, deprive it of its beauty, but man himself is supplanted."

"Who supplants who now?" Dyzma was indignant. "Just look around, we're throwing a harvest festival and the people are happy. And if a couple of those riffraff there die out, well, to hell with them. Those machines are growing the general prosperity, that's what."

He turned on his heel and left.

"He's right, he's right," the general nodded.

"But none too, hmm . . . none too courtly in his choice of words," the old landowner noted with a touch of surprise.

The provincial governor gave him an indulgent smile. "My dear sir, believe me: he's allowed, he can afford it. General Baron Cambronne was another one for courtliness! . . ."

The orchestra played. Clusters of peasants were beginning to flock to the manor house lawn. Finally, the reapers' procession approached, singing a Belorussian song with no words. In this wistful a-a-a-a, the austere melody, this rough, untrained sound, there resonated not so much the joy of a harvest accomplished but instead the wild song of the battlefield. Nina always wondered at this unsettling melody, which had been preserved for probably a thousand years. She didn't know why, but she was sure it was what American Indian songs sounded like.

Meanwhile, the procession was drawing nearer. At its head walked a sturdy young girl with wide hips and a bust so exuberant it seemed ready to burst through her homespun embroidered blouse. Her thick but shapely calves were visible below her short, red skirt, and—in contrast to the other girls, who wore silk stockings and polished, French-heeled pumps—her feet were bare. The leader of the procession must have been considerably poorer than her companions. She carried in her hands a large wreath woven from stalks of rye.

Baron Rehlf, standing next to Ponimirski, took him by the elbow and said, under his breath, "What a magnificent specimen! An absolute Pomona! A full-blooded human female. Just imagine what stomach muscles she must have, what thighs! I had no idea, Count, that here in the Borderlands, where the peasantry have been presented so miserably in terms of eugenics, I would see something so spectacular. As a matter of fact, they're *all* pretty. Hell, they're a race of their own. Inexplicable!"

George settled his monocle in place and gazed contemptuously at Rehlf.

"On the contrary, it's entirely explicable, Baron. The Ponimirskis have been lords of Koborowo for five hundred years, and to the best of my knowledge, none of my venerable ancestors were opposed to appreciating the folk's comelier half."

"Understood, understood," the baron nodded. "And yet the plebs still claim that we, the aristocracy, we involve ourselves in improving the race of horses and cattle only. But one look at the peasantry is enough to see that we're doing great work in that area, too."

"Excuse me," Ponimirski cut in. "What do you mean 'we'?"

"Well, the aristocracy."

"In that case, we misunderstand each other. I was speaking of the Family Ponimirski—the old aristocracy."

He removed his monocle, slipped it into his pocket, and turned away from the beet-red baron.

After several songs for the occasion, it was time for dancing and drinking galore. Because the evening was exceptionally chilly and the ladies had begun to complain, the company on the terrace decided to move into the house. Only Dyzma remained outside, not so much from a sense of duty as from the pleasure of some frenzied dancing with the wenches, and with the leader of the procession most of all. At one point, paying no attention to the gloomy expression on the face of her bridegroom-to-be, a broad-shouldered laborer from the mill, he took the girl by the hand and led her into the park.

She didn't resist the squire. There was nothing for her fiancé to do but go back to the festivities and get completely tanked with the rest of them.

Baron Rehlf, returning from a stroll in the park, where he'd wanted to extinguish his anger at that idiot Ponimirski, came to an involuntary halt at the sight of a certain little scene in progress, which inspired him to reflect, "So I was right, it's not only the old aristocrats who care about elevating the peasantry—it's also the new."

In the east, the night sky was beginning to fade into gray.

Chapter 24

The news came just before dinner, causing a general commotion. The cabinet had resigned and the resignation had been accepted.

Ulanicki received a telegram from Warsaw calling for him to return immediately.

For most of the guests at Koborowo, the change of government was a matter of direct personal relevance. For many, the odds of remaining in their posts were increasingly poor. Which was why no one could talk of anything else, and why Ulanicki was pacing the hall and uttering curses.

Madam Jaszuński even left before dinner.

Provincial Governor Szejmont called his office and instructed them to update him regularly on even the smallest details of the news coming out of Warsaw.

In the evening, the papers arrived. Their pages were overflowing with information and political rumors, multiple conflicting forecasts, various predictions and assessments of the situation. The one thing on which they agreed, though, was that the government had collapsed because it was unable to overcome the economic crisis and therefore must be replaced by an exceptionally strong cabinet, led by a man of extraordinary authority.

Among the many presumed candidates for the post of prime minister, there was one who stood out: General Troczyński, who had already made a name for himself as head administrator of the National Health Insurance and delegate to the International Congress of Culture and Art, and who had cemented his popularity with the publication of a pamphlet entitled "Strategic Mistakes of Napoleon the First, Alexander the Third of Macedonia, and Others." His previous work—a pamphlet entitled "Down with Communism!," as well as an oil painting, purchased by the Museum of the Republic of Poland, a self-portrait that depicted the general spearing a jaguar in one bold stroke—had long ago shed light on his merits and gained him early recognition.

In Koborowo, this candidacy was discussed at length, although—it needs to be said—without anyone raising any serious objections. During one such discussion over dinner, the only reservation anyone expressed was the baron's uncertainty about the choice of background color in the aforementioned painting.

"Nicky," Nina asked, "in your opinion, who should become the next prime minister?"

"I'm not sure . . ."

"Nevertheless? . . ."

"Well . . . if not Troczyński, then maybe Jaszuński? . . ."

A somewhat tipsy Colonel Wareda rapped his glass against the table.

"No, Nicodemus. Know who should become the next prime minister?"

"Who?"

"You."

There was silence. All eyes turned to Dyzma. He frowned, convinced that Wareda was having a laugh at his expense, and grunted disapprovingly, "Cool it, Wacek. You're sloshed."

Nina stood, an invitation for them to move to the sitting room. In the scuffle of chairs and feet, nobody heard the colonel's apologies.

"I suggest a boat ride on the lake!" one of the ladies called. "The moon is so beautiful tonight!"

Everyone enthusiastically agreed.

Indeed, it was an exceedingly lovely evening. The lake lay motionless, like a great slab of agate, and the sky was dotted with stars like tiny diamonds. Over everything shone the moon, which was, according to Governor Szejmont's calculations, at least five hundred carats.

As the boats paddled out with the soft splashing of oars, they began to sing.

"What a pity," Nicodemus sighed, "that there's no mandolin around here."

"Do you play the mandolin?" Miss Czarska asked in surprise.

"I do. And I especially like to play during moonlight boat rides. That's when inspiration strikes. The night, the moon, the sense of the horizon . . ."

Everyone burst out laughing, and District Governor Ciszko shouted, "Mr. President, must you make fun of our innocent singing?"

"Ah, sir," shrugged Madam Przełęska, "the former bank president has a lot on his mind!"

"I understand," the district governor backtracked. "I was just reading that they decided to close down the Grain Bank. What a bank it was! It has to be hard for its creator to watch it go down . . . Am I right, Mr. President?"

"And what if you aren't?" Dyzma answered with a question.

"Think about it," the district governor continued, "always and forever, it's been the case that simply knowing *how* to do things isn't nearly as important as actually making them happen. Everything was just fine when it was you, Mr. President, who was in charge of the bank."

"Maybe things will get better," Dyzma said.

"And yet!" The district governor waved his hand. "All it took was a couple of months for it to go bankrupt. A single man, just one man!"

"You're so right," confirmed Madam Przełęska with conviction.

"Cheerio, Nicodemus!" Ponimirski called from another boat. "Perhaps this calls for an Oxford rowing song? Shall we?"

"Sing, sing for us!" the ladies entreated.

"My voice is no good," Dyzma demurred with irritation.

"But it is, it is!" shouted George, enjoying his joke. "So you've forgotten how we used to bellow on the Thames? Lord Caeledin of Newdawn always said you sang like a—"

He didn't finish.

Nicodemus swung his oar, and Ponimirski, along with the rest of his boatmates, was splashed by an arc of water.

"I apologize," said Dyzma, "but cold water is the only thing that helps him."

They had just reached the shore. After a few minutes they came to the lane. There was an unfamiliar car in front of the manor house. It was very dusty, and the chauffeur was hovering over the raised hood.

"Who's this?" Dyzma asked.

"Director Litwinek."

"Litwinek?" Nicodemus raised his eyebrows.

Dyzma had met Director Litwinek during the official receptions at the Castle—he was the head of the secretariat there—but their relationship was not such that would entitle him to pay a visit to Koborowo.

They all went inside.

In the hall, Krzepicki was talking to a tall man with steel-gray hair. When Dyzma entered, they both rose, and there was a round of greetings and introductions.

"Well, how goes the government crisis?" Nicodemus asked casually.

Director Litwinek bowed. "I have the honor of coming here on account of that very matter."

"That very matter? How's that?"

Everyone waited tensely for a response. Litwinek reached into his briefcase and took out an envelope. He paused for a moment, and the silence was absolute. In a solemn voice, he said, "Mr. Bank President, sir. I come here by order of the president of the republic to ask you on his behalf to form a new government. Here is the letter, handwritten by the president himself."

He held the envelope in his outstretched hand.

Nicodemus flushed. His mouth fell open.

"What . . . that what?"

Litwinek, pleased with the impression he'd made, smiled slightly.

"The president of the republic hopes that you, sir, would be willing to form the new cabinet and assume its leadership."

Dyzma hesitantly took the envelope and, with trembling hands, pulled out a sheet of paper. He read what he could; the letters seemed to jump and squirm before his eyes.

Indeed, the handwritten letter confirmed what Litwinek had already said. He slowly folded the letter. His face was etched with worry.

"The president of the republic has no doubt," said Litwinek, "that you, sir, will not refuse him, especially now, in this time of severe political strain and acute economic crisis, when the country needs to be pulled out of its downward spiral. Difficult and monumental is the task before you. But the president believes that you, sir, only you, who has earned not only his trust, but the trust of the people, only you can pull this off successfully. Your towering authority, your formidable knowledge and wealth of experience virtually guarantee that you'll be able to form a government; under your firm hand, the country's prosperity will increase, this country that awaits, that longs for, a strong man. Allow me to convey my personal confidence as well—I believe that only you can do it, Prime Minister."

He made a low bow and fell silent.

It was the first time Litwinek had been in charge of such an honorable mission, and it was important to him that his words make a potent impression. He did not fail.

Raw emotion was visible on every face. Here, in their presence, the helm of the Ship of State was passing into the hands of a man, and not just any man, but a man of true greatness!

Nina, pale as paper, was clutching the arm of a chair to support herself. Wareda looked as if he were about to cry. Krzepicki stood erect, chin raised, casting proud looks at those present. From behind his shoulder, George Ponimirski's enormous eyes were wide with utter amazement.

Nobody dared to sit down.

Provincial Governor Szejmont made the first move. He went to Nicodemus and, bowing his head, shook his hand.

"Please accept my best wishes, from the very bottom of my heart, but not my congratulations, for at this historical moment, congratulations should be offered to *us*, the citizens of the state and also its loyal servants."

The other guests followed the governor's example. Nicodemus silently shook each of their hands, his face a bleak mask.

He was acutely aware of the magnitude of the honor he'd received. He, Nicodemus Dyzma, a miserable clerk from Łysków, could now decide the fate of a great nation, write his own ticket, his name on everyone's lips, everyone in the entire country, nay, the entire world!

But . . . but actually . . . What was really in it for him?

Warsaw all over again . . . a nervous life full of traps and ambushes, having to watch every word he said . . .

But power, enormous power over more than thirty million people! Thousands would give up their lives for just one day of power like that, and that title: Chairman of the Council of Ministers! . . . The Cabinet of Prime Minister Dyzma . . . The Government of Nicodemus Dyzma . . . The military presenting arms, warships saluting him with cannons . . . Whatever he said, they'd put it in the paper, print it in the daily news all over the world . . . Power, celebrity . . .

"I am kindly awaiting your answer, Prime Minister," Litwinek said.

Nicodemus came to. He looked around. All eyes were fixed on him.

He cleared his throat and rose from his chair.

"Give me half an hour to think it over," he said dully. "Mr. Krzepicki, come with me."

He headed for his office. Krzepicki followed him and closed the door.

"I'm wondering what I should do," Dyzma began.

"What do you mean, sir? Isn't it obvious! What an honor, what power!"

"Well, of course. But on the other hand, you see, this is a position of great responsibility. It's not just some bank at stake, it's the whole country."

"So what?"

"So I might not be able to handle it."

"You can handle it, sir."

Nicodemus clucked doubtfully.

"Yeah, but these days? All these crises, it's getting harder . . ."

"You'll figure something out, don't worry. I mean, after all, you've got no shortage of winning ideas, sir. And picture it, sir: you take office, people are satisfied, the national mood improves, you make a couple impressive moves . . . And if the economy takes a turn for the better! . . ."

"And if it doesn't? . . . C'mon, man, I'll make an idiot of myself, that's all there is to it."

"So what? We'll blame it on the bad economic situation and the global crisis. Big deal. Yours wouldn't be the first cabinet to fall."

Somebody knocked on the door. It was Nina.

"Do you mind?" she asked shyly.

"No, come on in!"

"Madam," Krzepicki said, wringing his hands, "just imagine: the president is hesitating!"

"Listen, Nee Nee, it's not an easy job. And for another thing, I like it here in Koborowo."

Nina's face was shining.

"Darling! You are so good to me! But, Nicky, I'm not such an egoist that I'd keep you here to the detriment of my fatherland. Only you can decide what is right. In my opinion, however, you should save the country."

"You think so?"

"You yourself know best what duty requires of you. But do not suspect me, God forbid, of snobbery. I assure you that I'd prefer to be here with you than to bear the title of Prime Minister's Wife. If I believed, however, that you were depriving our nation of your steady hand out of love for me, it would be very upsetting to me . . ."

"Hmm," Dyzma mused.

"Mr. President," Krzepicki began, observing in his boss some tentative movements toward a favorable decision. "Mr. President, I have an idea. Shortly after taking office, we'll leave for London."

"What for?" Dyzma asked reluctantly.

"What for? For a foreign loan! They wouldn't give it to just anyone, but you have enormous connections there. Presumably more than a few of your old colleagues from Oxford are running the show over there, occupying the highest posts and whatnot. And perhaps you can work something out with them and get a loan?"

Krzepicki did not realize that he had just sealed his hope's fate.

Nicodemus frowned and waved his hand for silence.

Right, he thought, I completely forgot about that . . . As prime minister I'd have to receive all kinds of ambassadors . . . Maybe even go to Geneva. Okay, so I could take an interpreter, but that would make it pretty obvious that I can't make heads or tails of anything other than Polish . . . other languages . . . And this lousy Oxford story . . . Besides, what do I need all this for?

He got up from his chair. Nina and Krzepicki looked at him anxiously.

"Well, I've made my decision," he said, going for a tone of steely determination. "I do not accept the position of prime minister."

"But sir—"

"Enough talk! I don't accept, and that's that. Case closed!"

Krzepicki sank into his chair. Nina stood petrified. Nicodemus smoothed his hair, raised his head high, and opened the door.

Silence fell in the hall as everyone jumped to their feet.

Dyzma, without closing the door behind him, took three steps toward Director Litwinek. He looked around and said in a low voice, "Mr. Litwinek, tell the president of the republic that I am grateful for this honor, but I will not become the prime minister."

"Sir! . . ." Provincial Governor Szejmont blurted out, but immediately lapsed into silence.

"But why? Why!?" Madam Przełęska cried hysterically.

Dyzma frowned.

"I have my reasons," he replied in a stiff voice.

"Sir," ventured Litwinek, "is your decision final?

"Every decision I make is final."

"Would you please write a few lines to that effect for the head of state?"

"I can do that."

Nicodemus nodded and disappeared into the office. There was an explosion of outraged exclamations as soon as the door closed behind him.

"Why? I don't understand, why?!"

"This is awful! The country is in a desperate, literally desperate situation! I truly can't think of anyone who would be more suited for this position than the bank president!"

Wareda nodded.

"He was insulted, he was obviously insulted that, contrary to his instructions, they let the Grain Bank go to ruin."

There was a moment of silence. They suddenly heard Dyzma's voice from behind the office door:

"Write it, goddammit, do what I tell you to! Enough of this!"

They heard the typewriter's subdued click-clacking.

"It seems to me," said Madam Przełęska, "that the bank president's decision was largely influenced by the state of his feelings, the love he feels for my niece. They were married just a few short months ago. The office of the prime minister requires more hours than there are in a day. And the president is a man of profound emotional depth, although he very skillfully hides it. We women can sense such things."

"Oh yes!" Countess Czarska agreed.

Rehlf shrugged.

"In my opinion, both you and the colonel are wrong, completely wrong. Insofar as I've been an observer of Mr. Dyzma's pursuits, and as far as I know him personally, the man is purely incapable of allowing personal matters to affect his decisions."

"He's a man of state, through and through!" exclaimed Governor Szejmont. "If he refuses now, there must be deeper political factors at work."

"But the country is sliding into the abyss!"

"It seems so to us," the governor smiled, "it seems so to us. But the fact is, it's not so bad. I'm sure that the bank president, whose understanding of economic matters is so much deeper than ours, does not consider the danger so great that he would have to personally come to the rescue."

"But he already came to the rescue once! And think how effective it was!"

"Cincinnatus," said the governor sententiously, "agrees to put down his plow only in the event of ultimate danger."

"Yes, yes!" one of the ladies cried in exaltation. "Then and only then will he stand at the helm and save our fatherland!"

"An extraordinary man," Director Litwinek said, his voice trembling.

"A great man," the governor seconded.

Suddenly, there was a long, squawking laugh from the corner.

Until now, Ponimirski had been quiet, no attention paid to him, his ironic faces unobserved. George had been listening, and finally he could stand it no more. He was reeling with laughter in his chair.

"What are you laughing at?" the governor asked in an offended tone.

George jumped up, his laughter trailing off, and made several attempts to put in his monocle, but his hands were shaking so much that he was unable to do so. He was agitated; this had clearly been the last straw.

"What am I laughing at? Not at *what*, ladies and gentlemen, but at *whom*?! I'm laughing at *you*, at *you*! At all of society, at all my beloved fellow countrymen!"

"Sir! . . ."

"Silence!" Ponimirski yelled, and his pale, sickly child's face turned red with rage. "Silence! *Sapristi*! I'm laughing at *you*! At *you*! The so-called elite! Ha, that's a laugh! I'm telling you that your statesman, your Cincinnatus, your great man, your Nicodemus Dyzma, is nothing but a common swindler who's leading you around by the nose, a cunning scoundrel, imposter, and complete and utter moron all at the same time! An idiot who has no idea about anything, not economics, not even spelling! He's a boor, without a hint of good breeding, devoid of even fundamental civility! Look at his yokel face and his ill manners! A complete nitwit, an absolute zero! I give you my word of honor that not only is this Oxford business all a lie, he can't speak a single language! A vulgar, shady character of the very worst sort, with the morality of a cutthroat grifter. *Sapristi*! Can't you see? I was wrong when I said that he was leading you around by the nose! You did it to yourself, it was you who put that swine up on a pedestal! You! You, bereft of any shred of critical reasoning! I'm laughing at *you*, you idiots! At *you*! Common rabble! . . .

He'd finally managed to put in his monocle. He gave everyone a look of pure contempt and left, slamming the door.

Director Litwinek, frightened and astonished, searched the faces of those present: they all wore a smile of embarrassment and pity.

"What did that all mean?" he asked. "Who was that gentleman?"

It was Madam Przełęska who responded.

"I apologize, sir, it's my nephew, the president's brother-in-law. Usually, he's calm, but . . . he is mentally deranged."

"He's a madman," the governor explained.

"Poor young fellow," Miss Czarska sighed.

"Ah," Director Litwinek smiled. "Of course, a madman."

PAGE 3   *taxi dancer*
In the early twentieth century, taxi dancers were paid dance part-
ners hired by entertainment venues to dance with their customers.
Taxi dancers' pay, like that of taxi-cab drivers, was determined by
the amount of time spent with customers.

PAGE 35   *mangle woman*
A lower-class woman who earned her living as a laundress would
use a mangle—a set of heavy rollers, often powered by a hand
crank, for wringing and pressing clothing.

PAGE 49   *Sapristi!*
Interjection; an oath derived from the French *Sacré Christ!*

PAGE 98   *"coming boor" types*
Kasia is referring to "The Coming Ham" ("Грядущий хам"), an
essay by the Russian writer and philosopher Dmitry Merezhkovsky. The title is a pun, referring to both the biblical
Ham—Merezhkovsky's work concerned what he considered the
crisis of spirituality in Russia—and the Russian and Polish word
for "boor" or "lout."

PAGE 122 *The Sejm's adoption of the act*
The Sejm of the Republic of Poland is the lower house of Poland's
bicameral parliament.

PAGE 131 *Bilitis and Mnasidika*
The Songs of Bilitis is a collection of erotic poetry about lesbian
love. The collection's author, Pierre Louÿs, claimed the poems
were found on an ancient tomb in Cyprus and were the work of
Bilitis, a contemporary of Sappho; they were actually written by
Louÿs himself in the late 1800s. Mnasidika is Bilitis's lover.

PAGE 140   *a modern Wokulski . . . the Necker of the twentieth century*
Stanisław Wokulski is the protagonist of Bolesław Prus's 1890 novel *The Doll.* "Wokulski" became synonymous in Poland with business acumen and entrepreneurship. Jacques Necker was a French statesman and the finance minister for Louis XVI.

PAGE 145   *he himself was Michorowki*
Duke Waldemar Michorowki, a dashing nobleman, is the hero of *The Leper.*

PAGE 145   *The Leper*
The Leper (*Trędowata*) is a 1909 melodrama by Helena Mnisz-kówna. The novel had a large readership but was uniformly scorned by critics.

PAGE 168   *a cry of "Evoe!"*
From the Greek εὐοῖ. The Liddell-Scott *Greek-English Lexicon* defines it as an exclamation used in the cult of Dionysus (Roman Bacchus).

PAGE 175   *I myself was the very Lycurgus*
Lycurgus of Sparta (800 BC) was the semimythical legislator who reformed ancient Spartan society and created many of its laws.

PAGE 222   *That's hilarious, you playing the mandolin*
The mandolin was typically associated with both rural and urban folk music across Southern and Eastern Europe. In the early twentieth century, amateur musical ensembles that entertained bar-goers would frequently include at least one mandolin player. It was not an instrument that inspired respect among the upper crust.

PAGE 254   *he needed to be sent off to Tworki*
Tworki was a notorious psychiatric hospital outside of Warsaw.

PAGE 259   *The Castle*
The Royal Castle in Warsaw was the seat of the Polish head of state (1920–22) and the residence of the president of Poland (1926–39).

PAGE 273   *met the newlyweds with bread and salt*
Welcoming guests with bread and salt is a traditional European gesture of hospitality. The custom is especially prevalent in Slavic cultures.

PAGE 277   *it's right out of Lombroso*
Cesare Lombroso was an Italian criminologist whose "born criminal" theory held that criminality was a heritable trait and could be identified through physiognomy.

PAGE 285   *General Baron Cambronne was another one for courtliness*
Pierre Cambronne was a general in the Napoleonic Wars. Legend has it that he responded to being taken prisoner at Waterloo with a single word: "Merde!" ("Shit!"). His reply became known as *le mot de Cambronne* ("the word of Cambronne").

PAGE 285   *An absolute Pomona*
Pomona was the Roman goddess of agricultural abundance and the protectress of fruit trees, gardens, and orchards.

PAGE 294   *Cincinnatus*
Lucius Quinctius Cincinnatus (5th century BC) was a patrician and statesman in the early Roman Republic and a fabled figure of civic virtue. Called upon by fellow citizens to lead the Republic in a war against the Aequi, he was appointed dictator of Rome. According to legend, he was plowing his farmland when a group of senators found him to notify him of his nomination. After a swift victory, he relinquished his absolute authority and returned to farming.

Lightning Source UK Ltd.
Milton Keynes UK
UKHW010828160421
382087UK00001B/167